BENEATH
THE
DEEP

ENDORSEMENTS

If you don't believe in sea monsters, you will by the time you have followed Morgan Sullivan into a place where science and faith are no longer at odds. If you do believe, you will not be disappointed by either the thrill and the mystery Andrea Chatman provides or the absolute realism of the circumstances surrounding a thought-to-be-extinct world. Family, love, and even obsession are as stunningly authentic in this story as the monsters themselves. Believe it or not—but take the plunge *Beneath the Deep*.

—**Nancy Rue,** award-winning author of the Reluctant Prophet trilogy and other books

BENEATH THE DEEP

ANDREA CHATMAN

PUBLISHING THE POSITIVE
Plymouth, Massachusetts

COPYRIGHT NOTICE

Cover and Interior Design: Jeff Gifford, Derinda Babcock
Editor(s): Marcie Bridges, Deb Haggerty

PUBLISHED BY: Elk Lake Publishing, Inc., 35 Dogwood Drive, Plymouth, MA 02360, 2021

Library Cataloging Data

Names: Chatman, Andrea (Andrea Chatman)
Beneath the Deep / Andrea Chatman

330 p. 23cm × 15cm (9in × 6 in.)
ISBN-13: 978-1-64949-451-1 (paperback) | **978-1-64949-452-8** (trade paperback) | 978-1-64949-453-5 (e-book)

Key Words: Geological oceanography, mystery, suspense, underwater habitat, mosasaur, family, relationships

Library of Congress Control Number: 2021950681 Fiction

DEDICATION

To the 'doodles' and the 'beans',
Auntie loves you.
May you always dream big dreams.

ACKNOWLEDGMENTS

What a journey this has been! This book would have never made it to print without a wonderful group of people that I can't thank enough:

First and foremost —Thanks to the Creator—without him there would be nothing to write about.

To Deb Haggerty, Marcie Bridges, Cristel Phelps, and the Elk Lake Publishing team—thank you from the bottom of my heart for not only giving my book a chance but for helping me to polish it to a shine.

To Nancy Rue—my mentor and friend, words cannot fully express how thankful I am for you. Thank you for your guidance and wisdom. I'm not sure this book would have ever been finished if I hadn't met you. Hoping to catch up one day soon! I miss your cappuccinos.

To Robin G.—Thanks for teaching me to Ask for Moon! Thank you for sharing your wisdom and experience and for encouraging me to go to my first writers' conference. It means a lot.

To Tim S. and Angie B.—thank you for giving me hope and encouragement when I really needed it. My first writers' conference was more than overwhelming, but you gave me the courage to keep moving forward when I really wanted to give up.

To Janice B.—you are a true example of pay it forward. I am so, so thankful for the day that I found your book, and you were willing to chat with a stranger on Facebook. You've helped me more than you will ever know. And I've been looking for books like yours my entire life.

To Leslie—girl, what can I say? My life would be so much less without you. You are the sister of my heart. Thank you for being my writers' conference 'wing man' and for introducing me to Nancy Rue. Thanks for your willingness to review the manuscript and your straight-forward honesty. Catlett is a better man because of you. Though he is still ... well, Catlett.

To Mom and Dad—thanks for believing in me and for reading the early drafts. Your love and encouragement have always given me the courage to go and do and try.

To family and friends—I love you all and am so thankful for each and every one of you. Thank you for the prayers and the encouragement.

And the coffee. To the baristas of Akamai Coffee Company—thanks for keeping me fueled! And for letting me hang out all weekend at your Kihei location.

And to my readers—thank you for your support.

On earth there is not his like,
A creature without fear.
Job 41: 33

Here there be dragons.
—Albertus Magnus

CHAPTER ONE

Seeing red. Quite an interesting concept, and one which could mean many things. Red in the cool depth of a ruby. Red in the fullness of a rose. Red in the flash of a warning light as Morgan Sullivan scanned her access card a third time. Red as in the rise of her anger. Red as in the color of fresh blood. Her brother was a dead man walking.

She shoved the card into her pocket and turned her back to the security camera as she pulled another from her bag. She pressed the new card against the scanner. Red. The edges of the plastic bit into her skin as her fist tightened around it. Her forehead fell against the door with a quiet thud. Not today.

Footsteps squeaked toward her. Not. Today.

"Morgan! Howzit?" Her intern's cheerful greeting grated against her raw nerves.

The building was supposed to be deserted. All she'd wanted was a quiet morning—to lose herself in her research. Forget the last twenty-four hours. Was some quiet too much to ask? Yeah. Apparently, it was. She forced a calming breath past her clenched teeth and pushed away from the door.

Then again, waste not …

"Hey, Keoni, could you come here a second?"

His sneakers squeaked against linoleum as he wandered closer without question. Like a lamb to slaughter. His attention focused on the tablet in his hand. Her fingers flexed.

"I thought you were in Iowa." He was way too cheerful for seven a.m. She was so going to replace his coffee with decaf. "Did you see th—"

His words cut off with a startled squeak as she grabbed his lanyard and ran his card through the scanner. The red light mocked her, and the door shivered beneath the pounding of her fist. This was so unfair.

"Nate locked down your lab before he left." Keoni's tone was apologetic, but his eyes were laughing. He had a terrible poker face.

She released his lanyard, and he scrambled back a few steps. This wasn't his fault, it was Nate's. Keoni was not collateral damage. There were rules. She rubbed her fingertips hard against her forehead. Usually Nate left one way in, but she'd tried everything. He'd gone too far this time.

"I'm sure he thought you were in Iowa." Keoni said. "Why aren't you in Iowa?"

His words were like salt rubbed into a gaping wound.

"Uncle Daniel's busy," she said.

Doing what, she'd didn't know. Or care. If her uncle was too busy for her, then she was too busy for him. She had work to do. If only she could get into her lab. The window rattled as she hit the door again. Nate was so dead.

"Oh, well he's missing out." Keoni said. "Look at this."

She didn't want to look at anything. A tablet was thrust into her hands, and she blinked at the blurred image. Not. Enough. Coffee. In. The. World.

"Nate sent the feeds from the AUVs this morning." He tapped the screen before she could give it back.

She scowled at the mention of her brother's name. Nate had taken his team and their fleet of Autonomous Underwater Vehicles, or AUVs, down to the South Pacific on a three-month research expedition. The torpedo shaped AUVs were designed to dive to depths of up to 10,000 feet, deeper and safer than manned submersibles. They planned to use the vehicles to map the deep sea trenches off Tonga at a depth not yet fully explored.

The project was a scratch in the surface when the deepest part of the trench was around 36,200 feet at Horizon Deep, but research was definitely a step in the right direction. The on-site location also provided her brother a temporary respite from any attempt at revenge on her part. Though in spite of her current predicament, her scientific curiosity was enough to set it aside. For a moment.

"What am I looking at?" she said.

"Only the world's coolest footage ever." The screen jarred as he tapped it with a little too much enthusiasm. "This is from the Nautilus AUV taken around yesterday evening, Aussie time, in the Tonga Trench at a depth of 6,000 feet."

She could see the readings from green digital numbers in the corner of the screen.

"What the ..." She flinched as two gigantic paddles snaked toward the screen and shot past the AUV's cameras. The image jarred as they struck the drone and yanked it forward.

"Is that a giant squid?" She watched in awe as an eerie green mass of dark writhing tentacles closed around the AUV, and yanked the drone toward a huge clicking beak. A surge of adrenaline shot through her as the beak closed down hard on the camera, shooting spiderwebs across the image as the housing cracked beneath the intense power of the squid's jaws. "This is amazing, do you know how rare this footage is?"

Few people had been lucky enough to capture video of the elusive creature.

"Shhh ... watch this part."

The image clouded in a mass of inky black goop and the video shivered as the squid released the AUV. The spider webbed cracks grew more prominent as the damaged AUV drifted deeper. The digital depth read 6,200 ft. deep and counting. The cameras failed as the cracks gave way beneath the pressure, and the screen went black.

"This is awesome." She rewound the video and ran it again. "I'll bet Piper is thrilled."

Her sister-in-law was the team's senior marine biologist and her best friend since university. Due to the intense depth the creatures inhabited, footage like this was rare. There was so much they didn't know about the giants. The tablet was yanked from her hand, and then returned before she had a chance to protest.

"Look at this." Keoni jabbed the screen with his finger as the ink cleared to the intense dark of the trench. The light reflected off something at the very limit of the camera's range. A shape, maybe. Big shape. She fought the urge to roll her eyes.

"It's a whale." she said, preempting what she knew was coming.

"Maybe it's not." Keoni said as he plucked the pad out of her hands. "Pretty deep for a whale."

"Not a sperm whale." She reached for the tablet, but he kept it out of her reach, his focus never leaving the screen. "They can dive up to—"

"A depth of over 7,300 feet, blah, blah, blah." His dark eyes shot her a wounded look. "You used to be a lot more fun."

Her teasing grin faltered as his comment hit her like a bucket of ice water. He was right, she used to be a lot less cynical than this. When had she turned into such a Scrooge? A twinge of annoyance slithered through her. Four months ago, that's when. Keoni didn't deserve her bad mood. At least he was still her friend.

"I'm sorry, you're right." She stepped closer, peering at the screen. "What did Verne pick up with the sonar? Was it close enough?"

Verne was Nautilus's partner drone. The AUV's mission was to map the geography and geology of the trench with its suite of sonars. If the black mass was something other than an echo, there was a good chance Verne might have picked it up. The gleam of excitement in his eyes made her grin.

"Piper hasn't sent the data yet." Keoni said, bouncing on his toes. "But I'll let you know the minute she does." His watch beeped and he grimaced. "I have to get back to the sand sifters. Catch you later, okay?"

"Sperm whales eat giant squid." She hurled the words after him as he vanished around the corner.

"So do sea monsters." His laughter echoed faintly down the hall.

She shook her head. Sea monsters. Keoni thought everything was a sea monster. So did her uncle. She wondered if the video would be enough to lure her uncle back to the Institute. Probably not. Her smile faded as the heaviness that had plagued her over the last couple days returned. She turned slowly and stared at the locked door of her lab.

Her phone chimed. She slipped it from her pocket and scowled at the screen. Nate.

NATE: You know the use of unauthorized security cards is a felony.

Red filled her vision again as anger seared through her. So not true. The cards were both hers, sort of. Besides, it was her lab, and he had no right to lock her out of it. No right at all. Her thumbs flew across the keyboard.

MORGAN: So unprofessional. What are you? Five?

His reply was swift.

NATE: Which would make you ...

She glared up at the security camera.
Chime.

NATE: Your face is going to stick like that.

Her eyes narrowed as she stared at the camera. Oh, he was good. He'd turned everyone against her, including the security team. Talk about legal ...

Her phone chimed again.

NATE: Go home, you're on vacation.

Her frustration peaked. Her bag hit the floor with a thud, and the door shuddered beneath the force of her foot. She spun and shook her fist at the security camera, like a child, regretting the action almost immediately. Who knew who was recording what for the record. Her father had warned them both after the last time Nate had pulled a stunt like this. Sometimes she really disliked working for the family business.

Her hand fell to her side, and she slumped back against the wall and slid to the floor. She took a deep breath and let it out slowly, letting her anger leach into the cold floor. This wasn't about Nate, either. Not really, but he certainly wasn't helping. She glared halfheartedly at the camera. She knew he was right. She should be on vacation, but her plans had changed.

She wanted to work. She needed to work. To focus on something other than her uncle who was pushing her away. Again. Did that make her pathetic? Maybe. She didn't care. At least work was productive. What was she supposed to do now? Go home and binge on Netflix? Alone?

Her phone rang. Her annoyance slipped from her slowly at the name flashing on the screen, like air from a leaky balloon.

"Traitor," she said, without heat.

Piper snorted a laugh. Morgan bit back a smile, an edge of homesickness dampening the small flicker of humor. She missed them.

"Just so you know," Piper said, "I told him not to do it. I'm just an innocent bystander."

Morgan pointed an accusing finger at the camera across the hallway on the off chance they were still spying on her.

"You're married to him." Darn her brother and his charm. "You were my best friend first, or have you forgotten that?" She lost her battle with her smile as her friend laughed.

"Don't be so dramatic. I love you both." Piper's smirk was audible.

Morgan tipped her head back against the wall and stared at the ceiling tiles. "You know Nate's only doing this because he thinks he's safe. Tell him if he values his van, he'd better release my lab."

She wouldn't dream of touching his classic Volkswagen. At least, not personally. She'd just pay the neighbor kids to Saran Wrap it. A mischievous smile spread across her face, she squelched it as she remembered the camera.

"Just don't scratch the paint."

Her annoyance returned as she heard her brother's deep laughter in the background. She snagged her bag and pulled it to her, retrieving a notebook and pen. She flipped to a fresh page and scribbled a message, then held it up to the camera in a last-ditch effort to bring the security team back to her side.

AHI POKE AND BEER
ON ME IF YOU LET ME IN.

"Nate says to cease your immature attempts at bribery." Piper said, dryly.

Morgan's frustration flared. "This isn't fair."

"It wouldn't kill you to take a break." Piper said, gently. "You need a vacation. What about Daniel?"

The paper ripped beneath her grip as she flipped to a new page of the notebook.

"He said he's too busy." She said the words quickly, as if spilling them all at once could make them hurt less. "Said he will be home this summer, after the term ends."

She scribbled the tip of her pen down the empty page, staining the white with purple ink.

Piper was quiet for a moment. "I'm sorry. I wonder what's gotten into the old man."

"You and me both." She whispered as the hurt seeped into her gut.

Her uncle's reasons for denying her visit had been frustratingly vague, particularly for a man who specialized in detail. She should have just gone anyway.

"I'm sure he'll come around or I'll help you kidnap him," Piper's indignant tone made her smile. "I'm sure Nate would help too. Maybe we should send Daniel the latest footage from the drones. Find something even he couldn't resist."

"I don't know if a giant squid would work, though it is impressive," Morgan said. "Keoni thinks there is a sea monster chasing it."

Maybe they could enhance it with a bit of movie magic. She shook her head. No, that would never work. Daniel loved sea monsters, but he was a pro at spotting fake footage. Still, a fun idea.

"It might have been." Piper said with a laugh. "Verne picked up a large fuzzy blob. Probably a whale. We'll know more when we get a chance to process the footage."

"I could help with that, if you can get Nate to lift the lockdown."

Piper laughed. "He says nice try."

"If I have to break the lock, he's going to pay for it."

"That's a bit drastic, even for you," Piper said. "Besides, there's nothing that can't wait a week or so. If you are so desperate, you could always join us."

Yeah, right. "I don't find puking my guts out a relaxing venture."

Her seasickness was legendary. Piper had experienced it firsthand.

Piper sighed. "Then go visit your grandparents. Ride your horse. I'm sure he misses you."

Morgan smiled wearily—she missed him too. She let out a heavy sigh. Maybe a break wouldn't be too terrible. She might even charge her tickets to Maui to her brother's account. The thought cheered her a little.

"You're right," she glanced up at the camera, "tell your husband this isn't over. And congratulations on the footage—it was really impressive. We'll have to celebrate when you guys get back."

"Thanks. And I will." Piper said. "Now, go do something fun."

Morgan laughed. "I'll try. Bye."

Something fun. Nate wouldn't be back for another several weeks, which was plenty of time to plot a suitable revenge, and still go see her horse. Maybe she could get Keoni to help. He always had great ideas. She stuffed her notebook and pen back into her bag, then stood. She tipped a salute to the security camera in case her brother was still watching and headed toward the intern office.

Her phone rang. Her smile dimmed as she read the name on the screen. Her uncle. She stared at it for a moment, and considered letting the call go to voicemail. No. She wanted answers too badly. Answers he owed her.

"Nate fed the Nautilus to a sea monster," she said, in lieu of a greeting.

The expected laughter didn't come, forced or otherwise, and the voice wasn't her uncle's.

"This is Detective Anderson with the Willow Creek Sheriff's Office, to whom am I speaking?"

Icy tentacles of dread crept into her chest.

"This is Morgan Sullivan," she said. "Why do you have my uncle's phone?"

"Dr. Daniel Smithson?"

Her throat tightened. "Yes, that is right."

There was a pause.

"Ms. Sullivan, I'm afraid there has been an accident."

CHAPTER TWO

Please, God, no. Not Daniel. Not now ... please, please, please. Her feet were moving but she didn't know where she was going. Scenarios flashed through her head, each worse than the last. Daniel bleeding ... dying ... already dead.

Rain splattered against her face, jolting her from her thoughts. She blinked at the dark clouds. The wind was cool, and she forced a deep breath into her lungs as reality came rushing back to her. Sharp and bitter.

"Ms. Sullivan." The voice in her ear grew more insistent. "Ms. Sullivan, can you hear me?"

Right. The detective. Facts. She needed facts.

"Is he dead?"

"He's missing."

"Missing?"

Her knees weakened, and she sank to the edge of the curb. Her bag dug into her side, but she ignored it. The drizzle fell steadily as her whole world narrowed to the voice on the phone.

"When was the last time you spoke with Dr. Smithson, Ms. Sullivan?"

Guilt seeped through the panic.

"Yesterday morning," she said. "Or, at least, it was morning here. In Hawaii. I'm on Oahu."

Now she was rambling. She forced herself to breath, and her pulse to slow. Panic wouldn't help anything.

"Was Dr. Smithson stressed or worried?"

She dipped her head. *Yeah, a little.* They'd argued. She'd been planning to surprise him with a visit. Afraid he wouldn't let her come if she asked, but she chickened out at the last minute. And she'd been right. He didn't want her there.

"Um, yes, a little. I wanted to visit. He said he was too busy."

"Is that normal?" the detective said.

"No." He'd never been too busy before. Not for her. "What happened, Detective—?"

"Anderson." His voice was calming, empathic. "There was an accident in a science lab at Winston College. In one of the science labs. An explosion and a fire."

Her blood ran cold. "Explosion and a fire?"

She pushed to her feet, and her head spun with the sudden movement.

"He's not in the lab, Ms. Sullivan," the detective said, "We are positive."

A sharp knock against the glass door behind her startled her. She turned to find Keoni watching, concern on his face. She plastered on a smile and waved a hand as she headed for her car.

"His phone was found in the snow," Anderson continued. "Beneath a broken window."

She froze as the pieces snapped into place, and the words were out of her mouth before she could stop them.

"He went through the window? And now he is missing?"

"Yes." His words were gentle, straightforward. "A witness reported they saw someone come through the window just before the explosion. When they reached the scene, he was gone."

Daniel was missing. Possibly hurt. Lost in the snow.

He hated the cold.

She slid into her car, tossing her bag onto the passenger seat.

"I'm coming to Willow Creek."

"If you like." The detective paused. "We will do our best to find him, Ms. Sullivan. I promise you that. If you hear from him, please let me know."

She scribbled his number onto the back of an old receipt.

"Please call me if you find him or if you hear anything."

He promised and ended the call. She shoved the phone into a cup holder and started the car with a hard twist of the key. She ignored the trembling of her hands. Keoni was still standing at the door, still watching her. She ignored him too as she shifted into drive.

Oh Daniel, what have you gotten into now?

FISHING BOAT OFFSHORE OF THE ISLAND OF OAHU
MORGAN, AGE SEVEN

The surface of the water shimmered, urging her to come closer. Morgan reached out a hand, straining to touch it as the boat swayed beneath her. Her fingers danced tantalizingly close, the spray wetting her skin. She squeaked as she lost her grip on the rail and slipped headfirst toward the blue sea. And then, suddenly, she was hauled back onboard ...

She grinned up at her uncle, giggling as he tried to frown at her. He just shook his head and picked the bucket of bait up off the deck.

"No feeding the sea monsters, kiddo," Daniel said. "Your mother would skin me alive."

She giggled again and scrambled to scoop an escaped prawn up from the deck. She dropped it in her uncle's bucket.

"Nate says there is no such thing as monsters."

Her big brother thought he knew everything. Just because he was ten, and she was just seven.

Her uncle's blue-gray eyes narrowed. "Oh, does he now?" He patted the chair, and she scrambled into it eagerly. She leaned forward to wrap her hands around the handle of the fishing pole, taking care to keep her fingers clear of the lines. Just like he'd taught her. "What do you think?"

She preened and sat up straighter, then answered carefully and thoughtfully.

"My hypothesis," she said, "is that since no one has explored the entire ocean, there could be sea monsters. Like the Leviathan in the Bible."

"Good hypothesis," he said.

She beamed at him. Her uncle was the coolest. The boat bobbed as he took a seat beside her and offered her a pog. She loved passion orange guava juice. She only got to have the drink on special occasions. Her grandmother said it would rot her teeth out if she drank too much.

"A long time ago, sailors thought there was a sea monster called the Kraken." He deepened his voice into the one he used for scary stories. She loved when he did that. "The Kraken was a massive beast believed to rise up out of the ocean, wrap ships up with its tentacles and break them into pieces."

"That's a giant squid, Uncle Daniel," she said. "Not a monster."

He grinned and reached over to ruffle her hair. "We know that now, kiddo. But imagine how you would have felt if a giant squid attacked your boat." He grinned. "Or how the squid felt. He probably thought the boat was a whale. What a surprise that must have been."

She giggled.

"I bet wood doesn't taste very good." She scrunched her nose at the thought.

The story seemed rather silly, but a thrill ran through her at the thought of seeing a sea monster. She loved his stories. Especially when he told them out here—on the boat. She looked back over her shoulder at the island in the distance, a speck of green against the wide blue ocean.

Her uncle's chuckle eased her fears. He reached out and tapped the spine of the book wedged between her leg and the chair. His latest addition to her treasure box, Twenty Thousand Leagues Under the Sea by Jules Verne, a wonderful adventure about a submarine everyone thought was a sea monster.

"'The human mind is always looking for something to marvel at', my wise little Conseil," he said. "There is a little bit of truth in every legend. For those willing to seek it out."

A blast of cold air cut through Morgan's bones, shocking her awake more effectively than coffee.

Why Iowa, Daniel? And why in the winter? She winced and clutched her coat tighter as she picked her way across the icy sidewalk. She'd hoped to arrive much earlier—the town of Willow Creek was more isolated than she'd expected. The first flight available had been a late morning one, with three connections. She'd arrived in Des Moines a little after noon and rented a car for a two-and-a-half-hour drive, which had turned into nearly four through a late season snow shower. The only thing she disliked more than the snow was driving in it.

Her uncle was still missing. No one had any further information for her. No matter who she asked. The hospitals had no record of a Daniel Smithson, and the morgue wouldn't give her any information. In fact, they'd hung up on her rather quickly, with a 'no comment', like she was some reporter. Her phone had gone dead halfway to Willow Creek, her charger forgotten on her desk at home. At least her suitcase had still been in her trunk, where she'd left it after her plans had changed. And now, they'd changed again.

She hadn't told anyone Daniel was missing, or that she had changed her plans, other than a brief text to Piper before her phone had died to inform her sister-in-law she'd decided to go to Iowa after all. Her parents were on a rafting trip and out of touch for at least another week. She decided not to worry her grandparents until she knew whether Daniel was still alive, and if he was injured.

Or whether she was there to escort his body home.

She tried not to dwell on those thoughts. Not until she knew for certain. But she'd had a long time to think on the flights and the long drive, and they lingered like a dark cloud in the back of her mind. The snow melted into sleet, splattering the icy sidewalk. She pulled her scarf higher and lowered her head against the wind. Worry crept through her. Daniel was lost, somewhere out in this frozen wasteland.

She whispered a prayer for his safety.

The building shielded her from the wind as she turned the corner. She slowed her step as she studied the cluster of news vans blocking the street in front of the Willow Creek Sheriff's Office. A small crowd had gathered at the bottom of the stairs. There appeared to be no way around the people. She edged closer and blended in with a group of curious onlookers. The front door opened, emitting two men in uniform. A third man in a dress coat and suit followed a few steps behind. The crowd quieted as one of the uniformed men stepped up to the lectern.

"Sheriff Davis will make a statement regarding the incident at Winston College. Please hold your questions until the end."

He stepped back as the older man took his place. Sheriff Davis leveled a firm look at the reporters.

"At midnight on the 21st of March, an explosion occurred in the science building at Winston College. Investigators have confirmed the cause of the incident was an accident involving a leak in a propane line, and not an act of malice or arson. Our colleagues from the FBI have confirmed these findings."

Surprise swept through her. The FBI? Why was the FBI involved? Morgan shifted her gaze toward the man in the suit, and found him watching her. She looked away, unsettled, as the sheriff continued his statement.

"The Willow Creek Sheriff's Office will continue to hold jurisdiction over the case, with the assistance of the Winston College Security Office. We continue to search for a man believed to be a witness to the incident, Dr. Daniel Smithson, a professor at Winston."

Her heart stuttered at the mention of Daniel's name. She edged closer, straining her ears.

"Dr. Smithson was last seen on Wednesday night shortly before the incident. His phone was found near the scene. He is not believed to have caused the incident, but there is concern for his welfare. Photos have been distributed to all news outlets. Anyone having information concerning Dr. Smithson's whereabouts is asked to please contact the sheriff's office. Updates will be provided as more information becomes available. Thank you for your time."

He stepped away and headed for the door. The rest of the men followed, ignoring the barrage of questions and flashes from the cameras as they returned to the safety of the building. No one seemed to notice as she followed a few moments later.

CHAPTER THREE

She didn't get further than the reception area, which was guarded by a sweet but firm receptionist who reminded her a little of her grandmother. Once the receptionist had determined she wasn't a reporter, Morgan had been skillfully directed to a chair with a cup of coffee to help warm her while she waited.

An old radiator rattled ominously beside her. Morgan eyed it with distrust but couldn't find the will to move away from the warmth. A deep cold had settled into her bones, a cold she couldn't shake. She took a sip from the mug cradled in her slowly thawing fingers, though it did little to ease the ice which had settled in her chest.

Her gaze darted to the door beyond the desk. Sealed and quiet. Then to the camera in the corner. And finally, to her cheerful jailer, gauging her odds at getting through the door before someone stopped her. The older woman looked up from her computer and met Morgan's gaze with a comforting smile and a knowing look.

Yeah, pretty much what she'd figured. No chance at all.

"Detective Anderson will be out momentarily, Ms. Sullivan."

"Thank you."

The radiator ceased its shuddering, and Morgan inched closer. At least the coffee was decent. The pot was a Keurig and the only thing in the room newer than ten years. The wood paneling was weathered with age but well cared for. A yellowing and faded McGruff poster was partially hidden beneath posted notices. The furniture was mid-century, in olive green and brown. And the pair of solid wood doors were probably original to the building.

The scene reminded her of something out of one of those old shows she'd watched as a kid. Her brother would have loved it. She half expected Andy Griffith to stroll in. Her feet jiggled as she tried to warm her frozen toes. At this point she'd take Barney Fife.

Anyone who might be able to give her answers.

The statement the sheriff had given earlier only left her with more questions. Questions she'd mulled over and over as she waited. With her phone dead, she was left without an ability to do some research with the aid of Google. She really needed to get a charger.

Her sleep-deprived imagination continued to spin a series of scenarios as to why the FBI had been involved. There was biological terrorism. This was the farm belt after all, the heart of the nation's food supply, right? In this day and age, terrorism wasn't so unbelievable. But what would terrorism have to do with her uncle? His focus was deep sea environments, not agriculture.

She squeezed her eyes shut, willing her brain to think. The FBI hadn't taken jurisdiction. Maybe they were called in on all explosion-related incidents. Which kind of eliminated the kidnapping theory too. She knew that much from TV. The FBI had jurisdiction in the case of kidnapping, right? Or was the FBI's jurisdiction only true if the kidnapping crossed state lines? She shivered. Kidnapping wasn't good, but it was a little better than the thought of Daniel injured and alone.

Lost somewhere in the snow.

The door to the office opened, and she jumped to her feet. Two men crossed by to the outside door, one dressed in dark slacks and a sheriff's office uniform jacket, and the other in a weathered leather jacket and jeans. She sank back into her chair and watched from the corner of her eye as they shook hands, their words too soft to carry across the room. She braced against the cold as the man in the leather jacket ducked out into the night.

The remaining man turned and gave her a small smile. He looked as exhausted as she felt.

"Ms. Sullivan?" He took her hand in a warm grasp. "I'm Detective Wyatt Anderson. You made good time."

And broke more than one traffic law in more than one state to do so. She squelched the sliver of guilt as she shook his hand.

"Do you have any news about my uncle?"

A blast of cold air cut through the room as the door opened and a man with slicked hair in a navy suit hurried inside, followed by a man lugging a camera. Anderson grimaced and ushered her toward the door to the office.

"Let's talk inside," he said.

The noise beyond the door was deafening in comparison to the silence of the waiting room. The room was a bit more modern. Anderson led her across the room through a cluster of desks and people. Loud, angry voices carried from a glass walled office at the far end of the room. She looked over as the door slammed shut.

A man and woman in dark suits stood facing the sheriff. The man gestured sharply at Sheriff Davis and turned toward the room. The man from the press conference. His eyes pinned Morgan's with a calculated gaze. She felt unease as she stared back.

"Ms. Sullivan?"

She shifted her eyes toward the detective. His eyes filled with concern.

"Are you all right?"

She was so far from all right she wasn't sure how to answer him. She glanced back toward the man in the suit and relaxed as he turned his back on them.

"It's been a really long day," she said, forcing a smile.

She grimaced as the words registered. Of course, it to have been for the detective too. He just smiled and ushered her through a door into a small lounge with a kitchenette. The room smelled of scorched coffee and cinnamon rolls.

"I hope you don't mind the break room. Our conference room is occupied at the moment." He closed the door behind them and waved a hand toward a comfortable looking couch. "Please have a seat. Would you like a refill?"

She looked down to find the mug still clutched in her hand. She handed it to him with a small smile. "Thank you."

The couch cushions were soft, the room pleasantly warm, and she was tired. Not an ideal combination for her jetlag. She sat on the edge of the seat, her back straight, and hoped it would keep her awake. Anderson placed the coffee on the table between them with a basket of creamer and sugar, and a plate of cinnamon rolls.

"You look like you could use one of these." He smiled. "My sister makes them. She runs Queen of Tarts Bakery a couple blocks over. Best in three counties."

Morgan's stomach rumbled and churned at their scent. She slid one onto a napkin to be nice. Her coffee, she kept black. The bitter taste wasn't ideal, but it was warm and helped jolt her lagging synapses.

"What happened to my uncle, Detective Anderson?" She watched intently as he settled into the chair on the opposite side of the narrow table. "I saw the press conference. They said he is still missing?"

The detective opened a folder and slid a photo across the table. She swallowed shakily and pulled the photo closer.

Daniel smiled up at her, his blue-gray eyes crinkled in a laugh. His white blond hair was shorter than it had been in their last video call. His face was tanned and weathered from a career spent on the ocean, and she could see the essence of weariness in his eyes which had been present since last fall when this whole mess had begun.

"This man is your uncle?"

Her heart clenched.

"Yes, he is. Where is he?" she whispered.

She took a sip of the coffee in an effort to steady her emotions, then coughed as it scalded her throat. Anderson slid a stack of napkins closer to her. His gaze even more empathetic than it had been a moment ago.

"What is it?" she said. "Just tell me."

He leaned forward, his elbows braced against his knees, hands loosely clasped. Her heart sank into her toes. His eyes met hers.

"Ms. Sullivan, we suspect your uncle was taken."

CHAPTER FOUR

"What?" Morgan blinked hard, as numbness engulfed her.

No. Oh, no, no, no, this wasn't happening. She pinned the detective with a desperate look.

"You think he's been kidnapped? By whom?"

Who would want to take Daniel? Everyone loved him. He didn't have an enemy in the world. At least that she knew of.

"We don't know yet, Ms. Sullivan." Her eyes darted to his, and saw nothing but sincerity on his face. His steady voice was calming. "I promise we are doing everything in our power to find him."

She drew a shuddered breath. "Thank you."

He dipped his head slightly, and slipped a small leatherbound notepad and a pen from his jacket pocket. She took a sip of her coffee and stared down at Daniel's photo.

"You two are close?" The detective said, quietly.

"Yes." Her voice was faint. She cleared her throat quietly. "My brother and I used to spend summers at our grandparents' house. Daniel lived next door."

Being with him was like summer camp, only better. Daniel hadn't had children of his own. He'd passed on his love of the ocean, lore, and literature to her. Like a surrogate daughter. Her mother had encouraged their relationship, though she had still grumbled good-naturedly about her daughter following her brother into deep sea geologic oceanography over her own field of marine ecology.

The rustle of notepaper jolted Morgan from her thoughts. She met Anderson's assessing gaze.

"When we spoke yesterday, you said he seemed worried?" he said.

Had it only been yesterday? Their phone call felt like a million years ago. She squeezed her eyes shut, her last call with her uncle played through her head. Guilt swirled in her gut.

"He did, yes. He seemed more distracted than normal." Tears blurred her vision as she opened her eyes. She sipped her coffee, to loosen the knot in her throat. Anderson waited patiently for her to continue. "I wanted to visit, but he said it wasn't a good time. He said he needed to help a friend."

She blinked. She'd forgotten that part.

"A friend?" Anderson's pen scratched against the paper. "Did your uncle mention this friend's name?"

She squeezed her eyes shut. Her fingers pinched against the bridge of her nose. Memories of their last video chat danced through her mind. They'd talked about her research, and a few of his own. About their family. And then about her proposed trip. The call hadn't lasted much longer after he'd asked her not to come.

She shook her head. "No. No, he didn't."

Daniel hadn't shared much of anything with her about his life at Winston College. Not really. Or what had made him leave Maui so suddenly.

"Was that unusual?"

She sighed heavily. "Not lately, no. I only know of one friend Daniel had at Winston—Dr. Alan Dolan, the dean. He was a roommate of Daniel's from their undergrad days. He invited Daniel to guest lecture at Winston. He'd been trying for years to get Daniel to agree."

And after years of declining, Daniel had suddenly accepted out of the blue.

She took a sip of her lukewarm coffee in an effort to wash away the bitter taste the thoughts left behind. She stared at his picture dully.

"Do you think this 'friend' was involved in his kidnapping?" She met the detective's eyes.

Anderson leaned forward in his chair. "Maybe. I assure you, Ms. Sullivan, we are following every lead."

"What makes you think he's been kidnapped?" The word hurt to say. "Yesterday you said he'd been in an accident and came through a window?"

He nodded slightly. "There was an accident, and a witness said he saw a man jump through a window moments before the explosion. We found your uncle's phone in a depression in the snow beneath the window, and tracks leading to the sidewalk."

"There was a witness?" A faint flicker of hope wavered, and she sat up straighter. "Did they see who took Daniel?"

Her hope snuffed out at his hesitation.

"Unfortunately, no. He was struck by a piece of debris and knocked unconscious. Your uncle was gone when he came to."

Cold settled in her gut. She drew a shaky breath.

"How do you know he was kidnapped?" she whispered. "How do you know he didn't just wander off?" She shivered at the thought of Daniel lost in the snow.

She stared at the mug clutched in her hands.

"There were signs of a struggle between the depression and the parking lot, along with tire tracks." he said, his tone gentle. "A witness saw a van pull out onto the highway shortly after the time of the explosion."

She clenched her eyes shut. In her mind she could see it—Daniel struggling to his feet, staggering to the road, only to be grabbed by a pair of shadowy figures and shoved into a van.

"Do you know where it took him?"

"Not yet," Anderson said. "Do you know of anyone who might want to harm your uncle? Anyone he might have had a disagreement or issue with?"

She gave him a half shrug and met his eyes. "No one in particular. Everyone liked Daniel."

Anderson's eyebrow rose slightly. She frowned.

"Okay. Apparently not everyone," she said. "What about the lab? Why was he there in the first place? His office was in the English Department building on the other side of campus."

They'd joked about that fact. A scientist teaching literature—sea monster legends and myths.

Anderson flipped through his notebook then paused to consult a page. "Apparently he was there working on a set of experiments in preparation for a guest lecture the next morning. The accident was thought to have been caused by a propane explosion. The fire department also found traces of magnesium—"

"Flash powder." Heat rushed to her face. "Sorry, I didn't mean to interrupt. Was it a geology lab?"

"Yes. As a matter of fact, it is a geology lab," Anderson confirmed.

She smiled wearily. Once a geologist always a geologist.

"It was one of Daniel's favorite experiments when he taught Geology 101," she said. "Flash powder, used for photography lighting in the old days. It shouldn't have caused an explosion though."

Not the way Daniel did it. She'd accidently set a lab table and a book on fire once, but it had only scorched the fire proofing before she'd pounded it out. The propane tanks would have been stored safely beneath the tables. Or should have been. She caught a flicker of hesitation in Anderson's expression. A comment he had made earlier struck her.

"You said the witness saw Daniel come through the window before the explosion, not after." She pinned him with her stare. "What aren't you telling me? What else happened in that lab?"

Anderson held her gaze. "I don't know for certain, Ms. Sullivan, but I'm going to do my best to find out."

Her gut told her he knew more than he was sharing. She forced her face to relax. Anderson wasn't the enemy; he was just doing his job.

"What if it wasn't Daniel they were after?" she said, quietly. "Whose lab was it?"

"We are looking into the possibility," he said. "Has your uncle ever mentioned a Dr. Catlett?"

"No." She sank back into the couch. "Was it Dr. Catlett's lab? Have you spoken with him?"

Anderson nodded. He closed his notebook and set it on the table, his gaze calm and steady. "We have. Your uncle was supposed meet him at the lab. Dr. Catlett was delayed."

Delayed? The window of the break room rattled violently. She startled, her gaze darting toward the sound. Raised voices filled the squad room beyond the glass.

"Stay here." Anderson stuffed his notebook in his jacket pocket and left the room, shutting the door firmly behind him. But not before she caught a few words.

"... report to your superiors. I'll have your badge!"

The voices grew louder. She pushed to her feet and took a step closer to the window. The sheriff stood in the doorway of his office, red faced and shouting, as the man in the suit stalked across the crowded room. She took a step back as the man shifted his glare toward her. Cold anger burned in his dark eyes. He wrenched open the door to the reception area. The windows rattled again as he slammed it behind him.

Her eyes darted back to the sheriff, as he stalked back into his office, his face beet red. He slammed the door. What the heck was going on? For a small town, things were certainly far from quiet. She turned around as the door behind her opened. But it wasn't the detective.

"Morgan Sullivan?"

The woman in the suit. Her heels cut a sharp, purposeful cadence as she crossed the room. Her green eyes held warmth her partner's lacked, and a touch of ... familiarity? Morgan was fairly certain she'd never met the woman before.

"I'm Morgan."

She accepted the woman's outstretched hand.

"I'm Special Agent Cynthia Blake with the FBI. I don't have time to talk right now, but I'd like to speak with you later. About your uncle."

The door opened, and Anderson stepped inside.

"You need to leave, Agent Blake." His voice was weary but firm. "Now please."

Morgan's eyes darted between the agent to the detective, and back again. The agent inclined her head slightly in response, her eyes never leaving Morgan's.

"Be careful who you trust, Ms. Sullivan." Her words were quiet. She smiled. "I'll be in touch."

She turned and with a nod to Anderson, she left the room. Morgan watched the agent as she crossed to the outer door and left the squad room without looking back. Weird.

She raised an eyebrow.

"What was that about?"

Anderson grimaced. The sheriff bellowed his name through the glass.

"I apologize, Ms. Sullivan, but it appears we will have to continue our discussion later."

She opened her mouth to argue, but shut it at the look of weariness in his eyes.

"I look forward to it," she said.

He opened the door and beckoned to a deputy, a younger man with a shock of bright red hair and a smattering of freckles. She set her mug on the table and gathered her bag from the couch.

"Deputy Murry will see you out," He held out a card. "Please call me if you think of anything else. And Ms. Sullivan, we will do our best to find your uncle, I promise."

A small bit of tension in her gut uncoiled at the sincerity she sensed in his words.

"I believe you."

He smiled. "Do you have a place to stay? The inn and practically every bed and breakfast in the county has been overrun by reporters, but my mother-in-law runs the boarding house on the Winston campus. And she has a thing against reporters."

"Macy Roberts?" she said.

A faint edge of amusement trickled through her. Daniel had mentioned Macy—more than once.

The detective nodded. "Your uncle has a room there. Macy has one waiting for you if you want it, for as long as you need it."

Tears pricked her eyes at the kindness. She hadn't given any thought to where she would stay.

"Thank you," she said. "Please let me know if you learn anything new."

He promised to keep in touch, and she followed the red-haired deputy out of the squad room and through the lobby. She gave the receptionist a small wave goodbye and braced herself as she stepped out into the cold. The stairs and the street were void of reporters, the sky dim. A light snow dusted the pavement, and the air was still and heavy with the promise of more snow before the night was out.

She stood at the top of the stairs for a moment, her thoughts spinning.

"What in the world have you gotten into, Uncle Daniel?"

A blast of wind struck her. Pulling her coat tighter, she headed for the car. Her eyes darted at every shadow as she quickened her step.

Be careful who you trust, Ms. Sullivan.

She looked back over her shoulder. She'd half expected the agents to be waiting for her, but the street was empty. Too empty. Her eyes darted at the shadows as unease settled in her gut. She quickened her pace. It was getting late. Too many questions remained.

And time was running short.

CHAPTER FIVE

Winston College was a half hour's drive from Willow Creek, surrounded by snow-covered fields. According to its website, its main programs were built around agriculture, animal husbandry, veterinary science, meteorology, hydrology, fine arts, and business. The enrollment boasted fifteen thousand students.

The campus looked like a ghost town as Morgan pulled through the main gate. The clock on the dashboard showed just past six p.m. The snow-covered sidewalks were devoid of life. No guards. No lights on at the administration building. Nothing, apart from the glow of a few lampposts. The emptiness would have been less odd with spring break only a day away, but after the explosion, she would've expected more security.

Snow crunched beneath her tires as she eased the car along the icy road. She found the science building toward the rear of the campus—a towering brick structure along the shores of the lake. The unease in her stomach grew stronger as she drew closer to the building. She had to see the scene of the accident for herself. Might as well start at the beginning, though she wasn't foolish enough to believe she might catch something the police or the FBI might have missed.

Was she?

She knew Daniel better than they did after all. At the very least, maybe she'd have a chance at catching Dr. Catlett before he left for break and ask him some questions of her own.

"If only you had trusted me more." Her words slipped out in a whisper. "What were you hiding, Uncle Daniel?"

She edged her car into an empty space in the nearly full lot. Apparently, she wasn't alone after all. She buried her nose in her scarf and pulled her coat tighter as she stepped into the cold. Lights flickered in the far corner of the dimly lit lot like fireflies. Her heart stuttered as she moved toward them. Candles. A small sea of them, the soft flickering light illuminating solemn faces. Warmth trickled through the cold that had settled in her chest at the sight of strangers holding vigil for her uncle. What she'd told Anderson was true—everyone loved Daniel.

She slowed to a stop a few steps behind the group. A cold blast of air swept over them from the water, and the warmth faded with it. Yellow caution tape trembled in the wind. Her gaze strayed up the face of the building toward the second floor and the twisted frames of the windows. Dark scars of soot streaked out from beneath the plywood. The reflection of the path lamps against the snow gave the scene an eerie glow.

The air left her lungs. She could see the scene just as the detective described it. Daniel's fall through the window at least fifteen feet into a snow drift maybe three feet deep. The white-hot explosion and fire. Her uncle as he stumbled to his feet, only to be grabbed and thrown into a van ... she drew a sharp breath, the cold cutting into her lungs like shards of glass.

Oh, Lord, please help us. Please keep him safe, bring him home.

A hand touched her arm, and she startled. A girl stood beside her smiling a silent apology and offered her a candle. Morgan's hand trembled as she accepted it with a shaky smile. She bowed her head as the girl moved away. The heat warmed her frozen fingers. The small crowd had begun to sing, and she let out a choked laugh in surprise. A sea shanty. One of Daniel's creations. Some words were missing and stumbled over with a twitter of laughter, but the sentiment held strong.

"Into the deep we go." The words slipped from her lips. "Into the dark below."

Her gaze flickered upward toward the windows and back to the disturbed snow on the ground beneath them. Anger flickered through the cold as she traced the tracks which led to the road. She was going to find out what happened to her uncle and bring him home. He owed her answers.

Morgan quietly edged away from the group and extinguished the small flame. There was work to be done. She lowered her head against the wind and headed around the side of the building. Light spilled from the windows of the four-story glass front. She brushed the remaining tears from her eyes, then pulled the door open and stepped inside. Her attention was immediately caught by the curved wall parallel to the glass. A slab of slate, polished and gleaming, dotted with fossils of shells, trilobites, and feathered sea worms. The display was incredible.

"Let me guess. Geologist?"

She spun toward the voice, suddenly aware of the thick band of black fabric that cordoned off the entrance. A band she was currently leaning against. The sandy-haired man in a security guard uniform gave her a friendly smile. She gave him a sheepish look in return.

"Geological oceanographer," she said, approaching his makeshift desk.

He laughed, and she couldn't help but smile back.

"I don't think you will find many of those around here," he said.

She raised an eyebrow. "I heard you had a deep-sea oceanography professor in the Lit. Department."

"Maybe so." He shrugged. "How can I help you? This building has been closed off to students—safety protocols and all that. Exams have been cancelled, but the TAs are on hand if you have questions." He tapped his computer. "I've got the list right here."

He shifted the screen away from her view as she tried to read it.

"I'm looking for one of the professors," she said.

Keys tapped, and he gave her an apologetic smile. "Sorry. It looks like they are all out. Most of the building has been blocked off due to the damage."

She sighed inwardly. Worth a shot.

"Could I leave a message?" she said.

"I could try, but they might not get it until tomorrow."

Not ideal, but tomorrow was better than nothing. Though every minute Daniel was missing ...

"Who is it for?" the guard said, fingers posed over the keys.

"Dr. Catlett."

The friendly smile tightened, and wariness crept into his blue eyes.

"Are you a reporter?" he said.

A surprised laugh escaped her. Though she supposed it was a fair question.

"No, I'm not a reporter." She pulled her card and a pen from the pocket of her bag and scribbled her cell phone number on the back.

A flicker of recognition crossed the guard's face as he read her name. "You're Morgan Sullivan?" He slipped a card from the pocket of his shirt. "Dr. Catlett asked me to give this to you if you happened to come looking for him."

Her forehead furrowed in surprise. Okay ... how had Catlett known she was coming? She hadn't even known of his existence until a couple of hours ago. The whole ordeal was disconcerting. She took the card. Dr. Scott Catlett, Geologic and Hydrologic Sciences. She flipped it over. A number was scrawled in blue ink. No message. The guard watched her with unabashed curiosity. She smiled as she tucked the card into the pocket of her bag. "Thank you. One more question if you don't mind."

"I live to serve."

She couldn't help but return his grin.

"Is there a coffee shop on campus?"

There most certainly was. The best in the state, if the guard's recommendation could be trusted. She bade him a good evening and left with a recommendation to try the gingerbread, and to tell them Andrew had sent her.

KULA, MAUI
MORGAN, AGE NINE

The map crinkled as Morgan leaned in for a closer look at the fantastical creatures etched on the yellowing paper. She squinted. They didn't look real, but Daniel said they were. Her uncle was usually right. At least about sea monsters. She tilted her head to the side and squinted harder.

"Try this," Daniel said.

She took the antique magnifying glass from his hand with a grin. It was her favorite of all his treasures. She carefully wrapped her fingers around the smooth handle, balancing its weight with one hand. Pleased she no longer needed two hands like she had when she was little, she held it over the map.

"What do you see?" The worn floorboards creaked as he settled onto the floor on the opposite side of the map.

"I don't think this is a whale," she said.

The creature had weird teeth. And it looked like a warthog. A warthog with a mermaid tail. Too weird.

"Hypothesis?"

She squinted at the map. Well ... the creature it was attacking was supposed to be a whale. If whales had owl faces. Daniel said they were drawn by a man who hadn't seen them, just heard stories. The sailors must have liked telling tall tales.

"Well, it had flippers and big teeth." She leaned closer to the map for a better look. "And it ate whales. Maybe."

She rubbed the bridge of her nose with her forefinger like she'd seen Daniel do. Something about the picture made her think of one of his stories. She snapped her fingers.

"Like the German sub monster," she said. "Yeah?"

She'd read an exciting story about a German sub boat captain in WW1 in one of Daniel's books. They'd sunk a British merchant ship, and when the ship blew up a creature was thrown from the ocean into the air.

"It has flippers." She tapped the picture with her finger. "Four of them. Not two, like a whale. And really big teeth."

There was a second story, about another German sub that had been attacked on the surface of the ocean by a big creature with a mouth full of large teeth. Like a giant crocodile with a jaw strong enough to crunch metal. She imagined the creature as something brave enough to attack a whale.

"That was close to Ireland." She reached over and pulled the world atlas closer to the map and traced her finger along the page from the southern tip of Ireland to Norway. "And Ireland is kind of near Norway where this creature was."

She tapped the map with her finger.

Her uncle smiled. "Good hypothesis. What do you think it is?"

She beamed at him. "mosasaur."

She dragged another open book closer to the map, a book of prehistoric marine reptiles. The artwork depicted a large marine reptile, with large teeth and a crocodile-like body, but a blunted nose and curved flippers.

"It looks like the one the German captain described."

Daniel grinned. "Could be."

A wild yell came from outside the open windows, and she groaned. Her brother was back. Daniel only smirked when she looked pleadingly at him.

"We can finish this later," he said as he pushed himself up off the floor. "Record your findings. Meet us by the cave when you are done."

Excitement replaced the disappointment as he collected a scroll from his desk.

"Treasure hunt?"

He winked. "Aye, little matey. There be treasure."

The recommended coffee shop resided in a corner of the Student Center, a short drive from the Science building. Morgan grinned at the name as she carefully walked up the stairs.

AT WIT'S END.

Someone had a sense of humor. A fitting name for a college campus coffee house.

A heavenly scent washed over her as she stepped inside. Exotic coffee. Warm baked goods. Rich chocolate. Her stomach rumbled. She joined the short line at the counter and scanned the room. The shop, like the rest of the campus, was sparsely populated. A small group of co-eds was gathered around a couple of round tables near the ceiling-to-floor bookshelves. A couple sat at a small table near the windows looking out over the quad, and a dark head of hair was visible over the top of an overstuffed chair near the stone fireplace in the rear of the room.

She felt some of the tension bleed from her shoulders as she soaked in the comforting atmosphere. Coffee. Books. Fireplace. This place was heaven. The sort of place Daniel would have adored. She checked her phone while she waited. The charger she'd purchased at the gas station wasn't the best, but it had worked. Somewhat. Twenty percent was better than dead.

No messages from Dr. Catlett. She'd tried the number on the card as soon as she returned to her car, but he hadn't answered. Same with his office number. Unwilling to concede defeat, she'd sent a text to the cell number, asking if he would like to join her for a coffee. Still nothing. Her phone wasn't the issue. She had ten text messages from Keoni. Nate had finally sent the rest of the video feeds. Keoni was insistent the blob wasn't a whale. She squinted wearily at the image on her phone, it was still too blurry to tell.

"Rough night, huh?"

She looked up. The barista gave her a warm, vaguely familiar smile.

"Yeah, you could say that," Morgan said as she scanned the chalkboard menu at the counter.

She looked over to the row of glass bell jars filled with various colored spices and chocolate powder lining the shelf above a gleaming espresso machine. Her brain felt sluggish.

"So many choices."

"Leave it to me." The girl grinned and made her way to the espresso machine. "Any allergies?"

"None." Her stomach rumbled again as she scanned the boards. "I hear you have the best coffee in the state. A security guard, Andrew, said I should try your gingerbread."

"How do you feel about chocolate?" The barista's eyes twinkled.

"The darker the better."

The barista gave her an approving smile and reached for a glass jar. Morgan watched as she added a scoop of dark chocolate powder into the milk and then a smaller scoop of another lighter colored powder.

"Was Andrew a blond guy with a mischievous smile?" Morgan nodded.

"You've met my brother," she yelled over the hiss of the steamer. "He's biased, but I love him for it."

Ah, no wonder she looked familiar. The barista had the same sparkling eyes and grin as the security guard.

"I'm Leslie, by the way. This is my shop."

"It's a great shop," Morgan said.

The kind of place she'd practically live in. Ceramic clinked as a mug appeared on the counter before her, topped with whipped cream and dusted with cinnamon.

"Give that a try." Leslie said with a grin.

Mere words could not describe the drink. It was ... well to overuse a word, it was heaven in a cup. Sweet. Spicy. Thick. Rich. Comforting. The dark brew warmed her to her toes. Worth braving the cold for.

"I have no words," Morgan said.

"I call it the Dr. S. special," Leslie said, "After one of our professors."

Morgan smiled fondly and took another sip. This was something Daniel would have dreamed up. "Dr. Smithson?"

Sadness dampened the girl's smile. "Yeah. Of course, he was in favor of calling it the Sullivan. He thought you'd be a fan."

Morgan inhaled sharply, then groped blindly for the stack of napkins Leslie offered, as she coughed the drink from her lungs.

"I'm sorry," Leslie said, "Guess I was right, you are Morgan."

"How'd you know?" She took another sip to quell her coughing.

"That's a lovely tan for this time of year, especially for Iowa," Leslie said, and then shrugged. "And he showed me a picture once. You have his eyes."

Daniel hadn't said anything about this shop, but he'd showed her picture to a stranger. Not that showing pictures to strangers was out of character for him. He'd never really met a stranger who hadn't become a friend.

As if Leslie read her thoughts, she reached a hand across the counter and squeezed Morgan's gently. "I'm sorry. He is a good man. I am praying for him."

The tears choking her now had nothing to do with the coffee. Leslie gave her hand another squeeze and then moved back, giving her a moment. Morgan swallowed hard and pushed the sorrow away. There would be time to cry later. She cleared her throat quietly.

"Was Daniel here that night?" she said.

Leslie nodded. "He was. Stayed until I closed up around eleven."

Only an hour before the explosion. Questions raced through her mind. The door chimed and Leslie smiled brightly as she greeted the group of newcomers.

"Why don't you enjoy your coffee," she said, turning back to Morgan. "I'll dish up some supper and bring it out to you."

Food sounded wonderful. As did a chance to question the woman further. Morgan offered her credit card, but Leslie shook her head and waved it away.

"On the house," Leslie said. "Go relax by the fireplace, I'll just be a few minutes."

Morgan collected her coffee from the counter and headed toward the warmth of the fire blazing in the stone hearth. She slipped her phone from her pocket as she went. Still nothing from Dr. Catlett. And another five messages from Keoni. She lowered her bag to the floor beside an empty leather chair and sank into it. Every bone in her body melted into the comfortably worn leather. She let her eyes drift closed for a moment.

The fire crackled. Quiet voices ebbed and flowed. Paper rustled. Her phone chimed. Her limbs felt heavy as she fumbled for it. She struggled to open her eyes. She opened the message, and her pulse quickened. Dr. Catlett.

CATLETT: You shouldn't be here.

Confusion, and indignation, surged through her, burning away the weariness. Her thumbs danced over the keypad. She paused and let out a breath, deleted her response, then replaced it with one word.

MORGAN: Why?

A phone pinged from the chair opposite her. She glanced up into a pair of startling blue eyes, the color of the deep ocean on a cloudless day. A shiver trickled through her at the intensity of the man's gaze, and then he looked away, shifting his attention to the stack of paper balanced precariously against his knee. She watched as his pen darted over the page.

Her eyes shifted to her phone. Annoyance simmered through her as it remained silent. She sighed and leaned back into her chair. She rubbed her eyes and took a sip of her coffee. This was madness. Why leave her his number if he was just going to send her cryptic messages. She was exactly where she should be.

She glared at the phone. Her gaze flicked toward the man in the opposite chair. He was watching her. His jaw tensed and he shifted his attention back to the papers. She sipped her coffee and watched him warily out of the corner of her eye. He was kind of attractive. Dark hair, square jaw ...

He shifted forward and dropped another folder on top of the stack on the table between them. Her gaze settled on the leather jacket draped over the back of the chair. And then it hit her. The man at the sheriff's office. Her annoyance flared as she pinned him with a stare.

"Doctor Scott Catlett, I presume."

CHAPTER SIX

A faint smile pulled at the corner of his mouth; his attention focused on his grading. Her eyes narrowed.

"Morgan Sullivan." His smile faded. "You shouldn't be here."

Anger boiled through her. Who was he to tell her what she should and should not do? She forced her anger to calm. She needed answers, and Catlett was still her best, and only, lead.

She leaned back in her chair, her eyes never leaving his.

"Why shouldn't I be here? My uncle needs my help. Where else would I be?"

He grinned, as if in response to an inside joke. "You're just as your uncle described you."

She bit her tongue and forced a breath.

"I am at quite the disadvantage here. You seem to know more about me than I know about you. And you didn't answer my question, Dr. Catlett."

His pen scratched against the paper. The man was exasperating. She straightened in her chair and tried a different approach.

"Why was Daniel in your lab?" She watched his jaw tick, and the pen paused its movement. "Where were you?"

He finished his notes, capped his pen, and dropped it and the remaining paper on the stack. His eyes met hers with an unreadable expression.

"Daniel offered to guest lecture my Geology 101 lab. He was setting up the experiments."

So, she had been right about the flash powder.

"At midnight?"

He shrugged. Her uncle being in a lab so late wasn't an oddity. He'd kept strange hours, ever since the death of her aunt. Something about this guy didn't sit right with her. She watched his gaze sweep the room as he settled back into his chair.

She leaned forward. "Where were you?"

Catlett flinched so subtly she would have missed it had she not been watching. He turned toward the fire, his face expressionless, but she'd seen something in his eyes before he'd looked away. Guilt maybe.

"I was in my office, two floors up, grading papers," he said. "I was planning on joining him, but I was late." His jaw tensed.

"Do you know what happened to Daniel?"

He glanced at her, an intense sadness in his eyes. And then it shuttered away so quickly she wondered if she'd imagined it. The clink of ceramic startled her as a tray slid onto the table between them, edging the precariously stacked papers out of the way. Catlett collected them, and stuffed them into his leather bag.

"Two specials of the day," Leslie said, with a bright smile.

Morgan swallowed her frustration. Her eyes warning Catlett that their discussion was not over. He ignored her, shifting his attention to the barista.

"You are the best." Catlett smiled at the girl, his face relaxed.

Butterflies churned in Morgan's stomach as he turned the smile on her. She drowned them with a sip of cooling coffee as she stared at him, unflinching. Humor danced in his eyes. He looked away as he broke off a piece of gingerbread and bit into it.

Leslie returned his smile. "Are you headed out in the morning?"

"No," he said, his smile fading. "I'm going to stick around, help where I can."

More than likely the police had asked him not to leave town. Morgan watched as Leslie gave his shoulder a squeeze. He didn't deserve sympathy. He was probably the reason Daniel was missing.

"Let me know if I can help in any way," the barista said. He nodded his thanks. "I see you met Morgan."

Morgan forced a smile as Leslie looked toward her.

"Small world," she said, dryly.

"Dr. S. left this the other night," Leslie said. She pulled a book from her apron and held it out to Morgan. "I thought you might like to hold on to it for him."

She balanced her mug on her knee and took it. The book was a dog-eared copy of Daniel's favorite novel, *Twenty Thousand Leagues Under the Sea* by Jules Verne. He was always picking up copies at used bookstores wherever he went.

"Thank you." A wave of conflicting emotions washed over her, leaving her feeling drained. She bowed her head slightly, thumbing through the book while she gathered herself together. She paused at the sight of writing in the margins of some of the pages. Random markings, like some sort of code. They reminded her of the games her uncle had played with her and her brother when they were kids.

"I caught your uncle's lecture once," Leslie said. "When he first arrived, he held an open symposium on sea monsters in classic literature. It was really fun."

Morgan smiled despite the heaviness settling over her.

"It was something," Catlett said, amusement in his tone.

Her smile faltered as irritation competed with her fatigue. She set the book aside and picked up her mug. She stared at Catlett.

"Did he share his theories?"

He grinned at her. "About sea monsters living today? Yeah, he did."

"And what was your opinion?"

He shrugged. "He made a good case, but I can't say I would come across many sea monsters in my line of study." He paused for effect. "Groundwater aquifers."

Yeah, probably not.

"What about the theory about underwater rivers," she said, a challenge in her voice.

"Like Loch Ness?" Catlett shrugged. "Daniel shared that one. Nothing much in the aquifers of Iowa. At least not that anyone has noticed."

They shared a companionable smile for a moment before she remembered she didn't have reason to trust him. And he still hadn't answered her question.

"Well, I think the thought of a real live sea monster still out there somewhere is thrilling." Leslie said, her smile faded to a grimace as she stared out the window behind them. "Dr. C., that reporter I warned you about is heading this way."

Morgan leaned around the edge of the chair, craning her neck to see. The man with the slicked back hair she'd seen in the lobby of the sheriff's office was striding up to the building. Catlett stood and quickly gathered his things.

Leslie headed for the front door. "Use the back door, I'll head him off."

Morgan stood, blocking his way. "We're not done."

The expressionless mask was back in place when he met her stare.

"If you want to help your uncle, go home, Ms. Sullivan."

He stepped around her, then crossed the room to the counter and vanished through the kitchen door.

Indignation flared through her as she grabbed her bag and hurried after him. She heard the front door chime and Leslie's greeting as she slipped behind the counter and through the swinging door. The kitchen was empty. She ducked around a stainless-steel island and bolted for the backdoor. The metal bar clanged against the door, and she rushed out into the cold night. She stumbled forward as her foot caught against the edge of the threshold, right off the edge of the concrete platform and into a knee-high snow drift.

Perfect. She ignored the snow steadily seeping into her jeans as she scanned the area for the fugitive professor. He was nowhere to be found. Perfect. Just, perfect. The wind whipped around the corner of the building. She pulled her coat tighter and scowled as she slogged her way to the cleared blacktop.

The world tilted violently as her feet flew out from under her, and she found herself lying on the ground, the wind knocked out of her. Tears burned her eyes as she lay there gasping. She wasn't certain if the tears were from pain or frustration. They added to her misery as the wind froze each drop against her skin.

"I hate the cold!"

The snow continued to fall, heedless of her declaration. She carefully sat up, body aching, then eased to her feet and dusted the snow from her hair and clothes. The wind cut through her damp jeans, and she slipped again as she struggled toward the door. Annoyance flared to frustration as she struggled up the icy stairs, only to find the door firmly locked. No amount of knocking brought help.

Great. Fantastic.

She took a deep breath and let it out slowly, forcing herself to calm down. She tugged her coat closer as her head cleared and jumped off the edge of the platform back into the snowdrift, which seemed the lesser of two frozen evils, and a little more forgiving than the ice. Anger burned as she picked her way toward the front of the building. Her fingers and toes were numb, her feet soaked and her boots a lost cause. She hadn't planned to slog through snow when she'd bought them. She hadn't planned for any of this.

You shouldn't be here.

Her frown deepened at Catlett's words.

Go home, Ms. Sullivan.

She stopped in her tracks and spun toward the darkness he'd vanished into.

"I'm not going home!"

There was no reply, but she hadn't been expecting one. He couldn't make her leave. No one could. She wasn't leaving until she found Daniel ... or at least what had happened to him. She could do this. She was a scientist. Trained by one of the best. This was just another puzzle, and she was good at puzzles. All she needed were the right answers.

But all she had at the moment were questions.

She lowered her head against the wind and quickened her pace. Her pocket buzzed, and she fumbled for her phone. Her anger fizzled.

Her grandfather.

Her finger hesitated over the screen. Did he know about Daniel? Her shoulders slumped. She should have told them herself. The story was probably all over the news by now which wasn't fair to them. She shivered as the cold bit into her. Her heart sank into her stomach. She was a terrible granddaughter.

The call went to voicemail. The small bit of relief she felt only made the guilt stronger.

"Ms. Sullivan."

She startled at the unfamiliar voice. A man stood at the corner of the building, silhouetted against the light from the parking lot and blocking her way. Her fingers tightened around her phone. She glanced around. Of course, no one else was in sight. She took a step back.

"My mother told me to never talk to strangers," she said.

She grimaced at the tremor in her voice. Her whole body was shaking, from cold and fatigue, not fear. The man's chuckle did nothing to alleviate her concern.

"Your uncle said you were precocious."

She sighed inwardly. Daniel would not have used such a word. The man slipped a hand from his coat, and she took another step back. He held up both hands. A wallet flipped open in one. Metal reflected dully in the dim light. He took a step back into the light. Revealing himself as the man in the dark suit from the sheriff's office, with the cold eyes and bad attitude.

"Special Agent Jonathan Weston, FBI," he said. "We'd like a moment of your time."

Fat chance. Still, curiosity edged through her caution. She glanced around for his partner, Agent Blake.

"We?"

He tossed the badge toward her and signaled to someone out of sight. She caught the leather folder out of reflex and held it up to the light. A dark SUV eased to a stop beside Agent Weston. He opened the rear door and gestured to her.

"If you would, Ms. Sullivan."

She tapped the wallet against her hand as her eyes darted from the vehicle to the parking lot beyond. Her thoughts warred between the man's attitude and her own curiosity, weighing the risk.

"You do want your uncle back, don't you, Ms. Sullivan?"

Anger swirled through her. She considered tossing his badge into the snow and refusing.

"You know where he is?" she said.

Her heart fell a little as he shook his head slightly.

"But we know who took him."

She crossed the distance, handed the wallet back and, ignoring his smirk, climbed into the SUV. The door closed behind her, sealing in the dark. Perhaps this wasn't the best idea she'd ever had, but at least it was warm. Well, warmer. Didn't anybody in this frozen land believe in proper heat? She pulled her coat tighter.

"I'd like to apologize for my partner, Ms. Sullivan," Agent Blake smiled at her from the driver's seat. "It has been a long day."

Understatement of the century.

The warmth was diminished as her partner climbed into the front seat and slammed the door behind him. A clump of snow fell from her boot and splattered against the floor. She hoped the rental agency would charge the cleaning bill to Special Agent Bad Attitude. If this was a rental. Did the FBI rent cars? The SUV eased away from the curb and into the night. She settled back into the seat. No turning back now. She startled as the locks snapped into place. They clicked back up a moment later.

"For goodness sakes, she's not a prisoner, Weston," Blake said.

Weston turned in his seat, ignoring his partner. "Why are you here, Ms. Sullivan?"

Morgan suppressed a shiver. Her parents had raised her to respect authority, but they'd also raised her not to respect it blindly. She refused to be intimidated into answering questions. No matter who asked them.

"Who took my uncle?" she said.

She heard a quiet snort from his partner. Weston's face was shadowed. He countered with another question.

"Ms. Sullivan, what do you know about the work your uncle was doing at Winston College?"

His question caught her off guard and her frustration fizzled a bit.

"Not to be uncooperative, but I've already spoken with Detective Anderson." And they had jurisdiction. Right?

She kept her eyes on Weston's silhouette as the SUV turned off the well-lit avenue and onto a dark side street.

"Please answer the question, Ms. Sullivan," Weston said.

"Who took my uncle, Agent Weston?"

She was cold, wet, jetlagged, and nearing the end of her patience. And extremely tired of having her questions answered with more questions. The man was frustratingly silent. His partner cleared her throat softly.

"Please, Ms. Sullivan," Blake said. "Any information you might have could help us find your uncle."

"He said you knew who took Daniel," she countered.

Agent Blake turned toward her partner. Interesting. That seemed to have touched a nerve. Weston ignored her, which didn't bode well for her chances at answers. Perhaps she should just play along. More flies with honey, and all of that. She leaned back into the seat.

"Daniel was invited to guest lecture for a seminar class for the spring semester," Morgan said. "As far as I know his work entailed giving lectures and grading papers."

"Who invited him?" Weston said.

"You don't know?" *Okay, maybe not the greatest answer.* She let out a breath as she tried to reign in her emotions. "Dr. Alan Dolan, the dean. They're old college buddies."

"What do you know about the night of his disappearance?" Weston said.

She shrugged and folded her arms across her chest.

"There was an explosion, Daniel went through a window and now he is missing." She stared at the back of Weston's head. "And you know who took him."

A thick silence filled the vehicle.

"Not to be uncooperative," she said, "but isn't this case under the jurisdiction of the Willow Creek Sheriff's Office? I wish I knew more, I really do, but Daniel didn't tell me anything. At all. If you aren't going to either, please just take me back to my car."

The words came out in a rush, like water bursting from a dam. Sudden and potentially destructive. She instantly regretted it, and resisted the urge to rub her eyes. She buried her hands in her pockets. The agents glanced at each other, and she swore she saw Blake smirk, though it could have been a trick of the light from a streetlamp. They had turned into a better lit street. The flashes of light played with the dull throb in her head. Just when she thought she'd ruined her chances, Weston spoke.

"Your uncle took the position at our request," Weston said.

She stared at the man in disbelief, her brain spinning.

"Daniel's a spy?" Her voice squeaked.

Blake coughed. "Not exactly. Your uncle was assisting the FBI with a rather sensitive case. We can't tell you anything further regarding that case, other than we know your uncle had a source at the college. Someone he was trying to convince to come forward as a material witness."

Huh. Okay then. She gave in and dug her fingers into the bridge of her nose. "Why Daniel?"

The agents glanced at each other.

"He came to us," Blake said.

Morgan considered this, as well as Daniel's odd behavior since his friend's death last September. Another accident. A car and a cliff. She sighed and dropped her hand as Weston turned in his seat to face her. She pushed further back into the stiff cushions and held his stare.

"We believe your uncle was going to meet with them the night of his disappearance," he said. "It is imperative to our investigation that we know the identity of his source."

Why tell her? Why didn't Daniel tell the agents? Something felt ... off. Her uncle didn't act without reason. At least, not usually.

"Why are you telling me this?"

"You knew him best," Blake said. "People will empathize with your situation. They will talk to you."

Morgan's brain stuttered. Knew him? Ice settled around her heart at the past tense of the word. "You think he is dead?"

The vehicle eased to a stop. Blake turned in her seat. There was sadness and compassion on her face. Morgan rejected it, refusing to accept that Daniel might be lost forever.

"We will do everything in our power to find your uncle," Blake said.

A car and a cliff. A lab and an explosion. A death and a disappearance.

"Have any of the others come back?" she said, playing on a hunch that Daniel was not the first.

A flicker of surprise crossed the woman's face.

"We will do everything in our power to find him," Blake repeated, an edge of steel in her voice.

Morgan released the breath she'd been holding. Maybe there was still a chance.

"How can I help?" she said.

"Just keep your ears open, Ms. Sullivan," Blake said.

A blast of frigid air sucked the warmth from the car as Weston opened his door and slid out, revealing her own car waiting just a few feet away.

"Be careful," Blake said. "We'll be in touch."

Morgan glanced at the woman and then at the open door and her partner standing stoically beside it. She wasn't getting any more answers tonight. She slid from the car. A light snow still fell. Weston shut the door as soon as she was clear.

"Ms. Sullivan, what do you know of the Leviathan?"

Weston's words caught her off guard. She turned and looked at him. He stared back—his face impassive. Why was that of importance? Could this night get any weirder?

"The sea monster?" She stared at the agent. "Probably a mosasaur. Mentioned in the Bible at least five times, most notably in Job chapter 41." And Daniel's pet obsession. But what did it have to do with his disappearance? Weston handed her a business card.

"Be careful, Ms. Sullivan," he said. "Be cautious of any sudden job offers."

He opened the door and climbed inside before she could gather her thoughts. She stared as the vehicle vanished into the darkness. The night was silent—the strange heavy kind of silence—like an out of body experience, or a dream, when disbelief sets in. Surely this couldn't be real. Could it? Her head throbbed. The whole situation was like the plot of a spy novel.

Morgan watched as a small cluster of co-eds hurried by, their laughter shattering the quiet. Her world had been shaken to its core, and yet life moved on. Life always moved on. She unlocked her car and slipped inside. Cold air blasted from the vents as she turned the key. She fumbled to shut them off, then sat back and folded her trembling hands, blowing what little heat she had left into them. Her thoughts muddled like searching for pennies in a mud puddle.

She closed her eyes in concentration. Okay. Daniel worked for the FBI. She would bet money he'd gone to them. This seemed slightly more plausible considering his recent behavior. Ever since the death of his friend in a supposed accident, Daniel had shut himself away, delving deep into a project he'd kept quiet from everyone. Even her. And then he'd abruptly left for Iowa. She'd searched his lab in Maui, more than once, but had not found any answers. Not. A. One.

He'd looked tired during their last video call. Worried. Distracted. Even more than usual. When she'd questioned him, he'd dismissed her concerns with a smile and changed the subject. Their new normal. Three days later, he'd gone missing.

A heavy sigh bled through her.

"Why didn't you trust me, Daniel?"

Would it have made a difference if he had?

CHAPTER SEVEN

Her pocket vibrated. She opened her eyes and turned the heat on full blast. Her phone slipped from her frozen fingers and bounced onto the passenger seat. Great. She could see the headlines now.

Niece of missing professor found frozen to death in rental car. Police suspect cause of death to be victim's own sheer stupidity.

She vigorously shook her hands and picked it up again. The phone had fallen silent. The number was unfamiliar, from an Iowa area code. Another vibration indicated a voicemail had come through. Morgan hit the speaker phone and set it on the center console, and then pressed her blue-tinged hands against the heater vents. Her fingers tingled.

"Hi, Morgan. This is Macy Roberts. I'm a friend of your uncle's." The woman's voice hitched for a moment and then continued. "I have a room for you at my boarding house for as long as you need."

Morgan swallowed hard against the knot in her throat as she listened to the directions on how to find the house. She already knew the address by heart from the care packages she'd sent her uncle, trying to make him homesick.

"The snow is going to get bad tonight so be careful on the roads," Macy continued. "See you soon, sweetheart."

She smiled wearily at Macy's kind words. And picked up the phone and entered the address into the map app.

Thankfully the boarding house wasn't far away. The snow gave way beneath the windshield wipers. Morgan stared at the warm light spilling from the windows of the coffee shop. Her body ached with exhaustion. Not even Leslie's magic mocha was enough to tempt her back out into the cold.

She dug into her bag for a granola bar. All she wanted was a hot shower and a warm bed, along with the hope tomorrow she would wake in Maui, and this would all be a bad dream. A pair of business cards fluttered into her lap. She devoured half of the bar with one bite before reaching for the cards. She glowered at Catlett's and stuffed it back into the side pocket, but lingered for a moment on Anderson's.

Should she tell the detective about the FBI? Did he already know Daniel had worked for them? She tapped his card against the steering wheel. Her gut told her to wait. Something didn't feel right. Then again, maybe it was just a lack of sleep. She returned it to the pocket and added Weston's to the collection before zipping her bag shut.

The snow had begun to fall faster since she'd returned to her car. Big fat flakes threatened to swallow her windshield. She flicked the wipers onto a faster setting and eased the car out of the space and onto the deserted road. Maybe Mrs. Roberts would be able to provide additional insight. After all, Daniel had lived there for almost three months.

She smiled sadly. He'd spoken of Macy often—and warmly. She'd teased him about his admiration for the woman, Mrs. Roberts having lost her spouse like Daniel. Morgan had wanted him to be happy, though the thought he might stay in Iowa filled her with sadness. And now he might not even return at all. She shoved the thought back into the recesses of her mind and focused on the road.

Staying at the boarding house would give her a chance to look over Daniel's room. Maybe she'd find some clue as to the identity of the mysterious source the FBI was so keen to find. And maybe why Daniel had gone to them in the first place.

The boarding house was located at the back of the campus, on the shores of Lake Winston, not far from the Science Building. Light spilled from the windows of the two-story ranch style building as she pulled into the nearly empty lot. She zipped her coat and gathered her bag before climbing out into the cold for what she hoped was the final time that night. She grabbed her small roll-a-board suitcase from the trunk.

The door opened as she made her way up the cleared path to the wraparound porch. She stepped aside quickly as a younger looking man came rushing by, panic on his face.

"I meant what I said, young man," an older woman said as she shook her finger at him, "if you darken my door again tonight, you will regret it."

He turned a few feet out of reach, an earnest plea on his face. "My apologies, Mrs. Roberts. I mean no disrespect, but the paper—"

The older woman took a step forward. Morgan bit her lip against her smile as he scuttled backward into the snow.

"Don't make me call your mother, James Messer," she said.

He turned and fled. Morgan smirked. She liked this woman already.

"You must be Daniel's Morgan."

She turned to find Macy beaming at her.

"I am." She returned the woman's smile.

"Come on inside, sweetheart. You look frozen to the bone."

Morgan did as ordered, her smile lingering. She knocked the snow off her boots and stepped onto the porch.

"It's a pleasure to meet you, Mrs. Roberts. Thank you for your invitation."

She followed the woman inside. The house exuded warmth and comfort, and for the first time since arriving in Iowa, she felt the weariness begin to leach from her bones.

"Please, call me Macy." She took Morgan's coat and hung it on a hook beside the door. "When did you get to town?

Are you hungry?" She took Morgan's hand and winced. "You are frozen through! Come along. Just leave your bag beside the door."

Yep, just like home. Her grandmother would love Macy. She followed the older woman down the hallway to the rear of the house, through a doorway, and into a cozy kitchen.

"Have a seat, sweetheart," Macy said as she waved a hand at the table next to an honest to goodness cast iron woodstove.

Morgan sank into a chair nearest to it and soaked in the heat with a sigh of relief.

"Thank you for your hospitality, Mrs. ... Macy." She corrected at the woman's pointed look. "I hadn't really given a thought as to where I would be staying."

"You are welcome to stay as long as you would like," Macy said as she set a bowl of steaming stew in front of Morgan. "Now, eat up. You look half-starved."

Morgan's stomach grumbled, loudly. "Thank you. It smells wonderful."

The stew tasted even better. As did the corn muffins with butter and honey. A tea tray settled onto the table as Macy joined her. "This honey is from my hives out back."

"And the butter?" Morgan said as she slathered it onto another muffin.

Macy laughed. "That is from the market in town." Her smile softened, almost wistful. "You look like him. Same smile, same eyes." Tears shimmered in the older woman's eyes as she turned her attention to pouring the tea. "Daniel is always talking about you and your family. He is very proud of you."

The bite of muffin Morgan had just taken lodged like a rock in her throat. She took a sip of water, masking her own tears. *Is.* That one word made all the difference to her. To have someone else believe he was still alive, and there was a chance he'd make it home. Macy's hand covered hers and squeezed it gently.

"Daniel loves to tell stories." Morgan said, with a rueful smile as she accepted a mug of fragrant tea.

Daniel had apparently talked about her a lot. With Leslie. With Dr. Catlett. With the FBI agents. And who knows who else, but somehow it didn't bother her with Macy. Something about this woman set her at ease. She could understand why Daniel liked her.

She wrapped her hands around the mug and inhaled deeply. Lavender and mint. Heat seeped into her fingers. They had a reddish tint now and tingled, but it was better than blue. She was finally beginning to thaw. She ran her finger along the rim of the mug as she debated where to begin her questions. She took a deep breath.

"Macy, did you see Daniel that night?"

Macy's eyes held a faraway look. "Yes. He was here for dinner at seven." Her voice faltered. She cleared it softly and continued. "He seemed preoccupied, even more than usual." They shared a knowing smile. Preoccupied was practically her uncle's default setting. Macy's smile faded. "Something was bothering him that night. He insisted he was fine, but I could tell. He just gave me that charming smile of his, and left to meet Dr. Catlett at the coffee shop."

Morgan hid her frown with a sip of tea. Interesting.

"I met Dr. Catlett earlier today. Did they meet often?"

Macy's smile grew fonder. "Those two were as thick as thieves. A funny pair but good for both of them, I think. Always discussing scientific theories and arguing late into the night." She stood and added another log to the fire. "More than once, I found them still talking when I locked up the house for the night." Her brow furrowed thoughtfully. "Dr. Catlett never said much before Daniel arrived. He has such a melancholy spirit for someone so young."

Melancholy? Cryptic and frustrating with a healthy dose of arrogance were the words she would have used.

"He is a good man." Macy topped off their tea. "He and Daniel both."

First impressions argued Catlett was nothing like her uncle. Something Macy had said caught her attention.

"Dr. Catlett is a boarder here?" Morgan glanced toward the door as if expecting him to swagger through.

"Yes, he is." Macy said. "Since last September. Did you get enough to eat?"

Morgan smiled. "Yes, thank you. Is he here now?"

She still had questions. Lots of questions. And now she knew how to find him. This time he wouldn't run out on her. Her excitement fizzled as Macy shook her head.

"I haven't seen him tonight," the older woman said, "but that isn't unusual, what with midterms and that awful incident with his lab ..."

The knot returned and Morgan swallowed shakily.

"Yeah ..." She wrapped her fingers tighter around the ceramic, wondering what she would do if Daniel ... Macy reached out and squeezed her arm gently.

"They will find him, Morgan," she said, "They will find Daniel. My son-in-law is on the case, and he is very good at his job."

But in what state would they find him? She sighed through her nose. There was no use in dwelling on speculation. Until she knew for certain, she would believe Daniel was alive. And causing all sorts of trouble for his captors, she hoped. She wouldn't stop looking. Not until she found him. He would have done the same for her.

After she'd eaten, Macy showed her to a comfortable looking room on the second floor, decorated in shades of rose and cream. Best of all, it was next door to Daniel's room. The older woman set both keys on the dresser and pulled Morgan into a gentle, motherly hug.

"I'm just below," she said. "If you need anything, anything at all, you just give me a holler."

Morgan smiled. "I promise and thank you."

She sank onto the bed as the door closed behind Macy and stared at the keys as exhaustion crept through her. Her body ached from her spill on the ice, and she had never been good with sleep deprivation. One of the reasons Daniel had refused to take her night fishing, even before an accident had put an end to the boat trips for good.

But what if there was something in Daniel's room that could help them? Could she really wait until the morning? The police had probably already looked, and maybe the FBI. But what if there was something that only she would recognize? She owed it to Daniel to try. She rallied her strength and pushed off the bed, collecting the keys as she made her way out.

The hall was quiet as she moved quietly to Daniel's door. There were at least eight bedrooms on the top floor of the house, including hers and Daniels. A sour feeling curled in her belly. She wondered which one was Dr. Catlett's. No light shone from beneath any of them, apart from hers.

She inserted the key into the lock and drew a steading breath before opening the door. She switched on the light. The room was a mirror of hers only slightly larger and in shades of blue, with a desk, a small bookshelf, and a comfortable looking armchair in the alcove by the window. She set the key on the nightstand and closed the door behind her.

There were few personal items. Paperback novels and textbooks lined the bookshelf. A photo of her family from Nate and Piper's wedding last summer stood on the desk. The air left her lungs as she drew nearer. Tears that had threatened to fall all day now flowed freely as her eyes settled on the object on the desk. Daniel's Bible sat open on the desktop, frayed and well worn. A pair of reading glasses rested beside it. As if he'd just stepped out of the room for a moment.

She sank down into the chair as sorrow swept through her. A sob shook her. Somehow his disappearance felt more real now with this evidence proving he'd actually been here. In this place. She pulled herself together with a shuddering breath and rubbed her blurry eyes. She slid the Bible closer. The book was open to his favorite passage of scripture. One he'd quoted to her often: Psalm 139 verses 7 to 10. He especially loved the last two verses.

"If I take the winds of the morning, and dwell in the uttermost parts of the sea ..."

She could hear his voice, strong and clear, finishing the words ... *even there your hand shall lead me, and your right hand shall hold me.*

The words gave her some measure of comfort. God knew where Daniel was right now. God was with him. She just wished she knew where he was too. Her body shuddered as she struggled to rein in her emotions, but it was a losing battle. She curled into the chair. She prayed for his safety, for wisdom, and that Daniel would make it home to them. She wondered if he was somewhere warm and dry, and if he was injured. The fall from the window had been significant, even with the snow.

Anger burned hot in her chest. Detective Anderson had said he'd been dragged. She wondered what the people who took him wanted with him. Her face hardened. She latched onto her anger, which was better than the helplessness threatening to overwhelm her. She forced her breathing to even, and her tears to slow.

We know who took him.

The FBI knew but they wouldn't tell her. But if they did know who had him, why weren't they out there looking? Why remain here? Why was this mysterious source more important than Daniel?

Ms. Sullivan, what do you know of the Leviathan?

And what did an ancient sea creature have to do with Daniel's disappearance? They seemed to be looking for everything except Daniel, despite their insistence they were searching for him. She closed the Bible and pulled it to her, hugging it to her chest. She would find the person they were looking for and ask them herself. He had to be someone whom Daniel had spent time with. Someone here on campus. She would find them and make them tell her. She wouldn't rest until she found the truth.

She stood and caught the back of the chair as she swayed unsteadily. The clock on the nightstand read nine p.m. which was only four in the afternoon at home. But she hadn't slept since the day before yesterday. Other than a few restless catnaps on the planes. She reluctantly left Daniel's room, taking his Bible with her, and returned to hers.

A shower revived her enough to remember her grandfather's call. There were three more texts from Keoni, but no other messages or calls. Nothing from Anderson. Forty-eight hours had now passed since Daniel had been taken. Time was running out. She climbed under the plush comforter before dialing her voicemail. She closed her eyes against the tears that returned at the concern in her grandfather's voice. Anderson had called them. She felt some small relief. At least they hadn't learned about it from the news. Though apparently, her grandfather had seen it there too.

The island news, or coconut wireless, moved quickly. Especially when national news picked up a story about one of their own. Daniel had grown up in the islands, married a local girl and had in turn been adopted into a large extended family. He'd taught at the University of Hawaii for a time. He was a well-known researcher, loved and respected by everyone who knew him.

And now they knew he was missing. They should have heard it from her.

She dialed her grandfather's number. To her relief, the call went to his voicemail. She assured him she was safe and she was sorry she'd left without telling them. Then she provided the highlights of what she knew, with the exception of the FBI and Daniel's involvement with them. She wasn't sure what to say, or if she should say anything at all about the FBI's involvement. She promised to call in the morning. Their morning, which was five hours behind Iowa. The difference might give her just enough time to track down the elusive Dr. Catlett.

After a quick text to Keoni, assuring him she would fill him in on all the details later, she turned her phone off, and was asleep the moment her head hit her pillow.

SULLIVAN INSTITUTE RESEARCH LABS, OAHU, HAWAII
MORGAN, AGE ELEVEN

Morgan watched the snowflake eel as it wiggled its long black and white-striped body through the hole in the coral. The tail vanished through the opening, and then its head reappeared. Mouth gaping, displaying sharp teeth. She stepped back from the tank with a shudder. One of her mom's interns had been bitten by one. She'd seen the scar on his calf. The scar was gross. And kind of cool.

She wandered out of the lab and across the deck to the shark pool. The wind ruffled her hair and the water on the top of the pool. Too much to allow her to see clearly. Nate said they'd brought in a new hammerhead shark two nights ago. The shark had been tangled in a net but had survived. Their aunt Leilani was overseeing its care. She'd promised to show it to Morgan, but she was off in some meeting.

Morgan hated meetings. They always seemed to last too long, and then everyone had even less time when they came back out. She decided to find the shark herself. She knew the lab well enough. Nate said it was ten feet long. He thought he knew everything now, since Mom was letting him help her with a couple projects. Morgan smirked. His projects were mostly scrubbing out fish tanks and mopping the deck. Sometimes he got to help work with the submersibles. She supposed cleaning was worth the effort.

At least Uncle Daniel's projects were always fun.

She skipped down the stairs to the underwater observation area and stepped up to the glass. And there it was. She took an instinctive step backward as the shark glided by. It wasn't ten feet long, but it was at least as long as the glass, which her aunt said was about six feet. She took a step closer as he followed the wall of the circular tank. Beautiful.

"Did you know that hammerhead sharks have 360° vision?" a voice asked behind her.

She squeaked and spun around. Her uncle smirked at her from the bench against the back wall. She narrowed her eyes at him.

"Did you know hammerheads are born with blue eyes?" she asked as she mimicked his tone.

"Really?"

She nodded solemnly. Then she grinned and raced over to join him.

"Their eyes turn brown as they get older. Helps them to see better," she said.

Her uncle looked suitably impressed. She straightened with pride. He chuckled softly and ruffled her hair. They watched as the shark spiraled from the top of the glass to the bottom, in a sort of ballet. She loved watching them.

"Did you know it is possible mosasaurs moved in a manner similar to sharks?" her uncle said. "For a while it was thought they moved like eels, due to the shape of their tails, but it appears at least some species may have had thresher tails like sharks."

Morgan watched the shark loop by, her mind morphing it into a much larger creature. A sea monster of massive size that could move as fast as Daniel said. What a scary thought. She'd seen the pictures in the books in his library. And once Daniel had taken her to a museum in Georgia where they had a full skeleton of the giant marine reptile. She'd always thought it looked like a big crocodile only with flippers instead of feet.

"Which is your favorite, Uncle Daniel?" she said. She knew already, but she loved to hear him talk about it.

Daniel just smiled. "The Tylosaurus is the most fascinating to me. It was one of the largest species of mosasaurs." He waved a hand at the tank. "It had a thresher tail like a shark, which gave it powerful speed, and a jaw that some scientists theorize could unhinge like a snake's, allowing it to swallow its prey whole."

He said the last with an ominous tone sending a delicious shiver up her spine. She giggled. Daniel tapped her nose lightly with his finger.

"And it had a hardened protrusion at the tip of its nose, which no one can seem to agree on the purpose of."

"What do you think?" she said.

Daniel shrugged. "I think it may have used it to ram things. It seems like the most fun."

"Uncle Dannniellll ... that is not very scientific."

He reached over and tickled her.

"Hey, whoever said science wasn't fun?" he said, as she gasped with laughter.

He let her go, and she scooted over to the far end of the bench—out of reach. After a moment, quiet settled back over the room.

"Uncle Daniel?"

"Yes?"

She scooted closer. "Do you think there is a Tylosaurus still alive today?"

Daniel smiled at her. "Wouldn't that be something."

She shivered again and leaned against the arm he had stretched across the back of the bench. The thought that a sea monster could be lurking somewhere out there in the ocean scared her. But it was kind of cool too. Kind of.

"Do you think we will ever see one?" she said.

"See what?" They looked over at the stairs as her aunt appeared, a bucket hanging from her hand.

Morgan jumped up. "A sea monster!"

Leilani smiled, but an eyebrow raised as she looked over Morgan's head toward her husband. "Sea monsters?"

Morgan groaned and covered her eyes as he pulled her aunt into his arms and kissed her. Grownups were silly. But she smiled. She loved her new aunt and was happy Uncle Daniel was happy.

"Hey, new species are discovered every day," Daniel grinned. "Giant squid, colossal squid, megamouth shark—"

Morgan groaned again, louder, and turned back to the shark tank as her aunt cut him off with a quick kiss. Lelani laughed.

"It's time to feed the turtles," She held the bucket toward Morgan. "Want to help?"

Boy did she ever! The turtles were so cute. Morgan took the bucket and headed up the stairs.

"Did you know there was once a giant sea turtle called an Archelon?" Daniel's voice echoed up from behind them. "It was as big as a car."

"Uncle Dannniellll!"

CHAPTER EIGHT

Morgan startled awake, thoughts of giant turtles and Daniel swirling through her muddled mind. Trapped between dream and reality. Sadness crept through her as she remembered where she was and why. The clock beside the bed read two thirty a.m. Too early to get up. The room was quiet, apart from the hum of the heater. She pulled the comforter higher against the cool night air and tried to settle back to sleep.

Thump!

She bolted upright at the noise and sat in the dark, ears straining to hear anything above the sound of her racing heart.

Wump!

Something struck the wall behind the headboard of her bed.

Daniel's room. Someone was in Daniel's room.

She threw back the blanket and swung her feet to the floor, ignoring the cold of hardwood beneath her bare feet as she moved quietly to the door. She grabbed a heavy figurine from the table as she passed, just in case, and eased the door open. The hall was dark, apart from a nightlight at the end of the hall. The house was silent. She eased her door closed and crept closer to Daniel's. For a moment, she entertained the idea he might have returned. But that tiny bit of hope fizzled as a light passed beneath the door. Daniel wouldn't use a flashlight in his own room.

She pressed her ear to the door. She could hear movement, but it was faint. Her hand closed over the doorknob, testing it cautiously. Unlocked. Her pulse raced. She'd locked it when she had returned to her room. Hadn't she? Her heart seized as the knob turned beneath her hand by a force from the opposite side of the door. The door swung inward. She panicked and shoved the door as forcefully as she could.

A yell of pain came from the dark room as the door made contact. She clutched the knob with both hands and yanked the door shut and held it with all her might, as she screamed loud enough to wake the dead. A door slammed down the hall, and footsteps pounded toward her.

"There's someone in the room!"

Anger burned through her, overtaking reason. She twisted the knob and slammed the door open, bouncing off the wall with a thud. A bone chilling gust of wind cut through the darkness. An older man, with sleep mussed hair and flannel pajamas, pushed past her into the room and switched on the light. The room was empty but the window in the alcove was open. Snow dusted the carpet and the armchair.

"What in heaven's name?" Macy said. "Are you all right?"

She was far from all right. But she nodded as she slumped back against the wall, shaking in the wake of the adrenaline. She folded her arms over her chest in an effort to hide the tremors. This was definitely not a story her family would hear about. Ever.

"Macy, call the sheriff," the man said as he pulled his head back inside the room. Macy turned and hurried back down the hall. He closed the window and locked it securely. "Whoever it was is long gone now. Is anything missing?"

Morgan swept the room with her eyes. Nothing looked out of place, though she honestly hadn't gotten a good enough look earlier to be able to say for certain. Books sat orderly on the shelf, clothes hung in the open closet, and Daniel's glasses were still on the desk where she'd left them.

"I don't know."

"Maybe Macy will," the man said. He ushered her toward the hall. "Come on, we'd better leave this for the sheriff."

She gave the room one last sweep before leaving.

"Did you get a look at the intruder?" he asked.

She squelched another tremor as she shook her head. "No, but I hit him with the door. The yell of pain was too deep for a woman."

She felt some small sense of satisfaction the man probably had a very large bruise on his face. Maybe even a broken nose.

Footsteps signaled Macy's return, she appeared at the top of the stairs.

"Wyatt is on his way," she said. "Campus security should be here any minute. Alan, you might want to get dressed. They will probably need you." She squeezed Morgan's arm gently. "They will want to talk to you too, sweetheart."

More questions. Great. For the second time she found herself in Macy's kitchen tucked into the corner nearest the woodstove, a mug of hot chocolate in hand. She stared at the ceiling and listened to the sound of heavy boots clomping overhead. Campus security had arrived shortly after Macy's call. Detective Wyatt Anderson and his team had yet to arrive. The snow was falling fast and thick outside, making the roads challenging, even for those used to driving in such conditions.

The snow had also provided cover to the intruder, as it quickly filled in the tracks he left behind. Security had followed the impressions as far as the icy road, but the tracks had ended there. There was blood on the snow near the edge of the roof. A faint smile pulled at the edge of her mouth. Maybe they would be able to at least gain his identity.

Macy couldn't say for certain whether anything was missing from Daniel's room. There was a power cord for a computer, but no computer. But Morgan hadn't remembered seeing one in the room the night before. Daniel had probably taken it with him the night he disappeared.

A plate of snickerdoodles appeared on the table. She gave Macy a weary smile and took one, though she wasn't hungry. The jetlag didn't help. Her body had no idea what time it was. Daniel's Bible sat in front of her. She'd grabbed it on her way out of her room, like a security blanket. She snagged one of the bookmarks, and it opened to another of his favorite passages. Job 40 and 41. The behemoth and the leviathan.

Daniel believed their descriptions matched the Brontosaurus and the mosasaur—the largest of the land creatures and one of the most fearsome of the largest sea creatures in recorded history. The descriptions did match well. The passage mentioned Behemoth had bones like bronze and iron and a tail like a cedar tree for balance And the Leviathan ... a fearsome creature no man could capture, the sight of which would leave its foes quaking in fear. Similar to the descriptions of the mosasaur.

Agent Weston's question itched at her brain. She rubbed her forehead. Her hand paused and then fell as she leaned closer. There, etched along the margins, were tiny symbols. A shout came from the hall. She startled and a slosh of chocolate splattered her sweatshirt. She mopped at it uselessly with a napkin. The front door slammed, and she jumped again.

"In the kitchen," Macy called toward the hall as she handed Morgan a damp kitchen towel. "Knock the snow off your boots first, young man."

Young man? Surely Macy hadn't let the reporter come back. Not after she'd told him not to. Morgan grimaced at the stain her scrubbing had only made worse. At least it was an old shirt. She tossed the towel on the table. The kitchen door swung open, revealing the elusive Dr. Catlett. She retrieved her mug and sank deeper into the corner, watching as he wrapped Macy in a hug.

"Are you all right?" he said. "What's going on?"

"Everyone is fine, just a bit of excitement." Macy caught his chin in her hand as he pulled back. "What in good gracious happened to you?"

Morgan watched with hyper focus as he gently extracted himself from Macy's grasp. "I'm fine. Just ran into someone who was in a hurry to get somewhere."

He turned. A bruise stretched from his left eye to his hairline.

Catlett's step faltered as his eyes met hers. His smile faded. Macy, clearly oblivious to the sudden rise in tension, pushed him toward the table.

"Sit down while I get you some ice."

His eyes were wary as he took the chair diagonal to Morgan's. Her eyebrow rose of its own accord as satisfaction curled in her chest. She stifled her Cheshire cat grin.

"Dr. Catlett," she said, calmly with an edge of concern, "that looks like it hurts. What'd he hit you with?"

Her high school drama coach would be proud. Catlett gave her a faint smile and leaned back in his own chair. "You should see the other guy."

She stared. He stared back. The front door opened, and voices filled the hall, heralding the arrival of Detective Anderson and his team. Macy handed Catlett an ice pack and went to greet them. Morgan waited until Macy left the room and then pounced.

"Working late?" she said.

He opened his good eye, ice pack covering the other. "Papers don't grade themselves."

"Must be hard to find the time while running from reporters."

His mouth twitched downward. He set the ice pack on the table and rose. She pushed back her chair to follow but relaxed as he reached for the coffeepot.

"Have a nice chat with the FBI?" he said.

Irritation snuffed out her satisfaction. She glared up at him.

"You were watching?" *From where? The woods, like a creepy stalker?* How did you know they were FBI?"

He hesitated, for a fraction so brief she nearly missed it. "I met them at the station."

His shoulders tensed. Clearly, she had touched a nerve.

"Do you know where my uncle is, Dr. Catlett?"

She remembered his hesitation, and the guilt she'd seen in his eyes, when she'd asked him the same question at the coffee shop. Catlett turned slowly and met her accusing stare. The sadness in his eyes stole her breath.

"I wish I did."

And then it was gone. Shuttered once more behind his expressionless mask. She watched silently as he sank back into his chair. He looked as exhausted as she felt.

"Why did you tell me to go home?" she said.

He picked up the ice pack and pressed it against his face with a wince. For a moment she almost felt sorry for him.

"Because it isn't safe."

"Is that a threat, Dr. Catlett?"

The ice pack hit the table with a squish, and she forced herself not to move as he leaned forward, his eyes blazing. His bruise stood out in stark contrast with the sudden paleness of his face.

"What? Why would you ..." His head dropped, breaking the stare. He let out a slow controlled breath, then retrieved the ice pack and carefully settled it back into place. "No, Ms. Sullivan. It is not a threat, simply an observation."

She stared at him with disbelief. What did that mean? The kitchen door swung open, and Macy returned with Detective Anderson in tow.

"Dr. Catlett, Ms. Sullivan."

The man looked as if he'd aged a decade since she'd last seen him. Dark smudges lined his bloodshot eyes. She believed him when he said he was doing everything in his power to find Daniel. She managed a small smile as he settled into the chair beside Catlett.

"What happened to you, Dr. Catlett?"

Catlett ignored her pointed stare as he lowered the ice pack. He wouldn't be able to dodge the detective's questions so artfully.

"I collided with a guy in a ski mask out in the parking lot." He waved a hand in the general direction of the door. "Probably the intruder. I chased him for a while but lost his trail somewhere around Maple."

Sure he did. Morgan shut her mouth with an audible snap. Her face flushed as the men glanced in her direction. She took a sip of lukewarm cocoa, then darted a glance toward Catlett. Her eyes narrowed as she caught him watching her, a flicker of a smirk on his face.

"What can you tell me about him?" Anderson said, as he accepted a cup of coffee from Macy. He pulled a small, battered notebook from his jacket pocket. "Did you get a good look at him?"

Tall. Dark hair. Broad build. Killer eyes ...

"He was about my height," Catlett said, "Kind of lanky build. Like I said, he was wearing a ski mask, and gloves."

Anderson nodded as he scribbled a notation in his notebook. "Mind if I ask where you were this evening between nine o'clock and now?"

Catlett pressed the ice against his eye. "I was in my office, until about a half hour ago when I arrived here. Around three o'clock."

His explanation sounded kind of familiar. Like his alibi for the night Daniel went missing.

"I thought the Science building was closed off," she said.

She felt the heat return to her face as their attention swiveled her way. Anderson raised an eyebrow.

"My office is two stories down from the lab, and on the far side of the building," Catlett said. "It was cleared this afternoon."

"Anyone with you?" Anderson said.

Catlett nodded. "My TA, Luke Weatherford, until around midnight, but after that I was alone. The security guard was at his desk when I left around two forty-five. Andrew Van Buren. Why nine o'clock?"

Her thoughts halted at his question. She backtracked quickly through the conversation.

"Dr. Smithson's office was ransacked sometime after nine," Anderson said. "His teaching assistant found it a little after ten."

Morgan inhaled a sip of chocolate and erupted into violent coughing. Liquids were lethal tonight. His office ... why hadn't she thought to check his office? Macy pressed a glass of water into her hand and gently patted her back.

"Apparently someone is looking for something," Catlett said, quietly.

"Are you all right, Ms. Sullivan?" the detective said.

No. Not at all. She nodded.

"Do you feel up to recounting the incident with the intruder?"

"Yeah." She walked the detective through the whole affair, from the sounds that woke her to the arrival of the campus security. She noticed, with some satisfaction, when Anderson glanced at the bruise on Catlett's face.

"Was anything missing from the room?"

She shrugged and glanced toward Macy, who had taken the empty seat beside her. "I'm not sure. I was only in the room briefly last night."

Macy confirmed nothing was missing that she knew of.

"Any idea what they might be searching for?" the detective said.

She really wished she did. "Did you happen to find a laptop in Daniel's office when you searched it?"

Anderson hesitated. "We did find it, but not in his office. His bag was found in the wreckage of the science lab. Our tech guys are looking into it, but it looks like it may be a lost cause." He looked at Macy, a touch of concern in his dark eyes. "On that note, we haven't found any keys. There doesn't appear to be any sign of forced entry to the locks on your front door or the doors to Dr. Smithson's office or room. Now I don't want to alarm you, but it's a fair bet your intruder could have let himself in with Dr. Smithson's keys."

A chill tickled up Morgan's spine. Or maybe he had keys of his own. Her eyes darted to Catlett. His eyes were closed.

"Use your deadbolts tonight and call for a locksmith first thing in the morning," Anderson said. "I'll post Murray inside the house until the locks are changed. I'd stay myself but—"

Macy squeezed his hand with an affectionate smile, tempered with a touch of worry.

"Don't you fret, Wyatt. I'll call Thomas first thing in the morning."

He gave her a weary smile. A phone chimed from the pocket of his coat. He excused himself and left the room. A deep feeling of unease settled over Morgan.

"Oh, Daniel." Her words were quiet but might have as well been a shout, so heavy was the silence blanketing the kitchen.

Macy squeezed her hand and stood, moving toward the coffeepot. Morgan's gaze shifted to Daniel's Bible, still resting on the table in front of her, mercifully spared from her hot chocolate episodes. She stared at the symbols etched into the margin. She straightened in her chair and leaned forward with intense interest, as she suddenly recalled the markings scribbled in the paperback novel Leslie had given her.

"What is it?"

She shut the book quickly at Catlett's question.

"Nothing," she said.

Great. That was smooth. She met his assessing stare with one of her own.

Focus, Sullivan.

"Macy says you spent a lot of time with my uncle," she said, "and you are new to the campus."

Catlett lowered the ice pack. "I'm sensing you have a question."

"What if Daniel just got in the way and they were after you?"

He raised his eyebrows. "If they were after me, why did they search Daniel's office and room?"

She sank back into her chair. He had a point. Unless he had been the one searching the rooms. In that case, he definitely knew more than he was letting on.

Before she could continue, Detective Anderson returned, and Morgan's heart sank at the solemn look in his eyes.

"What is it?" Catlett voiced the question that had refused to pass her lips.

The cold crept through her as she sat, ramrod straight in her chair, waiting for the news he seemed reluctant to share.

"The state police found the missing van," he said. "It appears the vehicle veered off the road and into Jacob's Creek."

Blood thundered in Morgan's ears. She barely heard Macy's gasp.

"There is a team on site, and the divers are on their way," Anderson said.

Divers? Her heart plummeted.

"Do you think he is dead?" She forced the words through her lips.

She could see the hesitation in the detective's eyes as he sought words to answer her question.

"We will know more soon. I'll call as soon as I can," Anderson said. He tipped his hat and left.

The heavy silence returned as they listened to the front door close. Daniel couldn't be dead. He'd promised her. She struggled to draw air into her lungs. Her body shuddered with each breath, like trying to breathe underwater. She slowly became aware of Macy's hand rubbing circles against her back. She latched onto the sensation, like a lifeline.

Morgan slumped forward against the table, bracing her head against her hands. She was on dry land. She wasn't trapped. She was safe. She could breathe. Her body gave another shudder as she drew a deep breath. And then another.

"That's it," Macy said, her voice soothing. "Just breathe."

She felt Macy's hand gently smooth over her hair. Embarrassment flooded through her as she remembered Catlett. She snuck a glance through her fingers, but he was gone. She wondered what he'd seen. Probably thought he was justified in telling her to leave, and she was weak. A mess. Maybe she was. She reached for her mug and sipped the cold chocolate. The taste pulled her fully back to the present and Macy's kitchen.

"There's no sense in assuming the worst, until we know for certain," Macy said gently.

She shut her eyes against the sudden rush of tears and prayed for a miracle.

CHAPTER NINE

Morgan scrubbed at her eyes. They were swollen and warm. She felt drained and empty. Macy had suggested she try to lie down and rest, but she couldn't. Not until she knew.

"Drink this," Macy said. "It will help."

A fresh cup of hot chocolate sat before her. She sipped it as she relaxed back into her chair. The warmth did help, as did the healthy dose of brandy.

"Thank you."

Macy slid into the chair across from her, a fresh mug of tea on the table before her. She looked every bit as weary as Morgan felt.

"You know, he feels a great deal of guilt for not being there that night," Macy said after a moment, gesturing toward Catlett's empty chair. "But it isn't his fault any more than it is yours."

Wasn't it? Morgan wasn't so sure. Her gut told her he knew more than he was telling. But she acknowledged Macy with a nod. She traced a knot in the wood of the tabletop with her finger.

"Daniel loves you, Morgan. Like you were his own daughter. He told me so."

Tears pricked at her eyes. She thought she'd run out of them.

"I know." The words came out in a whisper. "He told me too. After Auntie Leilani ..."

Macy's hand squeezed hers gently. "He told me about that too."

Her aunt had died when Morgan was still a teen. A rare cancer had taken her quick, too quick. Her death had nearly killed Daniel. But he had promised her ...

"He lived for you," Macy said.

Yeah. He had. Family was everything to Daniel. They'd all rallied around him. Lelani's family too. He'd found his purpose again, but he'd never remarried. Morgan was the closest thing he had to a daughter.

She drew a shaky breath. "He's been there my whole life. Right next door, literally, to my grandparents. My brother and I spent our summers there. He was the one who introduced me to the wonders of the ocean, including myth and lore."

"A family business." Macy smiled.

Yeah. It was. The Sullivan Institute. Founded by her parents, with Daniel as a partner. He'd never cared about the name. Only the science. Unlocking the secrets of the ocean and teaching others about them. Her parents were of the same mindset. Someone had to be the face of the company, and it wasn't in Daniel's nature to be at the forefront. The company had grown from five researchers to fifty over the past thirty years, with projects spanning the globe.

Nate had followed their father's footsteps into engineering, while she followed Daniel's into deep ocean science, much to her mother's good-natured chagrin. Though Morgan focused more toward the physical environment, Daniel's research resided with the creatures inhabiting the deep. The job was a dream come true and a challenge at the same time.

Her smile faded. "Something changed around last September. He lost a friend, a former colleague, to an accident. They said his car went off a cliff and into the ocean."

"How awful," Macy said.

Morgan looked up at the shock in Macy's voice.

"He didn't mention it?" she said.

Macy shook her head. Morgan bit her lip as she puzzled this new information. It was surprising Daniel had shared Lelani's loss with Macy, but not this.

"He changed," Morgan said. "Locked himself in his lab for days. Wouldn't let anyone in. Not even me. I even tried breaking in, but he caught me." She was a horrible thief. "He said he was fine and asked me to respect his wishes. He said he'd tell me everything when he was ready." But he hadn't. "Then, without warning, he closed up his lab and his house and moved here while I was on assignment in Australia."

His rejection still stung, like a fresh scar ripped open. She rubbed a hand against her chest, over her heart, as if she could make the ache fade. A heavy silence slipped over the room.

"I don't think Daniel intended to hurt you," Macy said, after a long moment. "I gathered from what little he said he was here because he believed he needed to be."

Morgan gave her a half-hearted shrug.

"Maybe so," she said, though she knew it was the truth.

Daniel wasn't a cruel man. He wouldn't have done something this out of character without a really good reason. She sighed. If only she could figure out who this mysterious source was, maybe then she'd have the answers she sought.

"Macy, do you know who Daniel spent his time with here?"

The older woman considered her question. "Well, other than Dr. Catlett, he spent most of his time with Dr. Dolan, the dean. Then there were his students, and his TA, Brittany Tate."

She'd never been one to back away from a challenge and this was a good start to finding him. Dolan seemed as good a place to begin as any. He was the one who had invited Daniel after all.

"Do you know if Dr. Dolan is still on campus?" she said.

"I am, indeed, young lady."

She turned toward the new voice. The man who'd been in flannel pajamas earlier stood in the doorway now dressed in a cable knit sweater and a pair of jeans. And his hair was less wild. He waved a hand as Macy rose. "Sit, sit, I can get my own coffee."

"Is there anyone who doesn't live here?" Morgan said, with a small laugh.

How very convenient.

Dolan chuckled. "I'm just a temporary refugee," he said as he joined them at the table. "The heating went out in my house last night. Macy was kind enough to take me in for a couple of days while they fix it." He sipped his coffee with a sigh. "Anderson's crew is finished upstairs. I passed Murray on my way down. He's pacing like a sentry in the front room. Maintenance will be here at eight to change the locks."

Morgan looked out the window at the lingering darkness and wondered what time it was now. She'd lost total concept of time between the events of the night and her jet lag.

"Any word from Detective Anderson?" she said.

Dolan shook his head. "No, not yet."

Disappointment warred with relief, leaving her feeling empty. The sound of boots on the stairs heralded the exit of the sheriff's team and campus security. Macy excused herself to see them out.

"I am sorry we've met under such unfortunate circumstances, Ms. Sullivan," Dolan said with a small smile. "Your uncle is a good man. He spoke very highly of both you and your brother Nate."

She smiled. "Thank you. And it's Morgan."

His smile widened. "As you are not a student, please call me Alan."

"May I ask a question, Alan?" At his nod, she continued. "Why did you ask Daniel here?"

He sat back in his chair, his face thoughtful. "Well, I've been trying to hire Daniel for years," he said. "That's no secret. He is an excellent instructor. I didn't think he'd ever take up my offer."

"Then why now?"

Dolan shrugged. "That is a good question. He called me up last December and asked if I would consider bringing him on as a guest lecturer."

"He asked you?" Somehow that wasn't as big a surprise as she thought it would be. "He told me that you recruited him."

Dolan shook his head. "Unfortunately, the science department is at maximum capacity right now. But he was insistent. Said it had to be this semester."

Interesting. The FBI had suggested he took the position because they asked him to.

"Why this particular semester?"

"He didn't say," Dolan said. "He asked what I thought about a guest lecture series in the English Department. They were only too happy to have him. His course filled quickly, despite the late addition. His lectures were standing room only."

Morgan smiled. "Sea monsters are always a draw."

As was Daniel. He could make almost anything interesting.

Dolan nodded. "True. It began that way, but after the first lecture, the students were petitioning my office for a course in the fall, if Daniel would stay on to teach it."

The thought filled her with equal parts pride and dread. "Was he planning to stay?"

"He said he'd think about it." His dark eyes studied her thoughtfully. "Honestly, I don't think he would have. He missed you all." He grinned. "And he hated the cold."

She laughed. The phone on the kitchen wall rang, its shrill trill made her heart stutter. She stood, but Macy beat her to it.

"Robert's Boarding House."

Fear shot through her as Macy sank back against the doorjamb.

"Oh, thank the good Lord." Macy said, her eyes on Morgan. "I'll tell them. Be safe now."

"Is it ...?"

Macy shook her head, with tears in her eyes. "There was a body, but it wasn't Daniel."

Morgan sank back into her seat as the heavy rush of relief left her trembling. "They're sure it isn't Daniel?" she said, needing to hear the words again.

Macy nodded her head as she sat down beside her. "Positive."

Morgan squeezed her eyes closed. *Thank God.*

She heard Dolan shift forward in his chair. "Who was it? Do they know?"

"Wyatt didn't say."

They probably wouldn't tell them since it was an ongoing investigation. Right? She opened her eyes while her mind churned with new questions. If it was the van Daniel had been taken in, where was he now?

"How far is Jacob's Creek from Winston?" she said.

"About thirty miles, give or take?" Macy said, to which Dolan nodded.

Thirty miles. She hadn't passed over a creek or any water between Willow Creek and Winston, at least none she could recall. But she had been driving in the dark. Most of the area appeared to be snow covered fields.

"What's between here and Jacob's Creek?"

"Well, there is the Messer Cattle Ranch, a couple of private homes, and the Cedar Spring Winery." Macy waved a hand. "Most of it is just pastureland and crop fields."

Maybe it wasn't the same van.

"And Jack Barton's airstrip," Dolan said.

Airstrip? There was an airport?

Dolan's pocket vibrated. "Please excuse me, ladies. No rest for the weary." He stood and made his way toward the door as he answered.

"There's an airport?"

Macy shook her head. "It's more of a small landing strip for crop dusters. Anyway, it's late, or very early. You should try to get some rest."

She didn't want to rest, but she could see the weariness in Macy's eyes. She stood and began to collect the dishes.

"Leave them, sweetheart. I'll take care of it in the morning." Macy smiled. "Or in a few hours." She pulled Morgan into a gentle hug. "I'm still praying for him. So is my Bible Study group. Daniel is a fighter."

Morgan squeezed her tighter. Yeah, he was. "Thank you."

"Now bed," Macy said, pointing toward the stairs. "Go."

She picked up Daniel's Bible and hugged it to her chest as she trudged up the stairs. The hallway was dark, and quiet. There was no police tape over Daniel's door, like in the movies. Everything looked the same as it had before. Exactly the same.

A sense of foreboding crept over her as she inched toward Daniel's door. She stopped before it and hesitantly reached out her hand toward the knob. She pulled back and then reached for it again. This was silly. The intruder was gone. There was a deputy in the living room, within calling distance. She was safe.

"Looking for something?" a voice said.

In retrospect, the shriek was a bit over dramatic. Even for her. She clutched a hand over her rapidly beating heart as she glared at Catlett. He stood in the open doorway of a room across the hall, hands in his pockets. If looks could kill, he would have been ash by now. She cringed inwardly as footsteps pounded up the stairs. Perfect. Deputy Murray appeared at the top of the stairs, out of breath, hand on his holstered gun.

"It's all right, Officer," Catlett waved a hand toward the end of the hall. "Ms. Sullivan thought she saw a mouse."

Annoyance washed through her. She wondered why Daniel had wasted his time befriending Catlett. He was usually a much better judge of character.

"Problem?" Dolan said as he appeared from the room at the end of the hall.

Great, now it was a party.

"The lady here thought she saw a mouse," The deputy's smile faded, and he beat a hasty retreat down the stairs at her cold stare. She was too tired to deal with this circus.

"I startled Ms. Sullivan," Catlett added before she could reply. "Trouble?"

Dolan shook his head.

"The sheriff asked to meet. School related." He headed toward the stairs. "Get some rest you two. Someone should."

And then there were two. She turned her ire on him.

"The body wasn't Daniel's," she said, pointedly. "In case you cared."

Catlett folded his arms loosely across his chest and held her eyes.

"That is great news," he said, with what appeared to be sincerity. "And for the record, I do care."

Maybe it was true. His surprise was not. He'd already known.

"I heard Macy from the hall," he said, as if he'd read her mind.

"Okay, goodnight then." She turned on her heel toward Daniel's door and wavered unsteadily as the room spun. His hand caught her elbow, steadying her.

"Easy there," Catlett said.

He smelled as good as he looked, like woods and soap. She inhaled sharply. How strong was that brandy?

"I'm fine." She shook his hand off.

Heat crept up her neck as she stepped away. She realized she was being rude, but at the moment, she really didn't care what he thought. She unlocked the door and pushed it open, flipping on the light as soon as she could reach it. Her heart raced as she recalled the intruder. She slowly stepped inside.

Daniel's room was just as she left it. Though a little more dust than she'd remembered. She ran her finger along the edge of the desk. Fingerprint dust probably. Poor Macy. She set Daniel's Bible on the desk and scanned the room.

"What are you looking for?"

Annoyance rippled through her. Why wouldn't he just take a hint?

"Nothing that concerns you."

Catlett blocked her attempt to shut the door. "Maybe I can help?

"You've been enough help," She ignored the flash of pain in his eyes and turned her attention to the bookcase. So far, the only thing out of the ordinary she'd noticed were the figures scribbled in margins of Daniel's Bible and in the paperback at the coffee shop. They itched at her brain. She'd seen those symbols before. In another book, maybe? Battered secondhand literature classic novels lined the shelf, along with a geology textbook and a hardback copy of a book on cryptozoology, the study of mythical creatures.

An eclectic collection but nothing out of the ordinary as far as Daniel was concerned. Most of the books were familiar to her. The rustle of paper drew her attention back to the interloper. Panic rushed through her veins. And more than a little anger. He was holding Daniel's Bible, flipping through the pages.

"Please put that down." Fear cut through her. She stood and attempted to take it from him, but he held it just out of reach. "Give it to me."

She moved again, but he sidestepped her.

"I can help."

Her frayed nerves snapped. "Give it to me and get out."

She regretted the words the moment she uttered them, but nothing he had said or done made her want to trust him. He held her gaze with an assessing one of his own. Then without a word, he surrendered the Bible to her. She hugged it to her chest, not caring how juvenile the action made her look. His eyes softened.

"Morgan, I'm sorry."

She took another step back, placing the bed between them, more for his safety than her own, she was sure. She was done. Done with apologizing. Done with questions. Just done.

"Please leave." Her words were quiet, void of emotion.

He tucked his hands in his pocket and stood there for what seemed like ages. Finally, he turned and moved toward the door.

"Yell if you need me," he said over his shoulder as he left the room. She could hear his smirk.

She grabbed a book from the shelf and hurdled it after him. The thump was muffled by the carpet, his laughter was not. Jerk. She stalked to the door and shut it, resisting the urge to slam it only out of respect for Macy. Twisting the lock, she leaned back against the door, as her anger faded.

She should get some sleep and leave this for tomorrow. She sighed and pushed away from the door. She knew as exhausted as she was, she wouldn't sleep until she had at least followed this small lead. Besides Catlett was probably still in the hall. She didn't have it in her to deal with him again tonight.

She collected the Bible from his desk and crossed to the armchair in the alcove and sank into it. Her thumb brushed against the weathered leather cover of the Bible in her lap. And again. The rhythmic motion was soothing. She opened to the first bookmark. Psalms 139, the passage it had been open to when she'd found it the night before. This had to be part of a code, she was certain of it.

Like the games he had designed when she and Nate were kids. The treasure hunts. The code needed a key. A phrase to unlock the sequence. As a child, her chosen phrase had been 'Nate is a brat.' Daniel's had varied.

"So, what is the key?" She knew what her uncle's response would be. She could almost picture him, seated at the desk, a smile his only response. "Okay then, I'll figure it out myself."

She flipped the pages to the Job passage, where she'd seen the other figures. There. The first three were the same. The fourth was different. She squinted at the bottom of the page where a phrase was scrawled in Daniel's writing: The human mind is always looking for something to marvel at.

She remembered the quote from Jules Verne's book *Twenty Thousand Leagues Under the Sea.* One of their favorites. She called her uncle "Professor Aronnax" for a whole summer, and he'd called her …

"You called me Conseil," she said.

Excitement laced through her as she stood and moved to the desk, collecting a pad of paper and a pen. She copied the figures onto the pad and then wrote three words beneath them. The number of characters matched the letters. Exactly.

"My wise Conseil," she said.

Aronnax's faithful assistant. Daniel's teasingly appointed nickname for her.

And the key to the code.

CHAPTER TEN

She quickly copied the fourth set of characters. Eight letters. Only five matched.

$$\_\_E\ A\ S\_R\ E$$

There had to be more to the key. She flipped back to Psalms 139 and copied the remaining three sets. A familiar thrill rushed through her as she filled in the letters.

My wise Conseil, with love Arronax.

Perfect. That gave her seven additional letters and nearly all of the vowels. She could work with these clues. She matched the letters to the word from Job 41.

Treas_re.

Treasure. She flipped the pages back to Job 40, but there were no additional characters. She tapped her pencil on the notepad. There were no other bookmarks marking pages. She grinned. Because that would make it too easy. There had to be some sort of link.

Leviathan maybe. Leviathan was mentioned by name five times in the Bible. Thanks to Daniel, she had the passages memorized before she could even read. He'd thought it was hilarious to have her quote them at family parties.

She flipped to Job 3 and traced the page to verse 8. Bingo. There in the margin was another set of characters. Just one word this time. Eight letters.

_ N _ _R I E _

Okay. Next one was Psalms 79. She tapped her finger beside verse 13. One word. Five letters.

H O L _ S

Holds, maybe? She flipped to Psalms 104 verse 26. Three letters.

T H E

Well, that one was easy, Last one was Isaiah 27 verse 1. Three letters again.

_ E _

Together it read.

_ N _ _ R I E TREASURE HOLDS THE _E_

She tapped her pencil against her forehead. She used to be better at this. Okay. Treasure. She squeezed her eyes shut and thought harder. Daniel and treasure. Daniel and the treasure hunts. Treasure and ... key? Her eyes flew open, and the graphite etched against the pad: *Unburied treasure holds the key*

She cheered. The treasure chest. Was it the treasure chest? Daniel had always buried that old thing at least halfway in the dirt. Chocolate coins. Books. She and Nate had never really known what they were going to find at the end of one of his pirate treasure hunts. He'd even hidden the keys to a car for her graduation. An old cruiser, but still it had been her own wheels.

"What are you hiding now?" she said.

And where was it? And what did it have to do with what was happening now? Her excitement ebbed. Probably nothing. He could have written the words ages ago. A chilling thought sent a thrill through her. What if he'd written it in case something happened to him? What if it led to his will, or a letter, or ...?

Her jaw twitched as she shoved the thought away.

She thumbed through the pages, just in case she'd missed something, but found nothing more. She checked the binding of the leather cover, but there were no signs of tears or separation or slight bulges that might hold a hidden letter. She sighed and leaned back against the chair.

Her gaze drifted to the bookshelf and a copy of Jules Verne's *Journey to the Center of the Earth.* She jumped up out of the chair and grabbed the book. She thumbed through the pages and smiled in triumph. She knew she'd seen these markings before. Daniel must have taken his inspiration from this novel. In it, the scientist Lindenbrock and his assistant Axel find a secret message hidden on a rock from an explorer who claimed to have made it to the center of the earth. The etches used by the explorer matched Daniel's in look but not in context.

There were markings in the margin next to the artist's rendition of the message. In Daniel's handwriting. She copied them onto the pad with the other: My wise Conseil.

Nothing more. She flipped through each of the books on the shelves. Even the textbooks, but there was nothing more. She put them back and stood slowly, grabbing the back of the chair as she wavered on her feet. The clock read a quarter after five. She really needed to get some sleep. Right after she took another look at the book Leslie had given her, which should still be in her bag in her room.

She tore the notes from the pad and stuck them into the Bible for safekeeping. Then she picked it up and left the room, taking care to lock the door behind her. She took a step toward her room, but a raised voice caught her attention. Light spilled beneath Catlett's door. He appeared to still be up too. She shook her head and headed for her room but paused as his voice rose again.

Her curiosity was going to get her hurt someday. She turned and crept closer to the door. His voice was muffled. She pressed her ear against the door.

"You're threatening me?" A chill ran down her spine at his tone. "Don't you think you've made enough of a mess? He can't be happy with you." His voice was deep and rough. She could only hear him and no one else. He was likely on his phone. "Yes, I know what is at stake if I fail."

Footsteps grew closer to the door. She held her breath.

"You listen to me, the girl is of no concern to you," he said. "I will deal with her. You clean up your mess."

Her heart froze, her breath with it. The door jolted beneath the impact of something solid, startling her into motion.

She quietly fled down the hall to her room, fumbling with the key as she reached it. She heard the lock on his door click open. Blood rushed through her head, leaving her dizzy as she jammed the key into her lock and shoved the door open.

She scrambled inside, forcing herself to close her door quietly behind her. She turned the lock and sank to the floor as her knees turned to jelly. Her heart pounded like a scared rabbit. His footsteps slowed as he neared her door, and then halted.

I'll deal with her.

He was involved. She knew it. Now he was coming for her too. His footsteps continued past her door toward the stairs. She slumped back against the doorjamb. Her head spun as she let go of a breath she hadn't realized she'd been holding. She clutched Daniel's Bible as every inch of her trembled with fatigue and adrenaline.

Catlett had been playing with her all along. He probably lied about not knowing where Daniel was. She would bet money he was the intruder she'd hit with the door. Not that she could prove it. She pushed to her feet in the dark room but didn't dare turn on the light. An edge of light from the streetlamp spilled in through the crack in the curtains. Her hands trembled as she checked the lock. Then she crawled beneath the comforter on her bed.

Exhaustion crept over her and within moments sleep claimed her.

Light streamed brightly through the curtains when she woke. A long sunny beam. Her head ached. Her heart ached too, though that couldn't be blamed on the jet lag. She drew a deep breath and let it out slowly. The soft bed and warm blankets urged her to drift back to sleep. She glanced at the clock by the bed and sat up straight. How could she have slept till ten o'clock?

She threw the blankets back and slid her feet to the floor. Everyone in Maui would be expecting a report soon, though she still had some time as it was only five a.m. She had nothing new to offer other than a cryptic code from Daniel, which may or may not have anything to do with his disappearance. And a potential threat from a man who had claimed to be his friend. She couldn't tell them about Catlett yet—not until she knew more. She grabbed her phone and opened the messages. Her hands shook.

There was a message from Daniel.

Absolutely impossible. Detective Anderson had called her from Daniel's phone, which as far as she knew he still had. Didn't he? Her hand trembled as she tapped the screen, some small part of her hoping against hope. Her breath left in a whoosh.

DANIEL: Leave now, or you're next.

What the ... She stared at the phone, unblinking. Her stomach twisted into a knot. Was this a threat or a warning? Who could have sent it?

Go home. She could hear Catlett's words as if he had spoken them. She wasn't going anywhere. Call it stubbornness or resolve, but she wasn't leaving until she knew what happened to Daniel. And no amount of threatening could make her. She dug Anderson's card from her bag and dialed his cell phone number. The call went through to voicemail.

"Detective Anderson, this is Morgan Sullivan. It's just after ten. I received a text from my uncle's phone, time stamped at six a.m. this morning. I thought you still had it."

Smooth going, Morgan. "It said 'Leave now, or you'll be next.' I've no idea what that means. Please call me back when you get the chance." She left her number and hung up.

She needed coffee. Her stomach grumbled. And food. Then she would hunt down Catlett and ask a few pointed questions. Preferably in a crowded place. Anderson still hadn't returned her call by the time she'd dressed and headed downstairs. Deputy Murray was in the hall, overseeing the installation of the new locks on the front door. He flinched slightly as he looked up at her. Her annoyance with Catlett strengthened.

Mouse, indeed. She plastered on a bright smile.

"Good morning, have you seen Dr. Catlett?" Probably too late but worth a shot.

The deputy gave her a bashful smile. "He left a couple hours ago, said to tell you to text if you wanted to meet up for coffee."

Okay. Maybe she wouldn't have to run him down after all. Leslie's shop would work. And it was a public place. Lots of people in and out. Of course, the FBI had collected her from the parking lot, and no one had seemed to notice. Other than Catlett. Stalker.

She shivered. Perhaps it wasn't too far from the truth. Morgan thanked the deputy and made her way to the kitchen. The room was empty, but a fresh pot of coffee sat in the warmer. Along with a note from Macy. She was running errands but had left blueberry muffins warming in the oven. The woman was an angel.

Her phone chimed.

CATLETT: Coffee. Wit's End. Noonish?

A little over an hour from now. Which might give her time to check out Daniel's office first. She sent a quick reply she would see him then. At least Macy stocked to-go cups, probably for the professors always on the go. Like Daniel. He lived on coffee.

She poured a cup, grabbed a muffin, and left the house. The sun shone brightly in a cloudless blue sky. The wind was gone, and it was almost pleasant. Even, she had to admit, pretty. She tucked her scarf up around her neck and made her way down the freshly shoveled path to the parking lot.

Her phone buzzed. She stared, puzzled. Keoni. He never called. Ever.

"What's wrong?" she said, "Why are you calling?"

His reply was a rapid string of what sounded like words.

"Keoni, breathe," she said, as she slid into her car. "Slow down. Please tell me you aren't drinking energy drinks again."

The last time he'd been drinking energy drinks she'd found him passed out on the floor of the lab.

"Maybe, but that's not important." His words were only a little slower. "Why haven't you answered my messages?"

She thumbed the call onto speaker, quickly checking over his texts. He plunged ahead without waiting for a reply. "I hacked into Daniel's server. There wasn't much there, but I managed to recover his browsing history. I think they took him, Morgan!"

Her reprimand died on her lips. "What? Who took him?"

"I don't know who," he said, "I just know they did. Daniel was looking into reports, news reports of scientists who had gone missing or died under strange circumstances. Like his friend, Dr. Yang."

A car and a cliff. An explosion and a lab. A death and a disappearance. Forty-eight hours ago she would have just brushed it off as another wild conspiracy theory. But now ... fear trickled through her.

"Missing from where?" she said.

"All over the world," he said. "Daniel was looking at reports going back at least twenty years."

Her stomach sank. Twenty years? Suddenly the FBI involvement made a little more sense.

"I've been searching the sites," he said. "There are rumors they are being recruited by a shadow corporation."

Any other day she would have laughed.

"Who don't take no for an answer," she said.

"Exactly." He sounded scared. "Morgan, if they took Daniel, they could still be around. Watch your back."

Leave now, or you'll be next.

"I'll let you know when I have more." He hung up without waiting for a reply.

She sat in silence for a long moment. The FBI had said Daniel took the job at Winston College at their request. Dr. Dolan said Daniel had requested a position for this semester. Her gut told her the story went something like this—Daniel's friend died in a suspicious accident. Daniel spent four months researching similar deaths and disappearances. Then he'd called Dolan, and then the FBI.

So, the question was, why had Daniel come to Winston?

The FBI had said Daniel had a source. Someone they seemed desperate enough to try to recruit her into finding for them. But Daniel hadn't shared the person's identity.

"Why, Daniel?"

She put the car into reverse and backed out of the space. Hopefully his office held some answers. Someone believed this enough to break in. She hoped they hadn't found what they'd been looking for.

The English department was housed in a building on the far side of the campus. An older brick style building over six stories tall, it brought back memories of her own university days. The physics department had dropped pumpkins off the roof of the English building every Halloween in the name of science. The pranks had been great fun until a pumpkin bounced off a contraption and straight through the windshield of the Dean's BMW.

She snorted. The memory was still funny to this day.

Daniel had told her his office was in the basement. There had been much lamenting over his lack of windows. She tried to use the dingy room as leverage to convince him to come back. But he'd just laughed and said at least it kept the cold out. He'd also mentioned the elevators were just as sketchy as the ones in the old science building on their campus. The kind she used to pray she wouldn't get stuck in, with a 50-50 chance she would. Daniel had once, for nearly an hour, which was one of the reasons he always carried a paperback novel with him.

She took the stairs.

The basement hall was well lit but cluttered and stuffy. And more than a little claustrophobic, smelling like floor wax and old books. Daniel must have felt at home, despite the lack of windows. She checked the directory by the elevators. His office was B117. The closest office to her current location was B101.

Of course, it was at the other end of the long, deserted hallway.

She made her way swiftly past the closed doors with their darkened windows. She slowed to a halt as she turned the corner. Even from several doors down she knew which office was Daniel's. The door was covered with notecards. The multicolored rectangles spilled from the doorway to pepper the walls on either side, like some sort of abstract art piece. Her heart twinged as she moved close enough to read the words.

Prayers. Thoughts. Wishes. All for Daniel.

"You can leave one if you like," a voice said.

Her head turned so quickly her neck cracked. A blonde headed girl in a bright pink sweater and jeans stood in a doorway across the hall.

"I'm sorry," she said, "I didn't mean to startle you."

The girl held up a stack of cards. A cup of brightly colored pens was clutched in her other hand.

"I was just replenishing the stack," she said as she set it down on a display case. "People have been coming by nearly nonstop since ..."

"The accident," Morgan said.

The girl nodded, her blue eyes shimmering, "Yeah."

"It is nice of you to provide the cards," Morgan said, turning back to the wall. She touched one of them. A prayer for his safe return. "Did you know him well?"

The girl's smile faded a little. She wrapped her arms across her chest.

"Are you a reporter?" she said.

Morgan almost laughed.

"No, I'm not a reporter," Morgan said. "Dr. Smithson is my uncle."

The girl's eyes grew wide, and her hand flew to her mouth.

"You're Morgan?" she said, "Oh, I am so sorry. I'm Brittany Tate. I'm ... I was Dr. Smithson's TA."

She brushed the tears from her eyes with the back of her hand. Morgan pulled a pack of tissues from her bag and offered it to her.

"It's nice to meet you, Brittany," she said, "Daniel talked a lot about me, did he?"

Brittany gave a watery laugh. "He did, yes. Mostly about the book selections he made for the seminar. Said you'd read them all multiple times."

Morgan grinned. "Yeah, well they probably all came from his library first."

"Except for the Lambton worm legend," Brittany said.

Morgan laughed out loud. "The graphic novel or the opera?"

Daniel called them both a ludicrous reimagining of a plausible historical account. The real legend of the Lambton worm was crazy enough. A 14th century English tale of a giant serpent that slithered out of a well every night to lay waste to the local countryside, until it was eventually slain by a knight. Daniel preferred firsthand accounts of legends as opposed to deliberate sensationalism. She just loved to drive him crazy by finding as many versions as she could. The crazier the better.

"Both," Brittany said. "I think he kept the novel, though."

She waved a hand toward the office door. Speaking of Daniel's office …

"Do you have the keys for his office?" Morgan said.

Brittany nodded. "Sure, would you like to see it?"

"Please."

Brittany vanished into her office and then reappeared a moment later with a set of keys.

"The police were here last night," she said, hesitantly. "Someone made a huge mess of it. I tried to straighten up, but it is still a bit of a mess."

"You were the one who found it?" Morgan said.

Brittany nodded. "I needed the mid-terms for grades," she said. "I called security right away." She pushed back the door and flipped on the light.

The room looked exactly as Morgan had seen from Daniel's video calls. Well, apart from the books and papers stacked haphazardly in piles around the room. There was a desk in the center, piled high with paper, and a pair of floor-to-ceiling bookshelves against the wall behind it, empty apart from a few books. She sighed, inwardly.

"Was anything missing?" Morgan said.

"Nothing that I could tell. But it's kind of hard to say," Brittany said.

"Daniel's not the most organized person."

Brittany laughed. Morgan smiled, and the girl relaxed a little.

"Not really, no," she said. "But he's not the worst I've worked for."

Morgan eased around the piles of books to the desk, scanning the room for anything familiar or just glaringly wrong. But nothing did. At least, not at first glance.

"What did it look like," she said, "when you found it?"

Brittany bit her lip and waved a hand at the room.

"Kind of like this but ... scattered."

A phone rang across the hall. Brittany almost looked relieved.

"Excuse me for a moment," she said.

Morgan moved around the desk to the bookshelves. She ran her fingertips along the covers of the few books stacked there, trying to recall what she'd seen in the videos. But she couldn't. Not really. She sighed and set the books back in order before bending to collect another stack. There were a lot more than she would have expected for the short time Daniel had been here. But he had always been a collector.

They were mostly classics which wasn't surprising since he was teaching a literature class. But none so far by Verne. Herman Melville. Tennyson. The Great New England Sea Serpent. Even Henry William Lee's lesser-known volume on the scientific truth behind sea monsters written in the late eighteen-hundreds.

But no Verne.

She flipped another stack onto an empty shelf. Bingo. She pulled the book from the shelf carefully. Its edges were worn, the pages dog-eared and familiar. An old edition of a collection of Verne's best-known stories. The one she'd bought him for his birthday, many years ago. His favorite. Her lips curled slightly upward.

Morgan sank into the chair behind the desk, and gently thumbed through the pages. Disappointment crept through her. There were no coded markings. No writing or scribbles of any sort. With the exception of her inscription, inside the front cover

To Arronax, with love, from your Conseil.

She closed it carefully and tucked it into her bag.

Leslie's novel bumped against it. In all the excitement at the house, she'd forgotten about it until now. She pulled it from the bag and flipped through the pages. The code looked familiar. Too familiar in fact. She slipped the note pages from the Bible in her bag and compared them.

Her excitement faded to more disappointment. There were only three words, written multiple times. The key words.

My wise Conseil.

But that was it. Nothing more. She sighed and rubbed her eyes. Maybe he'd been practicing. Like the words in the other Verne novel. Only there, he'd only written it once. But why write it at all? Especially when he'd had no guarantee she would find either of them. What if she'd never even come to Iowa?

She forced herself to calm down. She was here. She had found the code. In his Bible. The one book, if anything happened to him, would have been returned to her family. Other than the Verne collection, maybe. She pulled the Verne collection back out of her bag and flipped through it again. One page at a time. This time she noticed something, so small she had missed it: two sets of characters etched along the fold. She retrieved the coded pages and compared them.

Two new words.

*CAS_ER BISHO_*

CHAPTER ELEVEN

The missing character was the same letter. Based on similar codes Daniel had used, she made a guess on the letter.

CASPER BISHOP

Oookay. A name. An odd one at that. Maybe a literary character's name? She pulled out her phone to try a quick search and grimaced. There was no signal. Of course.

"We have a hard line for the computers," Brittany said from the doorway, "but cell service is pretty nonexistent with all this brick and dirt."

Figured. Morgan toyed with the idea of asking Brittany about the name, but something held her back. The code had been so well hidden, and besides, chances were, it had nothing to do with his disappearance anyway. Which brought her back to the question of what the intruder had been looking for.

"Brittany, who has been in this office since that night?" she said.

"Just myself," Brittany said. "And then the incident last night, whoever that was. Then the security office and Deputy Anderson." She waved a hand, distress on her face. "I called security, and they called the sheriff."

Morgan admired her for having the courage to work in this tomb on her own today after the events of the last couple nights. TAs usually got the longest hours and the tasks the professor was either too busy for or just didn't want to do. Daniel, of course, was different. He never treated his TA or Research Assistants as servants or asked them to do anything he wouldn't do himself. He was a mentor, and he never let an opportunity to teach go to waste.

"Did anyone come down here before that night," Morgan said, "other than students?"

"Dr. Catlett was here a lot," Brittany said, "nearly as often as Dr. S."

Not much of a surprise.

"Do you know Dr. Catlett?" Morgan said.

The girl blushed. "A little," she said. "He seemed to be good friends with Dr. S. Other than that, I don't know a lot about him."

Her tone suggested she wished that wasn't the case. Morgan couldn't blame her. He was good looking, but potentially dangerous, which was definitely a mood killer. Brittany tilted her head, a look of puzzlement on her face. Morgan forced herself to smile.

Brittany waved a hand toward the hall. "I need to run up to Dr. Nester's office to drop off some files. You can stay as long as you like. Just lock the door behind you if you leave before I get back."

Morgan nodded. "Thanks."

She glanced at the clock on her phone. She still had a little time before she was supposed to meet with Catlett. She wondered if Detective Anderson had tried to reach her yet. And who had sent the message.

Leave now, or you're next.

Maybe it wasn't so wise to stay here. In this basement. All alone.

"Get it together, Sullivan," she said.

She stood and picked up another stack of books. Still no other Vernes. She set the books on the shelf and grabbed another. None in that stack either.

Nor did she find any in the rest of the books which were only the paperbacks, and his old collection. Disappointment swirled through her. She couldn't imagine someone breaking in for his books. After all, she'd found the novels in both his office and his room long after someone had gone through his things.

She turned and swept her gaze over the room. Whatever they were searching for had to be related to why he'd come to Winston. What if the source hadn't wanted to be found? What if Daniel had tried to convince them to help the FBI and they'd turned on him instead?

Another shiver crept up her spine. What if Daniel had set a trap, with himself as bait and it had worked? Too well? She rubbed her arms briskly against the chill. Now she was starting to sound like Keoni. And what about the name?

"Casper Bishop," she said quietly. She turned and stared at the books. "Bishop."

"Knight," a voice said from the doorway, "King. Pawn."

She smacked her knee on the desk. At least this time she could claim the shriek was a cry of pain. The surge of adrenaline made her head spin. She waved Catlett back as he moved quickly toward her.

"Stay there," she said.

To her surprise he did as she asked, halting on the opposite side of the desk. She rubbed her knee hard, as she watched him from the corner of her eye.

"Are you okay?" To his credit, he sounded concerned.

Morgan moved her knee gingerly then nodded. She'd probably have a nice bruise but she'd live. Speaking of bruises ...

"Are you wearing makeup?" she said.

His forehead creased and he winced, though his bruises had miraculously faded almost to nothing. A small feeling of satisfaction passed through her as she recalled the impact of the door. Catlett settled into a chair on the opposite side of the desk, as if he owned the place. A surge of annoyance snuffed out her amusement. She bit back a scowl.

"Take up chess recently?" he said.

What was he …? Oh. Bishop. So that was what he'd meant by knight, king, and pawn. She didn't know a lot about the game, but she doubted Casper Bishop had anything to do with chess.

"Everyone needs a hobby," she said with a shrug.

"I thought snooping was yours," he said.

Snooping? She shot him an incredulous look. He almost looked surprised he'd said it.

"Did you need something, Dr. Catlett?"

He stared at her, assessing, as if he were trying to read her mind and steal her secrets. She stared back. A flicker of amusement danced in his eyes.

"Just to offer my help," he said. "Brittany said you were down here, straightening up the office."

She bit her lip against the retort he'd been anything *but* help. A twinge of fear coursed through her as the enormity of her current situation suddenly struck her. She was alone, in a deserted basement, with a man who had threatened to deal with her. Her eyes swept the office in what she hoped looked like a casual manner. Her hand tightened around the strap of her bag.

"We have it under control, thanks," she said, "Brittany should be back any minute."

A smile twitched at the corner of his mouth. "She'll be at least an hour," he said, "Dr. Nester is a talker."

A wave of panic choked her at his words.

Leave now, or you'll be next.

Was this how it happened to Daniel? Supposedly meeting a friend, in an empty building? Except here there was only one way out. And Catlett stood between her and her escape route.

She had to get out of here. Now.

"In that case, why don't we go get that coffee?" she said, with a tight smile.

She stood abruptly, moved toward the door, and tripped over a stack of books. A pair of strong arms halted her quick descent to the floor. Fear rushed through her.

I'll deal with her.

"Let me go," she said, struggling against his grasp.

She stumbled back against the wall as his hands fell away. Her knee throbbed and her head pounded.

"Are you all right?"

He stood a few steps away, hands loose at his sides. Genuine concern in his eyes. He probably thought she was crazy. But what did she care what he thought?

"Morgan, are you all right?" he repeated.

She bolted through the door and down the hall. Her knee twinged. She ignored it as she sprinted up the stairs and into the lobby. Footsteps echoed from the stairwell behind her. She shoved open the doors and ran for her car.

Bits of ice pelted her skin as she slid across the near empty lot. Her face twisted in disbelief as she reached the car and skidded to a halt. The trunk was open. A thin layer of white flakes dusted the interior. Maybe she'd popped it by accident?

She moved to slam it shut, but her hand faltered as it touched the cold metal. The driver's side window had been smashed in.

"Morgan, wait!"

Anger boiled through her, and she spun to face him, hands raised in a defensive stance. Catlett stopped several steps away, his expression unreadable. A siren blipped behind her. She turned toward the street and scrambled over a drift of snow to the road as a patrol car eased to a stop at the curb.

She looked back. Catlett hadn't moved.

"Did you do this?" The words were out of her mouth before they'd reached her brain.

His eyes narrowed. His jaw tightened. Anger shone in his eyes.

"What makes you think I did it?" He shouted back as he gestured toward the car.

Relief rushed through her as she watched Detective Anderson climb out of the patrol car.

"What's going on here?" His eyes swept the scene. "Ms. Sullivan, I've been trying to reach you. Are you all right?"

She shook her head and waved toward her vandalized rental. "My car ..."

Her eyes shot toward Catlett. He still hadn't moved.

"Stay here." He stepped over the snow drift and circled the vehicle. "What happened here? Have you called security?"

"We just found it like this," Catlett said.

Had he? He said he didn't do it, but he could have. Morgan folded her arms across her chest. She couldn't shake the trembling.

"I'll call them now," Catlett said, pulling his phone from his pocket.

Anderson nodded. "Thank you, Dr. Catlett."

The detective paused beside the driver side and opened the door with his gloved hand. He reached inside and pulled out a folded note. Morgan felt the blood drain from her face. She watched as he flipped the paper open. She took an instinctive step backward as the detective approached her.

"This is addressed to you," he said, quietly.

He held it open. The words chilled her to her core.

GO HOME, MS. SULLIVAN.

Go home. Her gaze flew up to meet Catlett's. Anger burned through the chill as she snatched the paper from the detective's hand and stomped her way through the snow toward him.

"You used the same words," she said.

He stepped back as she shoved it toward his face. She stepped closer, emboldened by her anger.

"I. Didn't. Do. This." he said.

His voice was calm, but his eyes burned. She took another step closer.

"What else have you lied about?" she said, "Where is Daniel?"

She was shouting. She didn't care. She was sick and tired of this crazy mess. She wanted the truth. She wanted her uncle back. She wanted answers and she wanted them now.

"I wish I knew," he said, quietly, "but I don't."

She stared at him, her gaze never flinching. He stared back. She almost believed him.

Anderson moved into her line of sight. "Easy, Ms. Sullivan."

There was nothing easy about this. She took a step back, then another. Paper crinkled as her fist tightened.

"I'm going to need that back," Anderson said.

Right, evidence. She let him take it, embarrassment heating her face. Her eyes flashed to Catlett's. He was watching her, his face unreadable. She turned and moved swiftly toward her car. She made it less than two steps. Her vision blurred as she took in the damage.

Go home, Ms. Sullivan.

Whomever had done this knew who she was. More lights flashed as another patrol car slid in behind Anderson's and Deputy Murray climbed out.

"Ms. Sullivan, security will have a few questions," Anderson said, "and then Deputy Murray will take you back to Macy's."

She swallowed hard against the knot in her chest and waved a hand at the car.

"I need to tell the rental agency."

How would she explain this? She hoped it was covered by the insurance. She'd scratched a car once by accident in a tight parking garage, but did it cover vandalism? Wait until her family found out. They were never going to let her off the island again. Anderson stepped into her line of sight again, slowly. She forced herself to breath.

"You can call them from Macy's," Anderson said. "We'll provide them a copy of our report and have it towed to Mason's garage."

Towed. Now she was without a car. She was beginning to feel trapped, and she didn't like feeling so helpless. At all.

Deputy Murray escorted her back to Macy's just after noon. He followed her into the house and took up his station in the front room. Anderson had ordered him to watch out for her. She supposed his presence should feel safe, but now she didn't know what she felt.

She'd asked Anderson about the message from Daniel's phone, but the detective said he would talk to her later, after he had finished with her car. The look on his face hadn't made her feel any better. She felt like she'd stirred a hornet's nest.

Someone thought she was a threat. Or at least wanted her out of the way.

Macy was still out. The house was still and quiet. Eerie. She went up to her room to make the call to the rental agency. She cast a glance at Catlett's door. He had still been in the parking lot when she'd left with Deputy Murray. Maybe she was wrong to suspect him, at least for the damage to her car. Maybe. She unlocked her room and stepped inside.

Her body went numb. Her room had been ransacked.

The contents of her suitcase were spread across the room, the bedding stripped and piled on the floor. The mattress had also been shifted. She closed the door and locked it. Then made her way back down the stairs.

"Deputy Murray, call Detective Anderson please." Her voice sounded foreign to her ears. Like she was watching the scene from a distance. "There's been another break-in."

She handed him the key to her room without waiting for him to reply, and made her way to the kitchen. She poured herself a cup of coffee and sank into the corner chair beside the cold stove. She stared at the mug, watching the steam curl in the air, seeking answers in the murky black of the liquid. But there were none. She pushed it away and buried her head against her arms.

Maybe it was all just a bad dream. Footsteps sounded in the hall.

The door creaked.

"Ms. Sullivan ..."

She drew in a breath. "Give me a minute, Murray. Please."

The door creaked again. And there was silence. The deep ache in her chest had returned. Not that it had fully faded. Dulled a little maybe, by the distraction of the chase. She shivered and pressed her eyes harder against her arm.

She hadn't found anything. At least nothing that would help find Daniel. But someone thought she had found something. Enough to vandalize her car and ransack her room. She had no idea what that they could be searching for. They had Daniel. She'd give them anything just to get him back. She sighed deeply and sat up slowly. She rubbed a trembling hand against her face.

Why now? Daniel had been taken two nights ago. Why were they searching now? Why not the night of the incident, or the following night? Why did they ransack his office and go through his room two nights later?

"What are you looking for?" she said, quietly.

She shifted, and her foot struck her bag. She stared down at it for a long moment. Could it be one of the books? Maybe not. They'd left the novel in his office, and the paperback in his room. Leslie had had the other paperback, but it held nothing different as far as she could tell. His Bible was the only thing she'd removed before the intruder broke in. She pulled it from the bag and laid it on the table and searched the pages again. Then the bindings, and the cover for a loose section ... but there was nothing.

She sank back against the chair. There was the code, and his 'unburied treasure'. A chill tickled through her.

"You couldn't be after the treasure," she said, "Could you?"

If so, their next stop would be Daniel's home, his lab, or even her grandparents' house and her family. Her breath caught. She was getting ahead of herself. Daniel would never put them at risk. Not intentionally. She forced herself to take a breath and calm down. Even if he had hidden the thing they were searching for, he'd left the location in code. A code known only to her.

She flipped through his Bible and pulled out the notes she'd tucked inside, and then stood and moved over to the stove. A box of matches sat on the ledge above it. She crumpled the paper, stuffed it into the stove and lit a match. She watched as the pages caught fire and curled into ash.

Besides even if someone could crack the code, they wouldn't know what it meant. Right? No one had asked her any questions about any codes. She'd just been told to go home. Three times. Heavy footsteps pounded in the hall. She dropped the match inside the stove and closed the grate, and was back in her chair, the Bible safely tucked back into her bag, as the door opened. She relaxed as Detective Anderson entered.

"Deputy Murray says someone searched your room," he said.

"Yeah."

She wrapped her hands around the mug of coffee, leaching the warmth into her chilled hands. He crossed to the counter and poured himself a cup.

"Was anything missing?"

She shook her head. "I didn't look."

She hadn't had the strength to do it when she'd found the room like it was. She wasn't sure she had it now. There was nothing important in her suitcase. Her wallet, her phone, her computer, and Daniel's books had all been with her. Just clothes and toiletries were left in the room.

"Feel up to looking now?" he asked, his tone steady and calming.

She took a sip of coffee, now bitter.

"Can I have a minute?" she said, quietly.

He nodded and joined her at the table. They sat quietly for a long moment. A thought struck her. One she hadn't considered before.

"Why did you call me?" she said. Her eyes met his. "When Daniel went missing. Why me?"

Daniel hadn't wanted her to come to Winston College. He'd made clear his desire for her to stay home before he'd vanished, probably to protect her from whatever mess he'd gotten himself into. His Bible and books would have been returned to the family eventually. She would have seen the code then. Even if they hadn't, she was willing to bet he'd left some sort of clues for her at home.

"Honestly," Anderson said, "you were the first number in his emergency contacts to pick up."

Disappointment slid through her. She took another sip of coffee.

"Speaking of your uncle's phone," Anderson said, "it's missing from the evidence box."

Her eyes darted back to his.

"How?"

His eyes hardened. "That is what I'd like to know."

There couldn't be too many people with access. Agent Weston's scowling face flashed through her mind. She wondered if the FBI still had access. But they didn't want her to leave, did they? They wanted her to find Daniel's mysterious source. A source she was no closer to discovering. She slipped her phone from her pocket and pulled up the message from Daniel, then slid it across the table. Anderson took it without comment.

"Any idea who could have sent it?" she said.

He shook his head. "Someone wants you to leave, Ms. Sullivan."

No kidding. She leaned back into her chair. Of course, now she had no car, which made it a little difficult. Apparently, the person who trashed it hadn't thought it through. Her gaze strayed to the smoldering stove, and a thread of worry crept through her. Maybe she should go home.

The door creaked open, and Murray appeared, his face apprehensive.

"Boss, you got a minute?"

Anderson met her eyes briefly, then stood and followed Murray out of the room. Fantastic. More good news, she supposed. Murray returned a couple minutes later without Anderson.

"Ms. Sullivan, do you feel up to looking over your room now?"

She didn't, but she supposed it was time. She grabbed her bag and stood, looping the leather strap over her shoulder. She clutched it close to her side and set her coffee cup in the sink before following Murray down the hall and to the stairs. Anderson wasn't on the bottom floor, at least not in the rooms she could see.

The dark foreboding feeling grew stronger. She climbed the stairs and paused at the top when she found a man with a campus security uniform and a deputy she didn't recognize in the hall. Her door stood open, but they weren't near it. They were standing outside of Catlett's open door.

She took a step closer. Had they finally busted him? If he *had* messed with her car, she he'd better pay for the damages.

"Ms. Sullivan," Murray said.

"What happened there?" she said, pointing to Catlett's room.

Murray just gestured to her room. "Please."

She cast one more look toward Catlett's door, then turned back to her own. She squared her shoulders and stepped inside. The once comfortable refuge now felt cold and tainted. Anger sparked through her as her eyes swept the room. Her clothes lay in a pile on the floor, her suitcase face down beside it. She bent and flipped it over.

"Ms. Sullivan ..." Murray began to speak, but she didn't hear his words.

She stumbled back. The inside of the bag was shredded, like someone had taken a knife to it. First her car, then her bag. Or maybe it had been the other way around. Whatever they were looking for, they now thought she had it. She stepped back around the bed just as Murray reappeared with the other deputy in tow. Anderson was standing at the top of the stairs when she reached the hall.

"Nothing is missing, but they were looking for something," she sighed.

"Any idea what they're looking for?" Anderson said.

Her thoughts flickered to the pile of ash in the stove downstairs. She shook her head.

"None."

"We've identified the body in the van," he said, quietly.

Her eyes darted to his. Wait, what? Confusion joined the fear, twisting her stomach in a nauseating swirl. He'd said last night the body wasn't Daniel's.

"It isn't—"

He shook his head. "We've identified him as a security guard from Winston College," he said. "George Cole. His boss said he called in sick on Wednesday night and hasn't been seen since."

She remembered he had told her at the station they suspected Daniel had been taken by two people. Who was the second one? And where was Daniel? She hugged her arms across her chest.

"He helped kidnap Daniel?"

"We think so." His face was grave.

A chilling thought crept through her.

"He didn't drown, did he?" she said.

Anderson shook his head. "He was shot. Forensics found the gun in the van." He hesitated for a second, then continued, "The gun was registered to Dr. Catlett."

Her eyes widened in surprise. "But didn't he have an alibi? Did you arrest him?"

Suspecting Catlett was involved was one thing, but quite another to have it confirmed.

"He's gone," Anderson said. "Room empty. He left the English Building shortly after you did. We put an APB out on his vehicle."

She slumped back against the wall. Well, now what? She felt the books press against her hip through the leather of her bag. Home. She looked up at Anderson.

"Can I get a ride to the airport?" she said.

Time to go treasure hunting.

CHAPTER TWELVE

Detective Anderson had an even faster idea than a car. By half past one, she was seated in a small two-man plane, winging her way over the frozen fields below. The ride was both terrifying and exhilarating. Her pilot, Jack Barton, owned the airstrip and was a longtime family friend of both Anderson and Macy. Gotta love small towns. He didn't talk a lot but she was fine with that.

Her brain felt like someone had thrown it into a blender and hit puree.

Macy hadn't made it back before she'd had to leave. Morgan hadn't even gotten the chance to thank her and apologize for the trouble she caused. Of course, if Anderson was right, it was Catlett who had brought the trouble, not her. But those facts didn't make her feel any better.

She smiled softly. When she found Daniel, she was going to send him back to finish what he'd started with Macy, whether he realized it or not. And she was going to tag along to see it through. Macy was amazing, and Daniel deserved a second chance at happiness.

But first, she had to find him. Detective Anderson had said the van in the river was suspected to be the one they took Daniel in. So where was he now? If Catlett was involved, as the gun suggested, had he'd been part of the kidnapping, or had he tried to rescue Daniel? The brief flair of hope surprised her. She scowled and buried it deep.

Catlett was a killer. Plain and simple. Right? She stared out the window at the frozen fields.

Honestly, she didn't know what to think. Catlett had an alibi for the time of Daniel's disappearance. Didn't he? Which would mean there was at least a third person. Her head throbbed. So, say this third person shot George Cole and took Daniel from the van before it went off the road, where had they gone? Macy and Dr. Dolan had mentioned a few things nearby. Did they have another car? Or...

"Mr. Barton," she said, "were there any flights out of your airstrip last Tuesday night, or maybe even early on Wednesday?"

The pilot shook his head slowly. "Not a one. But someone did cut a hole in my back fence though."

Her head jerked toward him. "When was that?"

"Last night, I reckon." He shrugged. "Nothing was missing. Just some papers rifled."

Last night didn't make sense. This incident was too late to have been related to Daniel though, right? Then again, she never had believed in coincidences. Why make a habit of it now? The plane banked. She looked out the window and watched as the fields slowly gave way to suburbs.

"That's awful," she said. "What kind of papers?"

"Nothing much. Old flight plans and schedules, weather reports."

She didn't know much of anything about planes, but that was just ... weird. Who would break in just to dig through old paperwork?

"Probably just some kids," he said. "Hold tight. We'll be landing in a minute."

She looked out the windshield to find the runway coming at them. She gripped the armrests of her seat as the small plane glided over the tarmac and landed with a smooth set of bumps. She laughed. Barton smiled.

"Nice landing, Mr. Barton."

"I aim to please," he said.

She laughed again. The small plane taxied to the far end of the field. She checked her watch. Des Moines International Airport was still a short drive away, but Anderson said he would arrange for someone to pick her up. She still had just enough time to make the flight if she hurried. With any luck she'd be in Maui by midnight.

A black SUV waited at the edge of the airfield. Resignation settled over her as she watched the FBI agents exit the vehicle. So much for hurrying. She climbed out of the plane and shouldered her bag. Barton pulled her carryon from the hold, and she mustered a smile as he handed it to her.

"Thank you, Mr. Barton," she said as she shook his hand, "for everything."

"Safe travels, Ms. Sullivan."

From his lips to the good Lord's ears. She plastered on a big smile as she turned to face the agents. Broad daylight didn't make Agent Weston's scowl any less intimidating. She wondered if it were permanently etched into his face. Maybe his mother had never warned him his expression would stick like that. She swallowed a laugh.

Weston glowered at her. She was playing with fire, but at the moment, she didn't care. Too little sleep, too much coffee, and too few answers, all added up to no more patience.

"Hello, Agents," she said. "Are you my ride?"

Unlike her partner, Agent Blake appeared to find her attitude amusing. These two were like yin and yang. At least someone had a sense of humor. "Hello, Ms. Sullivan, ready to go home?"

Morgan's fingers flexed against the handle of her carryon.

"Not really," she said, "but it seems like the best thing to do."

"Wise decision." Weston growled.

Blake rolled her eyes and gestured to her partner. His scowl deepened. He opened the rear door as his partner took the driver's seat.

Hello, déjà vu.

She shoved her bag onto the seat and climbed in after it. Weston shut the door firmly behind her. She met Blake's gaze in the rearview mirror and sank back against the seat as Weston climbed inside. All was silent as Blake started the vehicle and eased it through the gate and onto the road.

"You've attracted a fair amount of attention, Ms. Sullivan," Weston said.

Annoyance twisted through her.

"So it would seem," Morgan said, "unless busting car windows and ransacking rooms are some sort of twisted small-town hospitality."

She felt a twinge of guilt even mocking it. Everyone she'd met had been warm and hospitable. Well, everyone but Catlett. Her eyes darted to the review mirror.

"I think your source is Dr. Scott Catlett." Might as well get straight to the point. "Good luck with finding him, though. Apparently, he's on the run from a murder charge."

The agents shared a look. There had been something off about Catlett the whole time. She'd known he'd been hiding something all this time, behind those beautiful eyes, and his not-so-friendly attitude. Her gut had warned her he'd been lying, but it never suggested he was a killer.

"Thank you for your assistance, Ms. Sulivan," Blake said, "We will take it from here."

We know who has him.

Weston's words came back to her. She leaned forward, only to be thrown back against her seat as Blake took a quick turn through a yellow light.

"So, tell me who has my uncle." she said. "You said you knew."

The agents exchanged another glance, and her annoyance flamed into anger at their silence.

"What?" she said. "Was he taken by some sort of secret society kidnapping scientists worldwide for some unknown purpose?"

Brakes squealed as the vehicle took another quick turn, then slowed to a stop, inches from a metal gate. Blake lowered her window and spoke with a guard. A guard? Where were they taking her?

"Where—"

Weston shot her a warning look. For once, she held her tongue. The gate opened, and they drove through.

"Your intern should stick to his research," Weston said.

Ice water ran through her veins. She stared at the man. Apparently, Keoni had come closer to the truth than she thought. Unless this was some empty threat to scare her. And how had they known about Keoni's research?

"What my partner meant to say," Blake said, her voice soothing, "the best thing you can do now, is to go home and let us do our jobs."

She sighed internally. Because they had done such a good job so far. A car and a cliff. A lab and an explosion. Daniel had come to them, and now he was missing. He hadn't trusted them. Not fully. Not enough to tell them who his source was. Why had he protected Catlett? If it truly was Catlett ...

The SUV came to a stop, and Morgan looked up in surprise to find them at the foot of a stairwell leading to a plane. A big plane. Oh, wow. Okay, then. Good thing she didn't have a bag to check.

"Safe travels, Ms. Sullivan." Blake said.

The words felt like a mockery. The woman looked back over the seat as her partner exited the car. Her smile seemed genuine.

"You have my number," she said. "Let us know if anything strange happens or if Dr. Catlett tries to contact you."

Yeah, she'd get right on that. Weston opened the door, letting in a deafening wave of noise and an overpowering scent of jet fuel. She slid out of the car and dragged her bags out after her. A flight attendant met them at the bottom of the stairs. Weston showed her his badge and said a brief word. The woman nodded and waved to Morgan. Well, it beat TSA and waiting areas. She looked back as she reached the top of the stairs, but the SUV was already on the move.

The cold that had settled in her blood at Weston's threat still lingered as she slipped through the door and onto the jet bridge. She needed to warn Keoni to back off on his search.

The cleaning crew was just leaving as she was the first to follow the flight attendant onboard. Nice perks. Strange treatment, though. Almost like they wanted to be certain she left. Her seat was in the rear of the plane, last row, a window seat with no window. She didn't care. She stuffed her roller bag into the overhead bin and dropped heavily into her seat.

She pulled her headphones from her computer bag and shoved it under the seat. Chatter whispered from the front as people began to board. She stuffed the earbuds into her ears and plugged the jack into her phone. Her finger froze in mid-swipe as a message alert lit up the screen.

From Catlett.

CATLETT: I didn't shoot that man.

Her heart pounded in her ears, the noise nearly deafening with the earbuds. She glanced up involuntarily, her eyes scanning the plane for a familiar face.

The screen lit up.

CATLETT: Daniel is alive. If you value his life, please stay out of it.

The blood drained from her face. Her hand ached. She forced herself to loosen her grip and tap out a response with trembling fingers.

MORGAN: Where is he?

No reply. The plane engines rumbled, signifying preparations for takeoff.

Anger surged through her, but for once it wasn't strong enough to melt the cold gripping her heart. She typed one last message.

MORGAN: He was your friend.

The betrayal cut her deeper than she would have thought. She switched the phone to airplane mode, sank back into her seat, and closed her eyes tight against the nausea. If Catlett was telling the truth, her uncle was still alive. Daniel had left her something only she could find, and she would find it. Then she was going to go looking for him, and she wasn't going to stop until she found him.

UNCLE DANIEL'S LAB, KULA, MAUI
MORGAN, AGE THIRTEEN

Music blasted from her headphones. Morgan tapped her pencil absently in time with the beat. Her eyes narrowed as she pulled the book closer, her nose almost touching the page. This wasn't making sense. The science was ... wrong. Something nudged her boot, and she jumped. She shoved back the headphones and glared up at her uncle.

"You scared me," she said. When had he arrived? She had been waiting for hours.

"My apologies, kiddo." He didn't look sorry. "So, what has you parked on my porch on this lovely afternoon?"

Who talked like that? She wrinkled her nose at him. He wrinkled his back at her. She shook her head and sighed. Uncle Daniel, that's who. She grasped his offered hand and let him pull her up from the ground.

"I have a conundrum," she said.

Such a great word. She loved big words and using them. Especially to torment her brother.

"Ah," her uncle said, as he unlocked the door, "I do love a good conundrum. For instance, why is there a horse on my lawn, when there should be none or at the least, two?"

She wasn't allowed to ride out to Uncle Daniel's alone. Even though the trail was totally safe, and Sugar Cubes was the laziest horse on the planet. She glanced at the painted gelding, who placidly stared back before returning to his snacking on her uncle's grass.

"Grandma rode out with me," she said, "but she had to get back for a lesson."

Even though she could have done it herself. She was a teenager now, not a child, but she kept that opinion to herself.

"Good answer." Her uncle grinned and ushered her inside the lab.

The room was warm and dark. She wrinkled her nose again. The place smelled stale. He wasn't here often. Most of the time he and her aunt lived in their condo on Oahu. But he was at least here on the weekends. Especially when she and Nate were at their grandparents'.

"Where's Auntie Lelani?" she said as she tried to flip open one of the jalousie windows. The handle stuck. She pushed it harder, and the slats opened with a squeak.

"She's still on Oahu," he said, "A wounded turtle was found on the beach last night, and she had to stay. She says she misses you and loves you lots."

Her aunt had the coolest job.

"Is the turtle okay?"

"It will be fine." He dropped into the chair behind his desk and waved a hand toward the one she'd claimed as her own. "Tell me about your conundrum."

Oh, right. She opened her book and set it on the desk. He leaned in as she pointed to the text.

"This says the fossil record is a record of the evolution of creatures," she said, "but it isn't. It is stating it as a fact, but it is not, it's a theory." She stabbed the sketch beside the text. "A column like that one doesn't even exist! I told my teacher that, but she wouldn't listen. She just told me to stop interrupting."

Calling her teacher a liar had been a step too far, and Morgan had accepted the detention for her disrespectful attitude. But she wasn't sorry for saying it was bad science.

"What's your theory?" her uncle said.

She slumped back into the chair with a heavy sigh and frowned at the smile she saw flicker on his face. He knew the theories. He'd taught them to her, for goodness sakes. He folded his arms loosely over his chest and waited. She sighed. This seemed to be a teaching moment.

Fine.

"Well, I told her that if you take away the bones," she said, "and just consider the rock layers, there are too many issues for it to be a slow record of deposition over time." She held up a finger as she listed them. "Number one, many of the layers are too thick and too unformed. If it had been slow, there would be a settling out of grain size and striping in the layer. But there are examples all over the world of large layers of uniformed sediment, like in the Grand Canyon, and the cliffs of Dover, and Uluru in Australia. All supporting evidence of a large-scale water event."

She stood and paced the length of the room. Her uncle continued to calmly sit in his chair. How could he be so calm?

"Number two," she continued, "Carbon dating isn't consistent. Not when lava rock at the bottom of the Grand Canyon dates at the same age as the lava rock way at the top of the Canyon. And Number three, bones aren't preserved if they aren't buried fast. You need pressure to make a fossil. Otherwise, they just dissolve, and what about the soft creatures? Like the feather worms? How could they be so perfectly preserved if they were buried slowly? They wouldn't be. And don't even get me started on the jellyfish fossils that wouldn't even exist."

She threw her hands up into the air.

"So ..." her uncle said.

"The evidence points to a large water event," she said, "like a massive world-wide flood. If this is true, then the fossil record is actually made up of burials that happened in less than a year, not of the evolution of the creatures over millions of years. Ocean floor first, and then," she motioned toward the ceiling, "up. And they aren't all extinct. A lot are still alive today. Like the sharks, and the fish, and the feather worms. To say the fossil record is fact is bad science, Uncle Daniel. It's a theory."

The fossil record had to be observed, tested, and proven before it was a fact. That was real science, right? If they couldn't be absolutely proven, they were never called facts. No one had been there but Noah and his family. But there was evidence of a large water event in the rocks all over the world.

"My teacher doesn't even know much about science," she said, as she dropped back into her chair. "My friend said she really wanted to teach literature, but they made her teach both."

How could they do that? How were they supposed to learn to be scientists when their teacher didn't understand what she was teaching? Her uncle nodded thoughtfully and then reached over to the mini fridge behind his chair and pulled out a couple of sodas. He slid one to her and popped the top on his own. He took a long sip before replying.

"It is bad science to call theory fact," he said, "In truth they are both theories, Creation and Evolution, and it takes just as much faith to believe one as the other. It comes down to world view."

She knew this by heart, but she loved to listen to him teach it.

"We believe the evidence points to a large water event." he continued. "The Bible teaches such a flood occurred and destroyed all life on this planet, except for Noah, his family and the animals on the ark."

She bit her lip as doubt crept into her brain.

"What about the fish?" she said. "How did they survive?"

Her uncle smiled. "Excellent question. The Bible is very specific that land dwelling, air breathing animals were brought onto the Ark. They wouldn't have needed to do the same with the marine dwelling creatures as that was their environment."

She supposed a floating aquarium would have been impractical. Especially when it came to whales. And mosasaurs.

"But still," he said, "a lot of them would have died with changes in salinity, extreme cold or heat changes and rapid burial by the sediment layers laid down by the flood waters. But God would have protected many of the species, as he preserved Noah, his family and every creature on the Ark."

"What do you think happened to the marine reptiles?" she said, "like the mosasaur and the Pliosaurs, and all the others?"

All her life she had been taught the legends and stories of these massive sea monsters by her uncle. If anyone knew, he would. He grinned, his eyes sparkling as he leaned forward.

"Well, the post Flood world would have been very different," he said. "Less food, new environments, etc. A lot probably died off, or perhaps were hunted to extinction. But who knows, maybe one or two are still around. After all, the whales survived."

She rolled her eyes, even as a thrill tickled her spine. Maybe there was a little truth in the legends, as he always claimed. Like he said, the whales had survived. And if something that massive had, then why not?

"Regardless," he said, "you shouldn't call your teacher a liar in front of your class or any other time."

She felt heat creep up her neck. He knew about that, did he? The coconut wireless was way too fast and gossipy.

"I know," she said, slumping back into her chair. "Be respectful. Be truthful. Be tactful."

The mantra was practically her family's creed.

"Precisely," he said. "So, conundrum solved?"

She nodded. "For now."

"Good." He leaned forward, a twinkle in his eyes, and whispered like he had a big secret. "I've run across a new legend you are going to love."

She did love legends.

CHAPTER THIRTEEN

The plane jolted, and Morgan startled awake, heart racing. She clutched the armrests as the plane bumped again, and then settled into a taxi. Her pulse refused to settle as quickly. She sank back into the seat. Her body ached, and her head pounded. But she was home. Finally. At least, she thought she was. She'd lost track a layover or two ago.

"Aloha, and welcome to Maui!" a voice said over the speakers.

Yep, she was home, or at least her grandparents' home. And Daniel's. No more planes. She sank deeper into her seat, and looked out the window across the aisle. Rain streaked against the window, blurring the lights beyond in streaks of color. She stared at the blur of lights higher up on the patch of darkness she knew to be the side of Haleakala, the dormant volcano on the east side of the island. She'd called her grandparents as soon as she'd landed in LA and agreed without argument to come stay with them, though it had been her plan all along. She didn't want them to be alone.

She didn't want to be alone either. Even with the interrogation that was sure to follow. She didn't blame them. Daniel was missing, and regardless of her reasons, she had been a little reckless. Still, she wasn't sorry she went to Iowa. She was only sorry she had come back without him.

She slipped her phone from her pocket and thumbed it on. The time was just after eleven p.m. Maui time. Too late to return any calls. There were four messages; none from unknown numbers. None from Daniel's phone.

She melted back into her seat. She skipped the two from her brother and opened one from her grandfather. He'd been called away but was sending someone to pick her up. Which gave her a little longer to pull her thoughts together at least. The last text was from Keoni.

KEONI: On vacation. Going to catch some waves.

Confusion flickered through her as she stared at the words. Keoni didn't surf. At all. Which was almost as much of a running joke as her seasickness. Her eyes narrowed. What was he up to? She tried to call, but it went straight to voicemail. She hung up without leaving a message. She'd warned him to be careful via text during her first layover. Maybe he'd taken it to heart.

She hoped he had.

The line started to move as her fellow travelers shuffled off the plane. She slid her phone into her pocket and collected her bags. Nate could wait a minute. She trudged up the jetway and into the waiting area. And groaned, quietly. Of course, it had to be the farthest gate from the baggage claim. She clutched her bags tighter and willed her body forward. When all she really wanted to do was to sink into the floor and sleep.

A bit of the tension bled from her shoulders as she stepped out of the terminal and into the humid air. She breathed deep as she joined the flow of people heading down the escalator for the baggage claim. The rain was coming down in sheets beyond the overhang. Probably a late season cold front.

She loved winters in the islands. Cool and wet and green. Better than snow. So much better. Her smile faltered as the hairs on the back of her neck prickled. Someone was watching her. She glanced over her shoulder, but she didn't see anyone familiar. She quickened her pace as she scanned the area.

Had Catlett followed her?

The thought had crossed her mind, more than once. She quickened her pace. The feeling continued as she cut through the baggage claim and out onto the curb. The usual pickup spot was to the left, next to the wide-open space between ticketing and baggage. But in the rain, and this late, the area was dark and isolated, and wet. She moved a little way down the sidewalk, pausing, still in view of the crowd gathered around the conveyor belt.

A shiver trickled up her spine. Her grandfather's truck wasn't in sight. She slipped her phone from her pocket. Maybe her ride was running late.

A hand touched her arm.

Adrenaline surged through her, and she moved without thought. The resulting squawk of surprise was familiar. Keoni flailed his way out of the nearby planter, where she'd thrown him. Apparently, her self-defense skills hadn't been totally forgotten.

"Keoni, what are you doing here?"

She grabbed his hand and pulled him out. A few curious onlookers gawked. She smiled at them, shrugged, and yanked him closer to the curb.

"Wow, you are like a ninja." He combed his hand through his hair, which stood on end. "I got your message."

She rolled her eyes. "And decided to surf some waves?"

He cast a furtive look around and leaned in closer. "That was for them."

She was too tired for this. "Who?"

He gestured to the empty air around them. "You know, 'them'."

He stopped and waved sheepishly at someone over her shoulder. She turned to find the security guard watching them with suspicion. Perfect.

"But why are you here?" Not that she wasn't relieved to see him.

"Because he called me," a familiar voice said behind her, "and I asked him to come."

Her eyes blurred as she spun around and found her brother standing on the curb behind her. The truck idled behind him. Nate opened his arms, and she threw herself into them. For all his faults, which really weren't as many as she liked to pretend, her big brother gave the best hugs.

"You didn't answer my calls," he said.

She could hear the worry he didn't try to hide from her. She hugged him tighter.

"You locked me out of my lab." Her voice came out in a whisper.

"I'm sorry."

"No, you're not."

He snorted, and the knot of tension in her chest melted.

"You're right, I'm not." He pressed a kiss against her hair. "Are you okay?"

"Hey, guys, the security guard is giving us the evil eye," Keoni said.

Great.

"Come on," Nate said, "let's go home."

She pulled away and wiped her eyes as her brother grabbed her bag and threw it into the back seat of the extended cab. Keoni climbed in after it. She slipped into the front and smirked in fond amusement as her brother tossed the guard a salute before climbing behind the wheel. And they said she was the snarky one.

She scanned the sidewalks as they pulled away, but the faces were shadowed. The cab was dark and quiet, apart from the swish of the windshield wipers. The familiar scents of alfalfa hay and leather slipped over her like a blanket. A third aroma made her stomach growled, loudly.

A bag landed in her lap, and she opened it to find her grandmother's lilikoi muffins. Warm and fresh. She pulled one from the bag and bit into it, ignoring her brother's laugh. She loved her grandmother. So much. The only food she'd eaten since leaving Macy's was an airline snack box.

"Are those Tutu Evie's muffins?" Keoni said.

She handed the bag to him and melted into her seat as they turned onto the Hana Highway.

"Where's Piper?" she said.

"With the boat. One of us had to stay and wrangle the kids."

The kids being college students. She smothered her disappointment. Nate being able to get away at such late notice was amazing. His trip had been planned for months. The research was important. He would probably have to go back soon. A twinge of guilt turned her stomach. He probably needed to be on the boat now but dropping everything and helping out was what family did when there was a crisis.

She could feel the weight of his gaze on her despite the darkness of the cab.

"I'm sorry I didn't call," she said. "Things just happened so quickly."

So quickly she had difficulty believing all of this had begun less than seventy-two hours ago.

"What happened?" Nate said, his voice gentle.

She could hear Keoni shift in the back, and his head appeared in the space between the seats. A twinge of fear shot through her.

Your intern should stick to research.

She'd already put him in danger. If anything happened to him, she'd never forgive herself. He might not be related by blood, but he was Daniel's great nephew by marriage. Which made him family. Ohana. And Ohana looked out for one another.

"I'm going to have to tell it all again when we get to the ranch," she said, reluctantly.

"That's fine," Nate said. "We've got time."

She let out a heavy sigh. Why not? Once she started, the words flowed faster. She told them about Detective Anderson's call, and Willow Creek and Winston College, with a few selected edits, like the FBI and the intruder in the house. And the part of about Catlett's phone call, and his gun. And the damages to her car and the case tucked behind Nate's seat. Everything dangerous.

If she told him now, she'd have to go through the drama twice: once with her brother and the second time with her grandfather. Better to do it all at once. Maybe after she'd had some sleep. She did tell them about the clues Daniel had left behind. Silence settled over the car as she finished. She sensed Nate knew she was holding back, but for once he didn't press her on it.

"What do you think Uncle Daniel hid this time?" Nate said, after a moment.

"I really don't know," she said. "It could be anything."

She stared out into the dark, wet night. She hoped the trouble had stayed behind with the snow in Iowa. But she couldn't shake the feeling it had followed her home.

For better or worse, her grandfather had been out on a call when they'd made it back to the house. A horse had been injured trying to jump a fence in the storm. Even though partially retired, Matt Smithson was still one of the best equine vets on the island.

Her grandmother had given her a warm hug and an assessing look, then sent her off to bed. Evie Smithson was small in stature, but mighty in spirit. Nothing good was ever gained by arguing with her, nor did Morgan want to. She was exhausted. Her grandmother looked as if she'd aged a decade since she'd last seen her. Guilt settled in Morgan's gut, cold and heavy.

They should have heard about Daniel from her. From the intensity of her grandmother's hug, Morgan guessed she had been worried about more than just their son. She should have called them first.

Sleep eluded her, despite her efforts. Finally, she curled up on the window seat and stared out into the dark night. The moon shone brightly through a patch in the clouds. The breeze was cool and damp. She shivered and embraced it, using it to clear her muddled thoughts. She wrapped a quilt around her and snuggled into it. Her eyes grew heavy, and she let them close. The air was heavy with the scent of plumeria, wet earth, and more rain.

She was home. She was safe. She let her mind drift as she listened to the rain patter against the roof of the porch below the window and the toads croak from the garden below. There was a faint splash from her grandmother's koi pond, followed by another. She forced her racing heart to calm.

She was home. She was safe. The mantra calmed her. She was far from masked intruders who ransacked rooms, far from broken car windows, and killers pretending to be friends ... Her heart throbbed ... but her uncle was still lost.

If Catlett could be trusted, which she doubted, Daniel was still alive. And what if Keoni's theories had truth to them? What did Daniel have the mysterious 'Them' wanted badly enough to kidnap—and kill—for? No research was worth a man's life. Especially not research involving mythical sea creatures. Maybe it was something else. She made a mental note to check into Daniel's friend's research, Dr. Yang. The one whose death had begun this whole crazy adventure.

Agent Weston had mentioned Leviathan. Daniel had left his clues with the passages associated with Leviathan. But those two things were not necessarily connected. She pulled the blanket closer as a brisk gust of damp air whipped through the window. The internet was full of sites dedicated to cryptozoology. Some legitimate seekers of the unknown, the discoverers of creatures like the Megamouth Shark, the Mountain Gorilla, the Coelacanth, the Frilled Shark, and so many more.

Scientists like Daniel.

And then there were the enthusiasts. Amateurs who mistook fantasy for fact and refused to accept anything but their own theories. She'd been in the field long enough to meet several fanatics, in the truest sense of the word. Daniel had listened to their theories. He'd seen it as an opportunity to guide them toward the science, and in turn to the Creator.

Sometimes it worked. And sometimes their faith in their monster was stronger than the truth. She sighed. No. This wasn't the work of an amateur enthusiast. Explosions, fires, and murder seemed extreme even for the strongest of "true believers". She thumped her head lightly against the window frame and opened her eyes.

She stared out into the darkness toward Daniel's property. She'd left her keys at home in her rush to leave Oahu. Her grandfather had a set, which meant she would have to wait until daylight to do anything. The rumble of an engine sounded above the rain, and she smiled. She tossed the quilt on her bed and grabbed a hoodie from the chair. She tugged it on as she slipped into the hall. The house was quiet and still. She made her way silently down the stairs to the ground floor. Light spilled into the hall from the open door of her grandfather's study.

"Shouldn't you be in bed, young lady?" a voice said from behind her.

She turned, and the grin slipped from her face. Her heart seized. For a brief, irrational moment, she almost believed the man silhouetted against the light from the kitchen was Daniel. And then the light switched off, and her grandfather joined her in the door of the study.

"I'm sorry, kiddo," he said, "I didn't mean to startle you."

She forced a breath into her lungs and blinked hard against the tears. Her grandfather set his coffee on the hall table and gathered her into his arms. He smelled of coffee and horses and home. Her breathing hitched, and his arms tightened in response. And all at once she felt as if she were six years old again.

"My brave girl." His voice was soft, soothing. "I'm sorry you had to deal with all of that on your own."

No chiding for not calling them. No lecture for dashing off into danger. A few tears slipped free, and she hid her face against his shoulder, struggling to regain control. She wasn't six anymore, she was an adult, fully capable of looking out for herself. Nate was already treating her as if she were made of glass and likely to shatter. She couldn't have the rest of the family believing the same.

"Have you heard from Mom and Dad?" Her voice was steady, though the sniff ruined the illusion of control.

"Not yet," he said. "But according to their schedule, they should be back in range in a couple of days. I tried to get word through the rafting company to have them call us."

Maybe they would know something more by then. She pulled away and wiped her eyes on the back of her sleeve. Her grandfather caught her chin and raised it gently, then tilted her face from side to side, examining her with a practiced eye. Didn't matter that she wasn't a horse.

"How are you holding up?"

She sighed. Different words, same question. At the moment, she was still on her feet, and home. It was enough for now.

"As good as I can be, I guess," she said, "How's the mare?"

He released her chin with a knowing look. He was onto her attempt to deflect.

"Her leg should heal in a couple of weeks, and hopefully she'll be a little wiser next time."

Hopefully, but doubtful. Horses were practically accidents waiting to happen. Her grandmother's mare had managed to shave the hair off her nose once, in an empty arena, and they still hadn't figured out how it had happened. Her grandfather retrieved his coffee and ushered her into his office.

"I thought," she said, "Grandma didn't like you drinking coffee this late."

He gave her a conspiratorial wink. "She doesn't but it is decaf. So, it doesn't count."

Yeah, that was an argument she didn't want to be a part of.

Of all of the rooms in this house, her grandfather's study had always been her favorite, for the simple reason almost every bit of wall space was fitted with bookshelves, each bulging to capacity with books of all sizes and topics. Apart from Daniel's lab, and the stables, this room had been her sanctuary. She sank into one of the leather chairs across from his desk as he took the other.

"So. Want to tell me about Iowa?" Guilt weighed heavy in her heart, but there was no condemnation in his gaze, only concern.

"I'm sorry," she said. "I should have called, but everything happened so fast."

"Tell me." His words were gentle.

He listened silently as she told him the entire story. Beginning with the call from Deputy Anderson to her arrival in Maui. Every single thing Detective Anderson had shared. Everything about Scott Catlett, and the FBI. Macy Roberts, and the intruder, everything Dr. Dolan had shared. The body in the van. The clues from Daniel. The threats, and her car. Catlett's texts.

Everything.

The tension melted away as she finished, leaving only weariness, and intense sadness. Silence settled over the room as she waited for her grandfather to speak. Finally, he let out a long, slow breath.

"Do you believe Dr. Catlett's message?" he said, "that Daniel is alive?"

She wanted to. "I don't know."

He nodded, thoughtfully. "You've had a busy couple of days," he said.

A burst of laughter caught her off guard, but once she started giggling, she couldn't stop. Feeling on the verge of hysterics, she struggled to pull herself together. A glass was pressed into her hand.

"Drink this."

The dark red liquid burned a path down her throat. She coughed and took another sip. Her grandfather's one vice, a good port. She preferred a Cabernet, but it did help.

"Better?" he said after a long moment.

Her face felt hot. She hated feeling out of control. She drew a deep breath and let it out slowly. Then nodded.

"Yes. Thanks."

The leather of his chair creaked as he settled back against it. His eyes were sad and contemplative.

"I'm glad you are here," he said, "that you came home. It was the right thing to do."

She swirled the liquid in her glass. Was it? What if she'd brought the trouble back with her?

"Then we will deal with it together," her grandfather said.

His comment startled her, and she realized she'd spoken aloud. *Great.*

"Did Daniel tell you anything?" she said. "About what he was working on?"

Or why he'd left?

Her grandfather shook his head and sighed wearily.

"My son can be a mystery when he chooses to be. He gets that from your grandmother." His quick grin made her heart twinge. "I stopped in and had a look in his lab after he left and found nothing out of place. Everything was filed and neatly stored away, even his maps."

Quite out of the ordinary. Daniel's method of organization was controlled chaos. Her heart sank into her toes as an awful thought struck her.

"Do you think maybe ..." The words caught in her throat.

"That he thought he might not be coming home?" His words drove the fear deeper. "Possibly, but I do know this about Daniel." The authority in his tone drew her gaze to his. "Family is everything to him. If there is a way home, he will find it."

She nodded. A small spark of hope warmed her—faint—but still there. Her gaze settled on a bookshelf beside them. Adrenaline shot through her as she recognized a small wooden chest tucked into the bottom shelf. The chest wasn't much to look at, its surface scarred with time and wear. Not to mention all those times it had been buried in the dirt. She was out of her chair before she realized she had moved.

Daniel's treasure box.

She dropped to her knees and slid the box to the hardwood floor. Her heart raced in her chest as her fingers traced along the seam, searching for the hidden catch. The lid opened with a soft snick, and the hinges squeaked as she raised the lid. A row of hardback children's classics was nestled inside against a bed of worn blue velvet. Her books. Each one a gift from her uncle.

There is no treasure greater than knowledge.

Her vision blurred at the memory of Daniel's words. Her fingertips skimmed along the bindings as she searched for a particular book, *Treasure Island*. She narrowed her eyes in confusion as she found that one missing. Okay maybe the book wasn't the clue. She tapped her finger against the spines and scanned the titles again.

"My wise Conseil," she murmured.

A thrill of anticipation shot through her as she slipped a book from the box. Verne's *The Mysterious Island*. Sequel to *Twenty Thousand Leagues Under the Sea*. She ran her thumb along the pages and paused as they didn't bend. At all. In fact, they were glued together. She opened the cover, and a brass key fell to the floor with a loud clang.

"Unburied treasure holds the key," she said, with a grin. Literally.

CHAPTER FOURTEEN

The key was heavy and appeared to be an antique. As it should if it were a key to a treasure chest, or an old trunk. She grinned. Another clue. So like Daniel.

"Unburied treasure, huh?" her grandfather said. "Your grandmother always says that box looks like it's been buried and dug up one too many times."

"As any good treasure chest should."

Her grandfather laughed. "You sound like Daniel."

She laughed at the compliment.

"Looks like there may be another trunk." She handed him the key as he joined her. "Any idea what this might fit?"

The house held at least two vintage trunks and her grandfather's old sea chest from his navy days. There were also a few in the tack room in the barn, but none of those used a key like this. He shook his head and handed the key back to her.

"No." He ran his fingers through his thick snowy hair. "Probably at Daniel's. This explains why he was messing with this box before he left."

She had a feeling he was right. The trunk was probably hidden somewhere at Daniel's, though she couldn't remember a chest with a key of this size. And was certain she would have. She set the key on the floor and turned back to the treasure chest. The rest of the books were just books. No hidden keys or clues. Nothing in the lining.

Usually there was another clue, something to point her toward the next location.

"I can't believe he ruined a book," she said, ruefully.

She turned the book over. Maybe the clue was in the title. *The Mysterious Island*. Captain Nemo's secret base. She sighed. Maybe a reference to Daniel's lab? Something caught her eye at the bottom of the key shaped cutout. A scribble. She angled it toward the light. Two words: root beer.

"What is it?" her grandfather said.

A faint whisper of amusement warmed her. She shook her head with a snicker.

"Yo, ho, ho, and a bottle—"

"Of root beer," her grandfather finished.

Her mother hadn't been a fan of her kids singing about rum. Daniel had been the one to change it to root beer, which they had always celebrated the end of a successful treasure hunt with. The old kind in the brown bottles. Made her feel like a pirate.

Her heart twinged at the memory. What if this was Daniel's last treasure hunt? She picked up the key, smoothing her thumb along its rough edges.

"I'm going to find him." Her words surprised them both.

Well done, Sullivan. Why didn't she just spill all her secrets.

"Promise me you won't go looking for him," her grandfather said.

She darted a glance toward him and scrambled to her feet at his haggard look. His face was pale in the dim light. His hand settled on her shoulder, squeezing gently.

"Leave it to the FBI." His voice was firm, but faint. "Promise me, Morgan. I won't lose you too."

Her jaw shut with an audible click as any protests died on her lips at the sadness visible in his eyes. She wanted to agree, but how could she give up on Daniel? If Keoni was right, the FBI hadn't found any of the scientists missing so far, and now, they'd lost Daniel.

"Morgan, please. Keep it to the clues he left for you. He wouldn't want to put you in danger."

Cold settled into her chest. She could feel the key pressing into her hand as her fist clenched. And forced herself to nod, even though it felt like she was giving up.

"I promise to keep to the clues he left." She whispered.

Wherever they might lead.

He drew her into a comforting hug, as if he knew the price of her promise. Then again, he probably knew better than she did. She hugged him tighter.

"I'm going to ride over to Daniel's in the morning," she said.

He released her and met her eyes with a firm, but loving, look. Making her feel like she was sixteen again.

"Take your brother with you. I don't want you out alone."

Probably a good idea. She sighed and rolled her eyes in an effort to make him smile.

"Okay."

He met her gaze and smiled.

"Off to bed with you," he said, giving her one last hug, "you look like you're going to keel over any minute, and you are too big for me to carry anymore."

She huffed a small laugh with humor she didn't feel. The cold feeling had spread from her chest to her stomach, and was inching toward her toes. She stuffed the rest of the books back into the chest and slid it back onto the shelf.

"Goodnight, kiddo."

She murmured her goodnight and headed back through the quiet house to her room.

A key. Daniel's lab. And another book.

Lord, please protect him. Bring him home.

The prayer was becoming her mantra. Catlett had said Daniel was alive and to stay out of it. Everyone wanted her to leave the mystery of Daniel's disappearance to the authorities. But doing so made her feel like she was giving up on him. She slipped into her room and closed the door quietly behind her. The cool damp wind whipped the curtains. She crossed the room and closed it. The storm was growing stronger.

She didn't want to think about any of this anymore. Her brain was foggy. She tucked the key back into the book and stuffed it into the bottom of her pillowcase. Then she settled in, ignoring the lump the book made beneath her head.

Sleep crept over her, and for once, her dreams did not return.

A light rain drizzled against the leaves of the trees above her, releasing a calming scent of eucalyptus and damp earth. She closed her eyes and listened as it pattered against her raincoat. Her seat shifted beneath her, and she smiled.

"Patience, Sleuthy."

She opened her eyes and ran a hand along the damp, black neck of the horse. He shook his head as if in disagreement but stood still. She looked down over the valley below. The view of the valley was breathtaking, edged on each side with ocean, lush green in the center, the West side mountains rising behind. Dark clouds towered beyond the peaks, promising more heavy rain before the morning was out.

Sleuth turned his head toward the trail and whickered. She looked over her shoulder to find her brother approaching, astride her grandfather's Appaloosa mare.

"Good morning, Whisper Girl," The mare's ears flickered at her crooning. "Who's your grumpy friend?"

Her innocent smile slid into a smirk as her brother narrowed his eyes. Nate was not a morning person. Unless diving was involved. He pointed his finger at her.

"You were supposed to meet me at the barn."

No. She was supposed to take him with her to Daniel's.

Word had spread of Daniel's disappearance and the house had been overrun by extended family and friends by morning. The barn was the first place they'd look for her, once they figured out she wasn't in the house. She just hoped no one realized she'd left through her bedroom window. She loved them all, but she couldn't handle any more questions right now.

There was a Keurig in the office at the barn, so there had been no need to go through the kitchen. She even found her grandmother's stash of chocolate granola bars. She'd texted her brother after she'd tacked up Sleuth.

"We did leave a note." She cocked her eyebrow at him. "And we are waiting."

Nate's dark eyes narrowed, but the humor in them dampened the effect of his glare. He pulled a folded scrap of paper from his pocket. "Dear Slowpoke, Last one to the gate is rotten sushi. Love and Kisses, Sleuth."

She gave an exaggerated shrug. "I told Sleuth the love and kisses bit was too much, but what can I say, he's a big softy. Aren't you, big guy?" She tapped Sleuth's shoulder and grinned as he nodded his head in response. "Besides, you're here now, so let's go. I want to get to Uncle Daniel's before the rain."

Her grin was the only warning her brother got before she and Sleuth wheeled around and shot down the grass-covered path. Their last ride together had been too long ago. She let out an exhilarated laugh and urged Sleuth on. The big horse needed no urging. He loved to run as much as she did. She slowed him to a trot as they reached the trees. The breeze was damp and cold.

"We won, so you get to open the gate," she said, as her brother caught up.

Nate shot her a mock glare but dismounted and handed Whisper's reins over.

"You cheated."

She scoffed at him as he unlocked the gate and pushed it open. She clucked to Sleuth, and they passed through, followed by Whisper.

"It's not our fault you're sooo slow," she said.

She snorted at the look he gave her as he took the reins back and mounted Whisper. The world beneath the trees was quieter and a little drier. Pine needles blanketed the damp earth, muffling the hoofbeats of the horses. She breathed deep and exhaled slowly, soaking in the peace. They cut up to a side trail branching off the access road, giving them a nice, little shortcut.

"You look better than you did last night," her brother said.

The knot in her chest tightened as the levity faded. He was worried about her. And when Nate worried, he became overprotective. His protection had been nice when she was little and needed someone to help slay the monsters under her bed, but she was a big girl now. She sighed silently. Wait until he heard the whole story of what had happened in Iowa. He'd be insufferable.

"Thanks," she said, dryly. "What did I look like?"

"Death warmed over."

Lovely. She tossed a look over her shoulder at him. He looked tired. She almost felt sorry for dragging him out of the house so early. Almost. He looked beyond her and smirked.

"You might want to duck," he said.

Her retort died on her lips as she turned. She flattened against Sleuth's neck, barely in time to avoid the low hanging branch. The trail was a mess.

"Who's responsible for maintaining this trail?"

"Not sure. I don't think anyone's used it since last fall. Uncle Daniel always drove."

Sadness leached through her, laced with a bit of humor. Daniel had never really liked riding—he preferred to keep his feet on the ground. Her grandmother said he'd taken a scary spill once as a teen and broken a few ribs and a leg. From then on, he preferred being in the ocean. Her aunt had loved to ride.

Nate moved up beside her as the trail widened. She ducked another branch. "Maybe Grandma can add trimming the trail to the list of chores for the kids during spring break camp. She's been giving them odd jobs in exchange for lessons."

She snorted. "Is that why Giggles is sporting a hot pink mane?"

The long-suffering miniature horse was used to contending with the whims of children. She hadn't seemed to mind her new look all that much, though the roundness of her belly suggested sugar cubes and peppermints might have been the cause of her contentment.

"I heard you found Uncle Daniel's next clue," her brother said.

The book pressed against her back, secured in a drawstring daypack with the key nestled safely inside. Every ounce of her self-control had been tested as she waited for Nate at the gate. She shot a glance at her brother, wondering what else her grandfather had told him.

"Yeah." She urged Sleuth into a faster walk. "It was in the treasure box, like we thought. A giant brass key hidden in a copy of *The Mysterious Island*."

"Uncle Daniel ruined a book to hide a key? This must be serious."

She laughed. "Right?"

Books were sacred to Daniel. He might scribble in them, but even folding down the edge of a page had been frowned upon. He still used bookmarks. Gutting a book didn't seem like a very Daniel thing to do.

"There was another clue," she said, "written in the bottom of the hole. The words root beer."

She glanced at her brother in time to catch his look of realization. Enthusiasm blazed bright in his eyes. Nate loved a good hunt as much as she did. And Daniel's treasure hunts were the best. Sleuth turned his head to peer at her brother as he launched into a loud, and slightly off key, rendition of the pirate chantey. Daniel's addition didn't rhyme very well, but it was a lot of fun to sing.

She joined him for a line or two, in between bouts of laughter. The trail steepened, and Nate fell to the rear. She let Sleuth pick his path. A cool brisk breeze whipped through the trees. The heavier rains were getting closer, but they were almost to the lab. She shortened her reins and urged Sleuth into a trot as the trail leveled. Her pulse beat in time with the thud of hooves against the dirt. Dread warned with anticipation in a nauseating tangle as they drew closer.

What if someone had beat them to Daniel's place?

She slowed Sleuth to a walk and waited for her brother to catch up. She wasn't alone this time. Whatever happened, she knew Nate had her back. The forest opened into a clearing, filled with well-maintained grass. Sleuth let out a whinny, and, to her surprise, it was answered by a bleat. And another. And then the tinkle of bells as her grandmother's goats came over the small rise to greet them. Nature's lawnmowers.

The goats followed them as the horses edged along the perimeter of the fence line. Daniel's small plantation style cottage came into view as they crested the ridge, and to the right, his lab sat nestled beneath a stand of trees. Sleuth whinnied again as they approached the lab, and the sound pierced her heart. She rubbed a hand along his neck as she blinked back a sudden rush of tears. She half expected Daniel to poke his head out the door and greet them just as he always had.

"He's not here, Sleuthy." Her words came out in a choked whisper. "I don't know where he is."

She dismounted at the small paddock beside the lab. A damp black nose brushed against her arm as she loosened the saddle girth a notch. She rubbed her hand against his forehead. The motion calmed her.

"Are you all right?" Nate said.

She wasn't prepared for the rush of emotion this place brought. How real it made Daniel's disappearance. Her brother's eyes were damp. He reached out and pulled her into a tight hug.

"What if he never comes back?" she whispered.

Nate's arms tightened. "Don't give up hope. Let's stick to the facts."

Catlett had said Daniel was still alive. And her uncle would stay that way—if she didn't come looking for him. Nate didn't know whole truth. He was just an eternal optimist. Her brother sputtered and backed away abruptly, and she laughed as he fended off the large damp nose whuffing his ear. Sleuth was an attention hog. Nate took the reins.

"I'll see to the horses," he said. "Meet you inside."

Okay. She could do this. She made her way up the grassy slope, quickening her last few steps as the rain beat down harder. She dashed up the steps of the small porch and stopped beneath the overhang. The door was intact as best she could see, and a jiggle of the handle assured her it was locked. She pulled the keys from her pocket and found the right one. She hoped he hadn't changed the locks.

The door opened without issue, and she released a breath she hadn't realized she'd been holding. The room was intact. How anticlimactic. A bit of the tension slowly left her shoulders as she relaxed. She really had half expected to find it ransacked. Maybe the trouble had remained in Iowa after all. She left the door open as she disarmed the alarm. He hadn't changed the code either. His wedding anniversary, the only code he used not related to a book.

Her throat thickened with tears. If Daniel was dead, at least he and Leilani were finally together again. She closed her eyes and breathed a slow deep breath. Keep to the facts. Just keep to the facts. Daniel had cautioned her about creating theories before considering the facts.

If you put theories before facts, you were more likely to twist the facts to fit the theories.

Her nine-year-old self had taken his words to heart, and she'd thought he was the most brilliant man in the world—until she'd read the quote in a Sherlock Holmes story, *A Scandal in Bohemia*. Daniel was a walking search engine, since even before Google had been a thing.

She still thought he was brilliant.

She wandered slowly through the room. Everything looked the same as it always had, except ...

"It's too clean in here," her brother said, as he joined her, shaking the rain from his hair, "I don't think it has ever been this clean."

Another favorite quote of Daniel's was from Albert Einstein. Something along the lines of 'if a cluttered desk suggested cluttered thoughts, what did an empty desk suggest?' He'd taken the quote to heart it seemed. Daniel's workspace had always been a system of its own, a controlled sort of chaos. But this was out of the norm.

The whiteboards lining one wall were free of scribbles, the corkboard empty, his desk cleared and his books in orderly rows on the shelves built onto the rear wall. She saw no sea chests, nothing with a lock that would fit her key.

"You don't think he buried the next clue, do you?" Nate pointed to a shovel leaning against the shelves.

"I really hope not."

The red volcanic dirt left a permanent stain, and it was hard and slick. Most treasure chest burying when they were kids had taken place in fresh flower beds. But the chest hadn't been buried this time, so hopefully there was no digging involved. She moved closer to the bookshelves, as something odd caught her eye. Her brother caught it at the same time.

"I see *Treasure Island*," Nate said, "Or should I say, *Treasure Island*s."

There were many copies of the book, in fact, scattered throughout the shelves. Two side-by-side, another tucked between an Oceanography textbook and an autobiography by Jacques Cousteau. And another few on the shelf above. She took a step back.

"I count fifteen," she said. Which was overkill. Even for a bibliophile like Daniel.

"Fifteen men on a treasure chest." Nate muttered.

Daniel had changed the dead man part of the shanty too. "Yo, ho, ho."

As she scanned the books surrounding the copies, a pattern began to emerge.

"Only five are shelved with Verne books." She took a step closer to the shelf and ran her fingers along the spines.

"Two leather," Nate said, "three paperbacks. Anything stand out?"

In fact, one did. A paperback with a tattered spine tucked against a leather-bound copy of *The Mysterious Island*. She slid the book from the shelf. Nate looked over her shoulder, and she examined the battered cover and thumbed through the pages.

Nothing.

"Well," he said, "If at first you don't succeed, at least you have fourteen more times to try."

She rolled her eyes at him. "You're funny."

"I try."

A glint caught her eye behind the space the book had occupied.

"Nate."

She pulled the books from the shelf and shoved them into her brother's arms. A lock was set into the back at the base of the shelf. A tumbler lock with a three-letter combination. A symbol was carved into the wood above it. She traced the symbol with her finger. "Isn't that—" Nate said.

"A Kraken."

A mythical creature. A monster of the deep. She tapped her finger against the wood as her mind began to shift the clues at a rapid rate. The combination had something to do with the Kraken.

"Three letters," Nate said. "What do you think?"

"Well, Verne used a giant squid in *20000 Thousand Leagues Under the Sea*." She spun the dials. "JGV. Jules Gabriel Verne."

Nothing happened. Okay, so not Verne's initials. She was missing something. The clues had a pattern.

"The pattern," Nate said, reading her mind, "has followed book titles. So, what other books, or stories include Krakens?

Several most likely. She ran through the list in her head of the ones Daniel had shared. Books, stories and ...

"The Kraken." she said, "It's a poem by Alfred Lord Tennyson. One of Daniel's favorites."

She reached in and spun the tumblers. A. L. T. There was a loud click, like a bolt thrown back. She grinned at her brother, who grinned back, excitement in his dark eyes. But then nothing further happened. She looked closer. The Kraken emblem was raised. She held her breath and pushed it back in. A loud grinding filled the small space, and they both jumped back as a section of the floor dropped and slid away to reveal a large, dark hole.

CHAPTER FIFTEEN

Nate's low whistle broke the silence.

"Way cool, Uncle D.," he said.

Morgan laughed. "Did you say, 'way cool'?"

He jostled her playfully with his elbow and rushed for the hole. He beat her to it and stuck his head in. The gap was long and narrow. Like a box.

"What do you see?" She dropped to the floor and shifted closer, trying to see around her brother's big head.

He pulled his head back. "Nothing. It's too dark."

She looked in and caught a hint of reddish dirt at the bottom. She leaned back quickly as Nate swung his feet around and dropped into the hole. She snorted. And she was the one everyone called reckless? Nate vanished completely, which made the hole over six feet deep. Give or take. How had she not known about this? There was a flash of light and then the sound of falling chains.

"I found a ladder!" His voice had a faint echo, like he was standing in a cave.

She peered down into the space he had vacated. A chain ladder hung against the concrete wall.

"Is there room?" she said.

"Yeah." Nate's voice was fainter. "It's not bad if you like dark and creepy."

Who didn't like dark and creepy? Her, that's who. She took a deep breath and climbed down the ladder, while she did her best not to think about spiders. And centipedes. At least there were no snakes in Hawaii. Her boots hit the dirt floor, and she turned. A light glimmered faintly in the distance, down a long narrow tunnel. Great.

"Nate?"

"Back here."

She slipped her phone from her bag and switched on the flashlight app. Concrete gave way to lava rock as she made her way down the passage. The lab was built into the side of the hill, on low rise stilts. Lava rock wasn't the easiest thing to dig up, and blasting was often necessary. Most structures were just built around the rock. Daniel had cut back into what looked like an ancient lava tube.

The air smelled damp and musty, but the wind whistled from somewhere ahead. At least they didn't have to worry about suffocating. A low eerie moan echoed through the cavern.

"Beware the curse of the Pirate King."

She scowled. Her brother's cackling laughter still sounded like a strangled hamster. She panned her light along the jagged walls. The tunnel appeared to be blocked on one side by the foundation of the lab and the other by what appeared to be a cave-in. She panned the light upward warily.

"Nate, where are you?"

She stepped carefully as the path dipped downward into a cavern. Surely it couldn't be much further. Lava tubes could go on for miles, true, but why would Daniel go through the effort of building into one that did? And never tell them about it.

"Nate, this is not funny." His cackling sent a shiver through her.

She shone her light toward it, and for a moment all reason left her as the light caught a grinning skull. She bit back a scream. Thank goodness for shatterproof phone cases. Her brother's laughter echoed through the tavern. Jerk.

"I hate you."

"No, you don't." She could hear his grin. "I found an old friend of ours."

Friend? His light switched on, and she scuttled a few steps backwards. Nate lounged beside a rather authentic looking skeleton dressed in pirate garb, complete with a jeweled saber. The pirate skeleton's arm was outstretched, over the curved top of a battered sea chest. A chest with a large lock.

"Got the key?" he said, tapping the lock.

"Right here."

She slipped the bag from her shoulders and pulled out the book. The key fit snugly into the lock and turned with ease. The lid popped open like a jack-in-the-box sending the skeleton clattering to the floor. The light from their phones revealed a box-like shape, wrapped in a waterproof pouch.

"Not the most sparkly of treasures," Nate said. "I was kind of hoping for chocolate coins."

He reached inside the chest and lifted the bag from its resting place, carefully settled it onto the dirt floor.

"It's not very heavy," he said, "You do the honors."

He didn't have to tell her twice. She unzipped the pouch and looked inside. Another box. The wood gleamed beneath the light. Her excitement plummeted.

"What's wrong?" Nate shifted around beside her. "Morgan?"

She knew this box. Knew what it held. And she also knew what everything meant now. The clues. The elaborate hunt.

"Is that ...?" Nate said.

She inhaled a shaky breath and pulled the box from the pouch.

"Daniel's magnifying glass."

The one she'd wanted when she was little. The one he promised he would leave to her someday. Apparently, that day was today. She wasn't ready. She would never be ready.

"There's something else." Nate reached into the pouch and pulled out an antique envelope.

He handed it to her without another word. Her nickname was penned in old style calligraphy across the yellowed paper. *My wise Conseil.* Daniel's seal was stamped into the blue wax, a Pictish water dragon. Her hand trembled as she fingered the symbol.

"I can't ..." Her voice cracked.

Nate wrapped an arm around her and pulled her close.

"You don't have to," he said, his voice husky. "Open it when you're ready. There's no rush."

"Why didn't he tell us, Nate?" Tears spilled down her face. "Why didn't he let me help him?" She curled into him as he pulled her closer. His hand rubbed circles against her back, to soothe her. She didn't deserve his comfort. "I was so short with him. I was hurt when he wouldn't let me come, and he wouldn't tell me why. He tried to call back, but I didn't answer."

And then he'd gone missing.

"This is not your fault." Nate squeezed her harder. "None of this is your fault, Morgan. If Daniel were here, you know he would say the same thing." He gave her a tiny shake. "You hear me?"

She did hear him. Her head knew he was right, but her heart couldn't accept it yet.

"I can't say goodbye." Saying the words felt like a punch in the gut. "I can't. He's not dead. Catlett said he wasn't dead."

Nate's arm tightened a fraction of a second before her words sank in. Oops.

"What do you mean Catlett said?"

A shout echoed down the tunnel from the direction of the lab. They doused their lights in unison and a warning screamed in her brain. She had been followed. She clutched the box to her.

"Did you leave the door open?" Her whisper sounded like a yell.

"Wait here."

There was a skitter of rocks as her brother crept back down the tunnel. She slid the box and the envelope into her bag as quietly as possible. No one was going to take it from her.

The seconds stretched into hours, or so it seemed in the smothering darkness. Then the rattle of the ladder clanked through the cavern, like the sound of a ghoul dragging its chains. She scrambled to her feet as a shriek echoed through the dark, followed by loud laughter. Nate's. The sudden flood of relief left her knees weak.

"It's just Keoni."

She switched on her light as a grinding noise echoed through the passage. Nate reappeared a moment later, this time with a lantern and Keoni in tow.

"Wow!" Keoni darted across the room to the chest. "Is that a real skeleton?"

She forced a laugh and grabbed her brother's arm, hauling him back several steps. She leaned closer, her whisper sounding more like a hiss.

"Daniel went to pretty big lengths to keep this place hidden." And they ruined it by simply leaving the front door unlocked.

Her brother shrugged and whispered back. "He saw the hole in the floor. What was I supposed to do?"

He had a point. Daniel didn't have hidden secrets down here. At least she didn't think so. So far, they'd found nothing that had to do with his disappearance. In that case it was unlikely she was putting Keoni in greater danger by letting him see the cavern. Right?

"What was in the chest?" Keoni said.

"Just that pouch with a letter," Nate said, "and a gift for Morgan."

He turned back to her. His eyes were shadowed but she could feel the tension in his arm. His voice dropped back to a murmur.

"The front door is locked," he said, "and we found a button that triggers the passageway from this side." Which explained the grinding noise. "When we get out of here, you're going to tell me more about Dr. Catlett, and how he knows Uncle Daniel is alive."

He pulled away and crossed the cavern to join Keoni. The edges of the box pressed into her back. The weight pulled at her heart. This wasn't how things were supposed to happen. Daniel had promised he wouldn't leave her, but he had. She rubbed her arms against the damp chill. She sighed and swept the room with her light. Such an odd amount of effort just to store one chest, but then again, who knew how long this space had been here. Daniel loved his secrets. She paced along the edges of the cavern but found nothing else. A faint tapping sounded from the direction of the chest.

"Hey, guys," Keoni said, his voice muffled, "I think this thing has a false bottom."

She crossed the cavern and joined them in crowding over the box. Keoni ran his fingers along the edges of the bottom of the chest.

"It's a good two inches above ground." Keoni pointed to the exterior of the box.

"Maybe there's a latch?" she said. "Maybe along the top? Daniel had a chest that did that once."

She ran her fingers along the wood, and the hinges, and the intricate carvings along the sides, but no luck.

"None at the bottom either," Nate said, "and no space to slide a knife in."

"Hey guys," Keoni said, "what's this?"

A small keyhole, so small it looked like a natural knot in the weathered wood. Great. Another key. The box pressed into her back, and she sighed. Her heart sank as she debated opening it. She felt her brother's eyes watching her, but she didn't meet them. If she did, she'd just relock the chest and leave it. She slid the bag off her shoulder and pulled the box out.

"What's that—" Keoni's question cut off.

She glanced up to see Nate's hand on his shoulder. She gave them a faint smile. She slid her fingertips along the worn wood and pressed against the latch release. The lantern light reflected off the polished glass as she reverently eased the box open. Tears blurred her vision, she blinked them back.

She carefully removed the magnifying glass from its resting place, but there was nothing else in the box. She shifted the glass to one hand and gently prodded the satin lining.

"It's not here," she said.

"Maybe it's in the letter?" Nate said.

Her gut churned at the thought. That meant she'd have to open it too.

"Want me to look?" Her brother's tone was gentle.

And for some ridiculous reason his offer annoyed her. She could do this. She shook her head as she laid the glass back into the box. A faint rattling noise sounded from the handle of the magnifying glass. She picked it up and tilted it. The rattling repeated. A tearful laugh escaped her. Only Daniel. She set it on her leg and gently grasped the brass fitting on the tip of the handle, which twisted off with ease.

She tipped the handle and a key fell into her palm. A key that looked like it was just the right size for the lock.

"Wow," Keoni said, "This is better than an escape room."

She grinned. Yeah, Daniel was a genius at hiding things in an obscure manner. She handed the key to Keoni.

"You do the honors," she said. "You found the lock."

She sat back on her heels, the glass still clutched in her hand, and watched as Keoni inserted the key into the lock. The bottom tilted on a slight angle. Keoni slid his fingers under the edge and pulled up.

"Huh." She couldn't think of anything else to say.

Four small pouches. Clear pouches. All four contained portable hard drives. Maybe she was going to need to read the letter sooner rather than later.

"Not the best way to store one of these," Keoni said, as he lifted one from its resting spot. "At least not long term. The glue can wear off the parts and damage the drives."

Nate reached in and picked up another. "Maybe it was something he didn't want to keep on the servers."

Or maybe it wasn't related to his work.

"Speaking of computers, where is Uncle Daniel's?" she said. "I didn't see one upstairs. Did he only have a laptop?"

The other two shrugged. The laptop he'd had with him in Iowa was in the sheriff's custody, but Daniel would have backed up anything important. He'd had too many computers crash on him. And he had his own server at the office, but he'd spent the last four months here. Surely, he wouldn't have stored whatever he was hiding from them on the work servers. Secured or not. She made a mental note to check with IT as to the last time he accessed it.

"Keoni," she said, "do you have your laptop with you?"

He grinned. "Never leave home without it."

All right then. "Let's go see what he left us."

She returned the magnifying glass to its box, then placed it back in her bag. Nate added the hard drives. He gave her arm a squeeze and she gave him a weary smile in return.

"I like the Pirate theme," Keoni said, "but the rubber centipede is just sick."

Cold chills shot up her spine. Her head whipped toward the spot illuminated by his phone light. The critter wasn't rubber. A centipede the length of her forearm skittered across the chest of the fake skeleton and into a crack in the rocks. The light show as they all rushed to their feet could have rivaled a disco.

She slammed the lid of the chest shut and yanked at the key. Her eyes never left the hole the spawn of the devil had vanished into.

"Forget the key!" Her brother's voice held an edge of panic.

She couldn't blame him for panicking. He'd been bitten when they were kids. First it stung like fire, then it itched unimaginably. There might be no snakes in the islands, but these hellacious creatures more than made up for it. The dark underside of paradise.

"Don't they travel in pairs?" Keoni scrambled for the passage. "I heard they travel in pairs!"

The key slid free, and she darted after them. Nate pawed frantically along the edge of the wall where it met the slab. Panic warred with the irrational urge to laugh. Great, here came the hysterics.

"You lost the switch?" she said.

This was not good. She slid her arm through the loose strap of her bag securing it on her back. She wasn't about to lay it on the ground. Then she reached up to run her hand along the opposite side.

"It's not lost." Nate was yelling.

If they didn't find the switch soon, he might just try to break through with his fists. The panel opened with a snick, spilling light into the dark passage. Her relief was squashed as she was swept back into the passage by her brother's strong arm. In the opposite direction of the way out. Toward the spawn of Satan. No, no, no. He'd lost his mind.

"Na—"

A hand covered her mouth, and her brother hissed in her ear.

"That wasn't me. I didn't open the hatch."

They all froze as still as death. A shadow blocked the light from above. At the sound of a familiar chuckle, the air leached back into Morgan's lungs. Nate's hand fell away.

"Come on out," her grandfather said. Keoni slipped past and up the ladder. Morgan followed quickly, centipede not forgotten. She grinned up at her grandfather.

"Avast, me hearty," she said.

He just shook his head. "So, it was a treasure hunt?"

"Something like that," she said.

She moved to the side as Nate scrambled out of the hole after her and then triggered the passage to close. She looked from the panel to her grandfather.

"You knew about that," she said, pointing at the floor.

He just smirked, humor dancing in his gray eyes. Like father, like son. She shook her head. Her phone pinged as did Nate's. Repeatedly. Apparently, there hadn't been any reception in the cavern.

"That's the reason I'm here," her grandfather said. "Piper has been trying to reach you, Nate."

Her brother left the lab, phone pressed to his ear. The door closed firmly behind him. Morgan scanned through her messages. Piper had sent two to her as well.

PIPER: Have Nate call me. The AUV part is in.

PIPER: Call me anytime if you need to talk.

She smiled and texted back a thanks and a promise that she would soon.

"Morgan, come look at this." Keoni's dark eyes practically glowed. Only conspiracies gave his eyes such a maniacal gleam.

She shoved her phone in her pocket and joined him at the desk. He had plugged the first of the drives into his laptop. Data scrolled over the screen.

"What are we looking at?" her grandfather said.

Morgan leaned in closer. She stared at countless numbers. Five columns worth. And many, many rows. She glanced up at the title of the document simply labeled 'One'. Her heart began to race as she recognized the first entry.

01 0822565 57.3229 4.4244 WS

The screen jarred as Keoni tapped it triumphantly. "Do you know what this is?"

Morgan met his excitement with mixed feelings of her own.

"Two look like coordinates." Her grandfather said.

"They are the coordinates for Loch Ness, Scotland." She leaned back and folded her arms against her chest. "Drumnadrochit to be precise."

"This is Daniel's monster legend database." Keoni was practically vibrating in his seat.

Her uncle's life's work—and he had left it to her.

CHAPTER SIXTEEN

"This is only the holy grail of sea monster legends and sightings. There are over at least a thousand records in this sheet," Keoni said. She smiled; his enthusiasm was contagious. "But here's the most interesting part: the dates on this one stop in the mid-1700s."

"Uncle Daniel had research spanning centuries," she said, reaching for the stack of remaining drives. There were numbers scratched into the plastic casings. Dated by year.

"And the significance of number before the coordinates?" her grandfather said.

"It's a date. The day when St. Columba banished the Loch Ness monster," Keoni said. "It's actually the first official recorded sighting of Nessie."

She grinned at his enthusiasm.

"As the legend goes," she said, "St. Columba and his party were sailing up the loch when they witnessed some locals preparing to bury a man on shore. He sent one of his men to find out what had happened to him, but before the man could reach the shore, a monster rose out of the lake and tried to attack him."

Keoni picked up the story with a flourish. "But St. Columba shouted at the creature," His voice deepened dramatically. "'Leave this man alone, I command you in the name of our Savior, leave this place and be gone.'"

Morgan laughed. "Or something like that."

This was a well-established lore. There was even a tapestry depicting the event in St. Andrew's Cathedral in Inverness, Scotland. She'd seen it with her own eyes.

They shared a grin and turned back to the data on the screen.

"What else is on the drive?" she said.

Keoni minimized the screen. Behind it was a long list of folders, all numbered. No names. The first one started with 01.

"I'd guess it refers to the files," Keoni said. "One for each record."

He opened the folder matching the first record. There were documents, photos, video files, and hundreds of records. He opened a photo, and her breath hitched as she stared at Daniel's grinning face. The photo she had taken on a trip to Loch Ness, a high school graduation gift from Daniel. His face was relaxed. She could almost hear his laughter.

She looked up straight into her grandfather's knowing gaze. She looked away as her excitement faded. As fascinating as the data was, it wouldn't lead them to Daniel. This was the end of his last treasure hunt. No more clues. At least not here.

A memory pierced her thoughts. Maybe there was one clue left, the name etched in code into a book. Definitely worth a try.

"Keoni," she said, "does the name Casper Bishop have any meaning to you?"

He gave her a thoughtful look. "Maybe?"

"Who is Casper Bishop?" Nate said as he reentered the room.

A million-dollar question.

"Uncle Daniel wrote the name in one of his books. In code."

"Why?" Nate said.

"I've no idea," she said. "But it's the only remaining clue."

Keoni sorted through the pile of drives, grabbing the last one and switching it out with the current drive. The folders were structured much like the other drive, but with more current dates. Keoni opened a window and typed a string of words into a search bar.

"Now that you mention it, I think Bishop might have been involved in an incident," Keoni said. "Something somewhat recent, like in the last few decades. I vaguely remember Daniel saying something about it."

Why hadn't Daniel told her? He'd sent her an unending stream of articles and books. She didn't remember him ever mentioning Bishop. Why not?

"When did he mention it?" she said.

Keoni shrugged as he continued to scroll. "Last summer maybe."

"When last summer?" Her heart raced.

Keoni shrugged, his focus on the screen. "Before he took his sabbatical and moved to Iowa."

A list of files scrolled down the window. Keoni clicked on a document revealing a news article from 1989. The title caught her attention.

"Here it is." Keoni leaned back to give her better access to the screen.

Sea Monster-Seeking Billionaire Philanthropist Declared Lost at Sea.

She leaned closer and scanned the text. After an exhaustive three-month search of the South Pacific by authorities for his missing yacht, Casper Bishop, former CEO of Bishop Shipping Industries, had been declared lost at sea. Bishop had vanished after he had set out on his own to prove the existence of a sea monster he claimed was responsible for the death of his wife, Vanessa Bishop, five years prior.

The couple had set sail from Sydney on an anniversary cruise, intending to sail back to San Francisco via Honolulu, but they never reached Hawaii. Some fishermen had found

Bishop floating in a life raft off Tahiti three days later, half dead and raving how a sea monster had killed his wife. Foul play had been ruled out, and the sinking of the sailboat was declared a casualty of a large monsoon reported to have been in the general area.

But Bishop had remained adamant a monster had sunk their boat. Apparently, he died trying to prove it. The rest of the article was less than flattering, claiming Bishop had gone a little crazy before he'd disappeared. He had claimed the monster matched the exact description of the Biblical Leviathan.

Keoni summed it for her grandfather and Nate. "Some guy in the late 80s claimed a Leviathan attacked his yacht and killed his wife."

Leviathan. The word had been mentioned too many times in the past few days to be a coincidence. She scanned the document again.

"Leviathan?" she said. "Yes, he actually said Leviathan."

Keoni nodded. "I think that is why it caught Daniel's attention."

Leviathan indicated something gigantic. Not a sea serpent, but something more along the lines of a prehistoric marine reptile or one of its many cousins. Like a mosasaur. She remembered asking Daniel about it once, while watching a hammerhead shark swim.

"Does Daniel have the 1984 account?" she said.

Keoni pulled up the list again. "Yeah, it looks like it."

Morgan leaned closer to the screen as he clicked on another document.

Billionaire Philanthropist Claims Monster Killed His Wife on Anniversary Cruise.

Long title. She skimmed the text. The information was basically the same with one addition—Vanessa Bishop was survived by her husband, Casper, and their ten-year-old son, Alexander. A grainy black and white photo was included of a smiling couple and a boy posing on the dock beside what she assumed was the ill-fated yacht.

"I don't get it," Nate said. "Why is this important?"

Frustration washed through her. "I don't know. What does it have to do with anything? Everything? Nothing at all?" Her head was beginning to throb.

"Morgan ..." She ducked her brother's hand and moved to the far side of the room.

She needed space to think. This clue didn't fit the pattern. The other clues had all led her to the trunk, and the package, and the drives. Casper Bishop didn't fit. Other than to lead her to a particular legend. But Daniel had thousands of legends, and gigabytes of data. Why was this one important?

"Let's take a break," her grandfather said, his voice low and soothing. "The data isn't going anywhere. Why don't we take it back to the ranch? I know you skipped breakfast."

Her shoulders slumped and her frustration ebbed. She felt so drained.

"I had a granola bar." Well, half. Sleuth had snitched the other half. She wanted to think, not eat.

His phone rang, buying her a brief reprieve. "Matt Smithson speaking."

He left the room and she slumped back against the edge of the bookshelf. She pinched the bridge of her nose as the throbbing in her head intensified.

"Why does Uncle Daniel have to make everything so difficult?" she groaned.

"Well, if it was easy, it wouldn't be fun." Her brother settled beside her. "Right?"

She grinned at how much it sounded like Daniel's twisted logic. For once, she wished her uncle would just be blunt. But then again, maybe he had in his letter. Her gaze shifted to her bag, on the desk beside her. Her stomach churned. She sighed through her nose.

"Maybe this doesn't matter," she said, waving a hand at the computer. "Maybe it's just Uncle Daniel's version of busy work. To keep me out of trouble."

Nate chuckled and bumped her shoulder gently with his own. "Nah, even he knows that's a useless undertaking."

She snorted. Nate's phone rang, the theme from *Jaws*. She snorted again. So not comforting.

"It's Piper," Nate said, "I'm going to go take this outside, which means you have time to peruse the articles Keoni just pulled up." He headed out the door with a wink.

Keoni's eyes were still fixed on the screen. He couldn't resist a good mystery any more than she could. She pushed away from the bookshelf and crossed the room to the desk. She leaned over his shoulder.

"What did you find?"

"Looks like another sheet with dates and coordinates like the first one. This one has dates going back to the mid-1960s," he said. "And I found this."

He minimized the list and opened another file. She blinked in surprise. The format was intensely specific—like model input data specific.

"It looks like Daniel formatted the data," Keoni said, "for use in that program we were designing for that NOAA project. The one that modeled whale migration."

She knew the exact project Keoni was talking about. She had designed the physical environment model for it. Her intention had been to determine what effect, if any, large scale natural hazards, such as massive tectonic plate shifts, tsunamis, and undersea volcanoes, had on whale migration.

Daniel had been the lead consultant. His part of the program had considered the patterns of not only whales, but their food sources, and their predators. Daniel had apparently created a dataset for a different sort of predator.

"Do you have access to the model?" she said.

Keoni nodded. "Sure, but what about 'them'?"

"Who?" Oh, that them. "Right."

He swiveled the chair around to face her. "Daniel put this data on these drives for a reason. Maybe he was trying to hide it from someone."

"Then why did he format it for the model?"

The model was on a supercomputer. The servers weren't exactly public, and their firewalls were top of the line. Maybe he hadn't loaded it because it was personal, but then again, he had pioneered projects before which began as personal research ideas.

Indecision grated against her nerves. The temptation to try the data with the model was too great to pass up. And it wasn't like they would be risking the data getting out as long as they had a secure connection. Like the one in the satellite office in the Maui Technology and Research Park. She brightened at the thought, though her mood was immediately damped by one fact. Today was Saturday. The office would be closed for the weekend, and Keoni's key card was only good for the lab on Oahu. She needed her access back, which would take some tricky negotiating.

A car engine roared to life in the yard. Her brother stepped back inside and shut the door.

"Grandpa had a call," Nate said. "He said I'm supposed to keep you out of trouble until he gets back. Find anything good?"

She bit back the urge to stick her tongue out at him. She doubted her grandfather had said that. Nate got into more trouble than she did. Or maybe she was just better at getting out of trouble before she got caught. But she kept her thoughts to herself. She had bigger fish to fry.

"Maybe," she said. "First, I need my key card access back."

He folded his arms over his chest, and then to her surprise, he nodded. That was too easy.

"Fine," he said, "with a few conditions."

Frustration burned through her. "No conditions," she said. "What you did isn't even legal. I'm so telling Dad."

She heard a muffled snort from Keoni's direction. Immature? Definitely. What was it about her brother that made her revert into her six-year-old self?

"Who do you think authorized it?" Nate's grin was unapologetic.

Her fingers clenched into a fist. The world was against her, it seemed. Keoni let out a strangled squeak sounding suspiciously like a laugh. A high-pitched mousy laugh.

"He did not," she said.

"I'm afraid so. Mom too. You needed a break."

Betrayal on all sides. She quelled the urge to kick him. This was so unprofessional. Good thing Keoni was family. This had to be some kind of HR infraction. She wondered how much worse it would be if she locked Nate in Daniel's secret room.

"I need access to the model," she said, laying her final card on the table. "Uncle Daniel formatted his data for it. I need to know why. Please, Nate. It will only take an hour or so. The model will probably run for at least twenty-four hours." Depending on the amount of data and how much of the globe it covered. "Keoni and I can pop down to the tech park and be back in time for dinner."

Nate narrowed his eyes. "Not before you tell me about Catlett and how he knows Uncle Daniel is alive."

Her jaw snapped shut. Right. She'd kind of hoped he'd forgotten.

"Uncle Daniel wasn't at Winston College on a whim," she said, shoving her hands into the pockets of her jeans. "I think Dr. Catlett is a part of whatever he got caught up in. Catlett said he didn't know where Uncle Daniel was, but he later said Daniel was still alive."

"And he knows this how?" Nate said.

Hot anger laced through her as she threw up her hands. "I don't know, the man is insufferable. For all I know, he did shoot that—"

"He shot someone?" Nate's voice went deathly calm.

She froze. Oh boy. The cave with the centipede was looking better and better by the moment. She met her brother's gaze with a steady one of her own.

"Allegedly shot him, yes." And now she was defending Catlett.

Nate's eyes blazed. "Did he threaten you?"

She shifted her gaze. "More like strongly encouraged me to leave." And had possibly vandalized her rental car and left a threatening note.

"Has he tried to contact you since you got home?"

She folded her arms across her chest, matching his stance. "No."

"I'm staying."

A wave of affection cooled her anger.

"I'm fine, Nate," she said, squeezing every ounce of assurance she could into the words. "No one is interested in me. I'm safe here. Daniel didn't leave anything for me that will lead me to trouble. Besides, they need you on the boat. You're the only one who can repair that hunk of junk you call an AUV."

She let her arms fall to her sides as she met his stare with the best puppy dog look in her little sister arsenal. He sighed heavily and his shoulders relaxed. She bit back a smile.

Nate raised an eyebrow at her. "What about Sleuth?"

"You can lead him back," she said, "or ride him and lead Whisper. They shouldn't give you any trouble."

He dropped his head and nodded. "Fine," he said, "but forget your card. I'll have someone meet you at the office." He held up a finger, "And kick you out in time for dinner, whether or not you are done by then."

She held back a cheer. "Agreed." She glanced over to the desk where Keoni sat, unabashedly watching the debate with humor dancing in his eyes. "Keoni, pack up the drives and let's get out of here."

Nate offered his hand and she took it, giving it a firm shake. He gave her a rueful laugh and tugged her into a tight hug.

"I'll probably be gone by the time you get back," Nate said. "Promise me you'll be careful."

She bit back a retort at the worry she heard beneath his words.

"I promise."

She hoped she could keep it.

CHAPTER SEVENTEEN

Forty-five minutes and a quick stop for coffee later, Keoni pulled the car into a parking space in front of a tall, two-story tan building in the Maui Research and Technology Park. Above it, a little further up the hill, was the building containing the supercomputer her model resided on. She didn't necessarily need to be in close proximity to the machine to run the software, but in this case access to the secure lines helped. She glanced at the vehicle next to theirs and rolled her eyes.

"Keoni, isn't that your grandmother's car?"

He gave her a dramatic sigh, "Yeah. She was at the house this morning."

Trust Nate to pull out the big guns. Anuhea Kenolio had been a part of the company long before Daniel had married her sister, almost since its foundation. Morgan loved her like an auntie, and feared her, in a good way. Whatever Auntie Anu said to do, you did it. No questions asked.

"Okay," she said as they walked up to the door, "efficiency is the name of the game. Let's get this done as quickly as we can."

"And then go get a burger," Keoni said.

She glanced back across the street at the Brewery, the best burger joint and only brewery on Maui. "If we have time."

Keoni grinned. "There's always time for a burger."

She laughed and tapped on the glass door, and then pushed Keoni through ahead of her as it opened.

"Ah, my prodigal," Auntie Anu said, "Give your tutu a squeeze."

Morgan bit back a laugh at Keoni's long-suffering look as his grandmother crushed him in a hug. He loved her, she knew that, but his family was large and nearly as smothering as her own. At least, she was lucky enough to have only one older brother. Keoni had five. Auntie Anu released him only after his face was a sufficient shade of red and turned her attention to Morgan. The older woman pulled her into a tight hug. Morgan had always loved her marshmallow-smothering hugs.

"Oh, baby girl," Auntie Anu said, "I am so sorry. How are you holding up?"

A fresh wave of sorrow washed through her. She wondered if her tears would ever dry out. She hugged the older woman tighter.

"I've been better, Auntie," she said. "Trying to keep busy."

Auntie Anu pulled away and framed Morgan's face with her hands. Her dark eyes shimmered behind a sheen of tears. "I'm sure Daniel is all right. Wherever he is."

Was he? She could only hope. Morgan hugged her again, hiding her tears against the older woman's shoulder.

"I hope so."

"The family has been praying nonstop since we heard," Auntie Anu said, "and I've added Daniel to the prayer list for the church. The Lord knows where he is, and he will watch over him. Always."

Morgan swallowed hard as she read between the lines. Yeah, even if Daniel was no longer here on earth. Even if he was in Heaven. She pulled away and wiped her eyes with the back of her hand. She couldn't let her mind wander there.

"Did Nate fill you in on what we need?" she said.

Auntie Anu waved a hand toward the hall and led the way.

"He did indeed," she said, amusement dancing in her dark eyes. "I have an empty office you can use, but he said to lock you out at five o'clock sharp."

Morgan glanced at her phone—just after one thirty. They had plenty of time.

"I'll be in my office if you need me," Auntie Anu said.

"Mahalo, Auntie," Morgan said. She waved Keoni in ahead of her. "Do your thing, genius."

He wasted no time in hooking his laptop to the ethernet cable and setting up a secure connection into the network.

"Go ahead and log in." he said, sliding the laptop toward her.

Nate had been faithful to his side of the deal so far. Now to test the final part. She pulled up the remote login and entered her credentials. The login worked like a charm. Maybe she wouldn't Saran Wrap his van after all. Maybe. He still deserved something for locking her out. Parental support or no.

"Okay, I'm in," she said, "Let's take another look at Daniel's data."

Keoni watched over her shoulder as she pulled up the input files. Daniel had over a thousand separate records. Impressive. She had no idea he had collected so many stories, or there were so many to collect. There were too many records to process in their time limit. She copied the file to Keoni's laptop.

"Okay, we need to limit the records, so let's consider filters." she said.

"Well, you said Daniel wrote Casper Bishop's name in the book," Keoni said, "so how about focusing on all records in the South Pacific, with a focus on Leviathan?"

"Agreed." She set the filters and hit the enter key. "Huh. That's interesting."

Five hundred records remained. Daniel had been busy.

"Process time projection is 24 hours," Keoni said.

"We don't have that much time. Okay, Bishop's sighting happened in 1984, and the last in 1989. So, let's try all records for the past forty years."

The search narrowed it down to a hundred records. An impressive number of sightings, but much more manageable as a test case for the model.

"How long?" she said.

"Few hours, give or take."

A tight time frame, but doable. The first test would be a simple pattern construction, tracking the locations, looking for similarities in habitat and food sources, and maybe even forecasting future locations. Assuming the data represented real creatures. A thrill of anticipation fluttered through her.

"I wish Daniel was here to see this."

"You can show him when he gets back," Keoni said.

She could have hugged him. She slid the keyboard back to him.

"Go ahead and format the data to the new settings."

"On it, boss."

His dark eyes gleamed. This was probably the highlight of his monster-seeking career so far. Daniel was the master, and he'd left them his legacy. They looked up as a knock sounded on the outer door, down the hall. She glanced at Keoni. He just shrugged. She stood and peeked out into the hall. She ducked back into the office, her heart pounding so hard she felt like it might rip right out of her chest.

"What's wrong?" Keoni said as he rose from his chair. "You are super pale."

Agent Weston's words still haunted her.

Your intern should stick to his research.

She swallowed her panic and forced her body to relax. She waved him back.

"Everything is fine—keep working, I'll be right back."

He didn't look convinced, but he did as she asked.

She straightened her shoulders and slipped into the hall, shutting the door firmly behind her. Whatever happened, she had to protect him. The entry was empty, as was the hall. Maybe she was hallucinating? Her aunt stepped into the hall, startling her.

"Morgan, you have visitors." Auntie Anu's expression was grave. "I put them in my office."

Or maybe she'd seen exactly what she'd thought she'd seen.

"Thanks, Auntie," she said, "I saw them."

"Would you like me to join you?"

Morgan shook her head. "No, thank you. I'll be fine."

Her aunt squeezed her arm. "If you need me, just yell and I'll come running."

Morgan forced a smile. She had no doubt. She straightened her back and took a breath, steeling herself before she stepped into the room.

"Hello, Ms. Sullivan." A familiar voice said.

The light, airy decor of her aunt's office, and the bright sun shining through the windows, did little to make the agent's tone any less cold than it had been in the snowy dark of a street corner in Iowa.

"Agent Weston, Agent Blake." She nodded to each. "To what do I owe the honor of this visit?"

Her heart plunged. Please let him be alive. She walked around the desk and took a seat in her aunt's chair. She needed breathing space and a solid barrier between them. Something felt off. She wasn't sure what. What were they even doing here?

"Have you found my uncle?" she said. "It's been over the ideal seventy-two hours. Isn't that what they say in all the cop shows? Though I can't say how accurate the number is. If it's anything like the science in disaster movies, well ..."

She knew she was rambling. About nothing. Though it did seem to have an effect on Weston. She wondered if his scowl was permanently etched into his face. Neither agent answered her. The spacious office suddenly felt small and the air thinner. Her brain mutinied against the plan to remain calm, and every worst-case scenario imaginable paraded through her thoughts.

"Is he—"

"Breathe, Ms. Sullivan," Agent Blake said calmly. "This isn't about your uncle. Or at least, not directly."

Her thoughts came to a screeching halt. Then why were they here?

"What do you mean not directly?"

So much for cool and collected. Why did she feel like they were playing with her? But why would they?

"We have reason to believe Scott Catlett is on Maui," Blake said.

She sank back against her chair, willing her heartbeat to slow. Her gaze darted between the agents.

"Well," she said. "Maui is the number one island destination in the world. Millions visit every year. Maybe he's here for the sun. It's pretty cold in Iowa."

Blake coughed. She could have sworn she'd seen the woman smile.

"Has Dr. Catlett attempted to contact you since you left Iowa?" Weston said.

"Yes," she said. "A couple texts right before I left, but nothing since."

"Why didn't you contact us?" Weston said.

"I meant to," she said, "but it's been so busy since I got back. You know, with all the grieving family and what not."

Blake rested a hand on her partner's arm.

Morgan sighed. "I meant to, but it slipped my mind. He said he didn't shoot George Cole and that Daniel is still alive."

She slid her phone from her pocket and brought up the messages. Then she handed the phone to Blake.

"Ms. Sullivan, your life may be in danger," Blake said.

I'll take care of the girl.

She felt the blood leach from her face as Catlett's words came rushing back. She studied the agents. A strong sense of unease slid through her. She wanted to trust them. Had Daniel? Apparently not enough to tell them who Catlett was. Blake handed the phone to Weston. He pulled a notebook from his suit pocket and jotted a few notes down.

"We'll look into this," Blake said. "If Dr. Catlett contacts you further, I advise you to call us. Right away."

"Do you think he's right," Morgan said, "about Daniel being alive?"

"Perhaps," Blake said, exchanging a look with her partner.

Not much of an answer. The unease grew. "Do you think Catlett is dangerous?"

"He's wanted for murder," Weston said.

Morgan leaned forward. "A murder he says he didn't commit."

"He doesn't have any previous records," Weston continued as if he hadn't heard her. "He doesn't seem to have much of a history at all."

Not much of a history at all? "What do you mean?"

Weston folded his arms across his chest. "According to our records, Scott Catlett first appeared ten years ago."

Morgan blinked at them in disbelief. "How is that possible? The man has a PhD for goodness sakes," she said. "His academic record alone should go back further than that. Are you saying it's fake?"

"Ms. Sullivan," Blake said, calmly. "We are here because we'd rather not see you disappear like your uncle did."

Morgan flinched. "Do you think there is a chance I could?"

"Not if you keep out of this." Weston said.

Her stomach clenched. "How am I supposed to keep out of this if I don't even know what this is?" She bit out the words through clenched teeth.

"Just keep your head down, Ms. Sullivan, and you should be fine," Blake said, quietly, "Call us immediately if Dr. Catlett attempts to contact you again."

The agents stood, signaling the end of the conversation. But she wasn't done yet.

"Who is Casper Bishop?" she said.

Weston cocked his head. "Who?"

He shot a look at his partner.

"I'm not familiar with the name," Blake said. "Is it important?"

Morgan sighed inwardly. It had been worth a try. "I just heard it somewhere and thought I would ask."

"Be safe, Ms. Sullivan," Blake said, with a pointed look. "And be smart."

Abruptly, they turned and left the room. Morgan slumped back against the chair. Too weird. They'd come all this way to tell her in person when they could have just called. Couldn't they? And how did they find her here? Had they been following her all along? She shivered as a thought crossed her mind.

Were they using her as bait to catch Catlett?

The real question was whether Catlett had followed her and if so, why? And if he wasn't who he said he was, then who was he? And how had he gotten into Winston with fake credentials? This called for some serious internet stalking. She grabbed her phone and opened a browser.

"Are you all right, love?" Auntie Anu said.

Morgan forced her face to relax into a smile. She was beginning to dislike that question. She wasn't all right, but she had a plan, which made things a little better.

"I'm okay, Auntie." She rose from the chair. "The agents were just checking in. They haven't found Uncle Daniel yet."

Speaking of checking in, she glanced at the clock on the wall—just past two—which meant it was just after seven p.m. in Iowa. Time to do some checking in of her own. Auntie Anu squeezed her arm gently as she passed, her wise eyes observing.

"If you're sure you're okay..."

Morgan smiled warmly. Genuinely. "I am. Mahalo, Auntie," she said, and moved into the hall. "Excuse me, I need to make a call."

She pulled up Anderson's number and slipped into the conference room, closing the door behind her. The call went to voicemail after two rings. She swallowed her disappointment and cleared her throat softly.

"Hi, Detective Anderson," she said, "this is Morgan Sullivan. Listen, I just had a strange meeting with the two FBI agents who were in your office earlier. They think Dr. Catlett is here on Maui. I thought you might like to know. Anyway, please call me if you have anything new. Thanks."

She grimaced and rapped her knuckles lightly against the polished wood of the tabletop. If they had definite proof Daniel had been kidnapped, which she was sure he had been, and he'd been transported across state lines, which made sense, then the FBI would have jurisdiction. Right?

So, was Detective Anderson still in charge of the investigation into the guard's death? Or did jurisdiction fall under the FBI too? She scrubbed her forehead. This was too complicated. And headache-inducing. She dropped heavily into a chair and pulled up the browser on her phone. "Who are you, Dr. Scott Catlett?"

"Dr. Scott Catlett, Winston College." The search brought up the most recent stories covering the incident in Winston. She skimmed them, but they didn't provide anything more than what she already knew. She thumbed through the list and clicked on the Winston College link to his bio. Unfortunately, the link was broken. Maybe the college had taken it off-line on purpose. Couldn't be good for business to have one instructor missing and another wanted for the murder of another employee who was suspected of kidnapping said missing instructor.

"Dr. Scott Catlett, PhD." Huh. The search found only a couple of papers with his name, all within the last ten years, and a few conferences. No other universities. Strange for an academic. Publishing was a job requirement with the advancement of science. Papers meant grant money. She logged into the university library system and ran an author search, turning up a few more papers, but nothing dated further back than ten years ago. Just like the agents had said.

He didn't even have a LinkedIn page, and his name was apparently too common to determine whether or not he had a social media presence. At least he wasn't vain enough to use Dr. in his name. Still, someone would have needed to check his résumé and references, right? She sighed. At this point she wouldn't be surprised if someone had planted him at the college.

She needed more information, and there was one person who might know something. She pulled up her call log and tapped a number. Macy answered before the first ring faded.

"Morgan!" The older woman's voice was warm, but Morgan could hear the worry. Guilt swirled through her. "Did you make it home all right? I'm so sorry I wasn't here to see you off."

She should have called sooner.

"Hi, Macy. Sorry I had to run off so soon. Yes, I'm home."

The clatter and clanking of pots and pans sounded in the background.

"Glad to hear it," Macy said. "It's been a madhouse since you left, what with the sheriff's men going over what Dr. Catlett left behind. I don't understand it at all. I'm glad you left when you did, and that you're safe."

"Speaking of Dr. Catlett," Morgan said, "did he ever mention anything about his academic history, like what university he received his PhD from for instance?"

"No, come to think of it, I don't believe he did. So sorry, dear."

"What about friends?" Morgan said.

"Wyatt asked the same question," she said. "As far as I know Dr. Catlett kept to himself, other than when he was with Daniel of course. He seemed like such a nice young man."

The hot knife of betrayal poked at Morgan's heart. Had Catlett only pretended to be Daniel's friend?

"Would admissions have a copy of his résumé?"

Macy sighed. Morgan bit her lip. She had gone too far.

"Morgan, I really think it would be best if you left the investigation to Wyatt and the FBI."

Yeah, she knew she should, but of the two, Anderson didn't have jurisdiction over Daniel's kidnapping and the FBI agents were less than helpful. She hated feeling so helpless.

"Yeah," she said, "I'm sorry. You're right."

Voices rumbled in the background on the other end of the call.

"I'm afraid I need to go, sweetheart, but please feel free to call anytime."

"Thanks, Macy."

She hung up. If only she had Dr. Dolan's number. She could probably get it from the website, but with the media circus, he might not answer. Her phone chimed. A text from Nate.

NATE: Flying out soon. Try to stay out of trouble. Avoid main gate when you come back, reporters on site.

Oh, joy. Her phone chimed again.

NATE: Don't answer any inquiries. Grandpa is family spokesman.

She grinned. Poor reporters.

She brought the browser up again and tried one last search. *Scott Catlett, Casper Bishop.* The search list came up with the same news stories about Daniel's case, but none included Bishop. Further down were the same articles on Casper Bishop Daniel had stored in his records. None included Scott Catlett. The phone hit the table with a dull thud. She stared out the window, but the bright sun had no effect on her darkening mood.

"Who are you, Scott Catlett?" she said, "and what do you want with me?"

If anything. Maybe the agents were wrong. Then again, maybe he was out there right now. Watching. Waiting. A chill crept up her spine. Someday, her overactive imagination was going to get the better of her.

CHAPTER EIGHTEEN

A knock against the door jarred her from her dark thoughts. Keoni stuck his head into the room.

"Model is running," he said. "It will take a little while, so let's go get that burger."

She snorted as she tried to hide her rapidly pounding heart. Why did she insist on freaking herself out?

"It's always food with you." She wished she had his metabolism. "Fine, but if you don't have room for dinner tonight, I'm not going to save you from my grandmother's wrath."

Keoni clasped a hand to his chest as if she'd dealt him a mortal wound.

"I always have room for Tutu Evie's food," he said. "Are you okay? You look like you need a drink." He waved a hand toward the front door. "Come on, I'm buying."

She laughed, for real this time as she pushed up out of her chair.

"I appreciate the sentiment, but aren't you a bit under-aged?"

"I said drink," Keoni said. "Your own twisted mind jumped to alcohol."

"You've been spending too much time with my brother."

His answering grin was pleased. Uh-oh. She knew hero worship when she saw it. Looked like she was too late to stop the corruption.

"Come on," she said, hiding her smile. "I want cheese fries with that drink."

The weather had turned pleasant while they'd been in the office. The sun peeked out between the gray clouds, the air damp and fresh. There was even a rainbow. But she paid it only a passing glance as she scanned the area uneasily for any familiar faces. The pulse of a bass guitar blasted from the restaurant area, growing louder as they jogged across the street toward the building.

Her head throbbed in time with the beat. She grabbed Keoni's arm and steered him to the right as they entered the building, toward the open-air tasting room, where the music wasn't quite as loud. She glanced at the list of brews on the chalkboards above the bar and wished she liked beer. She really could use a stout drink.

"I'll do the ordering," she said over the music. "You go find us a table."

Keoni gave her a sloppy salute and headed for the back. The room was packed, but it was Saturday. And the beginning of the Spring Break season. Her eyes roamed around the room, but no sign of Catlett. She shrugged some of the tension from her shoulders and stepped up to the counter to place their orders.

One burger with everything and a side of fries, one order of cheese fries, and two craft root beers, on a tab. Keoni had offered to pay, and for once she was going to let him. The server gave her a numbered flag for the table, and the drinks. She stuck the flag into her back pocket and picked up the sweating bottles. The hair on her neck stood up.

She turned slowly, scanning the room. She was being watched. She saw no one, not the FBI agents, or Catlett, or Keoni for that matter. There were a lot of people, and this was a public place. She was safe, right? She wove swiftly through the crowded room toward the outside patio.

"Hey, number 17, join us for a drink!" an unfamiliar voice said above the noise.

Her gaze locked with a familiar pair of cobalt blue eyes and her body turned to ice. She took a step back. The man raised his hands. Right eyes, wrong face. He was blond, younger, not Catlett. He waved his hand at her, and she realized he was still talking.

She was losing her mind.

"Hey, sorry, didn't mean to startle you." He waved a hand toward a table nearby. A half a dozen co-eds waved back. "Come join us."

"No, thanks."

A hand rested lightly on her lower back.

"Sorry, she's with me." Keoni took one of the bottles from her hand. "Thanks, babe, I found us a table. This way."

She allowed him to steer her away from the man and toward the back of the patio.

"Isn't he kind of young?" Man, this guy was persistent.

She ignored him as she struggled to calm her racing heart. She raised the bottle to her lips and took a swig. The sugar and sharp taste pulled her back to the present. She felt a tremor against her back and realized Keoni was shaking. Her eyes darted to his face, which was beet red, with suppressed laughter. The jerk.

"Thanks, 'babe'," she said, dryly.

She sank into her seat and then popped back up as the table flag poked her shoulder. She pulled it from her pocked with a grimace and set it on the table. Number 17. She rolled her eyes.

"Nate was right." Keoni said, his eyes sparkling. "Can't take you anywhere."

She gave him a halfhearted glare. "The guy probably thinks I'm a cougar."

Whatever it took to make him back off.

"You're not that old." His eyes danced with mischief.

She snorted. "Thanks, I think." *Punk.*

She took another swig from her bottle and stared out over the rain-dampened garden.

"Besides you look younger than you are."

She almost spit her drink in his face, but instead choked. He pushed the napkin holder toward her and pulled papers from his back pocket. He held them out, like a shield.

"Sorry, that was too far."

Root beer was dripping from her nostrils, and he thought he'd gone too far. She blew her nose and shook her head with a laugh.

"You're insane."

He handed the papers to her. "Please accept my apology."

"Get me another root beer and I'll consider it."

She unfolded the papers and thumbed through them as he darted away. He'd printed the Casper Bishop articles from Daniel's files. Plus a few she hadn't seen yet. Her eyes narrowed. One included a rather interesting sketch of a mosasaur type creature. According to the article, it had been drawn by Bishop himself in an effort to prove the existence of the creature he had seen.

"Oooh, a marine saurian. And a big one."

Oh joy, Casanova was back. The blond man plopped into Keoni's vacant seat with an unapologetic grin.

"That seat is taken," she said. "My date will be back any minute. And he will not be pleased to see you."

"I'm Ian, by the way," he said, "And I think we both know that kid is not your boyfriend."

She narrowed her eyes. His grin widened.

"Please leave."

"Where was it sighted?" he said, gesturing toward the paper with his beer.

"Where was what ..." She was slipping. Majorly. "What did you call it?"

His eyes danced, and he leaned closer. "Marine. Saurian."

Marine saurian was a cryptid classification for large marine reptiles. Cryptid meaning not having been identified or proven. A term used by cryptozoologists and monster hunters. The question was, which one was Ian, and what did he want? This wasn't a coincidence, and she was tired of games.

"What do you want?" she said.

He flashed her a grin. "To find a quiet place for a friendly conversation."

Yeah, like that was going to happen. Where was Keoni? She eased back further into her chair.

"What's wrong with right here?"

His eyes glinted. "Your boy toy will be back any minute. Of course, he is a little preoccupied at the moment." He made a tsking sound. "Oh, fickle youth."

She hazarded a look over her shoulder. Keoni was at the bar, chatting animatedly with a pretty blonde woman she'd seen at Ian's table a moment ago. He wouldn't be returning any time soon.

She pinned him with a challenging stare. "Who are you?"

His smile went frigid. Dangerous. Her skin crawled. Her gut told her he was not a man to be trifled with. Her fingers tightened around the glass bottle. The place was crowded. She was safe as long as she remained here. Right?

"Call me a fellow enthusiast," he said. "Your uncle was one of the best. Rumor has it he left you his records."

Her smile froze as the blood drained from her face. The paper crumpled beneath her fingers.

"Ah, so the rumors are true," he said. "The people I represent would be willing to pay handsomely for a copy."

"Cheese fries and a burger?" a voice said, brightly.

Morgan blinked at the waitress as the woman slid a steaming plate of cheese fries onto the table. The scent turned her stomach. She set Keoni's burger on the table in front of Ian.

"Anything else I can get you?" she said.

The police? Ian's eyes held a challenge, as if he were daring her to make her move. The hairs stood on her neck.

Someone was watching. He probably wasn't alone. She couldn't take the chance that Keoni might get hurt. She forced a smile.

"No. Thank you."

The woman moved away, and Ian stood, slowly, as if he had all the time in the world. He leaned in close. Her fingers twitched, itching to hit him right in the center of that smug face. His smirk grew, as if he read her thoughts.

"Think about it, Ms. Sullivan," he said. "I'll be in touch."

He tucked a card beneath the edge of her plate and snitched a french fry before melting into the crowd. She didn't move. She couldn't. A glass bottle clanked against the table, and she flinched.

"Hey," Keoni said as he dropped into his chair, "Sorry I took so long. The bar was crowded. And then this really cute girl wanted to know the best place to find sushi."

Her brain spun through multiple scenarios. Each one darker than the last. She had to hide Daniel's data. Some place safe. Some place where no one would get hurt.

"I told her the Market was the best, but she didn't believe a grocery store could sell good sushi," Keoni rambled on around a mouthful of burger. "Are you okay? You look a little green."

She sucked in a breath and the world rushed back in. Loud and bright.

"You haven't touched your fries," he said. "Are you sick?"

She glanced at her plate. Her stomach twisted.

"Hey, I think you left your keys on the bar." The waitress was back.

Keys? Her keys were in the office, with Auntie Anu, and the data... She glanced across the street, panic crawling through her, like a million tiny ants. Auntie Anu could be in danger. She'd never forgive herself if she'd put her family in danger.

"Thanks," Keoni said, accepting the keys. "Hey, Morgan, isn't this Daniel's seal?"

The keys dangled from his fingers, a silver fob in front with a familiar seal etched into its face. The water dragon. She snatched them out of his hand and stood, her chair clattering back against the rail, and scanned the room for the waitress. Daniel's keys. These were Daniel's missing keys.

"Morgan?"

The keys no one had been able to find. The keys someone had used to break into Daniel's room at the boarding house and his office. She wove her way through the crowd to the bar. How did Daniel's keys get here? The waitress looked up with a smile as she approached.

"Where did you find these?" Morgan said, thrusting the keys under her nose.

The woman's smile faltered. "A gentleman found them on the floor by the bar. He said they might belong to you."

Gentleman. She turned, scanning the room for Ian, but he was nowhere to be seen.

"What did he look like?" she said. "Blonde and smug?"

The waitress looked hesitant. Morgan forced her body to relax and appear less threatening. She smiled ruefully.

"Sorry, it's just that there is this guy who just won't take no for an answer."

Understanding flitted through the woman's dark eyes.

"I totally understand," she said. "He was haole, tall, gorgeous blue eyes—"

"Blonde?" If it was Ian she was running straight to the FBI, bad feeling or not.

The woman shook her head. "No, he had dark hair, almost black. Really cute." She looked over Morgan's shoulder toward the door. "He just left. You might be able to still catch him."

Morgan bolted. She made it to the edge of the parking lot in time to see a white Nissan Sentra pull out. Anger, fear, annoyance flashed through her at a dizzying speed as the car slowed for a moment, and he waved. Scott Catlett. He was here, and he'd had Daniel's keys all this time.

"You lying, two-faced traitor!" She sprinted for the road, but he vanished before she reached it. She wanted to yell and cry and scream and just be done with the whole madness.

"Morgan!"

She was shaking and she couldn't stop. The keys cut into her fingers as she closed her fist around them. A hand touched her arm.

"Morgan?" Keoni appeared in front of her. His expression worried. Scared.

She couldn't let him get pulled into this. "It's too dangerous."

"What is too dangerous?" he said, his voice growing frantic. "Morgan, what is going on?"

"Home," she said. "I need to go home."

She had to return the drives to the chest, lock them away where no one else could find them. Daniel would understand. She looked over her shoulder at the patio. People were staring. She stared back. How had Ian known about Daniel's records? No one knew but Keoni, Nate, her grandfather, and herself. Right?

Anger boiled through her. What did Catlett want from her? They had Daniel. What more could they need? An arm slipped around her shoulders, hesitantly, like she might break or fight. She allowed Keoni to gently turn her in the direction of the office.

"Okay," he said, "let's go get our stuff, and I'll take you home."

She had to do it on her own. No one could know. No one would suspect she put it all back. She'd bury the key. Somewhere safe. Paper crumpled beneath her fingers. She looked down. Her hand trembled as she stuffed the articles into her back pocket as they crossed the road. Keoni tapped on the office door, and relief flooded through her as Auntie Anu appeared unharmed. The older woman's face darkened with concern as she ushered them in.

"What's wrong?"

Keoni gently pushed her through the door. "I'll be right back," he said.

He dashed back across the street before she could say a word. Back to the Brewery.

"Morgan Anne Sullivan," her aunt's voice was gentle, her tone firm. "You tell me what is going on right this minute."

An excellent question. One she didn't really have an answer to. At least, not one she could share without putting them in danger. She slid the hand clutching Daniel's keys into her pocket, her gaze never leaving the Brewery.

"I'm not feeling well, Auntie." True enough. "Maybe I picked up something on the plane."

She released a breath she hadn't realized she'd been holding as Keoni reappeared with a stack of takeout boxes.

"Oh, you poor baby." Auntie Anu gently pulled her toward a chair. "You sit here, and I'll go collect your things. Keoni will take you back to the ranch where you can rest."

Morgan forced a smile as she sank into the chair. Keoni slipped through the front door and dropped the boxes on the receptionist's desk.

"This was on the table under your plate," he said, offering her a small black card.

She stared at it as if it were a poisonous snake. Anger rushed through her, and she snatched the card from his hand and stood. Her anger faded as she met his nervous gaze. She shoved it into her pocket, and sank back into the chair, shaking, as the surge of adrenaline drained away.

"I'm sorry." She dropped her head in her hands.

"Keoni, go pack your things." Saved by Auntie Anu. "Take Morgan straight home."

She felt his questioning gaze as he headed for the back. He was going to grill her on the ride back. Lucky for her Nate was on a plane. A hand gently brushed against her hair, then moved to press against her forehead as she raised her head. Auntie Anu smiled gently.

"No fever," Auntie Anu said, "but you are too pale."

Keoni set her bag on the chair beside her. Morgan pulled it to her and looked inside. She brushed a finger against the case holding the magnifying glass. Daniel's keys pressed into her leg through the denim. All four drives were safely nestled in the bag. She pulled the strings closed and stood as Keoni entered.

Auntie Anu pulled her into a tight hug. "Be safe, and feel better."

Morgan squeezed her tighter as the fear she might not see her aunt again pierced her heart. The feeling of loss was nearly overwhelming. She had to pull it together. Or she'd never be able to sneak away.

"Thanks, Auntie."

She pulled away and followed Keoni to the car, scanning the area for danger, but there appeared to be none. She slipped into the car. Her phone chimed, and she pulled it from her pocket. She should probably let the FBI agents know she'd seen Catlett, and she had Daniel's keys, and about Ian ...

Her hands shook as she read the text.

UNKNOWN: Be careful who you trust.

The number was unfamiliar, but she knew exactly who had sent the message. She stared out the window, searching as Keoni backed the car out of the space. Her phone chimed again.

UNKNOWN: You are in danger.

No kidding. The question was, from who? And why? She hugged her bag closer. She had a bad feeling this had something to do with the drives safely tucked inside.

CHAPTER NINETEEN

They reached the ranch without further issue. Which was kind of surprising. She'd half expected someone to run them off the road and steal Daniel's data. She'd pretended to sleep most of the long ride back, and Keoni, for once, hadn't pushed it. Though she could practically hear the questions buzzing in his head.

A group of people were clustered around the outside of her grandparents' gate. Reporters, if the vans and the cameras were any indication. Just like Nate had warned. They passed on by and took the back way through Daniel's property. She'd been half tempted to ask Keoni to let her out at the lab, but she knew he'd never leave if she did. She convinced him to let her out at the barn instead.

"Are you going to be okay?"

She gave him a real smile. "Yeah, I just need a few minutes before I have to face the crowd at the house."

A few minutes to slip away while no one was looking. Once she returned to the house, there would be at least a half-dozen pairs of eyes on her at all times. They were probably already waiting for her. She'd bet money Auntie Anu had called. She'd have to move fast.

She waved as he drove on up the hill, before darting into the barn. The building was empty, not yet time for evening chores, though a few the horses were in their stalls due to the rain. She paused for a moment and breathed deep, letting the scent of hay and horses and earth seep through her frazzled mind. The knot in her chest unraveled and she relaxed a little.

She estimated she had just enough time to get to Daniel's and back before dark, if she hurried. She whistled softly, and a whicker answered. Sleuth's dark head appeared over his stall door.

"Hey, big guy." She rubbed her hand against his nose. "Up for a little exercise?"

He was always up for some fun. Especially if it meant treats. She laughed and pushed his nose gently away. She grabbed his halter from the rack. Within minutes they were tacked and ready to go. Voices drifted down from the house.

She had to hurry. She pulled the magnifying glass case from her bag and placed the letter inside it. Then she stuffed the case into the bottom of her trunk in the tack room.

"Just to be safe."

She hurried back to Sleuth and unsnapped the lead from his halter.

"Come on, dude," she said, to the twitching ears, "we gotta go."

She mounted and urged him into a slow trot and then into a canter as they reached the cover of the trees. The gate to Daniel's was open. She'd noticed the gate was open when they'd driven through, but she hadn't mentioned the fact. Sleuth tugged at the bit, and she gave him his head, leaning into him as he flew over the turf.

Ian, Catlett, Daniel ... it all faded away as the wind swirled around her. Sleuth pounded up the dirt road, the light too dim to take the path. This route would take a few minutes longer, but it was safer. She slowed him as they climbed the last rise to the clearing. He tossed his head but complied.

"Good boy."

His head bowed at her crooning words as he preened at her praise, and she laughed. He never failed to make her feel better. The clearing was empty. She rode up to the paddock and dismounted. She led him inside and slipped the bridle from his head.

"I'll just be a couple minutes."

She slid the bridle over her shoulder to keep Sleuth from chewing on it. Uneasiness crept over her as she neared the door. She drew a deep breath and forced herself to continue. She slipped Daniel's keys from her pocket and flipped through them. Her forehead wrinkled in confusion. The lab key was gone.

Maybe he'd left it behind.

She shoved the keys back into her pocket and pulled her grandfather's from her bag. She opened the door and stepped inside. The room was as they had left it, a little darker, but the same. She punched in the alarm code and locked the door securely behind her before crossing to the bookshelf and entering the code.

The passage opened with a quiet grinding, and she swallowed her unease as she climbed down the ladder. She switched on the lantern and hurried down the passage and tried hard not to think about centipedes the length of her forearm. The pirate king gave her a lopsided grin from the floor. She ignored him as she knelt before the chest and shoved the key into the lock.

Light glinted off metal as she looked inside. They'd left the smaller key in the hidden lock. Must have been all the excitement over the spawn of the devil. She pulled it open and replaced the drives inside.

A faint scratching noise whispered down the passage, and her heart leapt into her throat. She switched off the light and strained to listen. But there was nothing other than the pounding of her heart as it threatened to rip itself out of her chest. She switched on the light, relocked the compartment, and then the chest. She fingered the keys. And then slipped the chain from her neck and slid the smaller of the keys onto it. She needed to keep them separate.

She secured the chain around her neck and slipped it beneath the neckline of her T-shirt. Okay, now to get out of the creepy tunnel, and work on a good reason for running off when she'd been told not to. Without revealing the truth. She paused at the foot of the stairs, extinguishing the light, and listened. But all was silent. She quickly scaled the ladder and crossed to the bookshelf and triggered the passage. Okay, so far so good. She pulled the brass key and its book from her bag and scanned the books on the shelf.

Didn't they say the best place to hide something is in plain sight? She slid the book between a copy of *Treasure Island* and a kid version of *20,000 Thousand Leagues Under the Sea*. Then she grabbed Sleuth's bridle from the desk and headed for the door.

The doorknob turned with a small squeak. She stepped back quietly, her eyes frantically scanning the room for a weapon. A surge of triumph swept through her as she sighted one. She laid the bridle on the desk and eased the umbrella from the stand beside the wall, still hoping against hope the intruder was her grandfather, or Keoni, trying to teach her a lesson. She should have rearmed the alarm.

The door opened.

"Hey, Morgan," Catlett said.

She let out a yell and charged the door, slamming her body against it. He grunted in pain as his foot caught in the threshold. Good.

"I just want to talk," he said.

"Go away."

"I'm not going to hurt you."

Right, because she wasn't going to give him a chance to. She mercilessly stabbed his foot with the end of her golf umbrella.

"Like you didn't shoot that guard?"

"No ... didn't ... shoot the guard."

The door gave beneath a hard shove, and she went sprawling as it slammed open. Fear rushed through her, but so did anger. She latched onto it and let it blaze. All her distrust, dislike, frustration, fear ... she let it all go as she rolled to her feet.

"Are you planning to stab me again?" Catlett smirked, gesturing at the umbrella still clutched in her hand.

Yes. That was her plan. Maybe it wasn't a good plan, but it was all she had at the moment. She meant to live through this and see Daniel got justice.

"People know where I am," she said.

"Good, then you aren't as foolish as you appear to be." His eyes glinted with amusement.

She wanted to smack the grin off his face.

"The FBI is looking for you," she said.

Her arm was growing tired. Her grandfather had always managed to catch her in the act of rebellion. Where was he now when she wanted him to find her? She'd happily muck stalls for the rest of her life if it meant she would see another day.

"I know." He leaned back against the door and leveled a look at her. "I told you to stay out of trouble. You didn't listen."

Yeah, well better people than him had tried.

"You lied to me. You had Daniel's keys all this time."

His eyes softened. "Morgan—"

She saw the guilt, and her anger snapped. She lunged forward, brandishing her makeshift sword, fully intending to run him through. He stepped to the side in a smooth move, surprising her, and caught the end of the umbrella.

"I didn't lie. You never asked if I had the keys."

Her finger found the release button, and the umbrella shot open. She shoved it into him ignoring his startled yell. She grabbed the handle of the door and wrenched it open. He slammed his body against door, pinning it shut. His hand caught her arm before she could dart away. She kicked his shin. He grunted but didn't move.

"You. Are. In. Danger." His dark eyes penetrated hers. "From the very people Daniel was trying to protect you from."

Wait, what? "What do you mean Daniel was trying to protect me?"

His mouth pulled into a tight thin line. His eyes cooled, but she could sense his hesitation. He released her and stepped away. She watched as he turned his back and jammed his fingers through his hair.

Her fingers closed around the doorknob, but she hesitated. She should run. But, what if this was her one chance for answers only he could give?

"What do you mean Daniel was trying to protect me?" she said, again.

Catlett's shoulders rose and then fell as he sighed, heavily.

"Daniel knew you might come, if something happened to him." He turned slowly to face her. "If that happened, he told me to make sure you ended up on a plane home. He wanted you to be safe."

He looked bone weary. She snuffed out a small sliver of compassion and folded her arms over her chest.

"So, you wrecked my car."

His eyes narrowed. "Why do you insist on blaming that on me?" He threw his hands up in the air. "Fine, I left the note, but I didn't wreck your car."

"If you are so innocent, why won't you go to the FBI?" she said, "If you know who took Daniel, why won't you tell them? He trusted you." She took a swift step forward and poked his chest. "He protected you." She poked him harder. "The FBI was looking for you, but he wouldn't tell them who you were."

He caught her wrist, gently.

"There is a mole in the FBI," he said. "In all likelihood, there are several. Probably even one of the agents he was working with."

"I don't believe you."

His hand released her, and he took a step back.

"I know, but it is true."

He dropped into the desk chair and rubbed his hand over his face.

Thoughts of Keoni's 'them' whispered at the edge of her mind. Maybe he'd been right. Maybe it was some sort of conspiracy.

"Who are you?" she said.

He leaned back against the chair and stared at her. For a moment she thought he'd refuse to answer. Finally, he sighed.

"I am a recruiter. My real job at Winston College was to identify and recruit new talent, preferably young, imaginative, and highly intelligent talent, for a variety of positions in high-ranking research labs across the nation."

Okay, not at all what she had expected. What did that have to do with FBI moles and kidnapped scientists?

"I suppose you give them an offer they can't refuse," she said.

He chuckled. "No. They are free to turn it down, but few of them do. These are career launching offers for highly sought-after jobs in highly ranked labs. Woods Hole, Lawrence Livermore, Caltech ..."

"What about Daniel?" she said. "How does he fit into this?"

The pain in his eyes sent a shiver of fear through her.

"Your uncle has a skill set of particular value to my ... employer. I'd been at Winston an entire term before he showed up. When he did, I was instructed to become his friend and make him an offer." He smiled faintly. "But Daniel knew exactly who I was."

Her stomach twisted.

"So, you gave him to them."

His eyes flashed. "No. He knew they were looking for him. He offered to help me. I told him to leave but he wouldn't listen." She took a step back as he stood abruptly, upending the chair. "He wouldn't listen, and I was too late to stop them."

She sank back against the door. "How do you know he's alive?"

"Because he's too important to them."

"There was a guy at the restaurant. Is he—" Her voice faltered at the intensity of emotion in Catlett's eyes. "I'm guessing Ian isn't his real name."

"He's dangerous, Morgan." His eyes cooled. "I'm sorry for the dramatics, but I had to get you away from him. I promised Daniel you would be safe."

She studied him silently. He looked away.

"Why are you helping these people?" she said, quietly. "There has to be someone at the FBI who can help, or the CIA, or Interpol, MI5, or whatever. They can't all be moles." If he was even telling the truth.

"I can't take the risk."

But he could let Daniel? Her frustration flared.

"Why are you so afraid of them?"

He slumped back against the wall. Her breath caught at the intense anguish in his eyes.

"Because," he said. "They have my daughter."

CHAPTER TWENTY

A heavy silence hung between them. The vast array of emotions swirling in his eyes was overwhelming. He had old eyes, like Daniel's. Eyes which had seen too much sorrow.

"Your daughter?"

"Her name is Kaylee. She's six."

Acid burned in her stomach. Who were these people?

"Her mother?" She didn't know why she said it, but she had to know. Agent Weston had said he had family, but inferred they were gone.

His jaw tightened, and his eyes lowered. "She died shortly after Kaylee was born."

Morgan's heart clenched. Wife dead. Daughter kidnapped. No wonder Daniel had formed such a quick bond with him. Her uncle had always had a strong sense of compassion and justice. Which sometimes smothered his good sense. An edge of distrust wove through her sympathy. Even if his story were true, she had no reason to trust him. Especially after everything that had happened in Iowa.

"Macy said you've been at Winston since September."

"Kaylee's okay," he said, as if reading her thoughts. "It's ... complicated."

"Like shared custody?" The words were out of her mouth before she thought them through, but to her surprise, he gave a small humorless laugh.

"I didn't play by the rules." His jaw tightened, tension visible in every line of his body.

"Is that why they set you up?" she said. "I mean, assuming that you really didn't shoot the guard."

His glare sent a chill through her, though his anger seemed halfhearted. She raised her chin and leveled a challenging stare back at him.

A sudden pounding vibrated the door. Her heart jolted as she launched away from it, like a startled rabbit.

"Ms. Sullivan, it's Agent Blake. Please open the door."

How had the agents known where to find her? And why had they come? She hadn't told them about Catlett and the keys. Or the highly suspicious Ian. She meant to call them ... later. Were they following her?

Catlett appeared beside her. He was freakishly quiet and standing way too close.

"Did you call them?" His warm breath brushed against her ear.

She suppressed a shiver as she shook her head. He was still a suspected killer. Missing daughter or not. Another knock pounded against the door.

"Ms, Sullivan?" Blake said. "Your aunt called me. You left my card on her desk."

Okay, that made a little more sense, but not much. She might have left the card but why would Auntie Anu have called when she thought Morgan was sick—not that a suspected killer had followed her home from Iowa.

"Is there a back way out?" Catlett said.

She shook her head. The backdoor had long rusted from disuse, and even if they could force it open, the bougainvillea bushes would prevent their escape. Pretty flowers, nasty thorns. Besides, she wasn't going to run, and she wasn't about to let him disappear again. He owed her way too many answers.

Of course, she could just turn him over. But if he was telling the truth about his daughter, she'd never forgive herself.

There was always the passage, but she wasn't ready to make its existence known yet. And the big black horse in the paddock outside kind of killed the whole stay quiet and pretend no one was home idea. Looked like it was up to her.

"I've got an idea," she said, and raised her voice. "Just a minute."

"What are you doing?" His hand gripped her upper arm, and she glanced at it and then him, pointedly. He released her but remained close.

"Trust me," she said.

Oh, the irony. She gestured toward the corner behind the door. He fixed her with an unreadable stare, which she ignored. His jaw tightened but he did as she asked. She took a deep breath and schooled her face into a relaxed smile. Then she grabbed the bridle from the desk and opened the door.

"Hello again, Agent Blake." she stepped out quickly, forcing the agent to move out of the way, and shut the door firmly behind her. "I'm afraid I was just leaving. Daylight's almost gone, and I need to get back—"

"Don't rush off on my account," a familiar voice said.

Her spine stiffened. Maybe the fading light was playing tricks with her eyes, or maybe not. Ian smirked as leaned against the porch pillar. The leather of the bridle creaked beneath her fingers.

"I believe you two have met," Agent Blake said, amicably.

Morgan's eyes darted between the two. They knew each other. This could not be good. If Ian thought he was going to get Daniel's drives, he was in for a huge disappointment.

"Briefly," Morgan said. "And apparently he can't take no for an answer. This is private property, and it's time you both leave."

His smile tightened, and Catlett's warnings danced through her brain. She needed to leave. Now.

"Ms. Sullivan—" Agent Blake said.

Sleuth whinnied loud and shrill from the paddock. Good boy. Her heart beat a rapid pace as she took advantage of the distraction and stepped past the intruders, moving as swiftly as she could.

"It's getting late, and my family is expecting me," she said as she reached for the gate latch. "Perhaps we can finish this at the ranch, Agent Blake."

How strange her family hadn't come looking for her already. For once she wished for their smothering presence. Fear splintered through her at the sound of a cold metallic click.

"I had so hoped," Ian said, "we could do this the easy way."

"I said no guns," Agent Blake said.

Morgan slowly raised her hands, slipping the latch free as she did. She turned around slowly. Her heart thudded painfully in her chest. She shifted her head as Sleuth nosed her hair.

"He wants her unharmed," Catlett said, from the door of the lab.

She squeezed her eyes shut for a brief second, the sharp edge of betrayal pierced her heart. She didn't know why she was surprised. Her eyes darted between the three.

Where was Agent Weston? Ian stepped back and swung his gun toward Catlett.

"And you are wanted for murder." Ian smirked.

Catlett stared unflinching. "You're already in trouble for the mess in Iowa. You don't want to make it worse."

She swallowed hard as Ian gave him a noncommittal shrug. He waved a hand toward Agent Blake. "If you would."

"Dr. Scott Catlett, you are under arrest for the murder—" Blake said.

"Then again." Ian said. A sharp ping emerged from the gun, and Blake's voice fell abruptly silent. Morgan bit back a cry.

"Why did you do that?" Catlett said. "Are you insane?"

The agent lay crumpled on the grass as still as death. Morgan swallowed hard. Catlett stood on the porch, his hands loose at his sides. His gaze locked on Ian, hatred in his eyes.

"As much as I would love to pin this on you too and watch you rot in jail," Ian sighed dramatically. "I have orders to bring you back."

The rumble of an engine emitted from the road, and the edge of hope pierced through her panic. Then faded just as quickly as an unfamiliar SUV pulled up beside the house. The gate pressed into her back as Sleuth pushed against it. And Catlett lunged toward Ian.

"Morgan, run!"

She threw the gate open and swung into the saddle. Sleuth bolted for the woods. She buried her fingers in his mane as she tossed a glance over her shoulder in time to see Catlett fall to the ground. She dug her heels into Sleuth's sides, her breath coming in short gasps as tears blurred her vision. Make it home. Just make it home.

Sleuth stumbled, and she lost her grip. The ground rushed up to meet her. She tucked and rolled as best as she could. The air rushed from her lungs. The momentum sent her onto her hands and knees, and she crouched there, frozen for a moment as she struggled to breathe. Branches snapped behind her.

She forced herself to stand, ignoring the searing throbbing in her hip. Sleuth was a dark blur in the distance. At least he'd gotten away. If he ran straight back, he'd be at the barn in roughly ten minutes or so. All she needed to do was hide until help came. She plunged off the road toward the underbrush.

A sudden pain shot through her shoulder. Her legs turned to jelly, and once again the ground rose up to meet her, and darkness swallowed her whole.

OPEN OCEAN OFFSHORE OF THE ISLAND OF MAUI, HAWAII
MORGAN, AGE FIFTEEN

She was so dead. So, so dead. The sail above her head whipped uselessly beneath the onslaught of the wind, the ties eluding her outstretched fingers. The boat wobbled violently as she lunged for the rope, and elation swept through her as she caught the sail. The lines bit into her skin as she pulled it tight and leaned back, hauling with all her strength.

Daniel was going to be so mad at her for what she'd done to his boat. She was definitely grounded. Forever. She would love to be grounded if it meant she might live through this. Fear gripped her heart as the boat crested the wave. Cold water washed over her small vessel, swamping it. She tightened her grip.

The waves were getting bigger. Five feet, maybe more. She spared a glance upward at the boiling black clouds overhead. The storm was already on her. She hadn't meant to get caught in it. She'd just wanted to see the whales. Uncle Daniel had promised to take her, but he'd canceled. Again. Her aunt needed him.

She'd only meant this to be a quick trip before anyone knew she'd even gone. She hadn't needed anyone. She could sail. She was quickly regretting her decision.

Now, she hoped someone had noticed she was gone.

The clouds opened, and rain fell in cold hard sheets. The rope slipped. She tugged it desperately. The boat rose with the wave, and her heart sank as she caught sight of the land. A pinpoint of green against the vast gray ocean. She was caught in the current. She forced herself to breathe. The boat wasn't sunk until it sank, at least that was what her uncle liked to say. If she gave up now, she was lost for certain, but if she kept her head, she might still have a chance.

If someone was looking for her.

The mast gave an ominous creak as the boat slid down the back of the wave. A massive torpedo of mottled gray exploded from the water less than twenty feet from her. Her mind automatically jumped to her uncle's tales of the Leviathan and its massive teeth. Her scream turned into a gurgle as a wave caught her in the face. Her grip on the line faltered as she choked. She blinked hard to clear her burning eyes.

A whale. It was a whale.

Her relief was short lived as the mammoth creature hit the water and its wake crashed toward her. Her little boat spun, and another wave washed in from the other side, catching it in white, churning foam. The world upended. She rolled with the boat, and her wrist caught in the line, dragging her downward.

Her lungs burned. Black edged her vision. The boat pulled her down into the dark depths of the Pacific.

God, please help me!

A band of steel slid around her chest and tightened. The rope on her wrist went slack and she was propelled up toward the surface. She sputtered and choked weakly as her head broke through and fresh air invaded her lungs.

"I've got you, kiddo. I've got you."

Uncle Daniel.

CHAPTER TWENTY-ONE

Her mouth tasted as if something had died in it. A nagging sense of urgency tickled at her pounding brain. She swallowed thickly and struggled to remember what had happened. Her body ached. Her thoughts were disjointed, sluggish, like swimming through mud.

Morgan, run!

The command pierced through her murky thoughts. She jolted, and her body screamed. Or maybe she did. She whimpered and tried to open her eyes, but they seemed to have been glued shut. She breathed in slowly, struggling against the panic. She tried again, this time opening one eye at a time. She blinked.

The thing staring at her did not.

Her sluggish mind gradually realized she was staring at a large eye. Weird. She carefully tilted her head. The thing didn't move, just watched her, without blinking. She closed her eyes. So, she'd finally gone crazy. Or she was dreaming. She eased her eyes open and squinted. The hideous reptilian eye was still there.

Run ...

Panic laced through her as memories flooded her mind. She struggled to sit up. She'd been taken. She'd been taken, and Catlett had been shot. So had Agent Blake.

He wants her unharmed.

She wasn't sure who "he was" but they were off to a really bad start. She became acutely aware of a strap around her waist preventing her from sitting up. Her fingers found a latch and she hit the button, moving as the strap came free. Another rested above her knees; she released it too. And then the world tilted, and she slipped off the bench and onto the floor. Dull pain laced through her hip and shoulder. Sleuth ... she prayed he had made it home.

Tears pricked at her eyes as she pressed her throbbing head against the cold floor. Stupid, stupid, stupid. Why had she been so stupid? She tried to push up off the ground, but the action exhausted her. Her shoulder throbbed. Had she been drugged? The sharp pain, and the sudden darkness. Tranquilizer gun maybe?

She wondered what her family had been left to believe. Anger boiled through her, searing the panic. Someone had just made a very serious error. No one treated her family like this and got away with it. She would find Daniel, and they would find a way home.

They had to.

She drew a shuddering breath and pushed herself up, inch by painful inch, into a seated position. Her head lolled back against the edge of the bench, and she stared at the eye again.

"Clear your mind," she said, closing her eyes against the sharpness of the lights, her voice a faint whisper. "Think."

She opened her eyes slowly. The painted eye was still watching. She tilted her head back further. A reptilian eye in red against the dark metal. And it was on the ceiling ... so weird. A logo maybe? She drew a deep breath, let it out slowly, and then sat up. She rubbed her arms against the chill of the room. Cold sank through her as her eyes settled on a long black bag strapped to the bench opposite hers.

A body bag? She squeezed her eyes shut as her mind replayed Catlett's body falling. He'd tried to save her, and now he was dead. But why had he done it? What would happen to his daughter? Anger laced through her heart as she added one more wrong to the rapidly growing list against her kidnappers. A low groan echoed through the small room. She pried her eyes open.

She must be hallucinating. The bag moved.

Another muffled groan, louder this time. The bag flexed against the straps holding it secure. And then a series of muffled words that would have warranted a mouth-washing with strong soap came from inside it. She snorted.

"Hello?" said a voice from the bag.

Her heart shuddered. This must be a hallucination. She'd seen Catlett fall.

"Catlett?" she said, quietly.

"Morgan, please unzip the bag."

She blinked heavily at the bag. No way. She'd seen this in movies and it never ended well.

"Are you a zombie?" The words slipped from her lips in a hoarse rush of words. "I can't let you out if you're a zombie."

"I'm not a zombie."

Totally what a zombie would say. Or did they say anything? She couldn't remember. She hated those movies.

"Morgan, please. I'm alive, I promise."

Not certain she could stand, she slid across the short distance between the two benches. Her hip throbbed as she pushed to her knees. She hesitated, her hand hovering above the zipper. Then in one swift movement she grabbed the metal tab and tugged it, with all the finesse of ripping off a bandage. The heavy canvas opened to reveal a disheveled, but very much alive, Scott Catlett.

He smiled, and she frowned. The smile was foreign to her.

"Are you okay?" he said.

She stared at him. "What about this situation is okay?"

He frowned. She smiled. The frown was familiar.

"Help me out of this thing."

Must she do everything? The straps pinning him to the bench were snug. Someone hated him.

"Why are you in a body bag?" she said as she tugged the strap free.

"Sick joke, useless threat," he said. "Ian's a psychopath? Take your pick."

The whole thing was deranged. She and Nate had never taken their pranks that far. Of course, she'd never shot and kidnapped anyone either. She scrambled back, startled, as he sat up suddenly and ripped the bag fully open. Her back slammed into the bench.

"Sorry," he said. "Are you all right?"

She winced, "No."

She squeezed her eyes shut against the throb vibrating through her hip. She'd been thrown off a horse, shot and kidnapped. She was a billion miles away from all right.

"You were thrown?"

And now she was speaking out loud again. She heard the release snap free and the rustling of fabric. She rolled her head back against the edge of the bench and breathed until the pain dulled.

"Are you feeling any dizziness or nausea?"

His voice was close. She opened her eyes to find him kneeling beside her. His cat-like movements unnerved her.

"No," she said.

His eyes studied her. She stared back. How could eyes hold so much emotion? He was a paradox wrapped inside an enigma. And apparently, he'd tried to save her. Which made him what? An ally? A man with a guilty conscience?

He rocked back onto his heels. "I'm sorry you were caught up in this."

Too late for regrets. She grimaced and pushed to her feet, ignoring the dull throb and his proffered hand, and dropped heavily onto her bench.

"There is an eye on the ceiling." she said. "What's it mean?"

He didn't even look at it, just turned and slid a panel open beneath his bench.

"It's a logo."

Obviously. She stared up at it. A water bottle pressed into her hand. She looked down, and her heart gave a jump as he leaned toward her and settled a blanket around her shoulders. She grimaced at her rapidly beating pulse as he settled back onto his bench and took a long swig from his own bottle.

"It's Leviathan, isn't it?" she said as she found her voice again.

He saluted her with his bottle. She eased back against the wall and pulled the blanket tighter against the chill. The room was small and compact, with a door across from the end of her bench and another set into the opposite wall between the benches. She squinted at the latter one. Hatch. Not a door, but a hatch. A low hum thrummed in the background, faintly.

Her stomach twisted. She took a small sip of water as the pieces snapped into place. The bad taste in her mouth was seasickness. She rubbed her hand along the base of her neck and found a square patch. She gave it an experimental pull, and it peeled away easily. There was no logo, but the shape was familiar.

"Are we on a boat?"

Catlett's mouth quirked into a humorless grin. "Submarine."

Huh. She squeezed her eyes closed and waited. The nausea she was expecting didn't return. Interesting, but a good thing. Vomit and small spaces were not a pleasant combination. Maybe submarines affected her differently than boats. Or maybe the drugs hadn't worn off yet. She took a breath and let it out slowly. He was still watching her. She could feel it.

"We were on a boat," she said. "Before the submarine."

"Yep." He sounded certain.

She cracked an eye open. "How'd you know that if you were in a body bag?"

"The first round of drugs wore off on the boat." As if that explained everything.

She frowned, searching her memory. "I don't remember that."

"I think I have a higher tolerance for the drugs," he said.

"Like iocane powder."

He laughed. The long dormant butterflies in her stomach took flight. She squelched a smile and ignored them. She stuck the seasickness patch onto the bench beside her. The small act of defiance cheered her. She traced her finger along the edges, sealing it firmly to the metal.

"What happened on the boat?" she said. "How'd you end up in the body bag? What happened to Agent Bl—"

The questions spilled out of her like a torrent of water. Fast, fierce, uncontrollable.

"Easy." His voice was soothing.

She glared at him.

"You woke up, though not fully." His eyes darkened with anger. "You were extremely sick. Apparently, the idiot sent to find you didn't read your file." A dark smile twitched at the edge of his mouth. "But he got what he deserved."

"I have a file?" Her words came out as a squeak.

Catlett gave her a serious look. "Daniel has a file, you are a footnote," he said. "Or at least you were."

So, apparently Keoni's paranoia was founded. She owed him an apology. If she ever saw him again. She drew a deep breath and let it out slowly.

"So, what happened next?" she said. "I'm guessing I was drugged again."

He nodded and rubbed his thumb against the crook of his elbow.

"I was too, after I slugged Ian."

Which explained the body bag. She brushed her thumb over a bruise on her forearm. A needle mark? She breathed in and counted a slow exhale. This wasn't the time to panic. She had to think. They'd been drugged, smuggled off the island on a boat and then onto a submarine.

Okay maybe this was the perfect time to panic.

"And Agent Blake?"

His expression was unreadable. "She wasn't on the boat."

The nausea building in her stomach had nothing to do with the submarine.

"Who are these people?"

"Dangerous." The look in his eyes left her chilled. "Very dangerous."

She pinned him with a stare. "Are you?"

Catlett didn't answer. His eyes shifted to the door. He moved suddenly, crossing the space to her bench, settling inches from her. She flinched back in surprise, pressing into the corner of the wall. A metallic screech echoed through the small room.

Fear shot through her. "Who—?"

He held a finger to his lips. She fell silent as his posture went from rigid to a relaxed slump. He looked bored. He'd been through this before. She hoped he knew what he was doing. The hatch opened and a strange man in a black jumpsuit entered. She forced herself not to tense. He held a strange gun, probably a tranquilizer gun. He took up a position several steps out of reach. His eyes never left Catlett, who ignored the man and calmly sipped his water.

Morgan bit her lip. An Asian woman in a white jumpsuit entered a moment later. The black bag she carried suggested she was a doctor. The woman smiled gently.

"Ms. Sullivan."

Her voice was as soothing as her smile. Her accent was American, or Canadian maybe. Morgan wondered if she'd been recruited as well, or if she'd come willingly.

The woman's gaze shifted. "Scott."

The edge of Catlett's lips turned upward. "Doc."

"My name is Doctor Li," she said, her attention back to Morgan. "May I check your vitals?"

She had a choice? Her eyes darted to Catlett, though she didn't know why she was looking for his reassurance. His attention was on the open hatch. She wondered if he was planning to make a break for it. Where would he go on a submarine? Would he leave her behind?

"Ms. Sullivan?" She flinched as a hand touched her shoulder. "How are you feeling?"

A hand settled on her blanket-covered ankle, and she startled. Catlett squeezed it gently, his hand firm, grounding. She fought the urge to kick him.

"Breathe, Morgan," he said. "Doc's okay."

She let out another shuddering breath and nodded slowly. He released her ankle and turned his attention back to the door. The butterflies rushed back—with friends. She glanced up at the doctor and gave her a brief nod of consent.

"Where's your master, Stevens?" Catlett said, his voice slightly mocking. "Still licking his wounds?"

She stared at the back of Catlett's head, but the guard remained silent and still, as if he were carved out of stone. Li tsked softly as she pressed her fingers to Morgan's wrist, checking her pulse.

"I'm surprised he still hasn't learned how to duck." Catlett said.

"I've been ordered to sedate you if you continue," Li said, as if it were an everyday occurrence.

Morgan wondered how many times this scene had played out before.

"Why even bother when I could do it myself?" Ian stepped through the door.

Morgan froze. Ian was dressed in a black jumpsuit like Stevens, but the gun in his hand was not at all like the guard's. This one was definitely not a tranquilizer gun. The tensions in the room ratcheted as the two men stared at each other.

Claustrophobia pressed down on her. The room was tight with two, but it was nearly suffocating with five. Add a gun, and a man with a homicidal gleam in his eyes, in a submarine ...

"Nice shiner." She glanced at Catlett. "Your work?"

His face seemed frozen between bemused and smug. She smirked. The doctor gave a quiet cough she would have bet money covered a laugh.

"Are you quite finished?" Ian said, in a different accent than before, his eyes flashing.

She narrowed her own eyes. "So, you are British now? How very movie villain-ish of you."

Her voice faltered as Ian turned the gun on her. Catlett shifted back, and her head bounced off the wall. Pain shot up her spine as she found herself pressed tight into the corner, shielded by a hundred eighty pounds of muscle. Her claustrophobia reared, and she shut her eyes and tried to breathe. Voices were shouting, but the words were a confusing jumble. A cool hand pressed against the back of her neck, pushing her head into her knees.

"Breathe, Morgan," the doctor said calmly. "That's it, nice deep breaths."

Easy for her to say. She wasn't squished into a corner.

"He wants her unharmed," Catlett said.

"He wants both of them unharmed." The doctor's voice rose above the shouting. "You've pushed this far enough, Ian."

Silence fell over the room. She heard the clang as the hatch slammed shut, and Catlett slid away. Her feet hit the floor, the urge to run too great, but her knees refused to hold her. Hands caught her before she hit the deck and gently set her back on the bench. Voices buzzed softly above her.

"We may need to sedate …"

No drugs. No more drugs. A hand gently squeezed her arm. She looked into Catlett's eyes as he crouched before her.

"No more drugs." His voice was calm, but his eyes were blazing. "No more drugs, I promise. You need to breathe."

Her lungs felt like they were being squeezed by a vise. Her body shook. He took her hand and pressed it flat against his warm chest. Her startled gaze shot to his. His eyes were calm.

"Breathe with me, Morgan. In and Out."

She focused on the rise and fall of his chest. In and out. Her shallow breaths slowly deepened. In and out. Her head cleared, and the panic slowly ebbed.

"Good." He smiled. "Good."

Catlett released her hand as she pulled away. "I know you are scared, and you don't trust me, but I promise I will do my best to keep you safe. And to get you home."

She stared at him, feeling drained and confused, and embarrassed. She hadn't had a reaction that strong in years. A water bottle was pressed into her hand.

"Take a sip," Li said. "Small one."

She did and coughed as a bit trickled down the wrong tube. A gentle hand rubbed circles against her back.

"That's it," Li said.

Her hand fell away as Morgan sank back against the wall. They were alone in the room. Ian, the guard, and the gun, all gone. She glanced toward Catlett as he settled back on his own bench.

"Thanks."

He nodded. Li reached for her black bag, and Morgan flinched.

"No drugs," Li said.

She held up the blood pressure cuff, and Morgan nodded. Li reached into the side pocket of her bag and pulled out a folded square of pink paper. She handed it to Catlett. "Kaylee asked me to give this to you."

Morgan watched as he carefully unfolded it. His face softened into a sad smile.

He cleared his throat quietly. "How is she?"

"She's as spunky as ever," Li said, as she settled the cuff around Morgan's arm. "Practically running the place. She misses you."

Morgan's eyes met his. He hesitated and then turned the picture toward her. It was a child's crayon drawing of a mermaid in the ocean, with the words 'I love you, Daddy' scrawled across the top in blue. Her eyes shifted back to his and his fond smile left her breathless.

"We'll be docking soon." Li said, after a moment. "He wants to see you both the minute we do."

"What's his hurry?" Catlett's smile vanished, his tone hardened.

"Who wants to see us?"

"Captain Ahab." He didn't sound as if he were kidding.

Captain Ahab. The man who spent his life hunting his great white whale, only to die by its actions. A thought struck her, and several puzzle pieces snapped into place. The thought was farfetched, but nothing about this little escapade had been normal. And it fit Daniel's remaining clue.

"You mean Casper Bishop," she said.

The cuff tightened around her arm, too tight, and she winced.

"I'm so sorry," Li said. "But how did you ...?"

Her eyes darted from Morgan to Catlett. Morgan followed her gaze to the bemused look on Catlett's face. Catlett, who according to the FBI didn't exist until ten years ago. Wait, Bishop had a son.

"You're Alexander Bishop," she said.

Catlett didn't deny it. "I was a long time ago."

Huh. Okay then ... if Casper Bishop was still alive, and still searching for his monster, maybe Daniel was close by.

Her pulse quickened. "Is Daniel here too?"

Catlett looked at Li, who hesitated. Morgan's heart sank.

"He was sent out on a mission a couple of days ago," Li said. "But they haven't returned yet."

Cold seeped through her. "He's missing?"

Li smiled. "Probably just late."

The doctor's words weren't at all reassuring. Why would they need her if they had Daniel? Had they lost him?

"I need to use the bathroom," she said.

Li pointed to the hatch between the bunks. "It's right through there. The water's safe if you want to wash your face."

Morgan stood and swayed under a sudden rush of vertigo as the blood rushed to her head. Catlett reached out and steadied her. His hands were warm.

"I'm okay," she said.

She willed herself to move, but her feet felt as if they'd been welded to the deck.

"I will get you out of this, Morgan, I promise."

Forget the fact he'd been the one who had gotten her into this trouble in the first place. However, if she was honest, he wasn't entirely at fault. She looked up, and the lightheadedness returned. Along with the butterflies.

Li coughed. "I hate to break this up, but we are docking in thirty minutes."

Right. There were bigger issues. Like kidnapping, and secret bases, and guys with guns. She glanced up at Catlett. And ghosts from the past.

"I'd better ..." she said.

He released her and pulled the hatch open. She darted inside, pulling it firmly behind her. The door closed with a heavy clank. She started as her eyes met those of the stranger in the mirror. She groaned. A soft knock sounded against the door.

"I'm fine," she said.

She grimaced. Her reflection grimaced back. No wonder everyone was treating her like she was about to shatter. She looked like a reject from *Night of the Living Dead*. She tugged her hair free from its lopsided ponytail. A few leaves fluttered to the floor as she ran her fingers through it. A smear of red mud had dried against the left side of her face and down her neck.

Attractive. She let out a heavy sigh and turned on the water. Her shoulder throbbed, but she ignored it as she hunched over. The water felt too good. She was stalling, but she deserved some space. Too many thoughts were jumbled in her brain. She was in a serious pickle. Bishop had gone missing more than twenty years ago. What had he been doing all this time?

Whatever it was, the situation was extremely dangerous. She gripped the sides of the small sink and closed her eyes, whispering a fervent prayer toward Heaven.

For Daniel's safety and her own.

CHAPTER TWENTY-TWO

Li was gone when she finally exited the head. While Catlett took his turn, she sank onto her bench and stared up at the logo. Something crinkled beneath her. She shifted and pulled the folded paper out of her pocket. Keoni's copies of the Bishop articles. She darted a quick look toward the closed door and flipped through them. She paused on a photo of a smiling couple and their young son, standing in front of a sailboat.

She stared at the man. What kind of obsession could drive someone to these lengths? Kidnapping scientists and faking their deaths, abandoning his son, and holding his granddaughter hostage?

The room quivered slightly. She gripped the edge of the bench. The hatch clanked, and she shoved the copies back into her pocket. Catlett stepped out and closed the hatch behind him. She watched as he reclaimed his bench. He looked … different. His face was scrubbed, and his hair brushed back, but his eyes were the most startling. They were weary. She thought about the boy in the photo, and she was filled with an intense sadness.

She hadn't met Casper Bishop yet, but she already felt an intense dislike. For what he'd done to his son. And for stealing Daniel from her.

"Why Scott Catlett?"

He smiled faintly. "That is a long story."

And apparently one he wasn't going to tell her now. She let it go for now.

"I know this will be difficult for you," Catlett said. "But let me do the talking when you meet Bishop."

Not his father. Just Bishop.

"I'll try."

He snorted softly. Any further words were silenced as the main hatch clanked. They stood, and Catlett positioned himself in front of her as the door opened. Stevens stepped inside, and then Li appeared in the doorway.

"We've arrived," she said.

Morgan shifted closer to Catlett.

"And our escort?" Catlett said.

Li smiled. "He went on ahead."

Catlett's shoulders relaxed slightly, and Morgan did too. He stepped aside and motioned for her to follow the doctor, placing himself between her and the guard. She gave him a faint smile and stepped through the hatch. The corridor was painted a depressing gunmetal gray, like the room they'd vacated. She followed Li past several closed hatches.

They turned down a shorter corridor and crossed a threshold into a brighter hallway. Catlett's hand kept her moving as her step faltered.

"Are we under water?" she asked, and at Li's nod, "How deep are we?"

Her biggest dream, to live in a base at the bottom of the sea, had been made a reality. And now that she was here, she wanted nothing more than to see the sun again.

"Welcome to Atlantis," Li said.

Her eyebrows shot upward. "You're not serious."

"Sadly, she is," Catlett said dryly.

Atlantis? An amazing work of engineering, but seriously, they named it Atlantis?

"It does sound better than Sea Base 42," Li said.

Wait, what? Her eyes darted between the two.

"Forty-two," Morgan said. "Does that mean there are forty-one others? Or did it take forty-one tries to get this one right?"

Li just laughed. "I like her."

The maze of corridors was extensive, each branch seeming to stretch into infinity. Maybe it was a series of circles. How did it handle the pressure? The questions continued to build with every new corridor. Until she had to ask them, or her brain would implode.

"How big is this place? Where exactly are we?"

Through her head and out her mouth, the questions came at rapid fire speed. How did they ever manage to build something this large? And how had they managed to keep it hidden? Were they below an island like a Bond villain lair?

The hand on her shoulder fell away. Catlett was laughing. She glanced back. Even the guard was grinning. She couldn't help it. She was born to be a scientist. Questions were how she thought, answers were what she sought. A never-ending process. She wasn't going to apologize for it. A door slid open a few steps to her right. Her jaw dropped, and she darted through it before anyone could stop her.

She was in a lab. Large cylindrical tubes were positioned throughout the room. She moved toward the one in the center, her hand reaching out to touch the glass. The six-inch fish on the other side drifted peacefully, ignorant to her gawking. She caught her breath. It was magnificent, a creature she'd only seen in photos and videos captured by researchers, but never in person.

The glowing, transparent head was otherworldly.

"It's a ..." Her words were a faint whisper.

"Macropinna microstoma," said a gray-haired man in a blue jumpsuit. "Also known as the barreleye."

The fish was amazing. The first discovery had been tragically misunderstood due to the old scientific methods of dredging the deep with a net and dragging everything to the surface, which meant its head had collapsed. But here it was in all its transparent-headed glory. She watched the bulbous green eyes, entranced.

"I call it nightlight fish," a small voice announced beside her. "They won't let me have one though. So, I have to study them here in the lab."

She looked down into a pair of impish blue eyes framed by a small pixie face.

"Hi, I'm—"

"Kaylee!"

The girl's dark braids swung as she spun around. Her face lit up as she launched herself at Catlett with a squeal of excitement. "Daddy!"

Catlett caught his daughter up in his arms, spinning her as she laughed with delight. She wound her small arms around his neck, buried her face against him, and burst into tears. Li caught his arm and gently steered them into a quiet corner of the lab.

Tears pricked Morgan's eyes as she watched Catlett rock his daughter gently. His dark head bent against Kaylee's, whispering to her as he rubbed her back. His eyes met hers for a moment, and he gave her a damp smile. Stevens cleared his throat pointedly. Catlett glared coldly at the man.

Right, Bishop was waiting. Catlett whispered to his daughter, and she nodded. She raised her head and smiled shyly at Morgan. She smiled back, moving to join them as Catlett gestured toward the door. She cast one final look at the treasures filling the lab. She thought she heard him mutter the words 'just like Daniel,' as he led her back into the hall where Stevens was not so patiently waiting.

"I need to get back to the med bay," Li said. "Kaylee, why don't you come help me for a bit while your daddy talks to your granddad."

Morgan felt sick. So, the joint custody comment hadn't been so far from the truth. The little girl buried deeper into Catlett's arms. Catlett pressed a kiss against his daughter's dark hair and tickled her, making her laugh. "Go on, Princess. I'll be there soon."

The little girl nodded reluctantly and slid to the deck. She accepted Li's hand.

"Later, alligator!" She gave them an impish smile as she skipped down the hall.

Catlett snorted and shook his head. His eyes followed the pair until they vanished around a corner. Her heart ached. Stevens cleared his throat again. He gestured down the opposite corridor and they continued on their way.

Morgan craned her neck, trying to see through each open doorway as they passed. The color of the corridors changed somewhere from a white to a deep blue. There were more people moving through, all in a hurry. She scanned each face as they passed, and her scientific curiosity dampened. Something was wrong. Everyone seemed so ... tense.

"He's waiting." Oh joy, Ian was back.

Catlett edged in front of her as the man approached, looking as murderous as ever. At least, his gun was safely holstered.

"Well then, we can't have that," Catlett's voice was flat, tense.

Ian gestured for them to pass, but Catlett mirrored the gesture and waited. Ian glowered and turned on his heel, moving swiftly back in the way he'd come.

Catlett squeezed her arm gently. "Come on."

She nodded and followed Ian, Catlett's hand never leaving her arm. They turned a corner and paused at a wide door with the Leviathan eye logo etched across it. Catlett's hand fell away. Ian pressed a button on the keypad to the right of the door. A chime resonated inside, and the door slid open. Like Star Trek. Morgan stared at it in wonder. A hand gently pressed against her back and ushered her inside.

Her eyes grew wider as she stepped into the room. She so wanted a room like this. Shaped like a half dome of transparent glass. On the opposite side of the glass was the deep blue sea. The enormously deep blue sea. She moved closer, like a moth to a flame, pressing her fingers against the glass. Schools of bioluminescent fish darted by, like fireflies. Big and small and everything in between.

They were deep. She wasn't sure how deep, but from the few species she recognized, they were at least 2,000 feet. Which was ... impossible? Apparently not.

"Magnificent, isn't it?"

She turned at the sound of a new voice, heat rushing to her face. But the man standing beside her didn't seem to mind her distraction. In fact, he seemed pleased by it. She stepped away from the glass as he drew closer. Casper Bishop looked a lot older than the photos she'd seen—his face was weathered, hair streaked with gray, and his face shadowed by a well-trimmed Van Dyke beard. A much older, harder version of his son, his eyes were the same brilliant shade of blue, but colder.

His smile was cold. She'd seen the same exact smile before, on another much younger face. Her eyes darted toward the door where Catlett stood beside Ian. Interesting. She glanced back at her host. She couldn't help but grin at his wardrobe. A tailored jacket of dark blue velvet with silver buttons, the Leviathan logo etched into each one. Red cravat. White slacks and black boots.

"Captain Nemo, I presume."

His laughter seemed genuine, but his eyes held none of the warmth of his son's. In fact, she found the combination unnerving. He held himself like a man who knew his own worth, who wore power like a cloak. She sensed he wasn't someone to be trifled with, and yet here she was ... trifling.

"Forgive me, Mr. Bishop," she said. "It is truly an engineering marvel. We are, what, 340–350 fathoms deep?" Her math was a bit rusty, but 2,000 feet seemed reasonable.

He didn't seem fazed she knew his identity. A gray eyebrow rose slightly, and he nodded. "Very good, Ms. Sullivan," he said. "Four hundred, to be precise."

Impressive. The deepest habitat on record to date was the SEALAB III, run by the US Navy in 1969 off the coast of California's San Clemente Island at around 620 feet. And it had been classified knowledge until the turn of the century. So, who knew what was really possible? Though this seemed improbable. And yet here they were. Under 2,400 feet of water. At least if there was a leak, they wouldn't have to worry about drowning. They'd be squashed like a bug.

She stepped away from the glass and looked back at the door. Catlett was gone, as was Ian. She calmed as she found Catlett sprawled on a plush sofa. He smirked, enjoying this. She scanned the remainder of the room. They were in a study. There was no other word for it. Plush dark blue carpet underfoot. Matching paint on the walls, as if it were meant to merge with the sea beyond the glass. She stepped back as she found herself on the wrong side of a massive mahogany desk, which she'd been too distracted by the ocean to notice. Bishop didn't seem to mind.

She moved around to the opposite side of the desk.

"Why am I here?" she said.

"Straight to the point," Bishop said, with a slight incline of his head. "I appreciate that."

He waved a hand to the chairs opposite the desk. They were leather, expensive, and huge. She wondered how he'd managed to get them onto the base, let alone the room. She sat down on the edge of one, ignoring the throb in her hip as she straightened her shoulders. Bishop was watching, making no effort to hide his assessment of her.

His smile dimmed. Something had displeased him. She looked away to find Catlett in the chair beside her. This was going to be interesting.

Bishop's jaw tightened subtly. "Don't you have somewhere you'd rather be, Son?"

Catlett sprawled deeper into the chair. "Not at the moment., Father."

The tension was deafening, and for once, Morgan held her tongue. Thanksgiving must be a fun time here. Bishop chuckled, and a chill tickled up her spine. He clasped his hands and stood.

"You asked why you are here, Ms. Sullivan. Why don't I show you?" He crossed the room to the door. "Please follow me."

This felt wrong, but what choice did she have? She looked at Catlett, and he gave her a subtle nod. Okay, fine. What was the worst that could happen? She was already trapped in a fanatic's wonder of modern science. She stood, Catlett at her side. The door opened, and Bishop led the way through the corridor. Another guard in a black jumpsuit fell into step behind them as they marched down the deserted hallway.

The whole place was creepy. After a few moments, Bishop paused in front of a door. He slipped his glasses from his face and peered into the retinal scanner. The panel blinked green, and the door opened. Lights switched on as they moved inside. The room was huge. She felt her jaw drop as she moved toward the twisted wreckage of a submersible. She wasn't familiar with this particular design. Of course, in its current state she couldn't tell exactly what it had looked like originally. The metal on one side was torn, shattered, flattened, and twisted.

She could practically hear the screeching as the metal collapsed beneath the pressure. She eased closer, her attention focused on a row of marks along the edge, marks that looked like ...

"Teeth." She reached out and reverently traced the marks in the metal.

Not a shark. Shark teeth were pointed and jagged. This was a puncture, several punctures. Straight and clean, like a blade. And wide. Whatever it was had enormous teeth.

"This was found in the wreckage." Bishop said.

A thrill coursed through her. In his hand was a massive tooth. She took it carefully, her mind spinning as she slid her thumb along its edge. She knew exactly what it was. Daniel had one in a display case somewhere back home. Though his was smaller, roughly two to three inches of fossilized stone. A mosasaur thought to have been somewhere around forty feet long. This tooth was nearly four inches long, and unlike Daniel's, it was white and not fossilized.

"Where did you ...?" For once words failed her.

He gestured solemnly toward the sub. "This was one of our early expeditions, roughly ten years ago. The sub vanished with the crew. We found the wreckage three months later in the Tonga Trench."

He held out another tooth, this one an inch smaller. Yellowed with time, but like the other. Un-fossilized.

"I pulled this one from the wreckage of my yacht," he said, reverently.

He gestured toward a display case, which held a lone piece of shattered fiberglass with a partial name. She swallowed hard. Reading about a legend was one thing, but quite another to hold the indisputable evidence in her hand. She turned, but Catlett wasn't beside her. He was standing by the door, his face shadowed, unreadable. Her heart twisted.

She held the teeth side by side. At roughly an inch of tooth per 20 feet of creature, it was nearly eighty feet long now. She ran her finger along the edge. What if there was more than one? The thought both thrilled and chilled her. There had to be to sustain the existence of at least one ...

"If you are looking for an expert, you already have him," she said as she handed the teeth back with reluctance. "Daniel knows far more than I ever could."

Bishop's face grew even more solemn. He took the teeth and reverently placed them in a nearby case. "Your uncle was indeed every bit the expert I'd hoped he'd be."

Her heart plunged into her toes.

"His team took a sub out on an exploratory mission two days ago. We've had no contact with them for the past thirty-six hours."

"Maybe he got tired of your hospitality," Catlett said.

His hand rested lightly against her shoulder. She hadn't heard him move. Morgan forced herself to breathe, her eyes locked on Bishop. The question fell from her lips. Each word like glass, fragile, and ready to shatter.

"You think he's dead?"

He couldn't be. Not after everything they'd been through. Not after she'd come so far. The sympathy in the man's eyes turned her stomach.

"The last transmission was a mayday call. The sub was heavily damaged and sinking." Bishop said. "Their transponder went offline shortly after. I'm afraid he, and the crew, are gone."

Catlett's hand on her shoulder tightened. Numbness washed through her, as if she were watching a scene in a movie. Because it was all too surreal, and Daniel couldn't be gone. Not after she'd come so far. Her eyes strayed to the twisted heap of metal in the corner. All that remained of another submersible. Her stomach twisted.

"Why am I here?" Her voice sounded foreign to her ears. Catlett's hand fell away as she stepped forward, her eyes on the teeth in the case. Their wonder diminished. "I'm not an expert like Daniel ..."

"On the contrary, Ms. Sullivan." Bishop said, as he lowered the lid back into place. "You are very much an expert in your own right."

Her gaze followed as he gestured toward the far wall. She stared at the screen and the familiar data scrolling across it. Her thoughts jolted. Her hand rose to her throat, touching the key still tucked beneath her shirt. She hadn't even been able to protect Daniel's legacy.

"Your model is impressive," Bishop said. "Using it to reflect the potential effects of major natural hazards like tsunamis on whale migration is genius. And when you added in the Leviathan sightings ..." He turned to face her, excitement in his eyes. The light cast eerie shadows on his face. "You are exactly the expert I need to help me find this creature."

She stared at the screen. Cold crept through her body. Darkness edged at the corners of her mind. After what felt like eons, she met his eyes.

"If you'll excuse me, I'm not feeling well."

She turned and crossed to the door. No one made an effort to stop her, not even the guard. Her pace quickened as she turned down a corridor. She didn't know where she was going, just that she had to get away. Daniel was dead.

Her vision blurred. She blinked and broke into a run, ducking down another corridor. People. Voices. She stumbled, and a hand reached for her, but she caught her balance and ducked out of reach. And stumbled again. The world tilted and the floor was replaced with a blur of blue. Her head lolled back, and a face swam into focus.

Catlett. Why was it always Catlett?

His mouth was moving, but she couldn't make out the words. She felt as if she were drowning. She nearly had once before. Daniel had saved her then, but he wasn't here. He was gone. Her eyes slipped closed, and the darkness pulled deeper. She drifted, weightless. Voices whispered, insistent, but she ignored them. The darkness was soothing.

A bright light pierced the dark, searing into her skull, and her stomach revolted. The world tilted violently upright. Hands supported her as she heaved the contents of her stomach into a metal bucket. Pain flared up her spine ... she felt the sharp prick of a needle against her arm. Her head pounded. A hand rubbed her back soothingly, and her own hand flexed against the edge of the bucket. The room was trembling. Something cold settled against her neck, and she struggled to focus.

"Easy, Morgan," Dr. Li said softly, sounding worried. "That's it, just breathe."

Her body trembled as she drew a breath. And another. The rolling in her stomach eased. Her limbs felt like lead. Hands eased her against a soft surface.

"You're in the med bay," Li said, soothingly. "You're going to be fine."

She'd never be fine. A cloth settled against her forehead, cool and damp.

"That's it." A gentle hand squeezed her arm. "Just rest."

I'm sorry, Uncle Daniel. I'm sorry I failed.

Her mind drifted as the darkness eased closer. A warm hand squeezed hers, and Catlett's voice whispered, two words.

"I'm sorry."

His voice echoed the pain in her heart.

Me too.

She felt the tears as they traced warm rivers down her face. A thumb skimmed against her cheek, gently brushing them away.

"Stay." Her voice was faint.

His hand squeezed hers, anchoring her. "I'm not going anywhere."

She let the darkness wash over her.

SMITHSON RANCH, KULA, MAUI
MORGAN, AGE SEVENTEEN

The old screen popped out of the frame with a clatter. Morgan's heart skipped a beat. She froze, her ears straining for proof she'd been caught and would be dragged back into the throng of well-wishers who clogged her grandparents' home. Invading their sanctuary. Her sanctuary.

If one more person asked how she was feeling, she would ... well she didn't know what she would do.

She eased up onto the toilet seat cover and leveraged her upper body through the open window. A few years ago, this would have been easier, but she managed. She wrapped her fingers around the branch of her grandmother's ornamental lemon bush and hauled the rest of her body through. Rocks bit into her bare feet as she dropped onto the path below, but she ignored them and snapped the screen back into place.

A sharp rap pounded against the bathroom door. She ducked low as she heard the door creak open and darted along the back of the house. Clouds covered the moon, and she welcomed the darkness as she ran across the lawn toward the barn.

All was quiet when she reached it—the lights dimmed, and the horses bedded down for the night. She shoved her feet into her battered muck boots, grabbed a halter from the tack room, and crept down the row of stalls.

Widget, her aunt's bay mare, greeted her with a quiet whicker and a puff of grain-scented breath. Memories assailed her without warning, and she staggered beneath their weight. Moments never to be repeated.

Her aunt was gone, her ashes in a wooden urn in her grandparents' house.

She didn't want to remember her vibrant aunt that way.

The halter slipped from her fingers to the dirt floor as she reached up and tangled her fingers in Widget's mane. Her face pressed against the mare's neck, and her body shook beneath the force of the sobs she couldn't hold back any longer. The knot in her chest tightened, choking her.

She heard her name. Uncle Daniel.

His warm hand settled against her shoulder. She let go of the horse and buried herself in her uncle's arms. Guilt washed through her, adding to the pain in a confused whirl of emotions she couldn't control. He'd lost more than she had. She should be comforting him. She tried, but she couldn't be strong. Not anymore.

"I miss her," she said.

He didn't push her away or scold her for her selfishness. Instead, his arms tightened, and he pressed a kiss against her head.

"I know, kiddo," he said. "I miss her too."

She could hear the tears in his voice. She'd never seen him cry before today.

"We'll see your Auntie Lelani again one day." His voice faltered, dropping to a husky whisper. His hand smoothed over her hair. "She's alive and whole and happy. No more cancer. No more pain. Safe with Jesus."

She knew that. But she wanted her here. Her family was broken. A piece was missing. A gaping hole left behind. She felt Widget's nose press against her back, and the tears flowed faster as darker thoughts clogged her mind.

"I can't lose you too, Uncle Daniel." Her arms tightened around him, as if she could anchor him to this place, this time, forever. "I can't. Not ever."

She felt him sigh. His cheek pressed against her hair. Her scattered mind grasped onto a thought, and she continued in a rush, before he could speak.

"Not until we find Leviathan," she said.

Which meant forever, as people had been trying for ages. His chest rumbled beneath her ear with a quiet chuckle. His arms tightened.

"All right," he said. "Not until we find Leviathan."

CHAPTER TWENTY-THREE

Daniel hadn't kept his promise. He'd gone searching without her, and now he was dead. She pushed the thoughts aside and tried to return to the dream, where Daniel was alive, and she wasn't trapped in this nightmarish scenario. Her chest hurt, like someone had carved her heart from it and left a gaping hole behind.

The tears began again as she thought about her family. How much they must be hurting. She wondered what they'd been led to believe. If they thought she was dead. If they would ever know what had really happened. For a moment she was angry with Daniel for putting himself in danger. Sorrow snuffed the faint ember out. He'd been trying to help a friend, to right a major set of wrongs, but they were never his to make right.

She pressed her face against the pillow. Her body throbbed. A warm hand tightened around hers and she froze. She opened her eyes a slit, and then wider. Then relaxed as a faint smile crossed her face. Catlett was still there, his daughter curled in his arms, both fast asleep in an uncomfortable looking chair, both snoring faintly.

He'd stayed.

She wasn't sure what she felt about it. Her gaze settled on the little girl. She wondered what might have been if they'd met under different circumstances. If he'd simply just been a professor at the same college as Daniel.

Her smile faded as a fresh wave of sorrow swept through her. She squeezed her eyes shut. Her body trembled. Catlett's hand flexed against hers, his thumb gently brushing her skin. The snoring had stopped. She opened her eyes and found him watching, his eyes sad. He gave her a weary smile but didn't speak, which she was glad for. No empty platitudes or awkward words. Her eyes felt heavy, and she let them close.

"Thank you," she whispered.

He squeezed her hand gently. "You're not alone, Morgan."

Such a nice sentiment. He sounded sincere. For the moment, she let herself believe it. The door opened, but his hand didn't move.

"Good morning," Li said softly.

Morgan considered pretending to sleep, but it wouldn't make anything less painful. Only delay it for a little while. She opened her eyes. Li smiled.

"How are you feeling?"

Now, there was a loaded question. She decided to stick to the physical part of feeling. Her body hurt, her chest ached, and her head throbbed, but she wasn't nauseous, and the room wasn't spinning. She sighed.

"Like we've been here before," she said.

A quiet snort came from Catlett's direction, and she smiled tiredly. He squeezed her hand and pulled away. She caught it before he could. Heat rose to her face, but her panic ebbed as his hand covered hers.

"What do you remember?" Li said.

Too much. Her heart ached, as if it had been squeezed in a vise.

"How long have I been here?" Morgan said.

The doctor took her wrist and pressed her cold fingers against her pulse. Why were doctor's fingers always so cold?

"On the base?" Li said. "Ten hours-ish."

The doctor released her wrist and pulled a light from her pocket. Morgan winced as the brightness pierced her eyes. Her head throbbed dully, but the nausea stayed away.

"I thought doctors were supposed to be precise."

Catlett snorted again.

Li smirked. "I can check my watch if you like, or I could remove the IV."

Morgan raised her arm. She was not a fan of needles. There was a pinch, and then it was gone.

"You were out for nine of those hours," Li said. "But that was expected. I am sorry about the sedative, but it was necessary."

Morgan squeezed her eyes shut as the heat burned her face.

"Hey," Li said softly, "There is nothing to be ashamed about. You suffered a serious shock."

She opened her eyes and pushed up to a seated position. Or tried. A hand pressed against each shoulder pushing her down. Anger flashed through her, along with a twinge of pain as the movement ignited her bruised muscles.

"Easy," Li said. A low whine filled the room, and the bed slowly began to rise.

She relaxed as they released her. Catlett was standing beside her now, his daughter asleep in the chair. Her hand felt cold without his.

"Has there been any further word concerning the missing sub?"

Li shook her head, sorrow in her dark eyes.

"I'm sorry."

Hope disintegrated, leaving only the crushing ache of loss. Li exchanged a concerned look with Catlett. Morgan sighed. She had to pull herself together.

"I bet you would like a chance to clean up." Li gestured toward a door. "There's a shower through there and fresh clothes and towels."

Morgan nodded and swung her legs to the side of the bed. The room stayed in place. She carefully stood, wincing as she did. Li hovered at her elbow, ready to support her.

"Don't worry about using all the water," Li said. "That's one thing we have plenty of."

Morgan grinned. She hesitated at the door and looked back at Catlett. He nodded reassuringly.

"Take your time," he said. "I'll be back in a little bit."

He gathered Kaylee up into his arms. The girl let out a soft sigh and snuggled closer. Morgan's smile faded. She'd kept him here all night when he should have been with his daughter. His eyes softened as if he read her thoughts. He opened his mouth but hesitated, then smiled. A real smile making her knees go weak.

She slipped into the bathroom and closed the door behind her. She leaned against it for a moment. Deja vu flitted through her. This room was larger than the one on the sub. And it had a large walk-in shower. Her eyes widened. And the holiest of holy grails, a toothbrush.

A good rest, a hot shower, and clean teeth. Her grandmother's prescription for everything ailing a person, and of course, food. One step at a time.

She brushed her teeth first, eager to be rid of the bad taste in her mouth. Then she showered. The water pressure was perfect, and the hot water worked wonders on her aching muscles. She felt nearly human again as she dried off and dressed in the clothes Li had left for her.

The navy–blue jumpsuit was more comfortable than it looked. The Leviathan eye logo was embroidered in white on the left side. She traced it with her finger. All this built from one man's obsession.

Casper Bishop. The not so friendly ghost.

The base itself was incredible. At least what little she'd seen. And the teeth ... those teeth had belonged to something large. Daniel had always believed something could be hidden in the deep. Sea monster sightings had dropped dramatically around the age of steam travel. His theory suggested the creatures avoided the boats and were seen less because they could hear them coming.

The theory had merit. Hawaii had laws requiring boats to idle their engines when not moving, so whales would know they were in the area. Which made sense. But a mosasaur? Incredible. She wanted another look at the evidence and the results from the model. Whether or not the mosasaur did exist, perhaps she could use the data to convince Bishop to let her go looking in the same direction as Daniel. Maybe she could find him, or at least find some closure. A good plan, or at least the start of one.

She gathered her hair into a ponytail and stared at her face in the mirror. Her eyes were red-rimmed and still slightly swollen from the night before. Faint dark circles stood out against her skin, and she wished she had her makeup. But at least she didn't look like the walking dead anymore. Even if she still felt like it.

Her stomach rumbled. Food first. Monsters next. She opened the door and hesitated. Kaylee was waiting for her. The little girl gave Morgan an impish smile from her perch on the foot of the bed.

The girl held out a thermos. "This is for you. My dad says you need it."

Morgan smiled and accepted the thermos. "Thank you."

This was definitely Catlett's kid.

"I'm Morgan."

Kaylee jumped off the bed and took her hand. "I know," she said with the bravado of a six-year-old. "Come with me."

Morgan bit her lip against her laugh. Apparently, she had no choice in the matter. The girl pulled her out into the corridor and turned to the left.

"You have a horse named Sleuth," Kaylee said, as she waved at Li and the doctor waved them on with a giggle. "That's a weird name."

This time she did laugh. "His name is actually Sleuth's Enigma. It means something like a detective's mystery."

Kaylee looked up at her, her eyes serious. "That is weirder."

Morgan nodded, "I supposed it is."

"Come on!" Kaylee suddenly doubled her speed, dragging Morgan along behind her.

"If I come to your house, can I ride him?" Kaylee said.

Morgan wondered what the likelihood of that would be. She shoved the dark thoughts aside as she hurried to keep up.

"Sure," she said. "He would love you."

She hoped he was okay, and he'd made it home. She hoped he didn't miss her too much, and someone would love him. Kaylee pulled her around a corner, into a quieter corridor. She stopped beside a door and pressed her small hand against the pad.

"Do you like waffles?" the girl said.

Her stomach grumbled, and Kaylee giggled.

Morgan laughed. "I do like waffles."

The door slid open, and Kaylee tugged her inside. "Come see my dragons."

The little girl pulled her through a comfortable looking living area, and then into every little girl's dream for a bedroom. If every little girl dreamed of mermaids and sea creatures. The walls were a soft blue with swirls of turquoise and pink, and the bed was draped in pinks and blues and shaped to look like a giant shell.

Kaylee released her hand and hurried over to a cylindrical tank set against the far corner of the room. A pair of golden sea dragons drifted inside a small forest of seaweed. Morgan knelt beside the tank.

"Aren't they magical?" Kaylee whispered.

"Yeah, they sure are." She would have loved to have a pair when she was a kid.

She'd had access to various creatures and had visited practically every major aquarium in the world with her mother, but she'd always wanted a tank of her own, one with more than just a few hermit crabs. A green light flashed beside the tank.

"Watch this!" Kaylee pressed the button, and a stream of pink brine shrimp shot into the tank.

"Pretty cool." Morgan stood carefully, easing the pressure on her sore back.

A shelf filled with models caught her eye. Models of large ocean creatures. A killer whale. An octopus. A giant squid. And a large mosasaur, nearly a third of the size of the little girl. Kaylee darted over to it and pulled it down.

"This is my favorite one," Kaylee said, "It's a mosasaur." She said the word slowly, carefully pronouncing the word. She handed it to Morgan. "Grandpa said it was the monster that ate my grandma. A long time ago."

The words were matter of fact, as if it were simply the truth. Morgan's stomach twisted. What kind of person would tell such a horrible story to a child? A faint noise came from the door, and she turned to find Catlett leaning against the frame.

"All right, ladies, come and eat while the waffles are hot."

Kaylee squealed and ran for the door. Catlett caught her, flipped her upside down, and tickled her.

"Go wash your hands, little monster." He flipped her right-side up and pressed a loud kiss to her head.

Kaylee laughed and pushed him away. "Okay, Daddy, okay."

She squirmed out of his arms and disappeared around the corner. His smile was breathtaking, and Morgan's butterflies returned as he turned it on her.

"I'm sorry about your mother," she said.

His smile dimmed. Way to dredge up the past. Her face burned as she looked away and returned the model to its place on the shelf. He moved beside her, his eyes on the toy.

"She loved to sail," he said, quietly. "My father bought her the yacht for their anniversary. She was so excited."

His words were warm, his gaze far away, lost in a memory. "They left the day after my tenth birthday. I was supposed to join them in Sydney at the end of the school term, but they were gone before I could." Sadness crept into his tone. "The search went on for days …"

Tears pricked at Morgan's eyes, for the loss of that ten-year-old boy. For her own loss.

"I lost them both that day," he said. "My mother to the sea, and my father to his obsession."

The tears slipped free, and she shivered, her own wound too fresh. How many others had suffered in the wake of Bishop's obsession? Catlett's hand touched her arm. He was so close. She squeezed her eyes shut, fighting the urge to melt into him. She folded her arms across her chest. His hand fell away.

"I'm sorry, Morgan," he said. "For getting you into this mess."

A small laugh slipped from her lips, pained and sharp. "Something tells me it would have happened regardless."

"It shouldn't have. And I'm sorry."

She swallowed hard. He wasn't to blame. He was just as much a pawn in this twisted game as she was. He let out a small oof and jostled into her. His hand caught her shoulder before falling away.

"Kaylee." He growled, playfully.

A muffled giggle erupted. He stepped away and spun around, and the giggle exploded into a shriek.

"Morgan, help!"

A faint smile tugged at her lips at the sound of Catlett's deep laughter. She brushed her tears from her face, roughly.

"She can't save you. No one can. Bwahahaha!"

Morgan's smile widened. "Wanna bet?"

She moved quickly, and neatly extracted Kaylee from Catlett's grip. The girl dropped to the ground with a cheer and slipped behind Morgan, using her as a shield. His look of surprise faded into something deeper, and his eyes darkened as he took a step toward them. She narrowed her eyes.

"Give me the kid."

"Not a chance." She shuffled them back a step. "You'll have to go through me first."

Her heart fluttered as his gaze swept her from head to toe, assessing. She raised an eyebrow in challenge. Kaylee laughed, and her hands tightened in the back of Morgan's jumpsuit, tugging her backward. Catlett stalked toward them. She felt the blood rush to her face, but held his gaze, unflinching. What the heck was she doing?

"Last chance." His voice was low.

There was a soft thump behind her, and she stumbled back, stars shooting through her vision as her shoulders hit the wall, sending a flash of pain up her neck and through her head. Kaylee gave a muffled squeak but didn't loosen her grip. All playfulness fell from Catlett's face.

"I give up," he said. His voice was light, but his eyes were concerned. "Kaylee, let her go. It's time to eat."

His hands gently caught her elbows, steadying her, as Kaylee slipped by and darted out of the room, giggling. Morgan' eyes clenched shut. She forced herself to breathe, and then again, riding the pain.

"Are you okay?" he said.

She gave a small nod. She'd had worse, like the time Sleuth had refused a jump and she'd gone over the fence without him. Broken collarbone and three cracked ribs. She exhaled slowly, and the pain faded into a dull throb. She let out a slow breath, and opened her eyes, her face flushed. His eyes were rimmed in a lighter blue. She hadn't noticed the contrast before. Of course, she hadn't been this close to him until now.

"Come on, you guys!" Kaylee's voice startled Morgan, breaking her trance.

Her face grew warmer as she relaxed her grip on his shirt, leaving a wrinkled patch behind. She brushed at one until her brain caught up with her actions. His eyes were dark when she looked up, his face unreadable. His hands fell away as she stepped back. Her stomach growled.

"I heard there were waffles?" Her voice barely above a whisper.

Catlett stepped back. His grin returned as he waved her toward the door.

"And coffee," he said, collecting her abandoned thermos from the floor.

He gave it a swish and raised an eyebrow. She ignored him and headed for the door. At this rate, her face was going to be permanently stained red.

His voice trailed her wake. "You do like coffee?"

"Shut up."

Kaylee looked up from her waffle. "You're not supposed to say that. It isn't kind." She patted the seat beside hers. "Sit here."

"Don't be bossy, little miss." Catlett said with a laugh. He pressed a kiss to his daughter's hair and extracted the bottle of syrup from her hands. "And that is more than enough. Your teeth are going to rot out of your head."

Kaylee giggled at her father and patted the seat again. "Sit here, please."

Morgan eased her body into the chair. She forced herself to relax and smiled at Kaylee, and her syrup-soaked waffle.

"Mmmm! Looks tasty," Morgan said.

Catlett dropped a waffle onto the plate in front of her and then filled her mug with coffee. She took it with a smile. There were chocolate chips, real whipped cream, and rainbow sprinkles, which Kaylee was shaking over her waffle. Not a fish or sea-related food in sight, so obviously deliveries were being made.

"Do you like sprinkles?" Kaylee said.

"I love sprinkles."

The girl grinned and, without asking first, shook some onto Morgan's waffle before giving her father's the same treatment. Morgan hid her smile behind her mug. The coffee was excellent.

"So how big is Atlantis?" The name was still beyond weird to say.

"It holds at least fifty scientists and support staff," Catlett said. "Crew quarters, twenty laboratories, two docking bays, a mess hall with a kitchen—"

"I can show you around if you want." Kaylee waved her fork before stabbing it back into her waffle with a flourish. "Dr. Fritz is cool. He studies fish that glow in the dark. It's called bio-lumin-es-cence," she said carefully and seriously. "Dr. Titov works with him. She studies minerals in the water, and she likes cats."

The roster continued. Mr. Steve fixed pipes and submarines. Chef Mater made pizzas and the best French fries. Morgan grinned and nodded, her thoughts grasping at what Catlett had said. Fifty ... there were fifty people on this base. She wondered if they had come willingly, or if they'd been "invited" as she had been. She sipped her coffee.

This wasn't the time to ask. Not with Kaylee here. Catlett was watching her. She busied herself with her waffle, which was amazing.

"Dr. Yang and Daniel are the coolest though. They're helping Grandpa find his sea monster."

Morgan choked. She fumbled for her mug and took a gulp, sputtering as it burned a path down her throat.

"Dr. Yang?" She wheezed.

Catlett took the mug and pressed a glass of water into her hand. She downed half of it.

"Yeah, he's Daniel's friend." Kaylee said, oblivious to the look Morgan shot Catlett.

Dr. Yang was alive? Catlett gave her a small nod in response to her unspoken question. So, if everything had gone according to plan, Daniel's death would have been faked in Iowa? She felt the blood drain from her face. Had hers been faked? A hand gripped hers, and she forced herself to breathe. Kaylee rambled on.

"But they left a couple days ago on a submarine, so I've been helping Dr. Fritz."

The knot in her chest twisted, hard. A hand gripped her arm gently, pulling her to her feet.

"We're going to get more coffee." Catlett's voice sounded as if it were coming from a distance. "We will be right back. Finish your waffle, Princess, and please add some fruit, okay?"

He slid his arm around her as they moved through a doorway into a smaller room. Blood rushed in her ears, loud and dizzying. What if they thought she was dead? Daniel was gone, and she was never going to see them again.

"You're okay."

She was so far from okay. She couldn't even control her own body. He pulled her into his arms, and she let him. She pressed her forehead against his shoulder.

"You're okay," he repeated, his voice soothing. "Just breathe."

She forced herself to, matching her breaths to the rise and fall of his chest. His hand gently rubbed circles against her back.

"Does my family think I'm dead?" The thought sounded worse out loud.

His arms tightened, and he rocked them gently. "I don't know."

Anger flashed through her, and she grasped it and let it burn. She pushed him away and paced the small kitchen. He leaned back against the counter, his eyes tracking her, but she kept her own eyes on the deck. He was a victim too, right?

"How many people," she said, "are here of their own free will?"

"I'm not sure."

She spun to face him, her eyes pinning his. "Guess."

He combed his hand roughly through his hair and shrugged.

"Most of them?" he said. "It was pitched as a long-term, top-secret assignment. Once you are here, you stay. No contact with the outside world."

So, they were all trapped. In this giant, impossible, scientist-sized mousetrap.

"How is something this big even possible?"

"Anything one man can imagine; other men can make real." His words were dry, with a hint of irony.

"Don't quote Jules Verne at me," she said. "How is this base a secret? I mean, with all the maintenance, the supplies, the staffing ..." And what about supply runs? A contingent of fifty would need food, clothes, lab equipment, medical supplies, etc. Also, what about where and how the structure had been constructed in the first place?

"Expansive network," Catlett said. Like those two words explained everything.

Then again, maybe they did. She recalled his warning about the FBI, and his father's connections, and the extent of a network over twenty years in the making. This was insane and truly terrifying.

"What happened to Agent Blake?" she said.

"I don't know." But his eyes said otherwise.

"She's dead."

He sighed through his nose, regret in his eyes. "Probably. They don't leave loose ends."

Morgan's stomach rolled. She slumped back against the counter opposite him and as far away as she could get. Her mind spun through scenario after scenario. None of them were good.

A thought struck her.

"If Daniel was so intent on keeping me out of this, why did he write your father's name in his book? In code."

Her eyes flickered to Catlett's face in time to catch the flash of guilt. She froze in her tracks. No. Way. And yet, it was written all over his face.

"You wrote it." Her voice shrill.

"Morgan." He motioned for her to stay calm.

She smacked his hand away. "You wrote his name. Bishop, Knight, Pawn." His words from what felt like eons ago.

"It seems wisest to assume the worst from the beginning, and let anything better come as a surprise," he said quietly.

Another Verne quote, this one from *The Mysterious Island*. The very book Daniel had hidden the key in. Daniel's data. She'd seen it on Bishop's screen. Betrayal flooded through her. She leveled her finger at him. No more surprises.

"Did you steal Daniel's data?"

An alarm ripped through the room, earsplitting and nerve shattering, and the world washed in red.

CHAPTER TWENTY-FOUR

Her head spun from the surge of adrenaline. Her hands shot to her ears, and her eyes locked on Catlett's. Kaylee barreled through the door; her hands pressed over her ears. Catlett caught her up into his arms and grabbed Morgan's elbow and pulled her through the door into the main room. A screen on the wall was blinking. Catlett released her and pressed a button. The siren fell silent, but the light remained. Kaylee whimpered.

Morgan stepped closer, scanning the message as it scrolled across the screen. Medical emergency in the primary sub bay. Medical teams were to report to the bay immediately. All nonessential personnel were to remain in their labs or quarters.

Hope flickered to life. Daniel's sub.

"Where is the sub bay?" she said.

"Morgan—"

She found a button on the bottom of the screen, labelled 'map'. The screen shimmered as she pressed it. A map appeared, showing the path from Catlett's quarters, not too far from the bay. She turned for the door, dodging his hand as he reached for her.

"Morgan, wait!"

But she was already out the door. The noise in the hallway was deafening. Red lights washed the corridor in an eerie hue, like something straight out of every disaster movie she'd ever seen. She slid to a stop as the passage ended. Right or left? Was it right or left? A hand closed over hers, and Catlett tugged her toward the left, Kaylee still wrapped around him. Guilt flickered through her at the terror in the little girl's eyes.

She pulled her hand free and sprinted ahead as she sighted Dr. Li and the medical team. She followed them through a wide hatch and into a larger room. The air was damp and smelled like salt. Catlett caught her and pulled her to the side, as a team rushed through, wheeling several large boxes on a cart. She watched as the men followed the medical team up a ramp and through another hatch.

The alarms fell silent, but the lights remained. She shook her arm free and followed them, into the bay of a huge submarine.

"Ms. Sullivan." Bishop's voice echoed through the vast space, delight in his tone. "Welcome aboard the Leviathan."

Leviathan? How unoriginal. She stepped back as he approached. His eyes were lit with a fanatical enthusiasm.

"Your timing is very opportune," he said. "We've just received a signal from our missing sub, and you won't believe what they've sent."

"He's alive?" The surge of hope left her dizzy.

Bishop waved a hand. "Yes, yes, we believe so. The ship is damaged, but they were alive when the message was sent, less than an hour ago. But that isn't the most exciting part."

Anger flashed through her. "You know where they are?"

He pressed a tablet into her hands. "If you would like to accompany me, we will find the creature together."

"What—" Her words failed as she stared at the screen. A thrill of fear, deep and primal, ran through her. An eye glinted up at her. A ginormous eye. Yellow, reptilian, with a gleam of intelligence. Resurrected from the depths of time itself. The logo looked like a child's drawing compared to this.

She stared in shock. Daniel had found it. He'd found the mosasaur. She tapped the screen and watched intently as the video played. Bioluminescent lights winked and swirled, illuminating the edges of a large dark shadow as it neared the camera. She could make out a faint outline. Long snout, tapered flippers, tail ... A bright light pierced the water suddenly, illuminating the creature as it turned sharply and swept by—a row of long jagged teeth, black hide weathered and rough. When the light reached the eye, the creature's head swung toward the screen. The camera jostled violently, and the image went dark.

Her heart pounded. They'd been attacked. By a mosasaur.

"Do you have the sub's last known location?"

"I do," Bishop said. "You will help me find it?"

His words cut through her. The fanatical gleam in his eyes shone brighter. She had a feeling the 'it' he was referring to was not the missing sub. She shifted her focus back to the screen in an effort to hide the disgust in her eyes.

"Yes. I will." If there was the slightest chance Daniel was alive, she owed it to him to try.

"Splendid. Follow me." Bishop waved a hand toward another hatch. He turned without looking back and strode toward it. "Prepare to launch."

She looked over her shoulder for Catlett, but he was nowhere to be found. The deck hummed beneath her feet. She clutched the tablet and hurried after Bishop. They had Daniel's data and her model. If she could feed the sub's path into the system, she could use it to find them and still convince Bishop she would find his monster, and possibly save Daniel.

"Let's hope you are worth the hype, love." Ian appeared on her right, a cold smirk on his face.

She had barely registered Ian's words before the man was slammed into a bulkhead. She was pushed backward as the narrow corridor was swarmed with black jumpsuits and big guns.

"Enough." Bishop's command resonated through the space.

The crowd parted. Catlett hauled Ian upright, his hands still gripping his jumpsuit. She couldn't see his face, but Ian's eyes were murderous.

Bishop appeared at her side. "I must apologize for my sons, Ms. Sullivan."

She stared in surprise. Sons? Oh, this was just getting better and better. Catlett whispered something into his brother's ear and then shoved him into the wall before stepping back. His eyes met his father's, and the air crackled with tension.

"I will leave you behind," Bishop said coolly. "Both of you."

"It's what you're good at." Catlett muttered.

Bishop turned without another word and stalked down the passage. Ian glared at them as he followed.

"He's your brother?" she said, as they followed several paces behind.

His hand rested against her lower back, protectively.

"Half. Long story. Not now." His eyes blazed.

The deck beneath her feet shuddered. She grasped his arm as she caught her balance. They were really doing this.

"Where's Kaylee?"

His jaw tightened. "She's on the base. Safe. Where you should be."

Fat chance. Not while his father was planning to abandon the search for Daniel to hunt a very real sea monster.

"No one asked you to come," she said.

His hand gripped her arm as he pulled her to the side of the corridor. The emotion in his cobalt eyes stole her breath. His mask had cracked, and she saw it all. His fear, his anger and something she wasn't certain she was ready to define. His lips were white, pressed into a thin bloodless line, as if he didn't trust himself to speak. His hand trembled.

"Scott, it's real." Her use of his name seemed to catch him off guard. She held up the tablet. "Daniel found it. The creature, it's real."

He released her and stepped back, rubbing his hand hard against his face and through his hair.

"Help me find him," she said. "Help me find Daniel. Please."

He was the only one who might. She could try to do it alone, but she might not succeed without him. He knew this world. He knew Bishop. She didn't.

Catlett sighed and waved a hand in the direction Bishop had gone. She fell into step beside him. His hand returned to her back, and she relaxed a little.

They followed the bustle of activity up a narrow flight of stairs and through another wide hatch. The bridge was bigger than she'd expected. Bishop was standing at the railing which separated what appeared to be the command deck from the lower deck. A massive view port curved before them; lights glowed dimly beyond the inky black of the sea.

"Take us out," Bishop said.

"Aye, aye, Skipper," came the reply from the deck below.

Morgan caught hold of the railing as the ship shifted and the thrum beneath her feet intensified, and the sub moved away from the base. She watched in wonder as the lights grew brighter and took shape.

"Beautiful, isn't she?" Bishop said.

The view was breathtaking. The base glowed from its cradle, on supports holding it suspended above the sea floor. She couldn't tell how far down they went. The structure spiraled, like a shell, spinning outward in a graceful shape. Beautiful and impossible all at the same time. The ocean was an inky black beyond the reach of the lights. As if they were in space, instead of water.

The scene before her was like watching a sci-fi movie, with less CGI effect. Or safety. They rose above the structure, and she watched as the base was swallowed by the darkness.

"All ahead full," Bishop said.

The words were echoed from the lower deck. The base vanished from view, and the sea turned an impenetrable black, like staring into a dark pit. She half expected the creature to appear suddenly from the gloom. A hint of nausea swirled in the pit of her stomach. She swallowed hard as she looked away.

"How big is this sub?" she said, praying it was larger than the creature.

"One hundred and fifty meters from stem to stern, give or take a few." Bishop grinned. "More than enough to take on the sea monster."

Okay, good. They were too big to swallow, then. If it was a mosasaur, the common belief was it could unhinge its jaws like a snake. At 450 feet long, the sub was more than big enough to take on the mosasaur, even if were around 100 feet long. Or at least she hoped.

"This way, Ms. Sullivan," Bishop said.

She followed him through a door at the rear of the bridge and into a smaller room which mirrored his office on the base, with the exception of a large oval table in the place of a desk. Bishop crossed to a large screen nearly the full length of the bulkhead. The screen came to life as he touched it, displaying a highly detailed bathymetric map of the South Pacific. One with more detail than she'd ever seen before.

She took a step closer as he tapped it again, and Daniel's data splayed across it, like a fluorescent disease.

"Your work is quite impressive, Ms. Sullivan," Bishop said. "I had suspected the creature's path followed the trenches, but I hadn't realized how close it had crossed to the vicinity of my base, until now. How close it has been, all this time."

He sounded almost wistful. And hateful. Obsessive. This Ahab was determined to get his whale. The original story had not ended well for Ahab or his crew. Bishop had already sacrificed his relationship with his son for his obsession and destroyed countless lives. How much further was he willing to go? What else would he sacrifice?

"Where is the base?" she said. There were no markers on the screen other than the data points from her model.

Bishop turned and smiled. She suppressed a shiver.

"You must allow me some secrets, Ms. Sullivan." He tapped the corner of the screen, and a thin yellow line appeared, tracking along the edge of the Tonga Trench, the second deepest ocean trench in the world. "Here is the path your uncle's expedition took." He tapped the screen again, and a blue point appeared in the center, where it met the Kermadec Trench. "And this is, approximately, their last known position."

She folded her arms across her chest. "All that tells me is they followed the trench. I'm assuming your base, for safety reasons, isn't located near this highly seismically active area. In fact, if I had to guess, I'd say it is probably located further to the north. Say somewhere between Guam and Hawaii."

She really had no idea, but it was a sound guess. He was crazy enough to have it positioned near the trenches and the creature, but shrewd enough to want his investment to be safe and hidden. Which still left a lot of ocean floor. The many possibilities would take days to cover, time Daniel didn't have. Bishop chuckled.

"We are tracking the sub's path as we speak, Ms. Sullivan," he said. "I will find the sub, if you find my monster."

"I have your word on that?" For what it was worth.

He gave her an exaggerated nod. "Upon my honor, I will find it."

"Then I will do my best to find the creature."

His lips quirked into a cold smile. "See that you do."

He offered his hand, and she took it. Had she just made a deal with the devil? Bishop released her hand and headed for the door.

"You shall have whatever you require. Just ask."

Except for the location of the base, apparently. She watched him leave the room. The hatch clanked closed behind him, and the sound resonated through her. Like a death knell. She sighed and moved over to the console.

"I must be insane." She tapped the screen. The screen was fancy but not exactly work friendly. This was going to take forever.

"Crazy people don't think they're crazy," Catlett said. "Take my father, for instance."

She snorted and glanced over at him.

"I don't suppose you know where the base is?"

He shrugged. "I'm what he considers untrustworthy."

She shook her head. There was a faint clank of hard plastic against wood, and she turned to find a keyboard and mouse on the round table. She smiled. Perfect.

"You are amazing." She plopped into a chair and fixed her attention on the screen. She slid the tablet in the direction of his voice, not daring to look at him. "You need to see this." Anything to draw attention from her rapidly darkening blush. "It's from Daniel's sub."

While he was distracted, she familiarized herself with the workings of Bishop's system. It was a bit like her own, in fact more than a little. This looked like he'd pirated the data straight from her server, and not from Daniel's drives. She zoomed out a global scale and beamed. They didn't have Daniel's data, just those points she and Keoni had put into the model. A small victory.

She zoomed back to the South Pacific and toggled the data to draw in chronological order. The data was spotty and widespread. Not a perfect setup, but it might give her enough to work with. At least enough to convince Bishop. A thrill of excitement laced through her as she began to make out a definite pattern.

Daniel's data ended with a sighting in early 2005, but when combined with what she knew of the path of the ill-fated expedition, it looked as if the creature might have a definite migratory path. The spacing of the points was ... interesting. Almost as if ... her eyes widened.

"Oh, wow," she said. "I think there might be more than one."

CHAPTER TWENTY-FIVE

The words came out in a whisper, as if saying them any louder might attract the creatures to them. Assuming the creatures still existed, but then again, Daniel's video provided definitive proof at least one did. And if there was one, there had to be more, right? There was no way only one had lived for thousands of years. There had to be at least two if not more to keep the species thriving.

She glanced at Catlett, and her excitement ebbed. His face was pale.

"Scott?"

His finger flicked against the tablet, and the wall screen was replaced with the image of the giant eye. She shuddered. Seeing it at this scale somehow made it even more real. He tapped a key, and the video began to play, in slow motion.

"My father was right all this time." He pressed his hand over his mouth.

She bit her lip. Stupid. Why hadn't she considered the full implications before she'd acted so callously? She'd thought with the teeth, he might have already accepted the existence of the creature. But it was one thing to see a tooth, and another to have video proof of the monster that killed his mother.

"I'm sorry." She said, quietly.

She sat back and stared at the creature. The image didn't tell her much more than it was large and reptilian. The image fizzed out before the creature passed. There was no way to know its size or even type.

Or was there?

She watched intently as the video restarted. And there it was, an outline of the snout. She bit her lip, debating whether to ask. Before she could, Catlett squeezed her hand gently and passed the tablet to her. He stood and moved toward the far corner of the room, his back to the screen.

She waited for a moment, but he didn't seem to want to talk. Even if they found the creature, it wouldn't undo a lifetime of hurt and loss. This wouldn't bring his mother back. She let out a quiet sigh and picked up the tablet. She tried to lighten the image. The software wasn't great, but she managed to make it a little clearer. She watched intently as the muzzle glided into view and hit pause.

Her breath caught. There was a bulbous tip at the end of the nose, jutting out over the teeth, like a massive overbite. Oh, that figured ... if there were one to survive, of course it would be the biggest, and the deadliest. The hatch clanked open behind her.

"It's a Tylosaurus," she said, expecting Bishop.

"Its name is Tyler?" a small voice said from the doorway.

Morgan hit the power button on the tablet, and the image vanished from the screen. Her heart sank as she turned and looked at the girl.

"Kaylee Mae Catlett." Catlett's words held no anger, only resignation.

The girl darted over to the table and slid beneath it. Hiding.

"I just wanted to see it." Her voice was small and a little defiant.

His laugh was strangled. Morgan turned toward him, but his back was to her, his shoulders rigid and his fingers tangled in his hair. He turned and stalked across the room and through the hatch. Morgan ducked her head under the table to where Kaylee was huddled in the corner and motioned to the girl. She scrambled to her and crawled up into her lap. Morgan hugged her close, rocking her gently.

"I wanted to go with my daddy," Kaylee said, sobs shaking her small body. "I didn't want him to leave me."

Morgan's heart ached at the girl's words.

"Shh …" she said, pressing a kiss to the girl's head, "It's going to be okay. Your daddy loves you so much. You just scared him. He wants you to be safe."

The door closed behind them with a quiet click.

"Kaylee."

Morgan's chest hurt. Tears blurred her eyes as Catlett knelt in front of her, a stricken look in his eyes. This was all her fault. She was the reason he'd left Kaylee on the base. To keep them both safe. All her fault …

"I'm sorry, Daddy." Kaylee sobbed. "I just wanted …"

"Come here, baby." He held out his arms, and his daughter slid from Morgan's lap and into them. He gathered her close and stood. "I love you so much. I just want you to be safe." Tears streaked his face as he pressed a kiss to her hair. "I'm so sorry."

She read it all in his eyes. The torture his father put him through, put his own granddaughter through. Catlett had never wanted to leave his daughter. He hadn't been given a choice. Guilt swept through her. She had only caused them both further pain. How was she any better than Bishop?

She scrubbed the tears roughly from her face and opened the hatch. The bridge was in chaos. Lights flashed but no alarms sounded. She edged closer to the railing, eyes on the view screen. Two beams of light sliced through the dark water, illuminating a small cylinder resting on a ledge at the precipice of a dark canyon. Hope flared to life.

"Morgan!" She tore her eyes from the screen to find Li beside her. The doctor grabbed her arm. "They found Daniel's sub. Come with me."

Morgan looked back at the screen, but the sub was gone and ocean beyond the viewing port dark. She ran after Li, following her through corridor after corridor and through a double hatch until they reached an open bay as wide as the one she'd seen when first boarding the Leviathan. This one held a moon pool, a large one. A large crowd was clustered on the edge of the platform. Li grabbed her hand and pulled her.

"Medical team coming through," Li said. "Make a hole."

The whine of heavy machinery filled the room. Morgan watched as the small sub appeared slowly beneath the surface, and then breached through as the crane lifted it from the water and onto a cradle. Morgan felt the blood drain from her face as she stumbled to a halt. The tiny sub was practically monster snack sized, and a dent crushed into the side proved it.

A crewmember in an orange jumpsuit clambered up the ladder and tapped the top with a wrench. There was a pause, and then the screech of metal as the hatch on the top popped open. A deafening cheer went up from the crowd. Morgan felt the doctor squeeze her arm, but her eyes were locked on the door as a familiar head of gray hair appeared. The rush of relief left her weak, and at the same time she felt as if she could take flight. Daniel was alive. She watched as he made his way down the ladder to the ground.

"Uncle Daniel!"

Her feet barely touched the deck. She was almost to him before he saw her. His expression shifted from exhaustion to disbelief. She slid to a stop and threw her arms around him and buried her face against his shoulder. He smelled like scorched wires and sweat. He flinched, and she heard a hiss of pain, but he only hugged her tighter when she tried to pull away.

"You are not supposed to be here." His voice was tinged with pain and frustration. He pulled back, his hands gripping her arms, panic in his eyes. "Why are you here?"

"I thought you were dead," she shot back.

He stumbled back a step, as if she'd struck him. She'd never snapped at him before now. Argued, debated, and maybe yelled once, but never snapped. He'd never died and come back before either. Sadness filled his eyes, with an edge of defeat. He pulled her back into his arms and hugged her close.

"Not quite." He pressed a kiss against her hair. "Not quite. I'm so sorry. You were never supposed to be involved."

Her tears wouldn't stop, but for once she just let them fall. He was alive, and nothing else mattered. His arms fell away as she stepped back. His smile, though sad, was genuine.

"It's good to see you, kiddo."

She laughed and hugged him again. His arms tightened, and he tensed. He stepped back suddenly, pulling her behind him, shielding her.

"Bishop, she was off limits." She'd never heard him so angry, ever.

"Conditions changed." Bishop shrugged lightly. "She was the best replacement."

The room fell silent, as all eyes watched the impending standoff.

"Dr. Smithson, sit down before you fall down." Li said, as she appeared beside them.

The doctor calmly pulled Daniel down onto a bench. Morgan sank down beside him. She shot a look toward Li as he cradled his arm against his ribs. His face was too pale and pained. His eyes never left Bishop's.

"Two days." Daniel's words dripped with fury. "We were only out of contact for two days. I can do the math. You broke your word. We had a deal."

She considered the facts. The searches of Daniel's room and office at the college. Ian's offer to buy Daniel's data so soon after she'd found it. Her model with Daniel's data, scrolling across Bishop's screens.

"You were already in our network," she said, calmly, "waiting for me to add the records into the model. But the data I did add wasn't enough. It wasn't the entire set."

"I agreed to help him find his monster." Daniel said. His eyes flashed as he turned them on Bishop. "In agreement that you would leave her out of this."

But Bishop had taken her anyway.

"Your niece has a very particular set of skills." Bishop shoved a tablet into Daniel's hand. "Her computer model combined with your database provided the exact results I was hoping for. I just needed her to confirm the findings for me."

The screen was a mirror copy of the monitor in Bishop's conference room. Of course, he'd been monitoring her progress.

"Your monster is a mosasaur," she said, her words tight and sharp. "A Tylosaurus to be specific. It's thought to have been the largest of the species, the deadliest, and you sent Daniel and his team out in a bite–sized submarine. It could have swallowed them whole."

Bishop smiled. "But it didn't, Ms. Sullivan. I completed my side of our deal and delivered your uncle to you. It is time for you to make good on yours. Where is the creature headed?"

She tore her gaze from his and took the tablet from her uncle.

"Uncle Daniel, where did you encounter the mosasaur?"

Might as well call it what it was. Even though it felt beyond weird. He tapped his finger against the screen at a point just north of their last known location, about midway along the Tonga Trench.

"We were tracking along the inside edge of the trench, at a depth of about 2,000 feet," Daniel said. "It rose up from beneath us. A giant squid came shooting out of the trench, with the creature on its tail. We got caught in its wake but not before we captured the video I sent."

A thrill of excitement laced through her, tangled with a wash of fear.

"We saw the video," she said. "How big do you think it was? I couldn't tell from the clip."

A small smile flickered at the corners of his mouth. A gleam sparked in his eyes. There was her uncle. She smiled faintly.

"It was over eighty feet at least, if not larger." He squeezed her hand. "It was magnificent. It twisted and moved like a hammerhead shark, with long tapered fins and a tail like a thresher, not an eel. It dismissed us entirely until someone triggered the spotlight."

His grin was almost giddy. The monster had nearly killed him, and yet the scientific enthusiasm prevailed. She snorted softly, certain her grin matched his. The discovery was paradigm-shifting. In all honesty, she'd never really believed they'd ever find it, never believed it still existed. But Daniel had. The creature was real, and he'd been right all along.

So had Bishop. Her smile faltered. For a moment, she felt a miniscule of empathy for their captor.

"Eighty feet fits with the tooth Bishop found." She zoomed into the area on the screen. "Which way did it go?"

Daniel winced as Li pressed a butterfly bandage to the gash above his left eye. "North, best I could tell," he said. His eyes met Bishop's. "Check the logs. We have more data than I was able to send out."

Morgan looked up as Bishop spun on his heel and stalked away, waving a hand toward a cluster of orange suited technicians.

"Get a cable into the sub now." His voice was hard, and sharp, with an edge of desperation. "I want that data analyzed immediately."

From what she could see, they were already running several cables into the sub. She scanned the dents in the metal, shifted closer to her uncle.

"Where is Dr. Yang?" she said.

Li glanced up from her bag. "He had a nasty knock to the head. My team took him to the infirmary." She took her pen light and grasped Daniel's chin lightly, holding his face steady as she examined his eyes. "Any dizziness, nausea, or loss of consciousness?"

"None," Daniel said.

Just the gash to his hairline and a variety of bruises in varying shades. Not to mention the injuries he sustained falling from that window, long before he'd gone galivanting under the sea with Captain Nemo. Snow could only cushion so much.

"Looks like your hard head came in handy." Morgan said, dryly.

Daniel chuckled. "Touché."

He was infamous for downplaying injuries. She pinned him with a stare. He returned her stare with a weary grin.

Li smiled and released him. "Well, Dr. Smithson, I do believe you'll live. I'd still like you to come down to the infirmary so I can properly check those ribs."

"I'm fine, Doc."

He was not fine. She could see it in the pinched lines of his face.

Li gave him a stern look. "Okay, but we are going to revisit this when we get back to the base."

"I'll make sure he's there," Morgan said. Daniel shot her a bemused look. She raised an eyebrow. He let out a snort, followed by a wince. "Don't be a martyr."

Li turned her attention to Morgan. "How are you feeling? Any nausea?"

Morgan shook her head. Surprisingly no. Maybe the excitement was distracting her, succeeding where every therapist had not. Maybe her seasickness really was psychosomatic. Daniel's hand tightened around hers, and she squeezed it and pressed her shoulder lightly against his. He'd found her before she'd drowned, in the nick of time, but she never had been able to sail after that. And yet here she was, on a submarine. Leave it to something like a real-life sea monster to break her of it.

"I'd better go check on my team." Li said as she stood and collected her bag. "Try to stay out of trouble."

Morgan waited until she was out of earshot. She shifted to face Daniel. Her eyes locked on his. Questions spun through her mind, but one in particular slipped out first.

"Why'd you jump out the window?"

His expression froze.

Anger simmered through her.

"Don't shut me out again." Her words were clipped, sharp. "There is nothing left to protect me from. Not if the last several months have all been about this." She waved her hand around the room.

"You're right." The pain and the self-loathing in his words twisted her gut. It was unlike him. "I failed to keep you safe."

She sighed heavily. Not the answer she was looking for.

"Uncle Daniel ..." What could she say? That it wasn't his fault?

"I owe you a very long explanation," he said. "Which I promise I will give to you, but not right now. Right now, we need to focus on finding a way out of here."

She searched his eyes for a moment, and finally nodded. "I'll hold you to that."

He gave her an affectionate smile making her chest ache. "I expect nothing less."

She laid her head against his shoulder and squeezed his arm gently. "I'm so glad you aren't dead."

He laughed quietly. "Me too."

She raised her head and settled back beside him. They had to find a way out of this mess.

"Do you know where the base is?"

Her uncle shook his head. "He sent us out with a pilot from his hand-picked goon squad. All I can tell you is it didn't take long to reach the trench. Maybe a couple hours at most."

Bishop had taken even less time to find the sub. Perhaps they'd taken a more direct course. Or maybe the Leviathan was just faster. She tapped the screen, zooming into their supposed location. Without knowing the starting point, and without knowing for sure where the creature was headed, all she could do was make a fair guess.

"Do you have my heading?" Bishop said.

Speak of the devil. She suppressed a flinch at the man's sudden reappearance. She stood and handed him the tablet.

"According to the pattern in the data, the creature should head north along the trench toward Samoa." She tapped the screen. "From there, it will most likely track west toward the Papua New Guinea and then up toward the Mariana Trench. I know that leaves a lot of room for speculation, but I'm doing my best with the data I have."

She summoned every ounce of self-control to keep her tone steady and factual. Anger wouldn't help when dealing with a madman.

Bishop studied the map for a moment. His brow furrowed. "What do you know of the area?"

Morgan looked at Daniel. He gestured for her to continue.

"The section of the trench where Daniel encountered the creature is just above Horizon Deep, the deepest part of the trench at thirty-five thousand feet. The area has a history of seismic activity and has generated tsunamis in the past. Apparently, it is also home to a giant sea creature or creatures."

She spouted off the statistics as if she were reciting a lesson. The Trench was deep, dark, cold, and potentially deadly.

"And you are certain it will follow this path?" He traced an imaginary line between the data points.

Of course, she wasn't sure. They were dealing with a creature no one had seen in many, many, many years. She looked at her uncle, who nodded his agreement, and then turned back to Bishop.

"As certain as I can be."

A tech shouted something from a terminal beside the sub, and Bishop strode away without another word. She thought she saw a hint of worry in his eyes.

"You're welcome," she said. Psychopath.

"Have I ever told you how proud I am of you?" Daniel said.

She snorted as she reclaimed her seat. "I was trained by the best."

"Darn right."

She chuckled. So modest too.

Her smile dimmed. "I thought it would be safe to run your data through the model. Keoni had it on the secure server, but it looks like we were hacked."

Their firewall was supposed to be one of the best. If not, when they got out of there, she was going to have to bring it up with their IT department.

"It's not your fault," he said. "Bishop already had access to the model and the data, he just didn't have your knowledge and understanding of the parameters. Neither did I."

She straightened as a thought struck her. "Do you have access to model output for the rest of the data points?"

He shook his head, and she sank back against the bulkhead. Access to his model might have helped solidify her theory on the existence of more than one. Maybe they'd get a chance to test it later. Provided they survived the next twenty-four hours. One thing at a time. She watched Bishop out of the corner of her eye.

"Why didn't you just tell the FBI everything? About Bishop?

Daniel's face hardened. "I did at first, but something didn't feel right."

"That's why you didn't tell them who Catlett was?"

He nodded. "I would have if I'd thought it might help him get out, but Bishop's network is too interconnected. Telling them would have only put both Catlett and his daughter in greater danger."

"Agent Blake was working for Bishop."

Daniel glanced at her. He looked as if he'd aged ten years in the last ten seconds. She wondered if he'd slept since this whole thing had begun.

"That isn't surprising," he said, quietly.

She didn't mention Catlett suspected the woman was dead. Or their family probably thought they were too. Movement caught her eye, and she bit back a faint smile.

Her voice rose an octave. "And that so-called friend of yours broke my car window."

Daniel's expression went quizzical at the sudden change in topic.

"That was Ian," Catlett said as he joined them.

She met his eyes and arched an eyebrow slowly.

Daniel laughed. "I see you two are getting along."

Yeah. Splendidly.

"Hi, Daniel!" Kaylee waved from her perch on her father's back. Morgan was relieved to see her cheerfulness had returned. "Did you find the monster?"

Morgan's smirk faded swiftly as Daniel struggled to his feet with a wince. He shook his head as she tried to help him. "I'm okay."

Yeah, right, and she was Jacques Cousteau. She met Catlett's concerned look. Daniel ignored them both.

"Hi, kiddo," he said. "Yes, I did find it."

"It was a Tylersaur?" the little girl said, as she slid off Catlett's back and dropped lightly to the floor.

"Yes, it was." Daniel said. He offered his hand, and Catlett took it.

"It's good to see you, Daniel." Though the hesitant look on his face said he expected Daniel to hit him.

Her uncle smiled, warmly. "Likewise."

A bit of the tension faded from the younger man's shoulders. "I did try to keep her out of the way," he said.

Morgan grimaced as Daniel gave her a look.

"But you know how that goes." Catlett smirked.

Daniel sighed dramatically. "Indeed, I do. She's been like this since she was small."

She scoffed, and the two men grinned. She was in no way going to deal with a teamup against her. She didn't much care for the glint in Daniel's eyes as his gaze shifted from her to Catlett and back. She fought against the blush she felt creeping up her neck. She had to put them back on track, now.

"How many creatures did you see in that Trench?"

The levity fell away as Daniel took her abrupt change of topic in stride. Not a lot was known about the mosasaurs, other than what scientists had been able to decipher from their bones. What if they'd hunted in groups? Like alligators?

"Just one, I think," he said. "But we lost our sonar when we were hit."

The deck rumbled beneath their feet. They were on the move again. She stepped closer to Daniel as a contingent of black suited guards surrounded their small group. Ian wasn't with them for once. He was nowhere in the general vicinity in fact. Neither was Bishop.

"The captain requests your presence on the bridge." the leader said. He waved a hand toward the hatch. "If you would."

Like they had a choice.

CHAPTER TWENTY-SIX

Her uncle's face was pinched with pain when they finally reached the bridge. She shot a concerned look over his head at Catlett. There was a level of tension in the room which hadn't been there before. She didn't like this, at all. Bishop was standing in his place at the railing, and Daniel straightened as the man turned to face them.

The ocean beyond the viewing port was dark and foreboding. A vast void of emptiness. Like a vat of ink. Daniel stepped away as Bishop strode toward them. The man's crazed look had calmed, replaced by a look of hard determination.

"Ah, you're just in time. We are heading deeper into the trench. We're going to find this creature and kill it!" Bishop shouted boldly.

The roar of approval from his crew was deafening. Morgan opened her mouth, but snapped it closed as she caught Daniel's eye. He shook his head slightly. There was no point in arguing with a madman.

A voice came from the lower deck. "Lure deployed, Captain."

Lure? Morgan crossed the deck and leaned over the rail, her attention focused on the screen of a large station to the left of the viewing port. A ginger-haired woman in a blue jumpsuit toggled a set of joysticks, her eyes focused on a crosshair on the terminal screen, an infrared image of rocks and craigs, with an occasional flash of fins or tentacles.

"Bring it up on the main screen," Bishop said.

A giant mass skimmed into view a moment later, long tentacles trailing. The edge of a faux giant squid like creature shimmered with a rainbow of bioluminescence. Utterly cool. Must have cost millions.

"Take it down into the trench," Bishop said. "Let's go fishing."

"Absolutely not." Catlett's words were sharp and cutting, with an edge of panic. Morgan tore her eyes from the screen. "You are not going monster hunting with your granddaughter on board."

Her gaze darted to Kaylee who stood wide-eyed beside Daniel.

"But I want to see it!" Kaylee said.

Morgan smothered a smile. The kid was going to make a great scientist one day. If they all lived long enough.

"Take us back to the base," Catlett said. "Or send us in one of the small vehicles."

Morgan shook her head. "She's safer on the Leviathan." She met Catlett's cold stare with a steady gaze. "You saw what it did to Daniel's sub, and that was a glancing blow. If it is a Tylosaurus it could easily swallow half that ship and crush it." She smacked her hands together, miming jaws snapping.

And instantly regretted it, as she remembered Kaylee was watching.

"Take us back." Catlett's tone sent a shiver through her. "You have the data. You know where it is going. Return Kaylee to the base first."

For a moment, Bishop's eyes softened. But only for a moment. He looked out toward the void of the sea, and the crazy crept back into his gaze.

"I can't waste the time," he said. He signaled the guards with a sharp movement of his hand. "Take th—"

He staggered back as Catlett's fist connected with his jaw. Morgan pressed back against the rail as a scuffle ensued between Catlett and the guards. Kaylee whimpered, huddling against Daniel, her face pressed against his side.

Bishop's voice rang out through the bridge. "Enough!"

Everyone froze, including the men who pinned Catlett to the deck. He pulled a handkerchief from his pocket and pressed it against his lip. Morgan watched as Bishop's gaze darted from his son to his granddaughter. She saw regret in his eyes as he turned his attention back to his son. She thought he might bend.

"Put them in the conference room," he said. Then he turned his back to them and his attention to the screen.

"Mom wouldn't have wanted this," Catlett said as they hauled him off the floor. "She would have hated how much pain and destruction you've caused in her name."

Morgan's heart twisted at the look of utter betrayal in his eyes. Bishop stiffened but he said nothing. She stepped closer to Daniel as they followed the others into the conference room. Anger blazed through her as the guards unceremoniously shoved Catlett through the hatch. She pushed her way through them as he rolled up off the floor. The hatch clanked with a loud thud behind them.

"Daddy!"

Catlett braced as the small pink blur slammed into him. He wrapped her in his arms and cradled her close. "I'm okay, baby. I'm sorry."

But his eyes said differently. Tears blurred Morgan's own eyes at the pain in their dark depths. His jaw tightened. He pulled his daughter close, his entire world folded in his arms with no power to protect it.

Anger swirled through her as she stalked to the far side of the room. This whole madness had started because Bishop had lost his wife and now, he was willing to throw away everything he had left. And she had helped him do it. A warm hand squeezed her arm gently, and she turned into her uncle. He hugged her tightly.

"Where shall I go from your Spirit?" Daniel said. Psalm 139. His favorite verse. She relaxed as she listened to the familiar words. "Or where shall I flee from your presence? If I take the wings of the morning, and dwell in the uttermost parts of the sea, even there your hand shall lead me."

Uttermost parts of the sea. Nothing could be more real at this moment.

She sighed as she stepped back. "Bishop is going to kill all of us in his mad obsession."

Daniel squeezed her arm. "Then we're just going to have to find a way to stop him."

Right. Stop him or die trying.

"I need coffee," she said.

He chuckled. "I could do with a cup."

The deck jolted hard beneath them, and a siren spilt through the air. Her hands flew out, catching the edge of the table before she slammed into it. The room steadied, and the alarm fell silent a moment later, but red lights remained.

Her eyes swept the room. "Everyone okay?"

"We're okay." Catlett said.

Morgan's eyes shot to Daniel's. "Did we hit something?"

A thrill of excitement, tinged with fear, rose in her. Maybe they'd found the creature. A sharp set of clicks echoed through the room, like the creaking of a boat mooring. They increased to the steady rhythm of a drum. Deep and loud. The sound was familiar.

"Is that a whale?" she said.

This didn't sound like the whoops and whistles of the humpbacks frequenting Hawaii. This was different, something she'd only heard from recordings.

Daniel nodded. "Sounds like a sperm whale."

Catlett stood and moved to the table. He tapped the keyboard, and the blank wall was replaced with a live video feed. The image was washed with an eerie green glow. As they watched, a large dark shape glided into view. A sperm whale.

"Well, call me Ishmael," Morgan said as the whale shot toward the lure with one powerful swish of its tail.

"Your name is Morgan," Kaylee's voice piped up from the back.

Morgan swallowed her laugh as her eyes strayed to the numbers scrolling across the bottom of the screen. Her throat went dry.

"We're at three thousand feet," she said.

"How's the whale here, then?" Catlett said.

They watched as the lure did a looping spiral around the whale and shot back toward them. A shiver ran through her at the raw power of the whale. Magnificent.

"The sperm whale can dive to a depth of over 7,300 feet," she said. "It can hold its breath for an hour and a half."

Another click rippled through the vessel, louder than before, joined by a series of more clicks. Morgan could feel the vibrations in her bones. There was a theory the whales used the sound for echolocation, like dolphins, but the clicks of a sperm whale could shatter a diver's ear drums. The whale was testing something. Maybe the submarine.

The whale turned and thrust upwards, but before it could vanish, a second equally large mass crossed into the camera's view. A thrill of terror pierced through her, raw and deep, as a massive jaw closed around the tail of the whale. The mosasaur. The creature's head thrashed like a crocodile as the whale struggled against it.

"Uncle Daniel ..." Her hand closed around his arm; her eyes locked on the screen.

"I see it, kiddo. I see it."

Her eyes met his and she laughed. She gave his arm a shake. Her heart pounded. "You were right. You were so right."

They watched the terrible dance of the titans on the viewing screen. A dark cloud of water billowed up toward them. The whale gave a fight, and the creatures moved upward. She traced the silhouette of the mosasaur with her eyes as it glided past the screen. Massive and ancient, she held her breath as its tail swished by. A thresher shape, like a shark, as opposed to a long and slender one, like an eel.

"Well, that backs that theory." Daniel said, with glee. "Look at that!"

Morgan laughed. "Do you know what this means for science?"

A living breathing fossil. A tremor surged through the decking, and a bright flash of light washed the camera, then another. The room trembled and the view screen went dark.

"What was that?"

She sobered as she caught sight of Catlett's face, and Kaylee clutched in his arms, looking terrified.

"That was a torpedo," Catlett said. "He said he wanted to kill it."

Something told her it wouldn't be so easy.

"Can you get the cameras back up?" Daniel said.

Just as he asked, the viewing screen blinked on. This time displaying a different feed. This camera appeared to be from the bridge viewing port, just beneath the nose of the sub. A large dark mass sank past the camera into the abyss of the trench below.

"That's the whale," Daniel said. "See the flippers? There are only two."

Then where was the mosasaur? A low odd noise vibrated through the speakers, and her body trembled.

"Everyone brace yourselves!" She grasped her uncle's arm as the camera's view was filled with large teeth. They braced against the table as the creature struck the sub. The room shook. She could hear the creaking of metal, and muffled shouts from the bridge.

"Did you see that?" Daniel waved an arm emphatically at the now empty view screen. "Two rows of teeth."

She laughed, despite the fear. "Yeah, I saw it."

The low noise returned, and the sub jerked violently. Okay, this wasn't fun anymore. The greatest find of the century was worth nothing if they didn't live to prove its existence.

She watched as the mosasaur swept by. "Apparently the ramming theory is true, too."

"You owe me ten bucks," Daniel said.

She shot him an incredulous look, before she remembered the bet she'd made with him when she was a kid. She snorted.

"I'll buy you a shaved ice if we live through this."

"Deal," He took her hand and shook it.

"You two are crazy."

She looked to Catlett a bemused look on his face. She shrugged. Kaylee giggled.

"Pot, kettle," she shot back as she shifted her attention back to the screen. The room rocked again. "I think it's testing us. Think the sub can take it?"

According to Bishop the sub was large enough to prevent the creature from getting its jaws around them, but was it built to be rammed? Repeatedly? As if the mosasaur could read her thoughts, the deck trembled again. A new siren pierced the air.

"Maybe not." She could barely hear Catlett's shout over the noise.

She shot a glance toward him as he dropped into a chair. Kaylee had buried her head into his chest, her hands clamped firmly over her ears. His attention was on the screen, and his fingers flew over the keys. The view was replaced with a schematic of the ship. A section near the aft was blinking red, another toward the stern was orange. The shape of the sub was like none she'd ever seen before. Almost like ...

"Is this thing shaped like a giant mosasaur?"

"Yep," Catlett said.

Of course, it was. The room convulsed yet again and another section of the hull blinked red. Which answered her question about whether it was built for ramming. She glanced at the numbers at the corner of the screen. Nearing 3,200 ft. There was a whine, and the decking trembled and tilted. She gripped the table, her gaze locked on the numbers. And now they were going up.

"We're climbing." she said.

Another jolt. The creature wasn't backing down. This was so not good. The tilt leveled, and the engines whined. Apparently, Bishop wasn't the only one with a vendetta. A muffled wump sounded, with a fainter tremble. And for a moment everything was silent. Almost eerily so.

"What happened?" Morgan pushed away from the table and ran across the room to the door.

She couldn't see much through the porthole, but what she could see sent a shock through her. The bridge was in chaos. Smoke drifted up from the lower deck. Sparks flashed from the bank of equipment against the far wall. Bishop was nowhere to be seen. She grasped the door handle and turned it, but it was locked.

"We're locked in," she said, as she gave it another yank for good measure.

The deck shook, and she slammed against the hatch. The creature wasn't finished. A new siren split the air.

Catlett was on his feet and at her side before she could blink. "That's the decompression alarm. Here, take her."

"The what?" Kaylee wrapped her arms and legs around Morgan like an octopus, burying her face in Morgan's neck. Morgan squeezed her closer and stepped back as Catlett grabbed the handle and gave it a hard twist.

He pounded on the glass. "Let us out!"

This was not the way she'd thought she'd die. She wanted to be old and gray, with grandkids. Not trapped in a giant metal tube, sunk by a monster previously thought to be extinct.

"We're up to 900 feet," Daniel said.

She shifted her gaze and met her uncle's. The steady look in his eyes calmed her. She took a shaky breath, and then another. Okay, they were going to get through this. As her dad liked to say, fly the burning helicopter all the way to the ground. At least then you might have a chance to survive. But if you give up in the air, you're dead for sure. Of course, he'd meant it for helicopters, and this was a sub ... but, good enough.

"How do we get off this thing?" she said.

Catlett gave the door another jerk, as the floor trembled.

"There are life pods on the lower decks if we can get out of this room."

Good, they had a plan, or at least a part of one. She looked around the room for something they might use to open the door. Unless there was a way to use a chair, coffee pot or a pen ... not likely. She wasn't MacGyver. The room shook. Didn't this thing ever get tired? Her knees banged against the floor as it trembled again. Kaylee squeaked in her ear.

"It's going to be okay, Kaylee." She whispered to the girl. Her eyes found Daniel's as a disheartening thought rushed through her. "Think there is more than one creature?"

Daniel looked grim. "Maybe. Another section has just gone red."

Fantastic. Looked like that helicopter was going to burn after all. Or in this case, breach and be flattened like a pancake. And if they made it outside, they had potentially two creatures to contend with. Would the fun never end?

"Are we going to die?" Kaylee cried. Morgan struggled to her feet, resolve burning through her.

"Not on my watch, kiddo," she said. "I can tell you one thing—mosasaurs are no longer my favorite."

They just had to find a way out of this room. The hatch squeaked open, and the smell of smoke and scorched wires burned Morgan's lungs. Li leaned into the room with a cough.

"You guys ready to get out of here, or what?"

CHAPTER TWENTY-SEVEN

Suddenly, survival didn't look so bleak. Of course, they still had to make it to the pods. And then survive a massive creature who could probably crush the pod like a bubble, but one step at a time. Catlett took his daughter, and they followed Li onto the bridge.

The smoke was thicker in the hallway, swirling in thin dark clouds overhead before vanishing into the vents. She wondered where the vents led. Hopefully not down. Voices shouted from the deck below.

Bishop was on the stairs, shouting orders above the din. He spun toward them, his eyes wild. She gripped Daniel's arm and braced for a fight. They weren't going back into that room without one.

"Dad!" Catlett's shout barely broke above the din. "You've got to let it go!"

The craze in Bishop's eyes faltered for a moment, and she caught a glimpse of lucidity. He grinned and waved a hand toward the port.

"We've got it on the run, son!" Bishop said. "We've got the monster right where we want him."

Li gasped, and Morgan looked up in time to see a massive shape charge through the dark blue water, straight for them. The doctor's hand grasped her wrist, painfully, and hauled her through the hatch and into the corridor. She reached out blindly and yanked Daniel through behind her as the mosasaur struck the viewing port.

Li slammed the hatch shut and twisted the wheel.

"What about the people below?" Morgan could barely hear her own voice above the alarms. Bishop, the techs. Surely the doctor wouldn't leave people to die.

Li squeezed her arm as she passed by. "There is another hatch at the bottom, and it's not locked, if ..."

If the glass didn't break. Morgan had no idea what their current depth was, but they could see light in the water ... Maybe they wouldn't get crushed, not immediately. But the idea of being trapped in a sinking tin can full of water wasn't ideal either. Her eyes darted to Catlett's.

"How do we get out of here?"

He pointed down and grabbed her hand, pulling her behind him. She reached out for the rail, checking to make sure Daniel was behind her as they all followed Li down the ladder. The sub shuddered beneath another hit. These things just didn't give up. They were every bit as magnificent, and terrifying, as she'd dreamed. Though she'd never planned to meet one face-to-face. So, to speak. She wasn't a fan of things that tried to eat her.

They passed through another hatch and down another set of stairs, and then another, until she lost count. Daniel faltered on the sixth set, and she released Catlett's hand to help him.

"Almost there," Catlett shouted over the din.

Thankfully, the next hatch appeared to be the final one, as they spilled out onto a crowded deck. A wave of panic swept through her. This deck was too crowded. Too many people climbing through the narrow hatches into the pods. She caught a glimpse as they passed one. How big were these things?

Catlett grabbed her free hand and pulled her through the crowd after him. Her claustrophobia was creeping up on her. She breathed and pushed through it. She had to make it, for Daniel, for her family, and for the greatest find in the twenty-first century, provided she could prove it. And it didn't kill her first.

They reached the end of the first room with no luck. Catlett pulled them toward another door. The floor jolted, and the alarm fell silent. Was that good or bad? For the moment, she didn't care. There was a cry of pain, and then another from the corner. Li waved them on.

"I'll see you on the other side," Li said. And she vanished into the crowd.

Morgan hoped it was the surface, and not heaven. Not yet. She wasn't afraid to die, but she had so much living she wanted to do first.

"Come on," she said. She tightened her arm around her uncle's waist and hauled him toward Catlett.

"You'll be faster without me." He wheezed, his face pale.

No way, no how. She hadn't come this far to lose him now. She tightened her grip on his belt, ignoring the searing pain in her muscles as she pulled him through the crowd.

"Not a chance, old man," she said. "Do you know how much trouble I'd be in if I didn't bring you back with me?"

Daniel choked. "Grounded for a millennium?"

"Exactly." She was having a harder time speaking, and Catlett was getting farther away. The smoke circled overhead like some twisted sci-fi creature.

The room shook beneath another blow, and she slammed to the floor as Daniel fell into her. The stars were back, with friends. And then the weight was gone as a pair of strong hands pulled her back to her feet. Catlett. He was beginning to make this a habit, always coming for her. She could get used to this.

"Okay?" he said.

She gave her head a shake to clear it, which was a horrible idea. She forced a breath of scorched air into her lungs and coughed.

"Yeah," she said. She could always faint later. "Daniel?"

Her uncle was still standing, barely. He gave her a shaky grin. Catlett handed his daughter to her and took Daniel's weight, leading the way down through the maze.

Morgan tightened her grip and plunged in behind him. They reached the opposite deck, this one empty. All the hatches were sealed, all the pods were gone. Her heart sank. Okay, new plan. Maybe they could make it to the moon pool and find a working crane, and ...

"Come on, this way." Catlett said.

He passed through a hatch, pulling Daniel with him, but before they could follow, someone shoved her from behind. She went down hard, pain jolting through her knees as they struck the deck. Kaylee screamed, as Ian sealed the hatch with a clang and slammed the bolt shut. She struggled to her feet as the door trembled beneath a blow from the other side. Panic surged through her at the hatred in the man's eyes.

"Well, well, just the two I was hoping to find."

Oh, this just kept getting better. Kaylee whimpered as Morgan clutched her closer. She took a slow step back, and then another. Ian pulled the gun from his waistband and moved forward slowly, as if he had all the time in the world. As if a monster wasn't trying its best to crush them.

"We need to leave now, Ian," she said, calmly, trying to keep fear from her voice. "The sub is going to sink. We have to get out now."

"You can go." He waved a hand at the bolted door. "Just as soon as you give me the kid."

She'd rather free dive with the mosasaur.

"Not a chance." She choked as Kaylee's arms tightened around her neck. "I think her dad would prefer I didn't."

"Her grandfather would prefer you did."

The scoff slipped out at his words before she could stop it. His eyes darkened. Her arm burned beneath the girl's weight. She took a step back. Her foot hit something solid.

"Your father is still trying to kill this thing," she said. She slipped her free hand down, slowly, her fingers searching for the object. Her heart surged as they closed around smooth metal. "He told us to take her and go."

Not entirely true, but maybe he would have had the decency to do so, if he'd been in his right mind. She hoped.

"I don't believe you." Ian stalked closer, and she forced herself to hold her ground. "Give me the girl."

Her hand tightened on the metal. The room trembled, and she pressed her lips close to Kaylee's ear. "Get behind me."

Kaylee nodded hesitantly and loosened her grip. She slid to the ground. Good girl. Brave girl. Ian reached out and grabbed Kaylee. Fear shot through Morgan as the room shook again, more violently than before. She screamed—a banshee cry—as she hoisted the wrench in a sweeping arch toward Ian's gun hand. The gun went flying, and the wrench swung back around and into the side of his head.

He hit the deck and didn't move. The wrench fell to the deck with a clang. Morgan grabbed Kaylee's hand and pulled her toward the hatch. The bolt gave way beneath her shaking hands, and the hatch swung inward dragging them with it. They stumbled through, straight into Catlett's arms.

"Daddy!" Kaylee shrieked as he swept her up. "Did you see what Morgan did? It was amazing, like the movies!"

Morgan let out a huff of a laugh as she tried to catch her breath. His arm crushed her to him, and for a brief moment, she let him support her weight as her knees failed her. She cast a look back at Ian's still form. He still hadn't moved. She hoped he wasn't dead. Really.

"You're incredible."

She glanced up at him. "Tha—"

And he was kissing her. She had no hope of walking now. Her knees were permanently gelatin. She kissed him back. The room trembled beneath them. Right. Survival first. Daniel was smirking at them. She ignored her uncle as she pulled away from Catlett.

"Where now?" she said.

Catlett tightened his arm around his daughter and led them to a door on the opposite side of the room.

"Inside," he said. "Quick."

She faltered at the odd look in Daniel's eyes before he vanished inside. Catlett hugged his daughter, kissed her hair, and sent her through next. A horrible feeling crept through Morgan.

"How many does the pod hold?" she said.

He wrapped an arm around her waist and tugged her toward the hatch.

"Three."

Oh no. Not happening. She turned and dug her heels into the deck.

"You knew this," she said, struggling against him. "I'm not leaving you here. You just kissed me! Don't you know how it happens in the movies? If the kiss happens before the action bit, one of the people dies!"

"I'll take my chances." He kissed her again.

And then she was weightless and sliding down a short tube. She caught herself against a thinly padded chair and started to scramble back out, but the hatch slammed shut and sealed. She was thrust backward as the pod shot into the endless blue of the Pacific.

A wave of nausea writhed in her stomach. She swallowed hard as she struggled into her harness. Self-sacrificing ... jerk. She prayed he'd quickly found a pod, so she'd have a chance to yell at him in person.

"Are you—" her uncle said.

She cut him off with a watery glare. "Don't."

"My daddy is going to follow us." Kaylee said from the rear. "He promised."

He'd better. The pod sank lower, and the dark blue of the trench yawned up beneath them. Her fingers closed over the controls, her heart racing. The pod was small and spherical and nearly completely transparent. Great, so if the monster did swallow them, they'd get a clear view. She scanned the controls. There were two sets. Good. Her uncle had logged far more time behind the wheel of one of these than she had, which was almost none.

"Uncle Daniel, can you—?" Her words died on her lips as she took in his pale face. "Are you okay?"

His arm was cradled tight against his side, and he grimaced.

"I think I fractured my wrist in that last jolt. I'll live, but I can't hold the stick." His eyes held hers, "You can do this. I know you can."

Oh, this was getting better and better. Okay. She gripped the controls and studied the console. Her nausea rose again. She forced it back. She could do this, she had to do this. The pod jolted as another pod glanced off it, like a billiard ball. They needed to get out of here. At least they weren't upside down.

"The controls are simple," Daniel said. "Like one of those simulators your brother has set up in his lab."

Yeah, she'd thrown up in that one too.

"You can do it, Morgan!" Kaylee yelled from the back.

"Thanks."

She gripped the yoke and eased it to the left. The pod turned with it. Great. And then not so great, as the side of the submarine filled her view. She jerked the controls up and to a hard right, skimming up the side of the larger vessel. Kaylee shrieked again as they shot upward and joined a multitude of pods, like a sea of giant bubbles. They rose toward the faint green light above.

"Daniel, kill the lights."

He leaned over and flipped a switch to her right. The interior went dark, apart from the glow of the console and the lights from the Leviathan below. She stared downward. Every inch of the top of the ship from stern to stem blazed with lights. Bioluminescent shimmers pulsated along the hull like a huge living organism. The ship was unlike any submarine she'd ever seen.

The sub shifted, sinking deeper into the trench.

"Do you think Bishop is trying to give us a chance?" Morgan said, quietly.

She watched as a few more pods exited the ship and slipped into the dark of the sea. Maybe the man wasn't as mad as he'd seemed.

"Maybe so," Daniel said.

Then she saw it. Her jaw dropped as a large dark shape glided over the Leviathan, blocking the light. Its shape was massive, and beautiful, in a terrifying sort of way. She leaned closer to the window as the creature dove beneath the sub.

"If we live, we'll be so famous."

Daniel laughed softly. "All the evidence is on that sub."

"We'll figure something out." She whispered the words as she shifted closer, as if the creature could hear her. They weren't out of the woods yet.

"I want to see." Kaylee's head popped out from between the seats.

The mosasaur appeared again, sixty feet or so from the bow of the sub. Absolutely magnificent. The beast shot forward, propelled by its rapidly moving tail. Like a giant torpedo. A torpedo the size of a small submarine slammed into the ship, and the impact resonated through the water.

"Seat belts!" This was not going to be good.

Kaylee ducked back as an explosion ripped through the bow and the force of the blast sent them rocketing toward the surface. The girl screamed as Morgan gripped the controls, her arms straining to pull it under control. A light blinked on the console, and the pod suddenly began to descend, rapidly. Heading straight for the sinking submarine. Morgan yanked back against the controls, but they wouldn't budge. In fact, they jerked away from her, as if by unseen hands.

"Are we in auto-pilot?"

Daniel leaned forward and rapidly flipped switches with his good hand. "Doesn't seem to be a shut-off."

Her stomach dropped as the rest of the pods descended with theirs. They shifted slowly away from the sub, and deeper into the ocean. They were still too close. The sub lit with a second explosion, its bow tipping toward the trench. Their pod spun like a top. She shut her eyes and held her breath.

Suddenly, the pod steadied and moved away from the Leviathan like it knew where it was going.

"Do you think they're programmed to return to base?" What a fun thought.

"Probably," Daniel said.

They were still about sixty feet from the sub. Way too close. Her heart froze as the dark shifted beneath them, and a shadow formed eyes, and a snout, and the most terrifying set of teeth she'd ever seen. She tugged the controls with every ounce of strength she had left.

"Uncle Daniel!" Now the monster was right on top of them. And suddenly the pod shot to the left and down, and she had control again.

"You've got this, kiddo!"

Her arms trembled. "Hold on!"

The mosasaur closed its jaw with a hard snap, a sound she was sure she would hear in her nightmares forever. She skimmed the pod along its underbelly, narrowly missing a giant flipper and its massive tail as she shot them out into open ocean. Kaylee cheered from the back as she steered it back toward the surface.

"Good job, kiddo." Daniel squeezed her arm.

"Which switch killed it?" Her chest heaved as if she'd been running a marathon, and they weren't out of danger yet.

"The one back here," Kaylee said, "it was under the seat."

Well, what a brilliant place to put on an off switch.

"Good job, Kaylee!" She let out a laugh and turned the pod to face the sub in case the creature took another run at them, but apparently it had lost interest in them.

"There's another one!" Daniel said.

Her eyes shot to the stern of the submarine as a second, smaller shadow shot forward. There were two. Oh, wow, she'd been right. She had never been so sorry to be right. The creatures struck the sub as if the movement had been synchronized. And this time the whole ship lit with one massive explosion.

No ...

"Hold on!" She gripped the controls as the force of the shock wave pushed them up, and up and up. Like a champagne cork, they shot out of the water and into the brilliant blue sky. And then back down again. A flash of pain jolted through her spine as they struck the water, sinking several feet before floating back to the surface, like a fishing bobber.

Stunned silence hung heavily over the small pod. She peeled her fingers off the console and let out a shuddered breath.

"Everyone okay?"

"That. Was. Awesome!" Kaylee screeched from the rear.

Morgan laughed. Not exactly what she would have called it. The kid was a born scientist.

Daniel shot her a pained smile. "Let's not do that again."

"Agreed."

No arguments from her. Her heart was beating like a jackhammer. She stared down between her feet at the darkness. She could just make out a flash of light far, far below them. There was no movement—at least, none she could see. No creatures. And no pods.

Her stomach plunged toward her toes. Oh please, God, please. Let him be okay. Stupid self-sacrificing hero ...

"Do you see anything?" she said.

Kaylee popped over the console between them, pointing out the glass to Daniel's right.

"I see a boat!"

There was indeed a boat, a big blue and white one. She didn't care what it was, as long as it saw them and was too big to be swallowed. She looked down to the floor, again, just as a shadow rose beneath them. Oh shoot.

She grabbed Kaylee and held on tight. But there was no crushing. No rush of water or big teeth. Nothing but a gentle knock against the side of the pod.

"Hey look! It's my daddy!" Kaylee said. "Hi, Daddy!"

The girl wriggled out of Morgan's arms and into the space beside her, waving frantically. Tears flooded her eyes. She squeezed them shut as a rush of relief left her weak.

"Thank you, God."

Daniel squeezed her arm. "Amen."

She pried an eye open and glared half-heartedly as Catlett waved from the pod bobbing beside them. She was going to murder him, slowly.

A loud horn spilt the air, and she winced. The large blue and white ship sailed closer, its horn blaring a second time. Morgan blinked as the name came into view. She laughed, wild and uncontrolled, and on the edge of hysteria.

"Any idea how we should explain this?" Daniel asked, dryly.

What were the odds they would end up in the path of her brother's research vessel?

"Not a clue," she said.

CHAPTER TWENTY-EIGHT

In the movies, everything seemed so easy. The heroine saves the day, defeats the monster, and rides off into the sunset with the handsome hero. And they all live happily ever after.

In real life … not so much. She had never realized how much red tape existed until they'd popped into the path of a Navy-sponsored science vessel in a pair of unregistered and highly unusual submersibles. Add in the fact she was presumed to be dead, Daniel presumed kidnapped, and Catlett a presumed killer. Which was practically a one-way ticket to a lockdown, regardless the majority of the crew knew both her and Daniel. So much for the home team advantage.

Nate and Piper hadn't even been on the ship. They'd gone home for her funeral—she'd been sickened to hear. They also learned Ian had burned down Daniel's lab with a body inside. A body which had been presumed to be hers. She had a bad feeling she knew exactly whose body it was.

Ian was on the most wanted list of every agency in the alphabet. No surprise there. The surprise was, Catlett had saved his brother. Or maybe that wasn't such a surprise. Catlett was a good guy.

They hadn't even mentioned the sea monsters. The explosions were what had first drawn the ship to their location. A search was launched for the Leviathan and its crew, but no trace had been found of the sub or the other pods. Bishop's submarine had sunk in the area of Horizon Deep, the second deepest part of the ocean at nearly seven miles below sea level.

Morgan really hoped Li had survived along with the countless others trapped by Bishop's mad obsession.

After submitting to medical care and answering what felt like days' worth of questions, they'd all been shipped off to Honolulu where Special Agent Weston and the FBI met them on the tarmac. Many, many more hours were spent in windowless conference rooms, in endless debriefs, with the never-ending questions. Questions about the base and the sub and Bishop. Every detail of every minute.

She wished she'd been there when Kaylee told Weston about her superhero, Morgan, and how she'd sent evil Ian flying with her mighty wrench, just like Thor in the movies.

Morgan had liked that. A lot.

Ian had been sequestered in what she hoped was a very deep hole. Weston confirmed the man had murdered Agent Cynthia Blake, and Morgan was honestly sad to hear it. The woman had made poor choices, but no one deserved such a fate. The thought of what her own family had been through left Morgan itching to take another swing at Ian.

He had at least admitted to the murder of the security guard, and to Daniel's and her kidnappings, in hopes for a chance at a deal. A deal that would never come.

Morgan, Daniel, Catlett, and Kaylee had finally been released and sent by a small plane to Maui, where Agent Weston left them at the mercy of her family. The words 'smother love' took on a whole new definition, and she wouldn't have had it any other way. Even when the tears and the hugs and the eyes followed her every move, practically every moment of the day. She'd even awakened once to find her mother in the chair beside her bed.

Sleuth was the only one who hadn't smothered her. Though she smothered him plenty, which he loved and deserved. His arrival back at the barn that fateful day had alerted her family long before the fire had spread to the house or the cave below the lab. Daniel's data had been saved, though the building was lost.

Another botched job by Ian.

The quiet hadn't lasted long. Agent Weston returned after a few days, and the debriefing continued. The task force against Casper Bishop's network was finally gaining ground, especially with Catlett's support. Ian, on the other hand, was refusing to talk. Still, they had made a dent, no matter how small it was. Finding out the whole truth was going to take time and a lot of patience.

The summons back to Willow Creek was a blessed reprieve for all of them, apart from Kaylee who was quickly adapting to island life. Morgan's family had readily adopted the little girl and Catlett both. Such was the nature of Ohana.

Daniel and Catlett had been requested to return to Willow Creek to close out the issue of the explosion and the death of the security guard, nearly a month after it had occurred. Of course, Morgan had to go along.

Again, her family had been a little more than resistant to the idea, but she'd given them little choice. She'd survived crazed kidnappers, Bishop's ill-fated plan, and real live sea monsters. Iowa was sure to be duller this time around than her last visit. Right?

Shockingly, Nate had supported her fully and had given her the best gift ever—a signed and notarized promise he would never lock her out of her lab again. Though honestly, it seemed a bit anticlimactic.

She planned to frame it and hang a copy in his office, one in her own, and another in the security office for good measure. She also had Piper's promise he would honor it—or he would have to sell his precious Volkswagen van, as was stated in the fine print.

But when she set foot back in Iowa, her good mood plummeted. Along with the temperature.

CHAPTER TWENTY-NINE

Daniel waited until they'd reached Willow Creek to announce he was staying. At least until the end of the term. Dr. Dolan had requested it, and her uncle had agreed—just like they were back at the beginning. Before the lab accidents and kidnappings and sea monsters.

"It's still snowing!" Big, white, fluffy flakes. She ignored Catlett's snort as she followed her uncle down the front steps of the sheriff's office. "It's the middle of April. This place is insane."

"It isn't sticking." Her uncle didn't even try to hide his smile. "And it will be back to the sixties by next week."

"Right," she said, "and then there will be storms and flooding and tornadoes. Maui doesn't have tornadoes."

Catlett was laughing. She concealed her smile behind her scarf enjoying the sound of his laughter.

"Just hurricanes, volcanoes, earthquakes, and tsunamis," her uncle said.

"I can see my breath!" She smiled as the other two cackled like idiots.

At least this time, he had promised her she could visit whenever she liked, for as long as she wanted. She planned to, often. Starting now. She had at least two weeks of vacation time, and it would take at least that long for Keoni and Nate to start on the plan for the new AUVs. The official purpose of the drones was to map the slopes of the deep-sea trenches, to better understand the environments and the effects of plate movements.

Unofficially, they were monster hunting. They'd made the greatest find of the century but had no proof to back their claim. At least, not yet.

Morgan suppressed a shiver as the memory of the mosasaur flooded her thoughts. The massive, yawning mouth filled with jagged teeth still haunted her dreams— more often than she was willing to admit. This wasn't just a myth anymore. This was reality. The question was, did the world really need to know? What would they do if they did find out?

Catlett wrapped his arm around her shoulders, and she leaned into him as they paused at the foot of the steps. She felt his gaze but didn't meet it. He had enough of his own troubles. He didn't need to carry hers too. Maybe she'd let him one day, but for now it could wait. They were safe, and that was enough for now. Even if it meant freezing her tail off.

She leaned into his warmth.

"We still need your help with the project," she said to her uncle. "It was our dream, right? Or at least it was before it tried to eat us."

Daniel smiled. "Which I can provide from here until I get back to the islands."

"This summer?"

"This summer." His gaze held hers with the weight of a promise. He wouldn't shut her out. Never again.

"And you'll bring Macy?" Her grin was mischievous, and she laughed as he narrowed his eyes in a warning.

He had been mourning too long. He deserved to be happy, and she'd seen the smile he'd given Macy when she'd met them on the porch.

A small pink blur slammed into her. "Hey, Morgan! We're going to get ice cream!"

The madness was spreading.

"Don't you think it's too cold for ice cream?"

Kaylee grinned up at her. "Daniel says it's never too cold for ice cream!"

Morgan raised an eyebrow as she gave her uncle a pointed look, but his attention was on Macy as she joined them. "Yeah, well, Daniel's crazy."

Kaylee abandoned her for her uncle. "Daniel, do you want ice cream?"

He grinned down at the girl. "I would love some ice cream, if you would care to join me, my lady." He offered his arm with a formal bow sending Kaylee into a fit of giggles.

Macy's smile was radiant. Oh, yes, she was smitten too. Morgan wondered if Daniel would move to Iowa for good if they were to get married. She shook her head. For now, she would live in the present and not worry about the future.

"What are you thinking?" Catlett's warm breath tickled her ear.

She watched as Daniel headed down the street with Kaylee on one arm and Macy on the other. She smiled softly. "Reality provides us with facts so romantic that imagination itself could add nothing to them."

"Jules Verne?"

She nodded. The quote seemed fitting in the moment.

"Are you okay?" he said as they followed the trio down the damp street.

"With Daniel staying? Sure." She wasn't entirely thrilled but she'd made her peace with it. "And what about you? Have you made your decision?"

She turned to face him as he slowed to a stop.

"I think for now, it would be best if I take Dr. Dolan's offer to stay for at least the rest of the term," he said. "We just need some—"

Her heart sank.

"You need time, I get it. Totally understandable." She stepped back, forcing her smile to hold.

He snorted. "Will you let me finish for once?"

She waved a hand, and he caught it gently and tugged her to him. She met his eyes—soft and assessing. Her insides melted.

"We will never need time, or space, from you," he said. "I haven't felt this way, or really allowed myself to feel this way about someone in a really, really long time." He grinned. "You had me from the moment you threw that book at me."

Which was why he'd followed her to Maui. She could see it in his eyes.

"And when I hit you with the door?" She grinned. "Which I totally did."

He frowned, but it didn't reach his eyes. "Allegedly."

"I kno—"

His lips covered hers, silencing her laugh, and she returned his kiss. They could work this out. They'd survived monsters together. A little distance was nothing. Right?

"Besides," he said, as they parted. His voice was low and warm, and mischievous. "Kaylee wants to adopt you. Personally, I think she's just after your horse."

She laughed. "I'll share him, if she'll share you."

The warmth in his eyes sent a delicious shiver through her. "I'm sure we can work something out."

She pulled him closer and kissed him again. Oh, yeah. She'd never grow tired of this. Something wet and cold plopped against her cheek. The snow on the other hand ...

"Join me for a coffee?" she said.

He pressed a kiss against her forehead. "I'll follow you anywhere."

Oh, that was cheesy, but she liked it.

"Anywhere?" she said. "Because Daniel has a whole ton of stories left in his database. I hear there is this lake creature in Lake Champlain. Supposed to be some sort of Nes—"

She enjoyed hearing him laugh so hard. He tucked her against his side as they started back down the street.

"Why don't you just go after Nessie?"

She shook her head in mock shock. "Nessie is sacred."

After all, some myths were better off left alone.

Right?

URQUHART CASTLE, LOCH NESS, SCOTLAND
MORGAN, AGE EIGHTEEN

Morgan adjusted the lens of the camera, and her uncle's grin came into focus. She pressed the button and snapped a picture, trapping the memory forever.

"Save some of that film for Nessie," he said, laughing.

This trip had been good for him. She'd missed his smile. His real smile. This year had been tough, but they'd made it through. And here they were, standing on the banks of one of the most famous lakes in the world.

"It's digital, not film." She stuck her tongue out at him.

He waved her over to the wall, and she complied. The wind was cool and brisk and the cloud above the grey waters ominous. She thought it was absolutely perfect.

"Do you think Nessie is still in there?" she said. "Or did St. Columba really run her off?"

Her uncle shrugged. "People have been trying to find her for years with little luck."

She stared over the white capped water, her gaze rising with the sharp peaks of the mountains on the opposite side. The air felt alive. Like anything was possible. She considered St. Columba's story as her gaze returned to the loch.

"What if," she said, "the creature he witnessed was different than the creature people see now?" She waved a hand in the general direction of the River Ness, which connected the loch to the sea. "Maybe the river was deeper then. Or maybe the creature was trapped and just died off."

She raised the camera and snapped another shot.

"There have been a lot of witnesses since then," Daniel said. "What do you think it was that they saw?"

She grinned. "A really big eel or a sea serpent. Something like the creatures that have been sighted off the coast of California, or in Sydney harbor. Long neck, a mane similar to a horse and long thick body."

The wind ruffled her hair, bringing with it a scent of rain. She let the camera hang from its strap around her neck and buried her hands into her pockets.

"That would account for the humps," he said. "And it would definitely be harder to locate."

"But it isn't as fun as a plesiosaur." Ancient marine reptiles were always more fun.

Her uncle laughed. "No, I suppose not." He pushed back from the wall and headed for the narrow staircase. "Ready for lunch?"

She looked back over Loch Ness one last time before following. "Do you think she's really out there?"

Daniel paused on the top step and turned; his eyes shone with enthusiasm. She couldn't help but grin back at him.

"Definitely."

DEAR READERS,

Thank you for reading *Beneath the Deep*. I hope you enjoyed reading it as much as I did writing it.

Like Morgan and Daniel, I love a good sea monster tale—from the Kraken to Perseus and the Sea Serpent to the Loch Ness Monster and everything in between. My dream for this book was to create a story told from an aspect I had been unable to find despite countless years of searching—a sea monster story from the Creation Science point of view. While I have to admit the thought that a creature survived over millions of years does sound impossibly thrilling, what about a creature that survived a global flood and went on to survive thousands of years in somewhat relative secrecy?

As a geologist, I've always been fascinated by the dinosaurs and the great marine reptiles. Their bones have been found in the rock strata. We have irrefutable proof that they did exist. So, if the Flood of Noah was real (and I believe there is enough evidence in the rock layers worldwide to support that it was), what happened to the great marine reptiles? Years of history and legend are filled with stories of giant creatures lurking in the ocean, some benevolent and others deadly and terrifying. Leviathan has always intrigued me. The great mysterious dragon of the sea is mentioned in five different places in the Bible. A fierce creature of strength and cunning created to live and play in the ocean.

In 1538, a Swedish priest by the name of Olaus Magnus created a map of reported sightings of creatures in the North

Sea. He meant it to be scientific, a record of the great sea creatures as described by the men who sailed those waters. Today, his work remains one of the first and the greatest of all sea monster maps. Giant sea snakes, great tusked beasts, enormous lobsters, and other incredible creatures, most of which have been successfully matched to creatures about which we now have some understanding: whales, eels, walruses, etc. But some have yet to be linked to existing creatures like the giant sea serpent and the short-necked, razor-toothed creature which may possibly be a match to the infamous German U-boat monster during WWI.

As Jules Verne so aptly put it, "the human mind is always looking for something to marvel at." He poked fun at this in the first chapter of his novel *Twenty Thousand Leagues Under the Sea*. But that is what we do—we imagine, we dream, and we investigate. As our technology improves, so does our ability to search deeper into the dark depths of the ocean and ferret out its secrets. New creatures are being discovered every day. Creatures like the barrel-eye fish with its transparent head, the glass octopus, the frilled shark, and the oarfish—and larger species like the elusive giant squid, which was first discovered in 1873.

Who knows what really lives in the dark unexplored regions? Only time will tell. And until it does ... marvel on, my friends. And thank you for reading. I hope you look forward to the next chapter of Morgan's story.

Visit my website, www.andreachatman.com, for updates, fun, stories, legends, and more!

Andrea

ABOUT THE AUTHOR

Andrea Chatman is a coffee-fueled, sea monster-loving science nerd, and proud of it. She has a passion for science, unraveling mysteries, and helping others understand the wonders of God's creation. When she's not writing, she's saving the world from natural disasters as a disaster scientist, riding horses on the slopes of Haleakala, researching sea monster legends, and absorbing the beauty of Maui where she lives with her very opinionated cockatiel, Kolohe.

Andrea has a Bachelor of Science degree in Geology from the Old Dominion University with a minor in Oceanography, and a Master's Degree in Disaster Science from University of Richmond. She currently lives on Maui where she works as a disaster scientist, trying to help make the world more disaster resilient one country at a time. She has always had a love for science and a curiosity for the natural world. As the daughter of two geologists, her life has been one big field trip.

Andrea learned Creation Science from her father, who was the President of the Creationist Education Association,

Cincinnati, Ohio. She has always been fascinated with Genesis and the creation of the world, in particular Noah's Flood and how dinosaurs and marine reptiles fit into the story. Through *Beneath the Deep*, she explores the idea of the possibility that the myths of giant sea monsters are based on real creatures still living today.

Andrea has been a writer since junior high school, when a teacher requested that she not read non-school books in her class. She began to tell stories in her head, which eventually spilled out onto paper. She is an avid reader and loves a good story. She began working on *Beneath the Deep* in its current form in 2014.

Andrea has written several science articles that have been published in various publications, but prefers story telling. She is currently writing science-based devotional articles for Focus on the Family's *Clubhouse* and *Clubhouse Jr.* magazines for kids. Her first article entitled *Don't Blow Your Top*, featuring the Krakatoa volcano, was released in *Clubhouse* in March 2020, and her second article entitled *Hair Raising Creatures* was released in *Clubhouse Jr.* in April 2021.

Beneath the Deep is her first fiction novel.

Made in United States
North Haven, CT
20 September 2022

24340967R00180